Oswald's Revenge

A Paranormal Fantasy
~
{Book Two}

The Forest Immortal Saga

Kristina Schram

Mischief*Maker*Media

Published by Mischief Maker Media (USA)

First printing: September, 2014

Cover Design, Interior, and Technical Expertise: GorKee

Cover Photos: 1) Young Man in Hood, from iStockPhoto

Chapter Icon (Acorn Skull): Keegan Unzen

ISBN: 978-1-939397-13-3

Visit Kristina Schram on the World Wide Web at:
www.KristinaSchram.com

Acknowledgements

As usual I need to thank my awesome beta readers: Elizabeth Schram, Heather Duane, Gordon Unzen, Keegan Unzen, and Ian More. Your contributions have been most appreciated and extremely helpful in making these books the best they can be. All of you deserve a special tree-t.

I have a few die-hard supporters I'd like to thank, as well: My husband, Dan, of course, and a couple of good friends…Shelley Friederich and Bill Horvath, and my sister, Heather Duane. Each of you has contributed in your own way over the years: by sharing my Facebook posts, buying my books and spreading the word, getting my books at your library, and basically keeping my confidence strong when the going gets rough. Without your help, I'd go bark-ing mad.

Lastly, I thank those of you who read my books because you like them, and not because you have to. To my fans who seek me out to let me know you like my work, or who write kind reviews, thanks a *million*. You help keep my dream alive.

*To those who make preserving
the earth
their life's work.*

What would the world be, once bereft
Of wet and wildness? Let them be left,
O let them be left, wildness and wet,
Long live the weeds and the wilderness yet.

~ Gerard Manley Hopkins, from Inversnaid

There was given to me a thorn in the flesh,
the messenger of Satan, to buffet me.

~ II Corinthians, Chapter 9, Verse 19

He that studieth revenge
keepeth his own wounds green,
which otherwise would heal and do well.

~ John Milton

Chapter One

The Waiting Ends

The first riddle arrived on a Saturday morning in early October. Indian summer was teasing the inhabitants of Ranger, Maine—the temperatures were in the mid-seventies and perfect. Colorful leaves reigned supreme against the bright blue sky and everything looked normal, even mundane.

Gabriel Hawthorne, however, knew quite well that life—at least his, anyway—was anything but normal, and he had the terrible feeling that it was about to get worse.

Ever since Gabe had learned a few months ago that he was a changeling Dryad, he'd felt like he was living a borrowed life. His two younger brothers, Kris and Jer, along with their friends Abazi Wanibagw and Kimber Wistman, knew his family wasn't his own. The Dryads living in the woods surrounding their Maine farm also knew, but had yet to say anything, despite the self-proclaimed King of the Forest Immortal, Oswald, threatening to do so the last time he'd seen Gabe.

For the moment, neither Gabe's mom and dad nor his Grandpa Hawthorne seemed to know anything about him being a tree spirit (that was the hope, anyway), and Gabe planned to keep it that way. His dad was still recovering from a kidney transplant after diabetes had destroyed the originals and Mom was constantly worrying about their finances; they didn't need any more crap in their lives. Gabe and his brothers had readily agreed not to say a thing to their parents about their adventures in the woods this past summer, when Straif and his evil Dryad sons, Dorn and Feltry, had nearly killed them.

Grandma May, on the other hand…she definitely knew something. But what and how much, none of the brothers could tell. All they knew was that she was up to something. This past month, every time they saw her about town, she looked furtive and would jump nervously when they called to her. That might not sound so unusual, but

Grandma May wasn't a nervous person. She made *other* people nervous.

The brothers didn't confront her on it, of course. One, because she was a little scary, and two, because they had their own troubles to worry about. And now this…

Tacked to the hobbit-sized, hidden door leading to Gabe's turret room, the note looked cryptic and mysterious. The white rectangle of paper had caught Gabe's eye while heading out to the barn to lift weights, and fearing it was from Oswald telling his parents everything, he'd made a beeline for it.

But it wasn't that at all.

After reading it, Gabe looked around the yard and then at the woods. Nothing appeared out of place and no one strange was about, only his younger brothers coming out of the barn. They looked serious, twelve-year-old Jer's blond head tilted up to listen to his older brother, Kris.

Gabe felt a shiver run down his spine as he re-read the strange poem:

> *Follow the trail*
> *You'll find the key*
> *Go round and round*
> *And then you'll see…*
> *it.*

Who had sent it? Gabe wondered. Grandma May? It seemed like the kind of weird thing she would do. Still, why didn't she just out and tell them what she wanted them to know? Why the game? That wasn't like her. Grandma May typically had no problem telling you what was on her mind. In fact, sometimes Gabe wished she'd just keep her thoughts to herself, like when she harped on his driving. They owned an ancient, cantankerous Ford truck, and Gabe did his best with the ornery beast. But his best wasn't good enough for Grandma May, especially when he accidentally ground the gears.

Or maybe his mom had written the note. She'd been known to play devious tricks on her children, who were often entirely undeserving of such heinous treatment.

Still, neither Grandma May nor Mom had ever said a word about the existence of the little door, though they'd lived here in this house a long time—Mom had grown up here. He couldn't imagine they'd never once found the back entrance during all those years, but maybe they hadn't mentioned it to keep Gabe from sneaking out of the house. If they knew about it, then they could've been the ones to put the note on the door.

Watching Kris and Jer walking toward the house, Gabe immediately ruled them out as the perpetrators. Not that they weren't able—or willing—to mess with his head, but since finding out he could turn into a tree, which he'd refused to do again since his first transformation a few months ago, they'd been a little more cautious around him. Perhaps even more respectful, too, which was a nice bonus. Plus, he was the only one of them who owned a Wii U, which he'd traded up to after winning a 3DS in a raffle at his orthodontist's office years ago, and they didn't want to lose being allowed to play it by pushing things too far.

The kids at Gabe's new school—now *they* could be responsible for this prank. Ever since he'd started his junior year at Ranger School (unbelievably, kindergarten through twelfth grade were housed in one building), his life had been hell. First, there was Jake Morrigan, a senior and the most popular kid in school. He was also the meanest. Son of Candi Morrigan, local real estate agent and Gabe's mom's sworn enemy, he'd immediately taken a dislike to Gabe. Jake also wanted to date Abazi, Gabe's prickly neighbor whose father owned the store where Gabe now worked. But she'd yet to say yes to him.

Gabe wanted to tell Jake that he had nothing to worry about where Abazi was concerned—she didn't like Gabe, and he, well, he wasn't sure how he felt about her. Actually, it wasn't that she didn't like him *per se*; it's just that she liked to give him a hard time—*all* the time. When Jake had seen them talking together on the first day of school, he'd assumed the worst. They'd actually been arguing about Gabe almost hitting Abazi as she was climbing off her bike. He hadn't meant to, but the Ford's brakes were tricky at the best of times and had gotten stuck as he pulled into the parking lot. Next to him, Jer and Kris had been fighting over elbow room, which hadn't helped matters.

It wouldn't make a difference what Gabe said anyway. Jake had decided he didn't like Gabe and had proceeded to make his life a living nightmare. What made it worse was that Jake's younger sister, Jen, a sophomore, had a crush on Gabe (according to Abazi, anyway), and that peeved Jake off to no end.

Gabe sighed ruefully. Ever since moving from San Jose to Maine to take over the family blueberry farm business, his life had been crap. And there didn't seem to be anything he could do to change that.

The sound of his brothers arguing brought him back to the note. He slipped out from behind the web of bushes hiding the small door and went to meet them.

"I stuck the tomahawk *four* times doing a double rotation," Kris insisted.

"Learn how to count," Jer replied. "It was three times. The last time you missed the target completely."

"That's because you yelled just as I was about to throw."

"Remember what Abazi said… 'You have to know how to throw a tomahawk even when the conditions aren't perfect. *Especially* when they aren't perfect.' Like in battle!"

Both the brothers suddenly noticed Gabe. "What's wrong with you?" Jer demanded, his bright blue eyes suspicious as he looked his brother over. "Your hair's all funny." Gabe had a habit of running his hands through his thick, wavy hair when he was nervous, a habit that made it stand up in spiky tufts. Right now, he was feeling particularly nervous, so he probably looked like a hedgehog.

He held out the note. "I found this tacked on the secret door to the turret."

Kris quickly snatched it and read it out loud. "I'm not a poet," he said when he was done, "but that last part's a bit weird. Doesn't rhyme at all."

"That's what you focus on?" Gabe laughed. "Not the mysterious 'follow the trail, you'll find the key' bit?"

"I was getting to that." Kris grinned and swiped a summer-darkened hand back and forth over his brown Mohawk.

"Who do you think wrote it?" Jer asked.

Gabe shrugged. "Grandma? Mom? Kids at school?"

"Oswald…" Jer suggested.

"Or maybe Abazi did it," Gabe countered.

"Maybe Abazi did what?" a strident voice demanded.

The boys spun around. Abazi, wearing a colorful, beaded headband and her long black hair done up in two braids, marched toward them from the woods, her friend, Kimber, trailing behind. Not for the first time, Gabe thought Abazi had ears like a cat—she picked up on sounds Gabe never would. It was a skill that made her even more irritating.

"Gabe thinks you might have written this note." Kris offered it to her.

She snatched it from his proffered fingers and read it with a frown marring her broad forehead, slightly shiny from sweat. Her dark, scowling eyes found Gabe. "You think I wrote this drivel?"

He thought it best to take a neutral stance. "I think someone's playing a joke on me."

"If I were playing a joke on you, Hawthorne, it would be much better than this crudola."

"I did think it was a bit beneath your level."

Unexpectedly, her eyes sparkled. "Exactly. Mine would've at least rhymed all the way through—"

"That's what I said!" Kris broke in. "What kind of a loon writes like this?"

"Someone who isn't human?" Kimber suggested, panting a little as she joined them. The metal braces she wore on her legs for her cerebral palsy fit better now after Kris had made some pads and altered two of the hinges, but they still slowed her down more than she liked. She pushed her once-long blond hair, now cut in a bob, back behind small, delicate ears. She had once hid behind her long hair, but in getting to know the brothers, especially Jer, she'd been coming out of her shell more and more. Gabe and Kris treated her like a sister and Jer, well, he treated her more like a girlfriend.

Gabe mentally shook his head in disgust. How was it that his twelve-year-old brother had a girlfriend before he did? It didn't seem fair. Not that Gabe wanted to date anyone at school—not since finding out he was half-tree, anyway. They'd have to be barking mad to want to date him. He groaned. Now he was starting to sound like Abazi, dumb puns and all.

He turned his attention back to what Kimber had said. "You think it's one of them?" He pointed toward the monstrous trees that made up the woods back behind the barn, separated from the yard by a tall, prickly hedge, known to the Dryads as the Briar Borders. According to his mother, the hedge had sprouted up seemingly overnight, when he'd been four and returned after being missing for two days. Gabe wasn't sure if it was meant to keep him from the woods, or the woods from him.

Kimber's cheeks were pink, emphasizing the fairness of her skin. "Why not?"

Because I don't want anything to do with any of them, he thought to himself, remembering that awful time—the battles, Straif's horrible face, Oswald's anger.

"It makes sense," Jer said.

"But why now? And why the mystery? If they wanted something, why not just tell us?"

"Maybe something's going on again," Abazi suggested, retying the red rubber band at the end of one of her black braids. "Maybe Straif and his goons are preparing to come after you and this is Oswald and Hollie's secret way of letting you know."

"They could've just knocked," he replied moodily, feeling his chest tighten with anxiety. "Whispered it through the door or something. Why all the secrecy?"

Abazi shrugged. "I don't know. When have they ever done something that makes sense? Hollie pretended she was a baby so she could spy on you. Who does that?"

Kris laughed. "You have to admit that it got the job done. I wish I could do something like that."

Abazi punched him on the arm. "You would, you dork."

He pretended to be hurt, though, from the 'playful' punches Gabe had gotten from Abazi, his brother wouldn't have to pretend all that much. "I think it's cool—what they can do."

Gabe gave his brother a grateful smile, especially since he was one of *them*.

Abazi, on the other hand, gave him a mischievous look. "You only think it's cool because a certain tree spirit is quite poplar with you!" She burst out laughing, her shouts loud and carrying. "Get it? *Poplar—popular?*"

Kimber giggled and Jer joined in. Gabe felt himself smiling. Abazi's puns were so bad, they were actually kind of funny...sometimes.

When the last snort died away, Kris flourished his tomahawk. "So when do we start, people?"

Gabe glanced at his brother quizzically. "Start what?"

"Our next adventure, dunderhead! We need to figure out what that note means."

"I think we need to ignore it. It's probably a trap."

"What do you think the 'trail' is?" Kris asked the others, ignoring his brother.

"The spiral," Kimber suggested and Jer, who usually was the one to figure this stuff out, stared at her rapturously. He was a smart kid, but around Kimber he tended to go all dumb. "It goes round and round and it's a trail..."

Kris snapped his fingers. "That's really good, Kimber! Let's start there."

"And how do you propose we get there?" Gabe was not happy about this. "Fly?"

"Um, duh! We go through the woods."

"Do you not remember what happened the last time we went through the woods?" Sometimes Gabe couldn't believe his brother—how could he forget how scary that all had been? Gabe was still having nightmares, filled with black, spiky thorns and pale, sneering faces and deadly, lashing branches. But then again, Kris wasn't one of them, so it was easy for him to treat this all as one big adventure.

"We could follow that stream Oswald talked about—Shambolic Stream. I think he said it led them back home. We can start at the stretch of woods Mom said was safe for us."

"I think we should do it," Abazi agreed, watching Gabe as she spoke.

"Well, I don't," he grumbled. "It's asking for trouble. Straif wants me dead and he'll have no problem taking you guys out to get to me. It's too dangerous."

"We don't have a choice, Gabe," Abazi insisted.

"What do you mean? Of course we have a choice."

"No, we don't. That's why I came over. To tell you something." She paused, letting the drama build. Gabe thought a career in theater should be her calling, but she wanted to be president of the United States. "Remember how Mrs. Deacon and Mrs. Morrigan have been trying to get permission to clear the woods?" Gabe nodded slowly, already guessing what he was about to hear. Mrs. Deacon was a formidable woman who served on several committees and boards and thought it was her civic and Godly duty to put Ranger on the map. That meant further developing the town, which meant cutting down the trees.

Candi Morrigan, a very ambitious woman in her own right, wanted the same thing, but not for the town's sake. According to Gabe's mom, who'd gone to school with her, Mrs. Morrigan liked the idea of all the money and power such a venture would create for her and her spoiled offspring. Mom did not like Candi Morrigan, and the feeling was mutual. Mrs. Morrigan did, however, like Dad and made no secret of it, especially now that he was recovering his health.

"And…" he prompted.

"And…" She paused again.

"Just say it, Abazi!"

"They're bringing in a survey crew."

"Can they do that?" Gabe gasped. "Is it even legal?"

"I don't know, but they're doing it. While I was working at the store, I overheard that most venal of creatures, Candi Morrigan, telling that most skanky of creatures, Ronald Pruspin—he writes, if you can call the garbage he produces writing, for *The Ranger Rag*—that she'd give him an exclusive."

"So she's pretty confident they're going to get permission to cut down the trees?"

Abazi lifted one shoulder. "Or hope nobody protests enough, soon enough."

"But someone's protesting, right? Your dad? My mom?"

"Candi the Con-artist threatened my dad—subtly, of course—that he'd lose a lot of business if he said anything and he was gullible enough to believe her." She looked disgusted. "He thinks he's protecting me, but I'd rather he stood up to her, even if it meant starving."

"She's done the same thing with my mom," Kimber said. "I was there when she did it. She was very good at implying all sorts of things without actually saying anything my mom could fight against. And with my CP…well, she's scared to lose the store." She sounded guilty at the thought.

"I'm not sure our mom even knows anything," Kris noted. "She's been so busy with the farm. We're selling firewood now, so every free moment she has, she's out there cutting the stuff. She's obsessed with wood."

"Not to mention her writing," Jer added. "She's sold a few articles, and she's working on her book, too. I told her the other day that I brought a bear home for supper and she just said, 'That's nice, dear, just don't overcook it.'"

"And we can't go to your dad because he's sick," Abazi concluded. "So I guess it's up to us to do something."

"What are *we* going to do?" Gabe *really* did not like the direction this conversation was heading. He wished he'd never shown anyone the note.

"We're going to warn Hollie and Oswald and Dame Hazel about the surveyors, butt munch," Abazi said snidely.

"Did you just call me *butt munch*?"

Her brown eyes flashed at him, a challenge. "Yes, I did, *butt munch*. Just bear in mind that it could've been much worse."

"Do you two want to keep fighting?" Kris intervened, used to their constant quarreling, "Or act like adults?" Both their mouths snapped shut. "Anyway, I think Abazi is right. We need to warn the others. At the same time, we can see if we can figure out that note." His foot tapped the ground, as though waiting for the race to begin.

"This isn't a game, Kris," Gabe warned.

"I know that," he replied, his deepening voice unusually serious. "But if we don't do something, who will? Do you want the woods cut down? Do you want Hollie to die?"

Put like that, of course Gabe didn't want Hollie to die. He did, however, want Straif to die. And if the woods were cut down, forcing the Ko-goks to flee, maybe then Gabe could finally sleep at night. Straif would be gone forever and Gabe could at last relax his guard a little.

"So how is our going into the woods going to help her?" he tried. "It won't stop the surveyors, that's for sure."

Kris looked Gabe in the eye. "I don't know, but I'm going, whether you come with me or not."

Gabe, knowing he wasn't going to win, gave in. "So what do you propose we do?"

"What we've been waiting and preparing for all summer."

"And that would be…"

"To find out what's going on in those woods."

Funny thing was…Gabe didn't want to know.

Chapter Two

Wildrr

It was surprisingly easy to carry out their plan. Kris told Mom they were going to hike to the stream, which was true. She assumed the food they were packing was for a picnic, which wasn't *quite* true, but no one made the effort to correct her. What she didn't know was that their bags held weapons—a whole slew of them, from batas to tomahawks to whips made from willow branches. They were as prepared as they could be. Or so they thought.

Everyone remained quiet as they trooped out to the stream back behind the house. The area around the brook was filled with Black Alder trees, which are considered protective trees, and supposedly safe. According to an old, and much worn, tree book Gabe had found on the bookshelf in his turret room, this was a safe place.

Even so, an ominous feeling stained the air around them, as though the forest was waiting and watching their every move. Even Jer refrained from talking to Kimber, much as he wanted to, as was obvious by the number of times he opened his mouth only to shut it again.

The plan was to hike to the birch circle and warn Hollie about the surveyors. While there, they hoped to solve the riddle, then get the heck out of there. But when they reached the stream, Gabe noticed it looked different, and an itchy prickling ignited beneath his skin.

"Something's changed," he said loudly.

Jer scanned the area. "Wasn't there a bend further up, and didn't the stream run closer to the weeping willows?"

"That's what I thought," Gabe said, feeling a growing uneasiness. The stream had actually changed course drastically enough to be noticed. Unless there was major flooding, which there hadn't been, such a change couldn't happen in the span of a few months. "I'm not sure I like this."

But Kris was already halfway across the stream, balancing on a broad stone. "Come on, you wusses. It's just water."

"And these are *just* trees," Gabe grumbled, wanting to kick a mighty spray of 'just' water at his brother's stubborn back. But he refrained, mainly because he didn't want to get his shoes wet…or make any unnecessary noise. Something was not right here.

Kris only laughed and kept moving, his long legs soon reaching the other side. Gabe stifled a frustrated groan and helped Jer lead Kimber across a stepping stone bridge. Abazi followed after them, her head cocked. She was listening to something, and from her expression, she didn't like what she was hearing.

When they stood on dry land once more, he gave her a questioning look. She shook her head. "We better catch up to your berserker brother," was all she said. Biting down on an urge to have a hissy fit so he could get his way and turn back, Gabe followed after the others.

The sun filtered lazily through the yellow, orange, and red leaves, imbuing the air with a deceptive golden haze. Soon the leaves would all be gone, leaving only skeletal branches behind. Gabe shuddered at the image, which reminded him of the dark ones, and ducked his head low, not wanting to see anything but his feet, one in front of the other.

It was the only reason he noticed the movement—or more accurately, a little figure moving. His eyes widened, and without realizing what he was doing, he began to follow it. The little man stood about eighteen inches high, not even tall enough to reach Gabe's kneecap, and was heading away from the stream carrying a light blue bucket, with water sloshing over its sides as he hobbled along. An oversized cloth hat, the color of ripening watermelon flesh and covered in bunches of round, shiny black berries, practically smothered the little man's head, allowing only pointy ears, nose, and chin to show. He wore a deep green topcoat, peppered with twigs sticking out like spider legs, and blue and green striped leggings.

Without warning, the creature disappeared behind a large stone and before Gabe could stop himself, he called out, "Hey!"

The tip of a long, pointy nose, quivering like a dog's, appeared, followed by a single eye the size of a walnut. "Ye kin see me? It be not possible—" He leaped out from behind the rock, his hand darting into his topcoat. It quickly reappeared clenching a silver dagger. "'oo gave it to ye? Spit it out, ye blaggart!"

Gabe lifted his hands, showing he meant no harm. Even though the dagger was no bigger than a pen, he didn't want to lose an eye or a finger. Whatever this creature was, Gabe had the feeling it wouldn't be a good idea to rile him up too much.

"Who gave me what?" he asked, speaking as slowly and politely as he could.

There was a snort. "Art ye tellin' me ye dinna kent?"

"Could you elaborate on that?"

"E-lab-or-ate," the creature repeated, his eyes, in his round face, squinty with mistrust. "What sort of hoo-doo be that?" He waved the dagger like a cat's tail. "Speak up, dingbat! And this time, speak faster. A snail creeps along more quickly than the words out yer mouth."

Gabe swallowed. He didn't know whether to call for help or laugh. "It means, tell me more."

One large, round eye closed nearly in a wink. "Oh, well. Why didna ye say so in the first place?"

"I'm sorry," Gabe apologized. "I'll try harder next time to be more clear."

The creature nodded, accepting the apology. "I be wantin' to ken 'oo gives ye the drink of the elderberry."

"Drink?" Gabe repeated, clueless. "What drink?" Then he remembered the strange brew Dame Hazel had given them months ago. "Oh, yeah!"

The little man pulled back a bit, his free hand clutching at his chest. "There be no need to let the whole forest hear of it."

"Sorry. Dame Hazel gave it to me. She said it would help me sleep."

"Dame Hazel, eh?" The tip of the creature's nose twitched. "And 'oo be ye?"

"I'm Gabe," he offered. "Gabe Hawthorne."

In a flash, the dagger disappeared back into the folds of the topcoat and the small figure was limping toward Gabe, tiny hand outstretched. "Well, I'll be jiggered. I ken there be something special about ye. I be Wildrr of the Forest Realm, Sworn Protector of the Lady."

Gabe took the tiny hand, his mind whirling with the strangeness of what was happening. "Nice to meet you, Wildrr."

"The pleasure be all mine." The little man grinned, revealing tiny teeth the size of popcorn kernels, rather shaped like them, too. As Wildrr pumped Gabe's hand up and down, his round eyes shifted to the right, and then all the way back to the left, as though searching for something. Then he gave a quick nod, seemingly satisfied with what he saw—or didn't see. "Why not come with me, then, eh? I've got something ye might want to take a gander or two at."

Gabe couldn't take his eyes off the funny creature, so suddenly friendly. "You know who I am?"

"Eh? Caint hear ye right." Wildrr yanked on Gabe's hand. "We should probably hurry. There be something I want to show ye."

Gabe found himself being pulled along in a bobbing sort of jog; the tiny hand was much stronger than he would ever have guessed. They swerved around the standing stone, passing the abandoned bucket, now tipped over and empty. "But my brothers…and my friends…" He tried to pull away, finally succeeding with one hard wrench that sent Wildrr flying to the ground. "Sorry. I didn't mean to do that, but I have to tell them—"

But Wildrr was on his feet and his hand was in his coat once more. He pulled out an elaborately carved set of panpipes and began to play. The moment the pipes touched his lips, Gabe was lost. He couldn't have turned around if he'd wanted to, and funnily enough, he didn't want to. Entranced, he followed after the little man and the haunting melody, which made him yearn to see whatever it was Wildrr desired to show him—even if it was something terrible, or absolutely nothing at all.

The sun laid a golden carpet on the fallen leaves and they followed its path for some time. Abruptly, the music quit and Gabe shook his head to clear it. The stream, he noticed, was long gone; he couldn't even hear it anymore. He was on the verge of starting to worry about being lost when something fascinating caught his eye. In front of him stood a tree like no other, and yet which was strangely familiar to him.

Bone white, with bark peeled like dead skin, its slender trunk sprouted hundreds of dark branches akin to porcupine quills and its roots humped above the ground like writhing snakes. Bushes covered in black berries surrounded the amazing tree.

"Well, do what ye do, then."

Gabe glanced down at Wildrr, facing the tree with a reverent expression on his pie-shaped face. "In a minute… First, what *are* you?"

Wildrr frowned. "I told ye, dingbat. I be the Sworn Protector—"

"Yeah, I got that. But what sort of creature are you?"

Wildrr looked affronted, his little face wrinkling with the insult of it all. "I'm startin' to think I be the fool 'oo thought ye were something special."

"I can't know everything," Gabe retorted.

Wildrr blew a lungful of exasperated air through his nostrils. "I guessed that already, to be sure. All right, I'll tell ye. I be Faerie, and this be me realm." He indicated the woods surrounding the magnificent tree.

"You're a fairy…" Gabe breathed. "Wow." How much more unreal could his world become? Tree spirits that talked, streams that changed course, and now a fairy? What next? Goblins? Elves? The bogey man? He shivered. Hadn't he already met Straif, the ultimate bogey man?

Wildrr clicked his tongue. "I see this be a waste of me time."

"So what exactly did you want me to do?"

"Ye caint see?" He groaned in response to Gabe's blank look. "She be dyin'. Me Lady." A tear formed at the corner of his eye and Wildrr wiped it away with a harrumph. "Dinna kent why I bothered…"

"What about Oswald? Can't he help you?"

"Him? He be in hidin'. Straif has a price on his head. Stupid fool."

Gabe wondered if Wildrr were referring to Straif or Oswald as the stupid fool. "I didn't think Oswald was afraid of Straif."

"He tisn't—not for himself—it be for his band. For that spitfire, Hollie. Straif wants to lure ye back, haven't ye heard?"

Gabe thought of the note and a shudder shook him from head to toe. Could Straif have written it? It was possible, but Gabe couldn't imagine the 'nightmare-come-to-life' being that whimsical. "No, I hadn't heard that. And he thinks taking Hollie would get me to come?"

Wildrr looked smug. "He be right, eh?"

"Well, yeah, I guess so. Hollie's my friend. And my brother…well, he'd want to save her and I'd have to make sure he stayed safe so I'd go with him." Why was he telling a stranger all this? How did he know he could trust Wildrr? Very simply, he didn't. "Has he tried to take her?"

Wildrr nodded. "And he succeeded. Only she got away. She be a wily one." Again, Wildrr's eyes shifted, to the right and then back to the left. "At least give it a try before ye leave," he whispered. "She doesna have long, ye see."

Gabe suddenly understood. Like so many others in the Forest Immortal, this tree—the Lady—was dying. And Wildrr thought Gabe could save her. "But I—"

"All I be askin' ye to do is try!" Wildrr looked desperate, as though he'd do anything necessary to save his mistress.

Gabe's blunt fingernails dug into his palm. False hopes were about to be dashed, with him being the one doing the dashing. Then he remembered his own desperate hopes—that his dad would get better despite all the odds—and how they kept him from plunging into despair. And Dad *was* getting better. So maybe…

"All right. I'll try it, Wildrr."

Wildrr did a little dance of joy. "I ken I could count on ye!"

Slouched over, hand outstretched, Gabe walked slowly toward the tree as though approaching a wounded animal. "I'm not going to hurt you," he soothed. "I just want to help." He took one last step and his foot caught on a root. As he fell forward, one flung-out hand smacked against the smooth bone trunk and the other grasped a brittle twig sticking straight out, breaking it right off.

He stared at the broken twig, then down at his other hand, still resting on the trunk. It looked rather funny, he thought, feeling woozy. First it seemed to sprout numerous green leaves, then flowers burst forth—delicate white blooms that quickly transformed into clusters of berries red as drops of blood. As soon as the berries appeared, a searing pain roared through his body. He blinked at the agony and the illusion vanished, leaving his hand normal as ever and the pain a distant memory.

A violent shriek shook the air around him, threatening to blow his eardrums, and what had happened to his hand disappeared from his mind as though erased. He spun around to see Wildrr staring up at his Lady. "What have ye done to her?"

Gabe turned back to see branches shooting out from the giant tree, like needles piercing skin. The screeching increased and the tree began to thrash and struggle against her root-bound state. Gabe stared up at her, shocked.

"I'm sorry!" he cried. "How can I fix this?" But she only screeched louder, her limbs thrashing near Gabe's head. Dismayed and worried he was about to get beamed, he turned and ran past the stunned fairy, out of range of her swinging limbs. What was happening to her? What had he done?

"Lady! Oh, Lady!" Wildrr moaned, his cries blending so horribly with the tree's bellowing that Gabe wanted to scream himself. "Ye killed her, ye scab!" he shouted, suddenly angry. Gabe backed away, stunned. *Killed her? No!* "I be seekin' revenge! I'll kill ye with me own hands, see that I dinna do it!"

Gasping with fright and from the horror of what he'd done, Gabe ran, not caring where he ended up. "Ye murdered her!" Wildrr shouted, his words chasing after Gabe, catching him, implanting themselves deep in his mind forever.

He was a murderer.

Chapter Three

The Trail Goes Cold

Gabe felt hopelessly lost, both in the bleak woods and in his heart. What had he done? He hadn't just killed a tree, he felt like he'd killed a person. He looked down at his right hand, clenched into a tight, desperate fist and slowly uncurled his fingers to reveal the dead branch that had broken off in his hand. He was about to toss it away, as though on fire, but at the last moment, he stopped himself. Without understanding why, he tucked the twig into his coat pocket where it settled into darkness. Perhaps he meant to punish himself, hanging onto it, by not letting himself forget. Ever.

He stopped walking, suddenly realizing his situation. He was lost in the Forest Immortal, with enemies all around, and now a homicidal fairy was after him. He was in grave danger, as were the others. He started running again, faster this time.

"Ga-aabe!" he heard after a few minutes. Jer! That kid had a voice that could break windshields, and for once, Gabe was glad of it. He began to sprint toward the sound, and the trees seemed to be leaning toward him, closing in, creating a vortex of wood and desperation. He ran faster, breaking through to the stream. Winded, he glanced both ways hopefully, before spotting Jer's red windbreaker farther upstream.

"Where were you?" Abazi cried when he stumbled toward them.

"I-I was following…" He stopped to suck in more air. "I was following a fairy." He groaned inwardly. Put that way, it sounded as stupid as the expression Abazi's face was conveying so eloquently.

"And did he bring you to Santa Claus?"

"That's an elf," he grunted, finally able to straighten up. He loved to run, but madly sprinting long distances was not his forte.

"Elf, fairy—they're all the same. Made up."

"Abazi…" Kimber started. "Leave him alone for once." Everyone turned to stare at Kimber and she blushed, but didn't back down. "If we can believe in tree spirits…well, the rest follows, doesn't it?" Gabe smiled at her and she gave a short nod of acknowledgement.

"He could've at least said something instead of just leaving us in the lurch," Abazi grumbled.

"He kind of put a spell on me," Gabe explained, feeling like an idiot.

"A spell, huh?" Kris snorted derisively. "That's a new one. So what did he want?" His arms were tightly crossed to convey his irritation. Once embarked on a mission, Kris did not like to be deterred—especially by something as trivial as disappearing brothers.

"I think he wanted me to help a tree he was protecting."

"And did you?" Kris's tone implied Gabe had better make this waste of time worth it.

"I don't think so," Gabe hedged. No need to tell everyone that he'd made things worse. Far worse. "But I did find out why I could see him when I've never been able to see fairies before. We can all see them, in fact."

"How?" Jer demanded, intrigued.

"Remember when Dame Hazel gave us that drink? Well, apparently it had elderberry in it, which allows people to see fairies, maybe other creatures, too. I don't know."

"The old lady doped us?" Kris slapped his hand to his chest. "I feel so violated." Everyone laughed, the giddy sound at odds with the gloomy atmosphere of the woods.

"So we can really see them?" Jer's blue eyes were wide with excitement. Of the three of them, he was the one who seemed to believe the most in the possibility of a world filled with ghosts, fairies, and elves. When he was a little kid, they once visited a wooded park. Mom was feeling playful that day and told them she thought there might be fairies following along with them in the woods. Jer, four years old at the time, said he already knew they were there. When Mom asked him how he knew this, he said, "Because I can smell them."

"And what do they smell like?" she asked with a smile.

"Strawberries and lemonade," he answered, without hesitation. And for a brief moment, Gabe actually could smell strawberries and lemonade. For weeks after that, Jer begged his mom to host a tea party for the fairies, serving strawberries and lemonade, naturally. He wanted to catch one for himself.

To discover that they might actually be real, well, that for Jer was a dream come true. Of course, he didn't realize that this particular fairy was bearing a grudge that could kill them all. If he did, he might not be so thrilled about the little people being real.

"We should go back home," Gabe determined. "The fairy—his name is Wildrr—he said that Straif is trying to lure us into the woods. Hollie had to go into hiding because of it."

"Hollie?" Kris exclaimed. "Why her?"

"Straif thinks that if he can catch Hollie again, I'll come rescue her." As soon as the words left Gabe's mouth he realized the stupidity of saying this to Kris. First, because it would make him jealous, and second, knowing Hollie was in danger would only increase Kris's determination to continue this mad quest.

"*Again?* And why you?" Kris cried. "*I'm* the one who'd go after her."

"Well, yeah. But then I'd have to go after you."

"Oh," Kris responded, mollified. "So she's safe?"

"For now. She was able to get away the first time and Oswald has her and his band in hiding."

Kris gave a satisfied nod. "Then we'll just find the trail and that key and head home."

"The note could be a trap," Abazi pointed out. "Straif could've written it."

"I've already thought of that," Gabe replied. "But can you imagine Straif writing a poem? He would've at least drawn a skull somewhere and stuck it to the door with one his thorns of death."

"I suppose," she admitted. "So what do we do?"

"I didn't want to come in to the woods in the first place," Gabe declared. "So I'm for going home."

"We can't be that far from the spiral," Kris pointed out. "I remember hearing a stream near the spiral, when we were passing through the last time."

"I didn't hear a stream," Gabe said.

"Me, eith—" Abazi began, then yipped in pain. When Gabe looked at her, she was leaning down and rubbing her calf, as though someone had kicked her to get her to stop talking.

Gabe glanced suspiciously at Kris, standing next to Abazi, who returned the look, wide-eyed and full of innocence. "What was that, Abazi?" Kris asked, his voice high and light.

"Actually, I might have heard something like that, too," she mumbled.

Gabe glared at the two conspirators, both of whom refused to meet his eye. "Why am I the only sane person in this group? I get why Kris wants to throw his life away—because he's nuts. But you, Abazi? Why would you want to do this?"

She bristled. "Because I have a feeling about this. Okay, Hawthorne?" Her high cheeks were flushed beneath her warm, brown skin and he remembered she'd heard something earlier. He wondered what it was...the dark ones? Wildrr? Or maybe it was simply just that the squirrels were growing restless. Not that there were ever any squirrels around here.

Knowing he wasn't going to win with her—he *never* won with her—he turned to Jer, who looked mutinous, and Kimber, who looked a tad guilty. "I've learned to listen to Abazi's feelings," she said with an apologetic shrug.

Gabe didn't even bother with Jer. Where Kimber went, he would follow...like a love-sick puppy dog. Besides, he was most likely enjoying watching his oldest brother not get his way like he usually did.

He suppressed a sigh and said, "Then we'd better get moving." He glanced over his shoulder. He'd gone some distance from Wildrr, who was likely tending to his lost Lady, but at any moment the fairy might decide to make good on his threat and track Gabe down. Should he warn the others? He went back and forth for several seconds, but finally decided not to. Really, what harm could a fairy do? One swift kick would send Wildrr into the next county.

It was at this point that he noticed the others were making him take the lead, Abazi urging him forward. "So we won't lose you again." Holding back yet another frustrated sigh, he began to follow the stream.

Like the last time they'd been in the forest, there were no animal sounds and no undergrowth. The going was relatively easy, as nothing much grew alongside the stream, the trees keeping a distance of about twenty feet on each side. The more Gabe thought about it, the more he realized how odd that was. *It's like they're giving the stream room to move and change course. But why would a stream move? What good did that do?*

It was yet another mystery to add to the list. He pulled out the note and read it again.

Follow the trail
You'll find the key
Go round and round
And then you'll see...
it.

'You'll find the key...' It suddenly occurred to Gabe why Kris was so intent on making this trip. He wanted that key. Since he was a young boy, keys had held a potent fascination for Gabe's brother. He was always certain that each led to treasure, even when he'd never once found any. So to receive a cryptic note about a key was akin to handing Kris a treasure map. Besides, Gabe's key had earned him a turret room, so maybe Kris figured it was only a matter of time for him to score something equally cool.

Gabe himself wondered what the key would open and picked up the pace, his own curiosity stimulated. Despite the oppressive undercurrent in the woods, nothing bad had happened to them. No one had called to him, no one had tried to chase him or crush him with tree roots. Maybe they'd be all right this time.

Up ahead, he spotted a familiar landmark. Oak Alley, as Gabe liked to call it, was a corridor about a quarter mile long that led to the birch tree spiral. When he saw it his heart beat a little harder. He was excited to be here, but a little fearful, too; he could feel a sort of tension in the air.

"We're almost there," he told the others. "I guess you were right about the stream," he admitted, forcing his rebelling tongue to push the words out. Abazi looked away. Kris only grinned. "Or you got lucky," he added, determined to prove he wasn't as big a fool as they seemed to take him for.

Before entering the alley, Gabe stopped and gazed up at the giant trees. Strong and tall, they seemed almost majestic in their power. It didn't make sense that Oswald wasn't King of the Forest Immortal. He was one of these amazing trees, meant to lead. Not Gabe. Gabe preferred to just keep his head down and do what needed to be done. Nothing more, nothing less.

Using the books left behind on his bookshelf, he'd tracked down the type of tree he'd turned into. According to what he'd read, he deduced that he was a hawthorn, certainly nothing special. Hawthorns typically didn't grow very big, but their deadly thorns made up for their smaller size. Their wood was gray, and in the summer, the hawthorn tree's fragrant white flowers, with pink-tipped stamens, burst into bloom. Some thought the flowers smelled rather rank while others thought they smelled like apples. Further reading revealed that different types of hawthorn gave off different odors. Remembering the intoxicating scent he'd smelled when he'd first turned into a tree, Gabe was glad his was of the nice-smelling variety. He had enough troubles as it was; he didn't need to add stinky to the list.

People also seemed to be at odds with how they felt about the hawthorn tree. Was it good or bad? Well, apparently it was both. Elves and fairies considered the hawthorn sacred. Its wood produced the hottest fire, its leaves and blossoms were medicinal, and it could be used for spells for protection and to promote love and marriage. Greeks and Romans considered the hawthorn a symbol of hope. On the other side, medieval Europe believed the hawthorn was symbolic of witchcraft and death. Translated from Irish, hawthorn means harm. Gabe also came across the following rhyme: "Hawthorn bloom and elder-flowers will fill a house with evil powers."

Nice.

The worst of it was that the hawthorn tree was considered the sister tree to the blackthorn. Straif and his followers were blackthorns. Which made them all what? Cousins? Should he be calling Straif uncle? Whatever the relation, it was disturbing, because really, the two trees weren't all that different. In fact, it was hard to tell the difference between them. Blackthorns get their flowers before their leaves and hawthorns get their leaves before their flowers. Hawthorns have lobed leaves, like an oak leaf, and blackthorns have elliptical leaves, more of a teardrop shape. Another difference is that blackthorns have dark, nearly black bark, while hawthorns are more of a gray color, turning brown and cracked with age. Not white, the ancient symbol of goodness and purity, just less dark.

Again, *nice*.

It also seemed a strange coincidence that his family had distant ancestors who'd either picked or been given the name Hawthorne. But it could only be a coincidence since he wasn't actually related to the Hawthornes. He was a hawthorn, but not a Hawthorne. Philosophers would love the irony of his situation.

At any rate, the hawthorn tree didn't exactly give the impression of majesty. Oaks, on the other hand, were grand and strong and regal. In terms of tree lore, the oak was known as the King of the forest, associated with gods and goddesses, and thought to be very magical. If that weren't an advertisement for who the Dryads should follow, Gabe didn't know what was.

"Well, here we go," he said, speaking half to himself, as though needing a boost for courage. He motioned the others to go ahead of him.

The group was making good time through the corridor when Gabe felt a stinging crack on his forehead. "Ow!" His searching fingers didn't find any blood, but a small goose egg was already forming. "What the heck was that?" He glanced up at the trees. They returned his gaze, quiet and unyielding, as always. The others hadn't noticed his injury and had gained on him. He began to walk again, faster now.

"Ow!" Another missile hit its mark—in nearly the same spot. "Son of a—!" This time he searched for the missile that had whacked him good. On the ground by his left foot sat an acorn the size of a strawberry, light green topped by a golden brown cap, looking innocent, yet potentially deadly.

"What's your problem?" Abazi called back, ever the nurturer. "Did you trip again?"

"I've been hit on the head by an acorn *twice!*" The moment the word 'twice' was out of his mouth, the barrage began and the acorns flew at him like bullets. "Run!" he cried, leaping forward as the projectiles rained down on him.

It didn't take long for him to realize he was the only one getting hit. He sprinted past the others, desperate to escape the oaks. Just when he thought he was going to develop permanent brain damage, he burst into the birch spiral and the bombardment abruptly stopped. The others soon caught up to him, unharmed.

"Holy crap!" Kris shouted when he reached Gabe. "That was *awesome!*"

"Awesome? I'm *bleeding!*" A couple acorns had managed to gouge two cuts across his forehead. "How am I going to explain this to Mom?"

"She'll just think you tripped—like you always do."

"I suppose," Gabe mumbled, pulling a handkerchief from his pocket and dabbing at the blood. Every few seconds he'd stop and study the cloth, checking to see how much blood he was losing. It seemed like gallons.

Kimber, the last to reach him, hurried to his side. "Are you all right, Gabe?" Her voice was breathless and concerned, her sweet blue eyes wide with worry.

Seeing her anxiety, he thought he'd better sugarcoat things. Jer wasn't the only person who felt a desire to protect Kimber, even though she was actually pretty tough. "I'm fine. Just a little bruised."

"But you're bleeding!"

Kimber was fast becoming Gabe's favorite person in the world. "I'll be all right. It's just a scratch." His voice unconsciously deepened. "Nothing to worry about."

She gave him a shaky smile. "I would've been scared to death!"

"Well, I'm glad they were only targeting me."

"That was really strange," Jer murmured thoughtfully. "Why just you?"

"Because Oswald doesn't like me, remember?" he said, surprisingly calm. Maybe he was just relieved it hadn't been Wildrr. "And these oaks are his kind. So of course they don't like me, either."

"It all sounds to me a bit like Children of the A-corn." Abazi snickered.

Gabe bent down, picked up one of the acorns, and threw it at her. She easily ducked the half-hearted attempt. "I think that was your worst yet," he groaned, but with a smile. Right now he needed a little humor. He'd been attacked and it had been not only terrifying, but belittling, as well. No one likes to be hated, and that attack, as cold and ruthless as it had been, felt very personal.

Kris put his arm around his big brother. "Good thing you're fast, hm?" Laughing, he dragged Gabe along with him, moving him away from the oaks and into the spiral. The others followed after them, more cautious now, eyes darting upward every few seconds. "Didn't think anything like that would happen," Kris said quietly as he pulled his brother down to the ground for a breather.

Gabe sat, but pulled away from Kris's arm. It was his brother's fault, after all, for insisting they keep going. "Well, it did happen. Let's just figure out the stupid riddle and get out of here, okay?"

Kris nodded. "That's cool with me, but let's eat something first. I'm starving. We should probably get our weapons out, too."

Gabe wasn't hungry, but he ate anyway, his mind furiously working to avoid thinking about Wildrr and the Lady and the attack by the oak trees. When he saw that everyone was finished with their snack, he pulled on his backpack and stood up. "Let's get this over with."

The air in the spiral was cool, the light dim, and though Gabe felt better being here amongst the birch, he still felt far from safe. When they emerged onto the field, his worries changed to stomach churning fear. The giant sycamore that had served as their gentle canopy the night they'd spent here at Dame Hazel's invitation, was a blackened mess.

Isis was dead.

Chapter Four

An Unwelcome Visitor

Gabe skidded to a halt inches from the charred ruin of what had once been the grand Isis. "What happened to her?" Abazi gasped behind him.

"Struck by lightning?" Jer guessed.

"Or someone torched her," Gabe replied grimly. "I can't believe this was an accident."

"But she was so beautiful!" Kimber mourned.

"Straif did this," Gabe growled. "Or one of his stupid sons."

"We can't be sure—" Jer began.

"*I* can be! Wildrr said Straif was going after Oswald and his band. *He* did this. I just know it!"

"Calm down, Gabe," Kris soothed. "It won't bring her back."

"I *won't* calm down! They killed her! I don't know why, but I'm sure it wasn't for any good reason. They probably just felt like burning something." Gabe felt awful inside, like a part of him had died, too. Like maybe he should've done something to help her. Like he was responsible.

"Maybe Straif was looking for the key, too," Jer suggested.

Everyone turned to face him. "You think so?" Gabe asked.

"I don't know. If it's important, I don't see why he wouldn't want to find it."

"But where *is* the key?" Kris asked. "We went round and round, just like the riddle said."

"Maybe Isis was the key," Kimber suggested.

"But she's dead," Gabe said bleakly.

"Could the key be something symbolic?" Jer wondered. "Like something to do with a sycamore tree or the name Isis?"

"It's possible," Gabe answered thoughtfully. "But I can't think of anything off-hand."

Kris punched his palm. "This really sucks, you guys."

"We could still look around," Abazi pointed out. "I'd hate to have come all this way and miss finding our clue."

"You're right," Gabe agreed, and after a few more moments of staring at the blackened ruin, the group spread out and searched the field near Isis. With many muttered apologies to the once majestic tree, they searched through the ash and charred wood around her trunk. No one found anything, not even Kris, who braved the task of looking inside the last bit of trunk that remained standing.

"I think we need to go home," Gabe said tiredly, his hands black and aching. He couldn't take his eyes off Isis's ruined form and yet he would pay anything never to have to see it again. But he would see it again—the image was branded in his mind.

For once, nobody argued with him.

The group hurried toward home, weapons drawn, eyes searching. Their little adventure had grown too real. Isis's death had scarred them all. Luckily, the oaks did not attack again. Once Gabe thought he heard tiny feet following after them, but nothing made itself known. Back at the stream, he noticed it had reverted to its old course.

"It looks normal again," Jer commented, noticing, too.

"I imagine it does that to throw people off," Kris said, bending down to dip his hands in the cold water. "Get them lost."

"So Straif and his dark dorks can find them," Jer finished angrily.

"Probably," Kris acknowledged. "It's a good strategy."

They crossed the stream, then washed the soot off their hands and faces as best they could. Gabe said—though strangely, with some reluctance this time—"We can't go in the woods anymore. It's just too dangerous."

"But what about Hollie?" Kris demanded. "And the *key*?"

"Hollie's safe with Oswald. The key…well, I have no idea about that, and truthfully, I don't give a crap." He wouldn't soon forget how ruthlessly the oaks had attacked him and had no desire for a repeat performance.

"But maybe it's the answer to all your problems, Gabe," Kris persisted. "If we figure out this riddle, you'll know what's going on with you. Why you're a tree, who your real mom is—"

"Did it ever occur to you that maybe I don't want to know?" He *did* want to know—desperately—but he wasn't going to admit that to Kris, nor to anyone. He didn't even want to admit it to himself.

"Why don't we give it a few days?" Kimber proposed. "We can all think about the riddle and see if we can figure it out."

"I don't have much free time this week," Gabe said, feeling suddenly very tired. "I have two papers due on Wednesday and a history test on Friday."

"You can bet *I'll* be thinking about the riddle." Kris stood and dried his hands on his jeans.

Everyone else had the good sense not to say anything more on the subject, except Abazi. "I'm just hoping this is all a j-oak," she declared as she walked away from the stream, toward home. "Get it? Joke? J-oak?"

Laughing, she left them, not bothering to say goodbye. Kimber followed her, after telling Gabe she hoped he felt better soon. Only the sound of the rushing stream and Abazi's laughter could be heard as the brothers watched the girls go, not bothering to catch up.

~~~~~~

The next bad thing to happen was Wednesday, four days after their botched mission to find the key. During that time, Gabe had done his best to quell any conversation started by his brothers or Abazi about the riddle or about keys or about what to do next. Kimber wisely left him alone. He finished his two papers and studied for his test. He worked at Woodlands on Sunday while Abazi was up north visiting family. Her dad was trying very hard to increase her knowledge of her ancestors and culture, and Abazi was resisting the effort just as hard.

"They want me to do the sweat lodge next," she told Gabe on Tuesday. "I told them I sweat enough on my own, thank you very much."

Gabe had long ago decided that Abazi wasn't resisting her culture so much as that she simply enjoyed being rebellious. She was one of those people who would actually cut off her nose to spite her face. She just didn't like being told what to do. She and Jer had that in common.

Wednesday after school, he parked the truck by the barn, and while his brothers ran to the house, he followed at a more leisurely pace, his sneakers kicking up dust as he crossed the dirt driveway. As he moseyed along, his foot caught against a tuft of grass and he stumbled. He was fighting to regain his balance when his eyes caught a hint of white where the little door was hidden. His stomach clenched tightly.

Crap.

All he wanted to do was go over his history notes and finish up his math homework. He didn't want this. But despite what he wanted or didn't want to do, his feet had a mind of their own and began taking him toward the door. He pushed aside the thick undergrowth and made his way into the small space by the door. Same as before, there was another note. The familiar writing made his hands shake and he felt like someone was trying to force his Adam's apple down his throat.

He plucked the note off the door, but before he could read it, he spotted someone male heading toward the porch, which was odd. People rarely came to the house—Mom and Dad weren't exactly the outgoing type. Whoever it was looked way too young to be Grandpa Hawthorne or Dad himself. Gabe shoved the note into his pocket and hurried out from the bushes, only to freeze in his tracks. *Oswald.*

Oswald noticed him right away. Gabe's feet found their feeling again and he moved to cut him off. "What are you doing here?" he hissed, trying to block anyone's view of the trespasser.

Oswald stepped around him. Except for his curly, reddish-brown hair, dark eyes, and the pale scars over his left eye and along his jaw, he looked nothing like his usual self, his typical outfit of green cape, leather boots, and brown pants replaced by ordinary jeans, sneakers, and a red hoodie. In fact, the Dryad didn't look different from any other teenager, and that scared Gabe.

"I heard ye tried to pay me a visit," he replied in the Dryads' lilting accent. "So I came to return the favor." He climbed the steps. Gabe's brothers had left the inside door open so that only the screen door stood in the way. "Are ye not goin' to invite me in?"

"No!"

"Gabe?" his mother called from the kitchen, and his innards quivered painfully. "Is that you?"

"Yeah, it's me," he reluctantly admitted.

She came to the door. "Who's this?" She beamed at Oswald. He smiled back and bowed politely. Judging by the look on his mother's face, she was loving the gallant gentleman act.

"I'm a friend of Gabe's," he said, straightening up. Somehow he had lost his accent, now sounding more like a Mainer than Gabe ever would. "Oswald Eik."

"Really?" She looked very pleased. Gabe had had a lot of friends back in San Jose. Here, not so many. "Come in." She held the door for both of them. "You know, you look just like my brother, Richard." Her eyes studied him.

Oswald glanced over at Gabe, looking both superior and mischievous. "What a coincidence."

"If I didn't know better, I'd say you could be his twin. Hopefully not an illegitimate son?" She laughed. "Just kidding. Are you hungry?"

"I'm fine, Mrs. Hawthorne."

"Well, Gabe should be thanking you. I was going to have him chop wood this afternoon, but since you showed up—"

"I can still do it, Mom. Oswald isn't staying. Right, Oswald?"

"I had that one question I wanted to ask you, then you can get right to chopping *wood*."

Gabe frowned. "I really should get to work. My mom needs me—"

"Gabe!" she scolded. "You're making me sound like a slave driver."

"You *are* a slave driver," he mumbled.

She shook her head, then smiled at Oswald. "He doesn't know how good he's got it."

Oswald returned her gaze. "I think you might be right about that."

Something flickered across her face, then disappeared. "Here. Take some oatmeal raisin cookies." She scooped up several cooling on a wire rack and set them on a thick white plate she deftly pulled out of the cupboard with her other hand.

Gabe stared at her, suddenly worried. Those cookies were meant to be sold at the store. So why was Oswald getting such special treatment? Did Mom know something? Did she sense that he was her real son?

He grabbed the plate from her. "Thanks, Mom! These smell delicious! You're right, you know. I do have it good here." She gave him a funny look and Gabe decided to get while the getting was good. "We'll take these upstairs. Come on, Oswald."

He turned and hurried off, hoping Oswald would follow. When he heard footsteps behind him in the long, dark hallway that led to the turret, he breathed a sigh of relief. Using the key his Grandma May had given him, which he kept on a necklace around his neck, he opened the skull-handled door, once again reminding himself that he had to do something about those depressing knobs. Then again, truth be told, they were kind of growing on him.

He climbed the stairs, unlocked the second door, which had the tantalizing tree goddess carved on it, and pushed it open. The outline of a tree etched into the half-moon window that dominated one wall of his room was barely visible today without the sun to highlight it, and for that Gabe was grateful. The window faced south, overlooking trees, trees, and more trees, but by this time of day, the sun had already passed to the other side of the house.

Gabe indicated the bed. "You can sit there if you want." He thought briefly of tidying up—scraps of cardboard and duct tape from his latest project littered the floor—then dismissed the idea. He didn't want to look like he cared what Oswald thought. Not after his comment about how Gabe didn't know how good he had it.

Oswald leisurely lowered himself to sit on the end of Gabe's bed. He bounced on it a few times, as though testing it out. Gabe's cheeks went hot. "I'll take one of those." Oswald pointed at the plate of cookies. His accent, along with his officious manner, had returned.

Gabe reluctantly held out the plate and Oswald grabbed two cookies. He bit into one, then smiled. "Yer mom knows her way around the kitchen."

"She likes to bake," Gabe mumbled, feeling increasingly anxious. "So where did you get those clothes?"

"Borrowed them."

"And what happened to your accent—down in the kitchen?"

Oswald took another bite. "I can pass as yer kind when I want to."

"According to Dame Hazel you *are* my kind."

Oswald's eyes darkened. "Take that back!"

"Seriously? You're the one threatening to take my family because I'm supposed to be you and you're supposed to be me! So are you one of us or not? And if you are, how is it that you can change into a tree?"

Oswald bit his lower lip. "Dame Hazel isn't talkin' much about anything at the moment. I keep tryin' to pin her down, but she's a slippery sort. Just keeps sayin' it will all make sense in the end."

"And did she happen to mention when that end might be?"

"No. But I won't accept that I'm not the leader of the forest. It's me destiny, me heritage!" He sprung to his feet, poking his scarred finger into Gabe's chest with such force that Gabe stumbled backward. "I won't let ye have it!"

"Good!" Gabe cried. "Because I don't want it. I don't want to be a king!"

Oswald's eyes narrowed. "Everyone wants to be a king, Gabriel. It's the ultimate power."

"I'd rather have my family."

"I can't wait to prove ye wrong."

"Then you'll have a long wait."

"Just stay away from me land and me Rogues and from Hollie. Ye got her in enough trouble."

"Me? She came *here*. She disguised herself and spied on *my* family. Besides, I don't want to go into the forest. I hate it there."

"Then why did ye come? Don't tell me ye missed me?"

Gabe wondered whether he should tell Oswald the truth, then decided against it when he saw the scowl on his face. "We were bored," he answered, staring at the floor. The toe of his shoe traced an arc in the dust.

Evasion turned out to be the wrong tactic to take. "Well, then. I guess I'll just be havin' to make yer life more interesting."

"I…" Gabe started, but Oswald was already at the bookcase. He found the hook and had it undone in a blink. The bookcase moved smoothly away from the wall, revealing a dark opening.

"Ye come into the forest again, Gabriel, and I'll be waitin' for ye. And if ye think Straif is bad, just imagine him ten times worse and then ye'll have me." With that he was gone, disappearing down the pole like a dream.

Seconds later, what sounded like a herd of elephants shattered the stillness of the air. Kris and Jer pushed and wrestled each other through the door, falling in a pile on the floor at Gabe's feet.

"Mom said you have a visitor!" Jer's blue eyes searched the room. "Who?"

"Oswald decided to pay me a visit," Gabe replied glumly as he headed over to close the bookshelf and replace the hook.

Kris climbed to his feet, then helped his brother up. "You've got to be kidding me!"

"I wish."

"What did he want?" Jer asked, brushing bits of cardboard off his pants. Gabe made a mental note to sweep one of these days. Abazi would give him no end of grief if she saw how bad it was in here, not that she would ever deign to set foot in his room.

He drew in a fortifying breath, forcing his mind away from Abazi and back to the less mundane issues of kings and forests. "To threaten me, I guess. He found out that we were in the forest."

"Did you tell him why?" Kris demanded. Gabe shook his head. "Good man!" Kris patted his brother on the back. "No sense giving away all our secrets."

"Did you at least fish for information?" Jer wondered. "Like whether he sent the riddle?"

Gabe mentally smacked his forehead. Sometimes he missed asking the most obvious things. "Didn't think of that."

"It would've made him suspicious, anyway, and we don't want that," Kris put in. Likely he didn't want any competition for that key.

"Yoo-hoo!" a voice called from the stairwell. "I've brought lemonade!" A few seconds later, Mom strode through the doorway, bearing a tray of lemonade-filled glasses. Behind her padded Gypsy, the black and white kitten Gabe thought of as his own. She jumped on the bed and started cleaning herself. Gabe took the tray from his mother as she looked around the room. "Where's your friend?"

"He had to go."

She frowned. "But how did he get out? I was in the kitchen the whole time."

"The *whole* time?" Kris asked, his expression innocent.

Her head tilted to one side. "Well, I guess I did bring some laundry downstairs. But that only took about thirty seconds."

"That's probably when he went out," Gabe rushed to say. "He had to get home."

"Oh." She looked disappointed. "I didn't get to say goodbye. Well, I guess the important question is, did he like my cookies?"

Gabe was tempted to lie and say no. But he couldn't hurt her feelings to save his own. "Yeah, he liked them."

She smiled, pleased. "Good. He has excellent taste. You should invite him over this weekend, for lunch or something. Bring the tray down when you're done." Her eyes scanned the room. "And for heaven's sake, sweep this floor!" With that she was gone.

"I think we can rule out Mom as the riddle writer," Gabe said, feeling relief. He really didn't want her to be the one.

"How's that?" Kris asked.

"Because she had no idea how Oswald got out of the house. She really doesn't know about the hidden door."

"Makes sense," Jer said. "Unless she was covering, though she didn't really act like she was."

"I didn't think so, either," Kris agreed. "Though she sounds like she likes Oswald. How'd he manage that? Didn't she think he looked and talked a bit weird?"

"He looked and talked just like any kid. He dropped the accent and was wearing clothes like us."

Jer's eyes were worried. "You don't think he'd actually tell her who he is, do you?"

Gabe shook his head. "He might, especially if we go back into the woods. He warned me to stay away—from the Forest Immortal, from his band, and from Hollie."

Kris's eyes lit up. "He can't do that!"

Gabe held up his hand. "He can, and he did. So let's just leave it at that."

"But—!"

"But nothing. I'm not going to screw up this family because your ego's offended! Got it?"

Kris looked mutinous. "I've got homework," was all he said before grabbing a couple of cookies and leaving.

When he was gone, Jer laughed. "I don't think he's 'got it' at all."

Gabe plopped down on his bed and started petting Gypsy. "I don't think so, either."

Jer sat down next to him and together they finished their glass of sour, almost bitter, lemonade and the rest of the cookies. The second note sat forgotten in Gabe's pocket.

Chapter Five

Schemes

It was Friday afternoon, the beginning of a three-day weekend. Monday was Columbus Day and normally Gabe would have been ecstatic to have an extra day off from school. Not this time. Abazi had waylaid him after one of their classes and told him the latest bad news—which no one was supposed to know, but pretty much everyone did—that a company was definitely coming to Ranger to survey the forest. They didn't have time to discuss her news further, but Gabe had brooded on it for the rest of the day.

After school, on the way out to the parking lot, she caught up to him. "We've got to stop them, Gabe!"

"What do you want me to do?" he growled, feeling overwhelmed. In addition to spending the last few days worrying about Oswald's threat—thinking he was going to show up at any moment and make his claim on Gabe's family—he was positive he'd failed his history test. He'd misunderstood two of the essay questions and also had mixed up a couple of multiple choices. His papers were probably crap, too.

"You could man up, for starters."

"Man up?" He glared at her. "What the heck is that supposed to mean, anyway? If I told you to woman up, you'd be offended."

"I would, so don't ever say that to me." She tugged at her braid, thinking. "We need to do something, Hawthorne, and fast. I'm thinking sabotage."

"I'm in," Kris said, joining them. He waved off the gaggle of girls trailing behind him. They giggled, then slowly drifted away with several gooey glances over their shoulders at him, along with many more giggles.

"You don't even know what we're doing." Gabe rubbed his forehead irritably.

"So why don't you fill me in?"

Jer and Kimber came around the other side of the truck. "Are we planning something?" Jer looked excited.

Abazi filled them in on what was happening. "I was thinking about pouring sugar in their gas tanks, but now I've got a better idea. It will involve some exaggerating on our parts, however."

"You mean lying?" Gabe interpreted.

She ignored him. "You know how my dad always wants me to go native?" She didn't bother waiting for anyone to answer. "Well, I've decided to tell him that this weekend I'm going on a retreat to commune with nature and find my spirit guide."

"Where are you going to do that?"

She punched Gabe's shoulder. "The woods, dummy."

He stopped himself in time from reaching up and rubbing the sore spot. Dang, that girl could punch. "And get yourself killed?" Not to mention himself. He hadn't yet told anyone about Oswald's threat, but now might be a good time.

"I'm not going alone, idiot. You're all coming with me. We'll set up a watch, keep a fire burning. You can bet the Ko-goks don't like fire, and burning wood should serve as a threat to any other Dryads not to mess with us."

"It won't work. Our mom would never let us camp out in the woods. They scare her."

"What if you told her you were going to be camping on Mount Vidar? She might feel better about that part of the woods."

She might, which is why Gabe chose to ignore the suggestion. Instead he asked, "What do you plan on doing, Abazi, and why do we need to stay overnight to do it?"

She grinned. "Agree to do it and I'll tell you."

"And if I don't agree?"

"Then I'll tell your mom you're a speed demon and that you almost ran me over in the parking lot the other day."

"Nice try, but that won't stop her from letting me drive. She hates getting up early and Dad still isn't well enough to drive us to school."

"You can take the bus."

"Not home from any after school activity. We start basketball soon."

"Okay. Then you're fired."

"You can't fire me! It's your dad's store and—"

"And he'll do whatever I ask him to do." She gazed impudently at Gabe, arms crossed. "Haven't you picked up on the fact that I'm Daddy's Little Indian Princess? His Precious Pocahontas? His Sassy Sacagawea?"

Gabe bit down on his lip. He'd already come to rely on the money he earned working at Woodlands. It wasn't a lot, but it was enough to pay for his video game obsession or a new shirt, with some left over for college. Plus, he paid for gas and knew his mom was secretly grateful he did. He couldn't take that away from her. Besides, he still had that favorite child role to maintain.

"You're a real witch, Abazi."

Her expression was triumphant. "Why do I have the feeling you'd rather have called me something else? Something that rhymes with witch."

"I don't say that kind of thing in front of a lady." Then he made sure she saw him look directly at Kimber, who blushed and stared at the ground, though he thought he caught an amused smile playing around the corners of her mouth.

Abazi's dark eyes narrowed dangerously. "You listen to me, Hawthorne." She pointed a ringed finger at his chest. "You've spent the whole week acting like you're the King—telling us what we can talk about and what we can't. Well, I for one, am sick of it."

"Hear, hear," Kris interjected. "The King is dead!"

Abazi plowed on. "Dame Hazel might think you're King of the forest, but around here, you're just a god-awful pain in the butt who hasn't the guts to do what's right. So I'm taking over. You'll tell your mother we're heading up to the mountain where my dad says it's safe. And you will pack a good sleeping bag and food and matches and weapons, too."

Kris looked thrilled. "I'll bring the matches!"

"So what are we going to *do* exactly?" Kimber asked. "You know my mom won't like me out camping."

"My dad will make it okay with her. I'll just be sure to emphasize the whole spiritual importance of this journey, its sacredness, blah, blah, blah. Your mom will listen to him. You know she's got the hots for him." Kimber blushed.

Gabe shook his head doubtfully. "You really think they'll let you go with three boys, two of whom are teenagers?"

"They won't know you're going with us." Her eyes glittered with the deviousness of her plan.

He sighed and ran a hand through his thick hair. He needed a haircut. He needed a vacation. No, what he really needed was a new life. "You'd really get your dad to fire me?"

She nodded. "I don't want to because that would mean I'd have to work more, but I'm also not going to let those harridans get their way."

Gabe wondered if Abazi actually cared about the woods, or if she just wanted to get the upper hand with Mrs. Morrigan. The bossy woman came up in conversation several times a week. No. Make that several times a day. He wondered what she'd done, other than be herself, to make Abazi so angry with her.

"Fine. But this is it. I'm not doing anything like this again and if you threaten me, I'll be sure to do the same."

She tossed her head. "Whatever."

He hated that word, except, of course, when he was the one using it. "That's a promise, Abazi."

She stared at him coolly. "That threat is as empty as your head."

His fingers tightened into fists and his skin prickled uncomfortably as he willed himself to breathe deeply. No sense throwing a hissy fit in the school parking lot. She'd just use it against him at some later, and much anticipated, date. Or, someone would get it on video and stream it on the Internet. "So what's your plan?" he ground out.

"We're going to haunt the woods."

"Huh?" Kris's attention was back again. He'd been staring off into space for the last minute.

"We're going to scare off the surveyors. If you have any Halloween costumes or make-up, bring what you have."

"We're going to scare them away?" Jer sounded awed. "I can't wait!" Kimber gave him an affectionate look. At thirteen, she was only a year older than him, but sometimes she seemed decades older than all of them, even Abazi and Gabe who were both sixteen. "I've got an old megaphone. It's small, but it should do the trick nicely." He grinned happily.

"I guess I'll just tell my mom it's for a project," Kimber said. "No need to say what kind."

"That's the *spirit!*" Abazi cheered. "Any other ideas?"

"I can do a wicked good evil laugh," Kris volunteered.

"Excellent. How about you, Gabe?"

"I can turn into a tree. Is that good enough for you?" he asked drily.

"Sure. If you can actually do it again."

This time Gabe simply turned his back on her challenging eyes and climbed into the truck. "You'd better back up," he muttered under his breath as he started the engine. He revved it a few times for effect. She only batted her lashes, refusing to give way.

Kris and Jer piled in beside him and he shifted into reverse. "See you tomorrow after lunch, one o'clock," Abazi called as he backed up. "Meet us at the end of your driveway."

"We've got to figure out what to say to Mom to get her to let us go into the woods." Kris fiddled with the defunct knobs on the truck's dashboard as Gabe pulled out of the parking lot. "Something school-related might be best."

"Why don't we just tell her the truth?" Jer asked.

His brothers gaped at him and Gabe nearly drove off the road, the truck's tires hitting gravel before he pulled back onto the tar.

"I always knew you were crazy, little dude." Kris laughed.

"I know what I'm talking about," Jer persisted.

"Okay, which part are we telling her?" Gabe wanted to know.

"That Mrs. Morrigan is planning to send surveyors into the woods and we want to scare them off. We'll tell her we're camping out on the mountain, like Abazi suggested, so that we can catch them."

Kris nodded slowly. "It's crazy, but it just might work."

"The truth shall set us free," Gabe mumbled. But he had to admit that Jer's idea wasn't too bad. "All right. We'll try that. But let me do the talking." His brothers smiled their agreement.

Gabe parked the truck next to the barn and let his brothers run on ahead. They'd decided the other two should clear out while Gabe talked to Mom. When he entered the house, he found her making grape jelly from grapes he and his brothers had picked from the grape arbor (it seemed to Gabe that he was destined to have purple fingers—first blueberries, now grapes). Grandma was helping out by sitting at the table drinking coffee and giving directions.

"Hey, Grams."

She nodded at him. "How'd your test go?"

He was surprised she remembered. She'd stop in the store on Sunday and he'd told her about it. The whole time, however, she had seemed distracted, glancing over her shoulder every few seconds, clutching her giant hand-made bag close to her body. He'd bet good money that the old lady was up to something. But what?

"I think I failed it."

Grandma snorted. "Your mom always said things like that and not once did she fail. It would've done her good, though, to fail once in a while. Then she'd learn she could survive what she thought of as the worst thing in the world." She took a swig of coffee, giving Gabe a meaningful look with those shrewd, bright blue eyes of hers. He turned away. He was not in the mood for a lecture.

"What's up with your brothers?" Mom asked Gabe as he hung up his backpack and set his lunch bag on the cluttered counter.

"They're just excited to get a jump on our three-day weekend. Columbus Day is Monday," he prompted when she gave him a blank look.

She groaned. "That's *this* week?" He nodded. "Dangit! I haven't even started my fall cleaning. And now I'm going to have to deal with you three messing everything up while I'm trying to work."

"We don't do that anymore!" Gabe protested. "That's when we were kids."

"Yes, you do. And now the messes are even bigger. Your toilet paper, baking soda, and vinegar bombs come to mind."

He was about to further argue his case about how these experiments were simply him and his brothers engaging in the pursuit of science when he heard a light tapping coming from the staircase leading to the second floor. Kris and Jer, apparently listening in, were signaling him and it came to Gabe that he could use fall cleaning to help their case.

"Actually, we were thinking of going on a camping trip this weekend." He grabbed one of their own Macintosh apples from the bowl on the table. His teeth broke through red skin, into wonderfully tart flesh, and he chewed slowly as he waited for this to sink in.

"Camping?" Mom echoed. "Where?"

"Up on Mount Vidar."

She frowned. "I don't know…"

"You kids up to something?" Grandma demanded, and he cursed under his breath at her perspicacity. How did she always know?

"I might ask the same of you," he rejoined, thrilled to have thought up the perfect comeback for once.

Surprisingly, Grandma May blushed. "I don't know what you're talking about."

"Mom?" His mother was staring at Grandma May, looking both astonished and intrigued. "What's going on?"

"Nothing you need to worry about, missy."

Mom grimly tightened the lid on one of the jars. Usually Dad did this, but he seemed to be missing in action. "Spill it."

"Fine. Since you asked so nicely. Those harpies are bringing in surveyors."

Mom's green-brown eyes widened. "You're kidding me!"

"I heard that, too," Gabe admitted, figuring this was the best time to make his move. "They're surveying the woods this weekend."

"And you want to spy on them?" Mom supplied, quick to catch on.

Gabe's head dropped. "Something like that."

"Maybe sabotage them?" Grandma suggested, smiling secretively.

"Mom!"

"Ayla, those women are a menace. Next thing you know they'll be trying to buy us out of our property."

"They wouldn't dare!"

"Oh, yes, they would."

Mom looked suspicious. "Have they tried something with you?"

Grandma abruptly stood. "The mountain is a good place for the boys. It's time they got to know it anyway." She gave her daughter a meaningful look.

Mom sighed as she tightened the last jar and lowered it into the boiling water with a special clamp. "I don't know—"

"You've got to let them go some time."

Mom wiped her brow with the back of her hand. "I do want to clean this house."

"Well, there you go. You've got your excuse. I'm off." She headed to the screen door, then turned to fix Gabe with her icy blue gaze. "Bring those walking sticks I gave you last year for Christmas. They might come in handy." With those words, she was gone, down the driveway to her little cottage in the woods about half a mile away.

He heard the beeping sound of his mother setting the timer on the stove. "You'll be careful?" she said over her shoulder. "There've been recent sightings of mountain lions in the area."

"Mozi says those are just rumors to keep people out of the woods."

Mom raised an eyebrow. "You don't say. Well, in every rumor there's always a hint of truth. It's your job to ferret out that bit."

"What are you trying to say?"

"Just be careful," she sighed. "I'm not as worried about that stretch of woods up on the mountain, but still…"

"I know, I know. Lots of people have disappeared over the years."

"Never to be found again—" she reminded him in a dramatic voice. When he didn't respond, she finished, "Who most likely died a horrible death at the hands of some awful monster." His mom liked to exaggerate, but when she joked like this, he once again wondered just what she knew about those woods.

She headed for the cellar stairs. "I need to get the last load of laundry out. You might as well come and see if you can find that old tent of ours."

Gabe followed her down the dark stairwell into the dreaded basement, which he avoided whenever he could ever since a Ko-gok had attacked him through the wood chute. He searched the gray metal shelves in the corner while she pulled out clothes from the dryer. Not finding anything, he turned around to see his mom pull out a pair of his jeans. His stomach dropped.

The *note*. The second note. How could he have forgotten it? And now it would be ruined. His mom's rule was that if you valued something, don't leave it in your pockets, because she didn't do pocket searches before washing clothes. She had better things to do with her time.

He raced over to her. "I'll help." He grabbed the pants and hurriedly searched the pockets, pulling them inside out. There was nothing in any of them, not even lint. His eyes darted around, desperate now. Where before he wanted nothing to do with that note, he now felt an almost overwhelming urgency to find it.

"Looking for this?" His mom held up a crushed, white piece of paper. *Oh, crud.* "For once I decided to go through pockets. Kind of a yearly thing I do." She smiled and nodded appreciatively at her own wit.

"Uh, yeah, it's mine." He snatched it away.

"Love letter?" She grinned.

"Just something I'm working on," Gabe mumbled, quickly pocketing the note. He desperately wanted to read it, but didn't want to risk doing so in front of his mother. She would know immediately that something fishy was going on.

"So are you going to invite your friend, Oswald, to go camping with you?"

"Why would I do that?" he blurted. "I mean, he's busy this weekend. So you're okay with us going?" He half hoped she'd say no.

"I'm not thrilled about it, but it might not be a bad idea for you guys to get to know some of the woods. And if you should happen to come across anyone looking like they might be surveyors, feel free to scare the pants off them. But remember, if I'm questioned, I know nutink about anytink!" she said in her best Sergeant Schultz voice.

Gabe laughed. "Okay."

She handed him a pair of pants. "Why don't you finish up here? I've got to take those jelly jars out to set."

He took the pants and started to fold them.

She was halfway up the stairs when she stopped. "Try the attic. Now that I think about it, I probably put the tent up there. Your sleeping bags, too. Much drier."

"Okay, Mom." He let himself breathe again.

She disappeared through the doorway, into the warm, safe kitchen. When she was gone, he pulled the note out of his pocket and began to read.

Chapter Six

Your Eyes Are Blind

The second riddle turned out to be just as ridiculous and confusing as the first one.

Clue Number Two
(Since you ninnies couldn't
figure out the first.)

The answer is up
But your eyes are blind
Look high from the sky
And then you will find…
it.

After reading the note, Gabe stuffed it into his pocket. What the heck did it mean? He'd have to show the riddle to Kris and Jer. The question was, did he tell them he'd found it almost a week ago? Best not.

He quickly finished folding the laundry and carried the wicker basket upstairs. The sound of arguing voices met him, growing louder with each step. "But she's going to—"

"You stay out of it, Ayla!" Dad's voice, normally so relaxed, was surprisingly strong and vehement.

"I can't, Keith," she pleaded. "She ruins people. She could ruin us."

"I won't let that happen."

"You're forgetting what she did to—"

"I'm not forgetting anything."

Gabe wanted to eavesdrop longer, but the stair creaked beneath his shifting weight and there was silence. He took the last few steps in one stride and emerged from the doorway to find both his parents staring at him. Dad was sitting at the table, his hands clenching the pages of a newspaper, while Mom was wiping off a jam jar. He lifted the laundry basket. "Just bringing stuff up to Kris and Jer."

Dad gave him a strange look. "You're doing laundry?"

"Just helping out."

"And now you're going camping this weekend…" He was typically pretty easygoing, but he wasn't blind.

Gabe decided to go with the truth. "Mom told you about the surveyors?"

Dad heaved a sigh. "Yes, she did." Mom turned and busied herself with another jar. "And I'm not so convinced that what they're doing is a bad thing. Those woods could stand some clearing. It's healthy for them. Maybe healthy for all of us." Viewed one way, his words seemed innocent. Viewed another, well, they suggested that maybe Dad knew something about the woods and its strange inhabitants, that he wasn't entirely against getting rid of some of them. Gabe wondered which view was the correct one.

"Well, we're more interested in going up the mountain anyway," Gabe said.

The answer is up.

Gabe's heart beat a little harder. Could it be?

Look high from the sky.

The mountain. The answer was there. He had to tell his brothers *now*. They had to prepare. They could kill two birds with one stone. Scare off the surveyors, and solve those inane riddles.

"It's going to be cold," Dad warned, brandishing the newspaper. "Frost for sure. Maybe some flurries tomorrow night."

Gabe shivered. "Isn't that kind of early, even for Maine?"

Both his parents nodded, looking both concerned and a little bit excited. Weather anomalies had the power to bring out the little kid in everyone. Who knew what could happen? The blizzard to end all blizzards? An ice storm? Record cold temperatures?

He headed for the stairs. "I'll go look in the attic for the tent and sleeping bags." And fill his brothers in on everything. Well, *almost* everything.

"All the other camping gear should be up there, too," his dad called after him.

"Okay," Gabe hollered back. "I'll look for it."

He found his brothers in Kris's bedroom, tinkering with wires. Little Joe lazily batted at the ends. They swung about when they heard the door.

"Well?" Kris demanded.

"She said yes."

Jer's mouth dropped open. "How'd you manage that?"

"A little of my natural charm—" He saw their skepticism. "And Grandma May. She knows about the surveyors. Mom even kind of gave us permission to scare them off. Dad's not too thrilled about it, but he's not stopping us."

Jer shook his head in wonder. "It's a miracle."

"It's because she doesn't like Mrs. Morrigan," Kris put in, touching two wires together. There was a sizzling noise and a puff of smoke. He quickly pulled them apart.

"There's something else," Gabe said.

Two pairs of eyes focused on him. "Well…" Jer prompted. "Spit it out before I die of old age."

"Or," Gabe paused, "I could keep it to myself, and let you die of old age."

"Knock it off, you two," Kris scolded, sounding eerily like their mother. "We've got to work together now. We have a mission and nothing should get in the way of our completing it."

"Oh, fine." Gabe pulled the riddle out of his pocket.

Kris, having longer arms, beat Jer and snatched the note from Gabe. He read it aloud. When he was done, he looked at his brothers. "Who the heck is this kook?"

"A really bad poet?" Jer offered.

"Or maybe Grandma's up to something." Gabe filled them in on what she'd said about sabotaging the surveyors, and also his theory that the poem was talking about the mountains.

"You think she's doing this to get us out in those woods?"

"It's a strange way of going about it." Gabe cracked a knuckle. "She's usually so blunt. You'd think she'd just tell us."

"Either way," Jer said, "I think we need to follow up on it. Something's going on in those woods. Somebody burned Isis. My guess is Straif, but why did he do it, and how did he manage it?"

"The only way to find out is to go to the mountains," Kris declared with a grin.

"Fine," Gabe agreed. "I don't like it, but we can't let those surveyors go into the woods." His brothers nodded. "Mom and Dad said there's camping stuff in the attic. You two go fetch it—and don't get distracted…" He looked pointedly at Kris. "Just get the job done. We have a lot to do before tomorrow. We'll need food, warm clothes, weapons, and a plan to scare off the surveyors."

Before the last "s" was out, his brothers had leaped to their feet. Seconds later, he heard footsteps pounding up the attic stairs. He dumped their clean clothes on their beds, then headed to his room to put away his own.

Mom and Dad were working side by side at the counter, speaking in low voices, and didn't even notice Gabe pass by. After shoving his clothes into their proper drawers, he went around with a backpack and packed their weapons, including the staffs Grandma May had made for them. After re-reading the riddle, along with the first one, he sat down at his desk and copied them onto a piece of paper. Grabbing a Ziploc baggie from his stash, he shoved the folded paper inside and stuck it in his backpack.

What was taking his brothers so long?

He hurried up to the attic, ready to crack down on them because they were goofing around. They could never take things seriously, leaving him to do all the work. With a martyred sigh, he climbed the steps two at a time. Just as he expected, he found his brothers not working. Instead, they were standing stock-still in the middle of the attic staring up at the high ceiling. He froze and followed their eyes upward.

"I heard it, too," Jer whispered. "Like someone was throwing something at the roof."

Kris noticed Gabe. "Don't move. Something weird's going on."

Gabe stayed where he was, cocking his right ear upward. When he heard the cacophonous noise, he almost couldn't believe it. It sounded like they were under attack. His heart pounded crazily in his chest and his mouth went bone dry. "Come on!" he ordered and tore down the steps. Kris and Jer clattered after him.

"Whoa!" Dad cried as they hurtled through the kitchen. "Where's the fire?"

"I'm going to get you guys!" Jer yelled, hopefully throwing Dad off track. "And give you the mother of all wedgies!"

Gabe pounded down the porch steps and around to the back of the house. It only occurred to him as he rounded the corner that he could be running right into danger. He skidded to a halt, which was a stupid thing to do, being that his brothers were right behind him. The resulting impact sent him sprawling.

As the ground rose up to meet him, his eyes caught flashes of movement heading toward the line of trees. "Get off!" he hollered at Kris, whose arms were tangled in Gabe's legs. "They're getting away!"

"I'm trying!" But by the time they got themselves straightened out and on their feet, whatever had been there was gone. Kris's brown eyes were bright. "Another second and I'd've had them!"

Gabe stared at the trees. "The question is, who's 'them'?"

"Straif and his gang, of course," Kris answered.

Gabe swallowed hard. "I don't know. That's taking a big risk. It's still daylight. Anybody could have seen them."

"Not to mention the fact that the sun would've burned them," Jer added.

Silence descended as the boys thought about this. "Then who was it?" Kris wondered.

Gabe took one last look at the forest, which gave nothing away, then turned to go. He'd taken only two steps when he heard a loud crunch. He glanced down. Beneath his foot was a crushed acorn. He studied the pale chunks for a moment before realizing that some sort of writing was etched on the surface. He picked up a piece, but couldn't make out the tiny words. He grabbed another acorn off the ground, a whole one.

"What are you doing?" Jer asked, coming closer.

"I'm reading an acorn, what else?"

"Yeah, right. I *do* have a brain, you know." Gabe silently handed his brother the wooden missive. "Make like a tree and leave," Jer read in a low voice. "Ouch. That's really bad."

Kris grabbed up a handful. "Bugger off! Scram, ye wee feartie! Beat it, bampot! Oh, and my personal favorite, Scalamabooch!"

"That sounds like something Grandma May would say," Gabe remarked, feeling a little stunned and a *lot* weirded out as he read another one, "Usurper." He felt his face go hot. Someone was accusing him of taking something that wasn't his...something he didn't even want. But if what Oswald had told Gabe about being switched was true, then Oswald was the *real* Usurper.

"We have every right to go into those woods," Kris declared, his face alive with indignation. "They can't *ban* us!"

"Yeah!" Jer agreed. "They're our woods! And, well, especially yours, Gabe, if Dame Hazel was telling the truth."

"So you think it's Oswald and his gang behind this?" Gabe said slowly, throwing the acorn as hard as he could. It hit the side of the house and ricocheted off to land at his feet. He kicked it.

"Who else would it be?" Jer looked back and forth at them.

Who, indeed?

Still, even though Oswald hadn't been the friendliest toward Gabe, Gabe wasn't sure he would do something like this. It seemed so, well, mean. But the oaks had thrown acorns at Gabe, and now, here were acorns everywhere. It either had to be the Rogues, or Straif and his goons had braved the sun and open yard.

"We'd better get back inside. We've got a lot of packing to do."

"You still want to do this?" Kris asked, impressed.

"Not really. But I'm going to, anyway."

He'd never get another moment's rest until he knew for sure what was going on. Kris wasn't the only one who was curious about those riddles. Plus there were those surveyors to deal with. Not only were they troublesome, they could be in trouble if Straif got to them first. Big trouble.

There was something else Gabe wanted to know that he could only find out if he went into the forest. He wanted—*needed*—to know about his real mother. Was she still looking for him? Was she lonely? Would they ever meet face to face? And what would happen if they did?

The possibilities made Gabe shiver.

Chapter Seven

To the Mountain

The following day, after lunch, they met Abazi and Kimber at the end of the driveway, by the main road. The girls wore heavy jackets, thick gloves, wool hats, and sturdy hiking boots. Gabe and his brothers had to make do with some of Grandpa May's old winter jackets, worn work gloves Grandpa Hawthorne had dropped off several weeks ago to help with the wood cutting, and their sneakers. Living in San Jose hadn't required anything more than a windbreaker and a sweater—at the worst of times.

After greetings were exchanged, the boys quickly looped leather belts around their waists and set up their assortment of weapons. Everyone took a willow whip and a bata. Kris grabbed the tomahawk and Jer strapped on the bow and arrows, specially made with wood tips instead of the typical steel. Knowing the Ko-goks did not like the touch of wood, Jer had taken on the task of making the arrows with enthusiasm. Gabe slid a wooden staff through the belt at his back. They'd all wanted to take Grandma's walking sticks, too, but decided that a couple of them should leave their hands free in case Kimber needed to be carried.

"How did you convince your mom to let you come?" Jer asked Kimber. Her blue eyes were barely visible beneath an overlarge pink hat, and the tip of a bata stuck out of her jacket's right pocket like a turtle popping up for air.

"I told her it was this or start letting me wear make-up. She almost decided on the make-up until I added that I figured it would be all I needed to get this senior who I thought was absolutely *dreamy*"—here she fluttered her eyelashes and clasped her hands together—"to ask me out on a date. After that, she happily helped me pack." Kimber grinned mischievously.

For his part, Jer looked both sick to his stomach and ready to go after the guy and pound his head into the ground. Sometimes Jer had anger issues.

"I made him up," she quickly added, seeing Jer's face.

He didn't look entirely convinced, but he did let his fists uncurl.

"So what did you tell *your* parents?" Abazi wanted to know. She wore a beaded headband, just visible beneath her hat, and had woven her black hair into tight braids that fell down her back. She carried her own tomahawk and bata, tucked into a belt tied around her waist. "My dad totally fell for the whole spiritual line I gave him. It was almost sad, seeing him get so excited. He really needs to get a life. Living vicariously through me is totally pathetic."

"*Totally,*" Gabe agreed, nodding vigorously. She gave him a dirty look.

Kris rubbed his hands together and shuffled from foot to foot. Even though he was wearing gloves, he was still cold. Gabe, whom his mother had deemed hot-blooded because he'd happily wear shorts all winter, actually liked the cold. But even to him, this was pretty frigid. The temperature gauge on the porch read forty degrees and the day was overcast, with the feel of moisture weighing down the air. There'd been a thin layer of frost on the truck's windows this morning, even though the sky was overcast, and Gabe had traced his name in the ice. Mom had warned them it would get colder in the higher elevations. "If you're smart, you'll come home to sleep. If you're not, at least try to get a fire going. Then I'll know where to find your frozen bodies."

Abazi clapped her hands together. "Well, dudes and dudettes. Time's a wastin'. Let's make like trees and leave," she joked and all three brothers swung around to stare at her. She was already heading across the main road—without checking for traffic, of course—toward a break in the trees and didn't notice their gaping mouths. "There's a trail we can follow, but it's hard going. You wusses might not be able to handle it."

"Did you come over to the house yesterday afternoon?" Gabe asked suddenly. "Maybe throw something at the roof?"

She stopped where the trees began and spun around to face him. "I was working at the store yesterday afternoon. Besides, I have better things to do than to try and scare you losers. It's way too easy."

Aha! He had her now. "How'd you know someone was trying to scare us?"

"Because of that witless look on your face."

Scared witless. Gabe actually got one of her puns for once.

"So are you going to tell me about it?" she asked over her shoulder as she started walking again. They were in the woods now and the dark green of the fir trees set off the yellow and orange leaves of the oak and beech, making them appear to glow. The wind stirred and torrents of leaves swirled to the ground like ballerinas. Winter was coming.

"We think it was either Straif or Oswald and his gang," Kris answered. "They threw acorns at the roof of the house, then took off. All the acorns had messages written on them. One of them said, 'Make like a tree and leave.'"

Abazi chuckled appreciatively. "Well, whoever it was, they're terribly clever." She paused a moment. "So, it sounds like Oswald is making good on his threat to keep you out of the woods."

"How did you know about that?" Gabe stopped walking, and one by one, so did everyone else. His eyes fixated on his brothers accusingly.

Kris's head swiveled toward the sky. "Crows!" He pointed at the birds flying overhead, patches of black glimpsed through the nearly bare branches of a stand of birch. As though in answer, the large birds began to caw in unison, their hoarse, froggy voices piercing the air.

"Nice try, Kris. You told her, didn't you?"

"She called this morning. She needs to know, Gabe. We all need to know everything. This doesn't just affect you, you know."

"You're just mad because you can't see Hollie."

"You've got that right! You and Oswald are a lot alike, you know, telling people what they can and can't do. I'm sick of it. So's Abazi."

"Whoa, cowboy." She held up her hands. "I'll do my own talking, thank you very much." Kris frowned, then nodded at her, and she went on, "I don't know what Oswald's up to, but he's on the brink of starting himself a little war."

Gabe winced. "A *war*? With us? You'd better hope not. We're way outnumbered and way less prepared." Oswald's band, the Rogues, with their dark green cloaks and silent faces, reminded Gabe of ninja warriors. They would be hard to beat, if not impossible.

"I'm not saying we're going to fight him, but he might need to be taught a lesson. He can't just push us around like this."

Gabe felt himself relenting a little. He liked that Abazi had said *us*. He didn't want to be the one making all the decisions; he didn't want to always be the bad guy. But somebody had to look out for the others. As the oldest male, it was up to him to be that person.

Still…if Abazi really meant it, maybe he didn't have to do it alone. He pulled off a glove and reached into his backpack. "Fine. Then you'd better read this." He handed her the paper, pointing to the second riddle.

She read it out loud, her nose wrinkling up more and more with each word. "I don't know about you guys, but I don't like being called a ninny," was her response. Gabe thought it was typical for her to focus on the name calling part.

"Well, do you have any ideas about what it might mean?"

"No, but I say we go after Oswald, confront him on it."

"Great idea. I'm sure he'll invite us to tea and we'll have a little chat. It'll be fun!"

She glared at him until he looked away. "Nice, smart aleck. Remember when he said he and his band were heading home to the mountain? Right before they left us?"

Oh, yeah. Gabe also remembered that Straif had said the Rogues lived "up there," most likely meaning the mountain. And Wildrr had mentioned Hollie being brought to safety in the mountains. Funny he hadn't remembered all that mentioning of mountains before. It was as though he'd taken all that information and locked it away in his head. But why do that? Especially when it made him look foolish in front of Abazi.

Maybe because he didn't want to think about Oswald, didn't want to think about his threats and his bullying. How he'd walked into Gabe's house like he owned the place. Because Gabe realized when he let himself dwell on these things, he grew angry. And when he grew angry, well, something strange started to happen to him. He felt really weird, as though a creature lived inside him and wanted to get out. He wasn't sure what would happen if he ever let that creature get free, but he knew it wouldn't be good.

"I thought we were going to scare off the surveyors?"

"That's tomorrow. I overheard Mrs. Deacon tell Crappy Candi that the survey team was going to have to camp out in the woods because of how long it's going to take to cover that amount of land. And they're getting paid extra to do the job fast."

"Can't they just use an airplane?" Kris asked. "That's what I would do."

"They have to figure out where the boundaries are; no one really knows for sure. And since these woods are so thick, it would be too hard to see anything from above."

"They have to put boundary markers down at each corner of the lot," Jer added. "That's why they'll need to scout the entire perimeter."

"Straif is going to kill them!" Kimber gasped, sounding sincerely worried for the surveyors.

"So scaring them off the land might save their lives," Gabe deduced.

"I think that's a good way to look at it," Kimber said softly. "They might be really nice people, just trying to earn a living."

Jer gave her an affectionate, if slightly condescending, look. "You hate seeing anyone get hurt."

"Not necessarily, Jer," she said firmly. "Don't confuse kindheartedness for naiveté."

His eyes widened.

"Score one for my girl!" Abazi cheered, high-fiving Kimber. "All right, then. New agenda: Hunt down Oswald and demand to know what he's up to. Next, solve riddle. And tomorrow, protect the surveyors by scaring the crap out of them. Love it."

"Sounds good to me," Kris agreed, his eyes lighting up.

No one overtly disagreed with Abazi, which to her was as good as giving her plan their full and enthusiastic support. She turned to go and Gabe and the others followed after her. He kept his senses on alert, eyes open, ears tuned; this time he wasn't about to let himself get ambushed by a little person. Once was bad enough, twice would be embarrassing.

The slope of the trail rose swiftly and soon all conversation ceased, each of them focusing on using their oxygen for the difficult climb. Gabe was pleasantly surprised to find he was handling the effort pretty easily. Gearing up for basketball and their own 'warrior' workouts on the weekends had kept him in shape. He was, however, worried about two things. Kimber was one of them. Kris's adjustments to her braces had helped increase her balance and speed. Still, she was fighting against an incline that was nearly torturous.

His second worry was the unrelenting sensation, lifting the hairs on the back of his neck, that someone had been watching them for a while now. He turned his head to check on Kimber, then slowed to let her and Jer catch up. Jer had her arm, and she gave Gabe a grim smile as they passed. She was determined not to let the mountain win. "Thought I saw something," he said, not wanting her to think he was checking up on her. "Just keep moving, okay?" She and Jer nodded wordlessly, continuing their upward trek.

After scanning the trees and rocky slope and finding nothing, Gabe followed after them. He wasn't convinced no one was there, but for the moment, since he couldn't see whoever it was, he could only keep moving.

"This is the farthest I've been," Abazi declared after a half hour of hiking. A light sheen of sweat glistened on her brown skin. "Let's take a break and figure out where to go next," she added after glancing at a panting Kimber. Kimber and Jer plopped down on a rock, and Kris found an old log. After a moment, he pulled out his Klean Kanteen and took a swig from it.

Abazi's eyes found Gabe's. "Still going, huh?"

"Still going," he replied, noting she looked a little winded.

"Me, too," she pushed out, working hard not to sound breathy. She didn't quite succeed. He felt absurdly charged at the thought that he was beating her at her own game.

He moved closer to her. Knowing he was winning, he felt generous. Leaning over, he whispered, "Have you noticed that we have company?" She smelled of pinesap and fresh sage and lemons. He liked her scent, much to his annoyance.

"Since we started," she snapped, and he pulled back abruptly. "They aren't exactly trying to be quiet."

They could have fooled him. He hadn't heard a sound. Unlike the forest down below, there were animals up here. Squirrels, birds, and very likely deer, bear, and fox, too. A shiver caught hold of him as he remembered what his mother had said about mountain lions. Maybe the rumors were true.

"Two-footed, or four-footed?"

She squinted, then her scowl disintegrated into a grin as she moved to sit on a rock. "Good question."

"Okay, here's another one. Are they simply following us, or are we being herded?"

The grin disappeared. "For the moment, following us. But now that the trail's starting to fade…well, I don't know what they—it—will do then."

"If we start getting herded, then do we go along with it, or resist?"

She laughed. "I think you already know my answer to that."

Resist it was. Big surprise. Abazi would attempt to resist the pressure of a wall she was leaning against.

"Should we tell the others?"

"And have Kris go charging into the fray again? We can't take that risk."

She was right, but Gabe didn't like it. Knowledge was always better when it came to situations like this—not that he always followed this edict himself, like when he didn't tell Abazi and Kimber about Oswald. Still, Kris, with his berserker ways, did have a knack of bringing trouble down on all their heads. "I'll take the rear, then. At least keep my eye out so I can warn the others quickly if I need to."

"Suit yourself," she replied maddeningly. Why couldn't she just say, "Good idea, Gabe, you genius, you!"?

He bit his lip, then retreated to go check on Jer and Kimber.

Another five minutes passed, then Abazi stood up. "A rolling stone gathers no moss," she announced. "So get off your butts, cause I'm the boss."

Gabe and Jer helped Kimber to her feet. Kris stashed his water bottle and joined them. Gabe didn't like how quiet his brother was being. Typically he had something to say. He could only hope Kris was concentrating on what he'd say if he saw Hollie and knew nothing about their followers, be they man or beast.

For the next half hour, their way was impeded by the lack of a trail. Kimber tripped several times and Gabe stubbed his toe. It still hurt, and he wondered if he'd broken it, but it was probably just sprained. Just when he thought he would have to ask for a break, the way opened slightly, and they began to make good progress. Hopefully it was progress in the right direction. This was an awfully big mountain. Oswald and his gang could be anywhere.

And then, suddenly, there was nowhere else to go but straight up. The group stopped in their tracks and stood staring upward, mouths gaping at the rock face in front of them.

"I'm afraid I can't make it up that," Kimber said apologetically.

"There's got to be some way around," Abazi said, refusing to give up. "I'm going to scout the area."

"I'll join you," Kris said.

"Okay, you go that way and I'll go this way." She pointed off to the right.

Ten minutes later they both returned, looking glum. "It's like a bloody fortress!" Kris complained. "All it needs is a moat."

Jer's head slowly swiveled around. "Did you say fortress?" He didn't wait for Kris to respond, hurrying on, "Don't you see? It's Oswald's hideout. And you can bet there's some way in that's easier than scaling this cliff."

Chapter Eight

Strike Ye Dead

Gabe's heart pounded in his chest. Could it be? He hurried toward the cliff face, determined to find a way in. The more he thought about it, the more he was looking forward to seeing Oswald's world. The Dryad had been in Gabe's room twice now, so he had the upper hand. Perhaps knowing his enemy's world would even the playing field a little more, psychologically anyway.

"It would have to be an opening that you can't see standing face-on," he muttered, half to himself. "Maybe it's behind a bush or a stack of rocks. Or higher up."

In the end, it was all three. About ten feet up the cliffside, behind a scrubby pine tree and a stack of thick stones standing like playing cards, Gabe found the opening, black and narrow, but with a cool breath of air flowing through it. There was a small platform and he pulled himself over to stand on it.

"I found it!" he cried to the others. Kris was higher up on the face and Abazi was level with him, about ten feet to his right. Jer had stayed behind with Kimber.

"Good job, Gabe!" Kimber gave him the thumbs-up. "I can't believe you found it. It was almost as if you were meant to. Like you were guided there."

Gabe was about to protest that he'd only gotten lucky, but bit down on the words. Kimber was right—he had felt as though someone were steering him, inch by painful inch. His mind had argued against going in that direction; it simply had not looked promising. Yet he'd followed what the directions told him to do and found the opening. Despite his success, he had to admit the idea of being guided by unseen hands unnerved him.

Kris and Abazi joined him on the platform. "How are we going to get Kimber up here?" Kris asked.

"You don't have to say it so loud," Gabe hissed, glancing down at Kimber. She and Jer were talking, their blond heads bowed.

"What? It's not like she doesn't know she has CP. She can't climb this on her own."

"Yeah, Hawthorne," Abazi snipped. "Do you have to be so insensitive?"

Gabe's face reddened. "I was only trying—" he began, then stopped when he saw Abazi's grin. Boy, she liked goading him! "I just wanted to say that I've been working out. I'll carry her." He only just refrained from flexing his arm. Before Abazi could razz him further, he said hurriedly, "I'll go get her now."

He pulled off his backpack and headed down. Clinging to the stone, he nearly fell twice before he realized that there was a 'path' of sorts right below him. The stones here stuck out at just the right spots, making it an easier climb. Once on the ground, Gabe glanced up and saw why he hadn't spotted the climbing rocks. From this angle, they looked too large to be of any use climbing.

Kimber agreed to be carried, but despite Kris's claims, Gabe knew it bothered her that she needed help. The taut lines around her mouth practically shouted, "I hate this! I don't want to be a burden to anyone...*ever again*." Just like his dad felt. Gabe's father was getting better, but he still tired easily, and it drove him crazy to be dependent on others. Like Kimber, he wanted to be self-sufficient. Gabe was starting to wonder if his father would ever get back to the person he'd been before the transplant operation. Likely his father was wondering the same thing.

Gabe sent Jer up first, then followed him slowly. It wasn't easy navigating the steep face with Kimber on his back, even following the hidden path. Gabe was glad he really had been working out and running whenever he could. Sweat beaded his forehead and the skin around his neck where Kimber was clinging was starting to chafe. A rock gave way beneath his foot and he threw himself forward, grabbing hold of a protruding tree root at the last second. The stone bounced and clattered down the rock face where it landed with a thud.

That stone had nearly been him and Kimber.

When his heart settled down, he started moving again. Finally they reached the platform and Kris and Jer helped Kimber off Gabe's back, lifting her up the last bit. When she was safe, Gabe pulled himself up onto the ledge. They had made it. He felt strangely proud of himself. Strangely, because lately he hadn't been feeling too good about anything. He'd never been a super-confident person, but then having to move and start over at a new school, and having to deal with Jake Morrigan. Oh, and that whole 'Dryad/this isn't my real family' issue that he'd been trying to forget. That didn't help, either.

"I'll go first," Kris volunteered, looking like a child on his birthday.

Gabe pulled his backpack on. "Hang on. Let's scout ahead a bit. See what we're dealing with."

"Already did. Nothing but rocks and trees. No problem."

Gabe gave him a doubtful look. When it came to action, Kris wasn't exactly big on observing the little things. When drawing or building, he was as precise as a surgeon. But in life? Not so much.

He was already moving, though, so Gabe had no choice but to follow the others as they hurried after Kris's tall figure slipping between the rocks and disappearing like a shadow.

With a sigh, Gabe slid between the two rocks and then through another set. He felt like he was traversing the letter Z. The backpack made the passage a bit tight and at one spot Gabe got stuck, but he made it through after some shimmying and squeezing. Escaping from this place would not be quick and easy, he noted. Then he remembered his feeling of being followed, and his stomach squirmed uncomfortably.

The way didn't get any easier after the rock passage ended. On the other side, a stand of trees packed almost as tightly as toothpicks in a bottle greeted him. There had to be a path somewhere, otherwise they'd never get through.

Kris pointed to the left. "It looks like the land drops off over there. I say we go check it out."

Gabe felt slightly claustrophobic. He wasn't sure he wanted to head into all those trees, or if he'd even fit. He'd rather stay here, by the rocks. They were solid and safe and—

He suddenly realized he could no longer see the others. He hopped off the ledge and scurried after them, his shoes knocking pebbles off the stone trail. Before long, he discovered the closeness of the trees was an illusion. There was a path here, rich, black dirt covered by leaves and an occasional twig. The smell of decay caught his senses and he pulled it in, reveling in it. Odd, he mused, that the scent of rotting plants made him feel more alive.

He spotted Abazi's patterned hat and ran to catch up to her. "Don't go getting lost again, Hawthorne," she warned, not bothering to turn around. "I don't want to have to come rescue your skinny behind again."

"Again? When was the first time?"

"Um, when Feltry had you in his clutches?"

"Yes, I seem to remember you getting knocked out during that little scuffle."

"But only after I rescued you."

The bitter taste of bile filled Gabe's throat. "I rescued myself, Abazi."

"If your delusions help you sleep at night, fine. I'll give you that. But we both know the truth, don't we?"

Gabe had had enough. "Listen, Abazi. It's bad enough I have to spend my weekend on a suicide mission, but to have to listen to your annoying voice, too? No way. So just shut it for once, won't you?"

"Well, well, well," she drawled. "It seems Mr. Hawthorne has finally grown himself a pair." She laughed and skipped on ahead, once again succeeding in pushing a myriad of Gabe's buttons.

"Watch out!" Kris yelled from up ahead. "Whoa—!"

"*Kris!*" Jer cried, his voice echoing panic. Abazi and Gabe started to run.

They found Jer and Kimber at the top of a cliff peering down into a rock-strewn ravine. Kris lay in a heap at the bottom, his body wedged against a ten-foot boulder and his size twelve sneakers hanging over the edge of a brook.

"Kris!" Gabe yanked off his backpack and scrambled down the steep, mossy bank. "Kris!"

After nearly falling twice himself, Gabe finally made it down to his brother. Kris lay very still, his dark eyes staring up at the sky, his tongue protruding. Oh, dear Lord. He was dead.

"Kris?" Gabe reached out to touch his brother's cheek and his eyes teared up. "Oh, Kris. No!" *What have I done? What have I done?*

"Gotcha!" Kris sat up, his eyes wide and crazed like a zombie's. Gabe's hand turned into a fist and he promptly punched his brother in the shoulder. "Ow! Why'd you do that?"

"Because you're an idiot, that's why!" Gabe rose to his feet. "I thought you were dead."

Kris beamed. "Did you see my tongue? Was that a nice touch or what?"

It had been, but Gabe would never share that information with his brother, who really should be dead after pulling a stunt like that. "I'm going to go get my backpack."

After some hesitancy and studying of her options, Kimber agreed to let herself be carried down into the ravine. Jer carried Gabe's backpack, along with his own, reaching the bottom before them.

While Kimber gently scolded Kris for scaring them all to death, Gabe took the opportunity to look around. His breath caught at the amazing sight before him. In rushing to save Kris, and then hauling Kimber down, he hadn't really taken anything in.

They were standing at the bottom of a gorge, cliffs of dark gray rock rising up dramatically on both sides, tiny waterfalls slithering down in various spots. Along the space between the cliffs, a wide brook, dotted with fallen leaves spinning in whirls of water, rushed over moss-covered rocks. Tree roots as thick as Gabe's arm stretched out from the cliff sides like the handles of teapots. The smell of wet rock, decaying leaves, and fresh, clean water permeated the air around them.

Upstream, dark openings in the rock revealed themselves. Caves! Gabe couldn't believe his luck. He loved caves. One year, when he'd been nine or ten, his family had flown to Texas to visit Mom's sister and they'd all piled into minivans and driven to see Carlsbad Caverns. Since then, caves had held a special place in his heart. He didn't think there would be anything here as spectacular as Carlsbad—different kind of rock, he thought—but still, any cave was an adventure waiting to happen.

A loud whoop echoed through the ravine. Kris had seen them, too. Jer, who'd been preoccupied with fixing the strap on Kimber's bag, looked up.

"What?"

"Caves, Jer! Lots of them, I'll bet."

Jer looked pained. "Go on, Jer," Kimber urged. "I'll catch up. I'm slow, but I'm not completely helpless."

"I don't mind—"

"Well, I do. Now go before I get mad." She smiled at him.

"Yes!" Jer cried, bounding after Kris.

"Hey, peeps," Abazi called out, glancing warily around. "I don't mean to rain on your parade or anything, but don't you think we should be careful if this is Oswald's hideout?"

Everyone froze, Kris in mid-stride. *Stupid Oswald*, Gabe thought angrily. *Why does he always have to ruin things?* "Well, if he doesn't have the papers to show he owns this land," Gabe said loudly, "then he's going to have to force us out."

"Big words," Abazi remarked.

"I agree with Gabe," Kris said. "Oswald doesn't scare me."

A bird screeched and flew at them from out of the trees and Kris jumped. Everyone grabbed a weapon and readied themselves, but nothing happened and nobody came.

"Just a bird." Kris grinned sheepishly.

But none of them believed it was *just* a bird. Not even Kris. Still, they all silently agreed to carry on. What else could they do? They had wanted to talk to Oswald about the riddles and the acorn attack, and now here was their opportunity. If only he'd show himself. The waiting was killing Gabe.

Of course, it might not be Oswald watching them.

Maybe it was his mother…or father.

Or a hungry mountain lion.

Or worse, Straif.

"Come on," Kris said defiantly. "If we're going to get ambushed, we might as well have some fun before it happens."

"I agree," Kimber said as she hobbled toward them. "I've never been allowed to do this sort of thing, and I'm not letting anyone ruin it." Her cheeks were flushed and she looked ecstatic.

Gabe wasn't about to be the one to let her down. "All right. Just be careful everyone."

The first cave was high-ceilinged, but shallow—stretching back only about ten feet from the opening, and a giant slab overhead looked like it could fall at any moment. Water droplets plopped onto their noses and hats and down an occasional collar. A pool of clear water dominated the center of the cave and Gabe watched the drops splash into the smooth water, create seven or eight ripples, then dissipate. The walls were shiny with moisture, the floors almost equally so. The cave was neat to look at, but didn't go very far back.

He spotted Kris climbing out and followed after him, leaving the others behind. They scouted the area and soon found a well-worn path that ran alongside the brook. A tree root, sticking out from the ravine wall, made a good handle. When Gabe grabbed hold of it, it felt like marble, as though put to use many times. Once again he paused and looked around, wondering where they were, where Oswald was.

Gabe caught a flash of blue as Kris's sneaker disappeared into the next cave and he hurried after him. "Kris?" he called when he got close. The cave opening was smaller and lower to the ground than the first one. He'd have to get on his hands and knees to fit. Kris had peeled off his pack and pushed it ahead of him and Gabe did the same. Then he lowered himself onto his belly, feeling the cold stone through his gloves. Pulling himself along, into the pitch dark, the thought crossed his mind that if someone came, he would easily be trapped. He didn't even know if there was another way out. He started to back up.

"Keep 'em moving up there!" Abazi yelled behind him.

Thinking that this was a really bad idea, but unwilling to hear the names she'd come up with for him if he backed out, he continued to inch forward. There was a small opening to his right and he saw a flash of stream rushing past. There would be times when this cave would be flooded. But hopefully not today. He moved a little faster.

The floor of the cave tunnel was smooth enough, but he was glad when he could finally get up on his hands and knees. After several more feet of crawling, the cave opened up and Gabe was able to stand now. He pulled his pack back on and looked around. Kris had his flashlight out and was shining it around the cave. The image of two hunched shadows suddenly appeared on the glistening wall ahead of him.

"Kris, watch out!" Gabe cried, pushing Abazi back.

Kris immediately swung his bata outward as he did a full spin. The shadows didn't move. Gabe frowned and slowly made his way toward his brother. "Where are they?" Kris shouted. "Bring it on!"

The closer Gabe got to his brother, the more he became certain that what he'd seen were not shadows, but a strange sort of stain in the rock.

"Mellow out, Berserker Boy." Gabe grabbed Kris's hand and guided the flashlight to land on the shadows. "I thought we had company, but it was just this."

Kris laughed. "Just about killed me some imaginary cave creatures."

Abazi came to stand by Gabe, her shoulder touching his. "Nice going, rock for brains."

"Oh, and I suppose you knew what those were."

"Of course. Some people call them shadow figures, but they're just a natural discoloration in the rock."

Oh. "Well, you could've said something."

"And miss out on the show? It's fun seeing Kris all riled up, don't you think?" She gave Gabe an impish smile, almost conspiratorial, like they were in on the joke together.

"What?" Kris called out. "Are you two plotting against me?"

Gabe placed a hand on his heart and an innocent expression on his face. "Does this look like the face of a plotter?" Abazi snickered and Gabe felt goofily encouraged to continue. "I would never betray thee."

"Et tu, Brute?" Jer said behind him as he pulled Kimber to her feet.

"Never!" Gabe declared. "Unless you offered me money, then I might be interested."

"Fine," Kris said. "But wait until we explore all the caves before you stab me in the back."

"It is done, your royal hiney." Gabe made a grand, sweeping bow. Abazi and Kimber laughed and Gabe flushed, pleased.

"Well, then," Kris answered, not to be outdone. "Walk this way." He began to lurch along.

Gabe froze, his heart beating hard. *Kris!* How could he be so insensitive? Poor Kimber.

"That, I can do!" Kimber's voice rang out, surprising him, and her laughter filled the cave. Soon everyone was laughing and lurching. "And better than all of you, I can see!"

The competition was on. They shuffled and staggered and bumped their way out of the cave. Gabe hit his head twice. Once outside, they followed Kris upstream toward another cave system. This tunnel involved a really tight squeeze getting in. Leaving their backpacks behind, the others made it through, but Kris nearly didn't with his wide shoulders. Gabe worried he'd get stuck himself. He was easing his chest sideways through the narrow opening when a sound behind him made him freeze.

"Come out with yer hands up, scoundrel, or I be havin' to strike ye dead right where ye lie."

Chapter Nine

Whooping Like a Native

A sour taste flooded Gabe's mouth as he slowly scooched backward out of the cave, his knees feeling every bump and sharp rock along the way. The voices of the others had faded away as they went further into the cave. He hoped they'd get away.

"Ye can call yer friends out, too, intruder."

Gabe didn't recognize the voice and that worried him. Was it one of Oswald's crew? Straif's? Another fairy? Who?

Without saying a word, Gabe pushed himself to his feet and turned around, his hand on his bata, ready to pull it out. Before him stood a stooped, old man, gnarled and worn. His chin and nose curved toward each other to form the letter C; his eyes, small and nearly hidden in folds of olive-striped skin, peered outward, assessing, weighing. He was short; the top of his head, shod in a leather hat decorated with buttons, bits of colorful plastic, and bottle caps, barely reached Gabe's chest. The old man's swollen knuckles were wrapped around a staff; strangely shaped bones dangled from leather straps tied around it. He appeared to be wearing several layers of clothes under a robe-like jacket. His long feet were clad in fringed moccasins. Every few seconds he'd cock his head to the right and then to the left; his little eyes under bushy eyebrows wary and calculating.

Gabe felt a surge of optimism. He could take this guy.

"I told ye to call yer friends out."

"Leave them out of this. This is between me and your leader, Oswald."

The old man snorted. "Do I look like someone who'd be takin' orders from that whippersnapper? Hogwash and balderdash, sonny! He baint be *me* leader. Nobody be tellin' Filidh what to do but Filidh himself." He jabbed a twisted finger at his chest.

"This is your place?"

The wrinkled face collapsed into a grimace. "Used to be all mine. Until those scoundrels overran me gorge, makin' noise at all hours. Shoutin' and hollerin' like beasts. Worse than the Bean Sídhe."

"Banshee? Oh, right." As kids, whenever he and his brothers made too much of a stink with their crying, their mom would tell them to quit howling like a banshee.

"Well, ye ken me name. What be yers, stranger? And what be yer business in Filidh's province?"

"I'm on a mission," Gabe told him, not offering his name. Who knew if news of what he'd done to the Lady had made it this far.

"A mission, eh? To do what? Annoy Filidh?"

Gabe ignored the jab, even though he wanted to point out that *he* wasn't being the annoying one. "I need to find Oswald and ask him why he attacked my house."

Filidh cackled. "Attacked it, did he? Hm. The boy's got gumption, I'll give him that."

"Gumption? More like a chip on his shoulder. He thinks I'm trying to take his place here and I'm not." As soon as Gabe spoke the words he wished he could take them back. "I mean—"

But it was too late. The little man's eyes widened as much as they could with all that skin in the way. He stepped closer and a sharp whiff of wilderness and unwashed human filled Gabe's nose. "Ye be the one they call the Usurper? Well, I'll be a pig in a puddle."

"Where did you hear that?" Gabe demanded, shaken. Filidh only shrugged. "Well, it's wrong. I'm not trying to take over anything. I just want to be left alone. But when he throws acorns at my roof and leaves notes on my door—" He broke off, realizing that all along he'd never thought it was anyone but Oswald leaving those stupid riddles. The Dryad was obviously trying to get into Gabe's mind—rattle him, scare him off. "Well, if he thinks he can get away with what he's doing, he's got another think coming."

"Ye done with yer blubberin'?" Filidh snipped. "Just lettin' ye ken what some around here call ye."

"But you don't think I'm trying to take over?"

"I baint be sure I care one way or t'other. I gather stuff; I don't think on it much. It be what it be. Filidh's opinion on it don't be matterin' too much one way or t'other."

Gabe thought the old man protested too much, his eyes narrowing suspiciously as Filidh's head did its habitual back and forth swivel. "All the same, I bet you have an opinion."

Filidh's eyes sparkled. "Course Filidh do. But it'll cost ye."

"What's your price?" Gabe asked. He'd rather be ignorant than pay too high a price.

"It be high, that be for sure." He cackled. "I be glad I lured ye here."

"You were the one herding us?" So that's what Abazi had heard.

Filidh looked quite satisfied with himself. "And ye made an easy job of it. Like sheep, ye were."

"We knew you were there all along."

Filidh grinned, revealing pumpkin seed teeth. "Sure ye did." He jerked his head to his left. "Yer friends be comin' out on t'other side." Gabe looked upstream a ways to see Kris's head emerging from the stones. "We be meetin' again, Gabriel, King of the Forest Immortal," Filidh warned. "Be prepared to pay me price then." Two sharp cracks shook the air, and Gabe swung around to find Filidh had vanished, leaving only his strange, wild smell as evidence anyone had been there.

Gabe grabbed everyone's backpacks and hurried along the path to catch up with the others. Kris blinked at Gabe in surprise as he stood up. "How'd you get ahead of me?"

"I got stuck, so I backed out. Didn't want to mess up my bum knee." He'd sprained his knee once and whenever he needed an excuse to get out of doing something, he blamed his bad knee. His mom never fell for it, but his brothers would buy it on occasion. On this one, Kris did. He knew Gabe loved caves and wouldn't miss a chance to explore them if there wasn't a good reason.

"Bummer. Maybe next time." Kris took his backpack from Gabe and pulled it on.

"Yeah," Gabe agreed. "Next time." He wasn't sure why he didn't want to share his meeting with Filidh, or that Filidh was the one who'd lured them here. The reasoning escaped him, but he did know he didn't like feeling this need for subterfuge. There had to be a good reason for staying quiet, just one he didn't yet know.

"This place is so awesome," Kris declared, grinning as he looked around. "Hey, look! Stairs and a bridge!"

The group looked to where he was pointing. Twenty yards ahead and about thirty yards up in the air, a long bridge made from five or six logs strapped together crossed the ravine. Gabe wondered who'd built it. Probably Filidh, since Gabe couldn't imagine the Dryads using their dead for such a purpose. Of course, Oswald's band carried batas and staffs, both made from wood, so maybe there were exceptions. It certainly hadn't been Straif or his followers. They couldn't touch dead wood, not after partaking of blood from animals and eating their own kind.

Kris took off for the bridge and the others followed after, Abazi right behind him. Gabe and Jer helped Kimber up the stone steps, which, like the tree root handle, had been worn smooth, as though used for centuries.

"You go ahead," Jer urged when they reached the log bridge. "Kimber and I will make our way across."

"I'll scootch along the logs," she said, looking determined.

"Be careful," Gabe warned. "There's nothing to hang onto, and it's quite a drop," he added, unnecessarily, as he looked down at the boulders and tumbling white water. Jer nodded instead of arguing like he usually did. It *was* quite a drop. Gabe took his first step onto the bridge, then didn't look down once as he quickly made his way across the logs.

Another set of stairs met him on the other side and he scrambled up them after Abazi and Kris, both of whom had disappeared. "Don't get too far ahead, you guys!" When they didn't answer, his heart quickened. Where were they? He moved faster, his foot catching on a root and nearly sending him sprawling. Sweating now, he forced himself to slow down and watch where he was going.

Eyes on his feet, he nearly slammed into Abazi standing stock-still in front of him. Jerking to a stop, his head swung up to see what had caught her attention. Straight ahead, a waterfall, possibly fifty feet high, plummeted into a pool, fizzing the water into white before smoothing out and turning black as a mirror at night. It was amazing, and he watched it in awe as cool mist settled on his face. Abazi, too, was staring at the magnificent sight, her lips slightly parted and her eyes hazy with pleasure. Her hair, already coated with water droplets, glistened in the sunlight filtering through the treetops. Gabe felt like he could stay in this mystical place forever.

"Where's Kris?" he shouted over the roar of the falls, not wanting to break the spell, but also feeling worried about his brother.

She pointed. "I told him not to do it."

Gabe's eyes flew in the direction her finger pointed. To their right, a stone bridge crossed the pool. Dark and slick with water, the walkway looked very narrow and extremely dangerous. Gabe spotted Kris on the other side of the pool from them, grinning and giving him a thumbs-up. Then he gestured toward the top of the waterfall and Gabe saw what he'd missed before.

Another stone bridge…over the waterfall.

"Kris!" he shouted through cupped hands. "Don't do it!"

Kris just grinned and gave him the okay sign before following another set of stone steps up to the waterfall, which was even with the top of the ravine. He moved so quickly Gabe felt certain that the boy who tripped over own his feet several times a day was going to fall over the edge and smash his head on the rocks below.

But he didn't fall. Not yet, anyway. "I have to stop him," he yelled to Abazi.

She looked back at him, her face pale. "Is he always this crazy?"

"Pretty much."

Pushing past her, he faced the stone bridge. The long, gray stretch seemed impossibly slippery and narrow, but it was the only way to save his brother from certain death. Gabe took a tentative step, slipped, and jerked backward, smacking against the stone wall of the gorge. Winded and shaken, he shook his head to clear it. *Focus, Gabe!*

The next attempt was a success and he was off the ledge and onto the bridge. After that, each step was painfully slow as he scooted along. When he was halfway across, he steadied himself and glanced up to ascertain where Kris was. What he saw made him want to throw up. Kris stood on the high bridge, smack dab in the middle of it, doing a strange sort of victory dance and whooping like a native.

Don't ever say 'whooping like a native' to Abazi, he hazily made a mental note to himself.

He gestured with both hands as he yelled, "Get down! You're going to fall!" Kris touched his ear and leaned forward, a questioning look on his face. Gabe again motioned for Kris to come down. Kris laughed and started doing his dance again.

He might have been fine—might never have fallen—except for what happened next. A massive acorn flew from out of nowhere and cracked against Kris's forehead. His mouth popped into an 'O', his eyes widened, and he toppled forward off the bridge.

Gabe watched his brother fall as though in slow motion. This time he wouldn't be able to fake being dead. The pool wasn't deep enough, there'd be hidden boulders and Kris would smash his head and he'd drown and there'd be no pretending and laughing at his grand joke.

And Gabe could do nothing but watch his brother die.

Do something, do something, do something!

Kris was inches from the pool's surface when a tree branch whipped out and wrapped around his waist like a lasso, catching him mid-air. Just as quickly as it appeared, the branch retreated, pulling Kris up. As he neared the top of the gorge, the branch shortened until it was able to set him on his feet.

"That was awesome!" Kris cried. But his exhilaration was snuffed out when ten Dryads surrounded him and pointed staffs at his heaving torso. "Hey! What do you think you're—"

"Silence, trespasser!" The crowd parted and Oswald stepped forward. He wore his usual garb—green cloak and brown pants—the same as all the Rogues. It sounded dull, but it was, admittedly, a cool look. With swift, long strides, he headed, not toward Kris, but down the steps toward Gabe. When he reached the stone bridge, he didn't look down at his feet once as he advanced along it. Gabe stared at the Dryad leader, his heart beating in a sick rhythm of fear and anger. "Ye're trespassin'," Oswald accused. "We want ye to leave."

"What kind of stupid trick was that?" Gabe shouted.

Oswald stopped walking, his brows drawing together. "I save yer brother's life and this is the thanks I get?"

"I saw the acorn. One of your lackeys threw it—that's why Kris fell."

The frown deepened into a scowl. "Ye think we'd do such a thing?"

"I think you're capable of it, especially after what you did to our house yesterday."

Oswald looked genuinely confused. "We were nowhere near yer house yesterday—have not been there for some time now, other than when I came to visit ye. And that was just me."

He looked like he was telling the truth, his eyes grave and his jaw set, but Gabe wasn't falling for it. "I can't believe anything you say, Oswald. Not when you threatened to teach me a lesson if I came into the woods, not since you're calling me the Usurper."

"Where'd ye hear about that?" Oswald demanded.

"I have my sources," Gabe replied, his cheeks burning.

"Gabe!"

Gabe spun around to see Abazi shuffling toward him along the bridge. The quick movement shifted his weight too quickly and his body pitched backward. He flung himself forward and wrapped his arms around the bridge at the last second, saving him from falling into the pool. Oswald stared down at him, the slight tilt at the corners of his mouth showing his amusement. Gabe kicked his legs ineffectually as he struggled to pull himself up. His chest hurt from hitting the stone and he thought he was going to drop when he felt a slender tendril wrap around his leg. The humiliating image of him dangling upside down like an idiot in Oswald's grasp bloomed like a fungus in his mind.

"Don't you dare touch me!" he cried, and Oswald retracted the branch, smiling. Three more kicks and Gabe was able to swing his right leg over the stone walk, then pull himself up. Abazi wisely stayed back and let him do it himself. On the other side Jer and Kimber stood, waiting and watching.

"Smooth move, dipwad," Abazi remarked when he stood up.

"You're the one who startled me!"

"Whatever. Just thought you could use a little moral support."

Oh, great. Abazi, the cheerleader. He stalked toward her until she had backed up several paces. Then he glanced back at Oswald, who'd crossed his arms and was watching them, looking both bored and suspicious at the same time. Gabe leaned toward Abazi. "Oswald set us up. One of them threw an acorn at Kris so that Oswald could come to his rescue."

"Are you sure?" She looked skeptical.

"Of course I'm sure! He wants to be the uncontested King of the forest, and he wants my family." This came out sounding whinier than he'd intended and he quickly added, "He also wants revenge."

"Revenge for what?" she challenged, and he mentally cursed her. Couldn't she just for once accept what he said? Did she have to argue with everything that came out of his mouth? "Why would he want revenge against you? You didn't do anything wrong."

"I never said he was rational," he hissed. "For all we know, he's a lunatic. Look at what he's doing with those notes. Then there were those two acorn attacks, and he threatened to take my family. Now this. He's not even a real Dryad."

"Why don't we pretend to be friends with him? Throw him off guard?"

He pulled back. "I'm not that good of an actor."

"What if it meant saving your patootie?"

"Okay, that might work," he finally conceded.

"Just don't overdo it."

He bit down on a retort about certain other people overdoing it. "I won't." He turned around and headed back toward Oswald, Abazi right behind him. "Thanks for saving my brother," he said stiffly.

"What changed yer mind?" Oswald demanded, his eyes like a hawk about to strike.

"Abazi said she saw the acorn come from the other side of the stream. As far as I can see, you're all on that side." He pointed toward where Kris was standing.

"That would be the case…if I were an imbecile."

"What?"

Oswald raised his staff and made a circle in the air. Gabe looked behind him to see another forty or fifty Dryads step out from the trees.
Six of them jumped down to land beside Jer and Kimber, and while
they didn't touch them, the Rogues made it clear they weren't going
anywhere.

"Why did ye come here? I told ye to stay out."

"I came because your note told me to."

Oswald's features sharpened. "What are ye talkin' about?"

"I'm talking about the two notes you sent. The riddles."

"Two notes? Riddles?"

Gabe was pleased to see that Oswald looked none too happy. It
bothered him, though, that he looked anything but guilty. "Ye're either
lyin' to me, or something strange is goin' on." He pulled in a deep
breath; his dark eyes studying Gabe closely. "Ye leave me no choice.
Ye're comin' with me." He snapped his fingers and two of the Dryads
lifted Jer and Kimber into the air and started across the walkway.

"We're not going with you!"

Oswald nodded at the Dryads and they turned and dangled Jer and
Kimber over the water. "Hey!" Jer cried out, kicking. "Put us down!"

Gabe stared at his brother and Kimber, then glanced up at the sky.
He was trapped. He and Abazi had no choice but to follow after
Oswald. "All right, I'll come." The two Dryads lowered Jer and Kimber to the walkway, then followed after Oswald as they all crossed to
the other side.

Kris didn't even notice them coming. He was too busy talking to
Hollie, his face animated as he recreated the moment he got beaned by
the acorn, his head jerking back and his body convulsing as though
he'd been electrocuted. Gabe didn't even bother to roll his eyes. The
kid nearly dies and sees it as a moment to impress the ladies. No wonder he'd already been christened 'G' at school. The 'G' stood for gorgeous, by the way—yet another reminder of the inequities of life, especially since *Gabe's* name actually started with a 'G'.

Swallowing his growing discomfort, he stepped off the bridge. After
climbing the steps, he hurried over to where Hollie and Kris stood,
totally absorbed in one another. He needed to warn Kris about
Oswald, and quickly, before things went any farther. "You got lucky,"
he said in a low voice, which was actually not what he meant to say. He
really wanted to yell at his brother and tell him what a big dummy he
was and if he ever did anything like that again, Gabe was going to kill
him!

Kris turned. "Hey guys! Wasn't that awesome?"

"You know they were the ones who threw the acorn, don't you?" Gabe persisted.

Kris's eyebrows shot up. "What do you mean?"

"What are ye talkin' about, Gabriel?" Hollie demanded, her green eyes blazing with temper. She was wearing her typical green shift, which made the red in her tousled hair even brighter, and, as usual, no shoes.

"Way to keep it a secret," Abazi muttered.

"Your leader's a fraud," he announced, though he made sure not to speak too loudly.

"Oswald might be a bit full of himself, but a fraud he isn't."

"Then who threw the acorn?"

Hollie shrugged. "A squirrel?"

Abazi laughed, then quickly bit down on it. She and Hollie weren't exactly bosom buddies. "Or was it moose *and* squirrel?" she put in, unable to resist.

Hollie didn't get the joke, but Kris roared, which Hollie soon made clear she didn't like. "So, Gabriel," she purred, taking his arm, but looking at Kris all the while, "what brings ye to these parts?"

"You don't have to pretend with me, Hollie. I know you guys have been sending us notes to lure us here."

"Notes?" she echoed, sounding exactly like Oswald.

"The riddles…you know."

"I don't know what ye're talkin' about, Gabriel Hawthorne! And don't ye take that tone with me!"

He blushed and pulled back. "Sorry, Hollie, but I wish someone around here would be big enough to admit to harassing us." A cracking sound split the air next to Gabe's ear. He spun around. Oswald. His tree-arm retracted as he approached. "What did you do that for?"

"If ye've something to say to me or about me, say it to me face."

Gabe's fist curled up, ready to punch. "I already did. I think you sent me those notes, and I think you attacked our house. And if it wasn't you, then I'd like to know who it was so I can kick his—" Suddenly Gabe couldn't breathe. Oswald's tree-arm was wrapped around his neck like a boa constrictor. His fingers tore at the rough wood and he sputtered and choked.

"Are ye callin' me a liar?"

"Get…it…off…me!"

"I asked ye a question, Usurper."

"And...I...said..." Gabe stopped. He was starting to see spots and his vision was darkening and blurring. He felt himself rise upward like a ghost, and two seconds later, he flew through the air.

The water was icy cold and very hard when he hit. He plunged below the surface and attempted to fight his way back up, his mind spinning. His heavy winter coat weighed him down; his leather gloves made paddling nearly impossible. Head threatening to split open, he broke out of the water, gasping. Over the sound of his own gagging and panting, he heard laughter. He'd nearly died, and they were laughing about it.

He could kill them all.

Chapter Ten

The Face-Off

"*Y*ou jerk!" Gabe yelled. "I'm going to *kill* you." He mumbled this last part to himself, though he'd been tempted to shout it just as loudly as he had the insult. He was furious and humiliated, and he was cold. He felt like he really could kill Oswald right now. The worst part was that he was having trouble keeping afloat. Normally a strong swimmer, Gabe couldn't seem to make his limbs move. Soggy and numb, he began to sink.

When he saw the branch coming toward him, all his fury and humiliation soared up from his gut like a lion's roar. He reached out, grabbed hold of the limb, and in a blur of red vision, gave a hard yank.

"What are ye doin'?" Oswald shouted, and a moment later, he was in the water. But instead of swimming back to shore, he stroked toward Gabe.

Gabe smiled through chattering teeth. "Who's laughing now?"

"Not ye, *Usurper*!" Oswald's branch-arm shot out and smacked Gabe across the head. Stunned, he went under. He frantically kicked to resurface, but it wasn't easy going. His backpack was weighing him down like stones, and he struggled to pull it off.

"Gabe, you idiot!" His blurred eyes found Abazi leaning over the edge of the cliff, looking disgusted. "Stop this peeing contest of yours and get out of the water! You'll get hypothermia!"

Oswald's lips curled into an amused sneer. "Looks like ye've got yer girlfriend doin' yer fighting for ye."

"She's not my girlfriend," Gabe hissed, and before he knew what he was doing, his eyes had searched out the sun. "I need your power," he whispered to it. "Make me strong, make me a tree."

Like last time, Gabe felt himself begin to grow and expand, lengthen and solidify. His backpack slipped off and he flung it to the shore, though it didn't quite make it, slithering back into the pool. Within seconds, his arms had turned into a multitude of branches; his legs a solid trunk. Unlike the first time, his transformation happened very quickly and soon his tree form felt almost more real than his human body.

Seeing Gabe as a tree, Oswald turned into one, too. An oak tree would loom much larger than a hawthorn, but once transformed, Oswald and Gabe nearly matched each other in size. Oswald was the stronger of the two, but Gabe had thorns and possessed an unexpected cleverness that the steadfast oak did not. And so, the battle turned out to be fiercer than either of them expected.

Rising up, Gabe willed his limbs to lash out at Oswald, one stinging blow after the other. At first, Oswald easily blocked each onslaught. But Gabe was relentless, his feelings from years of living with a sick father, moving across the country, struggling to fit into a new school, and then—finally, terribly—finding out he was a Dryad, all came together in a perfect storm of emotions.

The sun warmed his limbs, sending bursts of energy through him, increasing his precision and allowing him to strike Oswald's vulnerable spots with his thorns. Gabe's smaller limbs distracted Oswald while his larger branches snaked around the Dryad's torso, lifting him into the air. Oswald cried out angrily, his limbs thrashing and flailing. Just when Gabe thought he had won, Oswald released a torrent of massive acorns, aiming them directly at Gabe's tree eyes and making him virtually blind, the shower of acorns like a dark blizzard.

Temporarily routed, he threw Oswald away from him. The Dryad flew through the air and smashed against the cliff wall, then he fell into the pool, sinking beneath its surface like a brick. Before Gabe could allow himself a congratulatory smile, he heard screaming, muffled, but clear enough. "Ye killed him!"

Several seconds passed before Gabe's tree mind registered what this meant. Oswald had yet to appear. Using his roots, Gabe waded toward the spot where Oswald had gone under, feeling sicker with each heavy step. Had he really murdered him? He hadn't meant to. He wasn't a killer. It was being a Dryad that had done this.

Never again.

Never again!

With each step, he forced himself to transform back to a human until soon he was swimming. Just as he reached the spot where Oswald had disappeared, something burst out of the water behind him. Oswald. Before Gabe could turn around, Oswald wrapped his tree limbs around Gabe's neck and lifted him high into the air. The light from the sun faded, then winked out.

"Stop it!" a voice screamed. *Stop what? Stop dying?* His mind snickered at the idea. *Would if I could.* The black shadow in his brain was growing bigger with each passing second, and soon it would take over and he would be dead.

Dead.

So this is what it was like—dying. Not so bad. A bit painful, maybe. Well, a lot painful, he realized now. Flashing lights in his head crackled like lightning strikes and his lungs screamed in protest. His neck throbbed. *Just let it be over. Just let me die...*

And then he was falling, back into the water, but he didn't have the strength to swim to the surface.

Within seconds, strong arms were around his waist, pulling him upward, and his splitting head broke free from his watery prison. He sucked in air, each draw of breath a pain and a relief. Hands were waiting to pull him up and then he was lying on the stone bridge, wet and weak, half-dead.

"That jerk nearly killed you!" Abazi was leaning over him, searching his face. The tips of her braids tickled his cheeks like little spiders. He wanted to bat them away, but he couldn't move his arms.

"What do ye think ye're doin', Oswald Eik?" someone shouted. *Hollie*, Gabe thought groggily. "Ye nearly killed him! And for what? To prove ye're a Dryad? To show ye're King?"

"Leave me alone," Oswald mumbled.

"I will not!"

"I said, leave me alone! I know what I nearly did, ye nyaff, now butt out!"

"Don't be bossin' me. Dame Hazel'll be hearin' about this, for sure."

"Ye always were a tale teller, Hollie. *Now leave me be!*" There was a flurry of movement as Oswald stalked off, followed by his band, then silence.

Gabe heard footsteps close to his head and they echoed strangely, as though someone were walking through his mind. He wished he could just go to sleep and pretend none of this had happened.

"Your leader is insane!" Abazi shouted at Hollie.

"He isn't me leader. I follow me own rules, thank ye very much!"

"Whatever. Just keep him away from us."

"He isn't normally like this—" Hollie began. "Well, he doesn't mean to be so ornery. It's just that lately— Oh, blighters! Forget Oswald. I want to know more about those notes ye keep goin' on about."

"We've gotten two so far," Kris told her. Gabe swiveled to see his brother crouched behind him.

"You're wet," he rasped, suddenly feeling very cold.

"As a puddle." Kris grinned, though it was a bit lopsided. His lips were blue and trembling.

"A puddle…" Gabe's head spun and he felt his whole body deflate.

"We've got to get him out of these wet clothes," Abazi directed. "He's probably already got hypothermia."

"Can ye carry him, Kristofer?" Hollie asked.

"Can a dog bark?"

"Ummm…" She appeared to be considering this.

"That means yes."

"Well, why didn't ye just say that? Come on, then. We'll take him to me cave."

"What good is a cave going to do?" Abazi demanded.

"A cave will be too cold," Jer added his two cents. "We need heat, maybe a place to build a fire."

"This is a special cave. Now come on, ye laggards, before he dies!"

~~~~~~

Abazi and Kris carried a barely conscious Gabe off the stone bridge and up to the top of the cliff. Then Abazi helped shove Gabe up onto Kris's shoulders, firefighter-style. Hollie took the lead and Kris followed after her, glad he'd been putting in extra workouts whenever he could. Gabe felt heavy as a cement blanket, cold as one, too. His wheezing didn't sound good, either. Not a worrier by nature, Kris nonetheless felt a stab of alarm and moved faster.

"Slow down!" Abazi called from behind him. Carrying his backpack, plus her own, was taking its toll.

He pretended not to hear her, making his strides even longer until he passed Jer and Kimber to walk alongside Hollie. "How far?"

"Not too much further," she replied. "So, are ye goin' to tell me what really brought ye here?"

"I told you, Hollie. We got a couple of weird notes and one of them led us here…into a trap."

"I can't believe Oswald would do that. He wants nothing to do with the likes of ye. So why would he lure ye here, to his home?"

Kris attempted a shrug. "I don't know. Strategy. Maybe he wanted to show us up in front of his followers. Demonstrate his power, you know. He certainly did a good job making us look like idiots."

"Ye did that on yer own." She laughed.

He gave her a sideways glance, taking in the cute way her nose crinkled up as she laughed. "Thanks for the vote of confidence." His eyes focused on his feet once more. He did not want to trip.

"I want to see those notes, see if I can tell who wrote them."

"They're in Gabe's backpack. We'll have to go back and get it."

"I'll do it later. I hope the notes survived the soaking."

"I'm more concerned that Gabe does."

She nodded seriously and they walked another hundred yards. "We're here." She gestured toward a tiny crack in the face of a stone wall. Well, not *tiny*. But certainly not very big, at about two feet high.

"You've got to be kidding me. I can't fit in there."

"If ye can't, yer brother's goin' to freeze to death."

"Crap." Kris rubbed his hand over his wet Mohawk, sending water drops flying through the air. He sighed, then crouched down, carefully sliding his brother off his shoulders. Gabe didn't exactly slide off smoothly, his hip catching on Kris's shoulder so that he ended up getting dumped onto the hard rock. He groaned, then curled up into a ball, shivering miserably.

"He's pretty bad off," Kris noted worriedly. "He didn't even yell at me for dropping him."

The rest of the group caught up. "This is it?" Abazi exclaimed. "Where's the opening?"

Kris pointed at the crack. "Anyone know how to flatten themselves?"

"It's all a matter of knowing how to twist your body," Jer said matter-of-factly.

"Well, count me out," Abazi declared. "I'm not a pretzel."

"I'm game," Kimber said. They all stared at her. "I'm in physical therapy, remember? I'm used to being put into all kinds of strange contortions." She grinned.

"I'm game, too," Jer announced heartily.

"Easy for you to say, Tiny Tim," Kris scoffed. "I'm twice your size."

"You are not!"

Gabe moaned. "All right!" Abazi yelled. "I'll do it. Though I feel like I'm about to enter Wonderland."

"I'll go first," Hollie said. "After I'm out of sight, put Gabe's arms into the crack. I'll pull him through."

"He's too heavy for you."

She frowned at him. "I'm a Dryad, ye knobby. Now let's do this."

"Sorry, Gabe," Kris muttered in his brother's ear as he bent down to do as he was told. Hollie slipped through the crack as easily as a lizard, and as soon as Kris saw she was gone, he tugged Gabe toward the opening until his arms were in darkness up to his elbows. With a push, he had Gabe on his side, ready to be pulled into the black hole like a slab of meat for butchering.

Kris burned this image into his brain for a later rendition onto paper. He hadn't told anyone, but he was writing up their latest adventures and sketching illustrations to be made into a book. If he could sell it, all their money troubles would be over and he'd be a hero. The thought made him grin. He felt a tug and realized Gabe was moving, inch-by-inch, disappearing inside the cave like a morsel into a monster's mouth. Another great image. A few seconds later, Gabe had been swallowed up and it was Kris's turn.

"Quickly now," Hollie called out, her voice hollow and strange. "He's startin' to shake something awful."

Lying down on his side on the cold rock, Kris drew in a deep breath and pulled himself through the narrow space. At one point his butt got stuck, but with some careful maneuvering, he slipped free, thankful to find his necessary parts all still intact. His head inside the cave now, he tried to look around, but saw only black ink. His other senses sharpened and he smelled something bitter, like hot tar. He didn't have time to think on it; Abazi was shouting at him to get a move on.

Once through, he crawled along the damp cave tunnel. His wet clothes felt heavy and he just now realized how cold he was himself. He wanted to stand up and run, anything to warm up, but he couldn't see anything and didn't want to risk knocking himself out. Where was Hollie? What had she done with Gabe?

Spurred on by cold and the thought of getting himself into another bad situation, Kris crawled faster. Just when he told himself he should maybe stop and lie down to rest a while, a dim light farther down the tunnel beckoned to him. He hurried onward until his head broke through into a large cave. Fumbling and shivering, he fell into the wide-open space. After blinking a few times, his eyes adjusted and he saw he was in a cavern, round and smooth and filled with all sorts of bric-a-brac. In the middle of the cave was a fire pit and thin wisps of smoke rose toward a hole in the ceiling, which let in a dim beam of light.

Thinking of little else, he stumbled toward the heat and knelt before it, hands outstretched. Realizing he still wore his gloves, he peeled them off and threw them on the floor where they made a squelching noise. Soon he was pulling off the rest of his layers. He needed heat directly on his skin.

"Get his shoes off," he heard from behind him.

"Who's taking off his pants?" Abazi demanded.

"I'll do it." Jer.

"He's blue!"

"Hurry now. Careful!"

The group dragged Gabe close to the fire. He had only his boxers on and was nearly as blue as the berries they'd picked this summer. Goosebumps marred his skin and he was groaning through chattering teeth. He looked on the verge of death.

Lightheaded, Kris watched as Hollie stirred up the fire. She added several handfuls of what looked like black stones, then three or four heaps of dried grass. The grass burned up quick as an explosion, throwing extra warmth toward Kris and Gabe. A sweet scent filled the air around them.

"Hang their clothes on that," Hollie directed, pointing at a nearby metal contraption that resembled a homemade coat tree. Abazi, Jer, and Kimber moved back and forth, working together silently. When they bent down near Kris and began picking up his discarded clothes, he looked down to find himself, like Gabe, dressed only in his boxers.

Oops.

No one seemed to take any notice, though. With a shrug, he scooted closer to the fire. Feeling better by the moment, he started looking around him, taking in Hollie's cave. The bric-a-brac sorted itself out. The floors and walls were covered with what some might call junk and others, treasure. But nothing, Kris discerned through the smoke, was made of wood. Metal, plastic, clay, and grass—those were the materials Hollie collected. She did not collect the bones of her kind. No, she only used those for weapons. *Was that ironic*, he wondered, *or fitting?*

"Feelin' better?" she murmured close to his ear. He felt her body heat, which helped warm him, and his gratitude to her at that moment was immense.

"Almost good as new," he asserted. "Though I still can't feel my toes."

She laughed. "Sit and put them close to the fire. I'll build it up."

"How's Gabe?" he asked as she dropped five coals into the pit in front of him. The grass came next.

She glanced over at Kris's brother, her thin face scrunched up. "Not good, I think."

"Not good?"

Footsteps rushed over to him. Abazi, Jer, and Kimber had heard. "What do you mean, 'not good'?" Abazi demanded.

Hollie never took her eyes off Gabe. "He's not warmin'. He has ice in his veins. It be a serious problem for Dryads."

"What can we do?" Kris asked, stunned.

"Ye can do nothing. Only he can."

"Then what does he have to do?" Jer wanted to know.

"He has to transform."

"Well, that's easy," Kris said. "He already did that once today. He can do it again."

"He won't," Hollie said flatly. "He said he'd rather die."

Chapter Eleven

A Night in the Mountains

Abazi's dark eyes flashed. "Then make him do it, Hollie. You're one of his kind. Say something and get him to do it!"

Hollie reared up. "Are ye daft? I can't just make him do it! Anyway," she quickly deflated, "he's more powerful than I am."

"Did he say why he won't change into a tree?" Jer asked quietly.

"When I ask he only shakes his head and mumbles, 'murder' over and over."

"Murder?" Jer looked surprised.

"He thinks being a Dryad changes him, makes him bad."

"That idiot," Abazi muttered. "Does he have to take everything so literally? Talk about stubborn. I'm going to go talk to him."

Hollie grabbed her arm, stopping her. "This is Gabriel's battle, Abazi. It's not for us to interfere."

"Are you serious? Gabe's my friend. I'm not just going to sit by and watch him die." She looked both defiant and guilty as she stomped over to Gabe's side. She crouched low and for a moment stared down at him. He looked like a piece of liver, purplish and wet. She took his cold, clammy hand in her own and leaned close. "I don't know what you're up to, Hawthorne, but if you don't turn yourself into a stupid tree, you're going to die. And if you die, I'm going to make your life miserable. Got it?"

"Leave me alone," Gabe groaned, his voice weak.

"I'll keep talking at you until you do this."

"I won't become one of those *things* ever again," he croaked. "So, Leave. Me. Alone."

"You'll die."

"Good."

"You don't mean that."

"Are you saying I'm afraid to die?"

"I'm saying you're being an idiot."

He turned away from her. "I don't care what you think. Now go away and leave me to die in peace."

Abazi stared down at him. Was she seeing things, or was he looking better? "There won't be any peace where you're going, Hawthorne. Just fire and brimstone. So you'd better make sure you live long enough to make amends for nearly killing poor Oswald."

"*Poor* Oswald?" he choked out. "He started it! You should be saying poor Gabe!"

Not her imagination—he *was* reviving. Already his skin looked pinker. "Oh, poor Gabe," she said in a sing-song voice. "Has a loving family and a special gift. Poor Gabe, strong and healthy."

"Gift?" he sputtered. "More like a curse. I won't do it, Abazi, so just stop trying to make me." He suddenly sat up and she fell back. "Where are my clothes?" he yelled, his face a definite red.

Abazi allowed herself a self-congratulatory smile. "You big faker."

"Faker?" Gabe gaped at her, eyes wide, lips twitching as he struggled to come up with a suitable comeback. "I'm not a faker!"

"Whatever. Your clothes are wet so you'll just have to sit there in all your glory." She snapped her mouth shut. Did she just say that last part?

Gabe's eyebrows drew together. "Glory?"

"Glorious idiocy!" Pushing herself to her feet, she stalked away to the other side of the cave. *Boys!*

"Ye're revivin'!" Hollie rushed to Gabe's side and Abazi's scowl deepened into a mask of fury. "How did ye do it? I thought ye were dyin'!"

"I was not," Gabe insisted, then looked around at the others. "Right?"

Kris's left eyebrow twitched as he studied his brother. "I don't know if you were dying or not cause I was fighting my own battle. I thought my nuts were going to freeze off."

"Kris!" Jer exclaimed, glancing over at Kimber, who was giggling. Seeing her reaction, Jer was seized by the giggles himself.

"What?" he said innocently. "I was just using one of Abazi's play on words. Though it would've worked better if I were a Dryad. Gabe's the one whose nuts are freezing—"

"That's an oak," Gabe corrected him. "They have nuts. I have thorns."

"Yeah, and you're a thorn in my side," Abazi muttered.

"Well, you're a thorn in my butt," he snapped back. It wasn't the best of comebacks but hearing it, Jer and Kimber roared with laughter. Kris laughed, too, and soon they all were laughing like little kids telling fart jokes around the campfire.

Gabe felt himself grow warmer with each passing second, and more aware of just how little he had on. "Got a blanket or something?" he asked Hollie, who was wiping tears from her cheeks.

She nodded, her eyes sparkling. "Are ye sure ye want to cover up, though? Might be best to keep yer skin exposed to the heat of the fire."

"I'm sure it will find its way through the blanket," he replied dryly. With a little smirk she handed a rough woolen one to him and Gabe wrapped it around his body, hoping it would work as a shield. The look Abazi was aiming at him right now was like bullets. Was she jealous? The thought warmed him even more than the blanket.

"How about ye, Kristofer?" Hollie asked, picking a blanket up off the floor from a corner of the cave.

"And deprive you of seeing my magnificent muscles?" He flexed his arm. "That would be cruel of me, don't you think?"

"I've seen better," she snorted and threw the blanket over his head.

He yanked the blanket off and pulled it over his shoulders like a cape. "You have not!"

She smiled. "Ye'll never know for sure, will ye?"

"Oh, I know for sure, little lady. These babies are pure gold." He lifted his left arm and kissed his bicep, then did the same with the right.

Jer groaned, his blue eyes darting over to see how Kimber was reacting to all this. She was looking at Kris, her expression innocent. "Your ego's as inflated as the Hindenburg, Kris," Jer commented. "And you know what happened to that."

"I'm sorry, little brother. If my guns scare you, I'll put them away." With a grin, Kris tucked his arms under the blanket. Jer scowled.

Gabe peeked at Abazi only to find her smiling at Kris. Gabe didn't like that smile. "So what do we do now?" he demanded, determined to get the focus off Kris, attention amoeba that he was. "We still haven't figured out what the note meant…why Oswald wanted us to come here."

"I already told Hollie my theory," Kris offered, stretching as he spoke. "I think Oswald set us up. To humiliate us."

"Then what about the first riddle? Nothing happened to us then." That wasn't exactly true, Gabe remembered with a shiver, but he wasn't about to bring up what he'd done to Wildrr's Lady.

"It was a practice run," Kris replied confidently. "To see if we'd jump through hoops. And boy, did we." His expression soured. "I should've seen it coming. Besides," he went on triumphantly, "there was that acorn attack."

"Now wait just a busy minute!" Hollie exclaimed. "I'm pretty sure Oswald didn't write those notes. That isn't his style. He's an oak. Oaks don't do trickery."

"Then who wrote them?" Abazi asked angrily.

"And why?" Jer added.

"Well, I know one thing for sure." Everyone turned toward Hollie. "I need to see those riddles. I've a good mind for figurin' whimsy."

"Shocker," Abazi muttered. Kimber elbowed her and gave her a look.

"I'm goin' after them. I'll be back soon." Hollie headed for the cave opening, then stopped. "Please don't leave while I'm gone."

"We won't," Gabe promised. "Our clothes are wet, remember?"

She tapped the side of her nose. "Ah, yes. How could I forget?" She gave him an impish smile, then disappeared down the tunnel.

When she was gone, Abazi asked, "Do you think she's right? About Oswald not sending those riddles?"

Gabe shook his head. "I think she's being loyal." Or dense. Or stubborn. "He wants to be King of the Forest Immortal and I'm in his way. He nearly killed me, you know."

"Because you nearly killed him," Abazi argued. "You should've seen his wounds. You two are bad for each other."

"If he lured us here to humiliate us," Jer put in, "why wouldn't he have pushed his advantage more when he could? Instead, he just stormed off."

"He's the one who was humiliated," Kimber said. "I know that look." She didn't say how she knew, though they could all guess. "The only way he won was to trick you, Gabe."

Gabe felt his cheeks go warm. "I thought oaks didn't do trickery."

"That wasn't trickery, *per se*," Kris said. "More like good battle strategy."

"Do you really think I could've won?" Gabe asked Kimber, who was watching him with a strange look on her face. "I mean, I couldn't have done it without…changing."

"Oh, yes. You would've won." She paused, her blue eyes searching his face. "There's nothing wrong with becoming your tree form to fight Oswald, Gabe. His intentions were to make you look bad. You were right to defend yourself."

"But I almost killed him. I almost died myself." His voice was barely a whisper. "I promised myself I wouldn't do it again."

"If I could do what you can, Gabe, I'd embrace that part of me." Kimber's eyes had grown surprisingly fierce. "You have a gift."

"It feels like a curse," he said heatedly. "Anyway, what does it matter? We need to figure out what to do next. Do we track down Oswald and demand to know what's going on? Do we go home?" Gabe said this last part in a hurry, avoiding Kimber's eye. He had the feeling he was disappointing her. He seemed to be good at disappointing everyone lately.

"I say we go after Oswald," Kris offered his two cents. "I'd like to teach him a lesson with the almighty fist." He raised his into the air and looked quite majestic until he spoiled the effect when his bicep distracted him. "Hey, I think my muscles got bigger! Must be from dragging your sorry butt all that way." He grinned at Gabe.

Gabe was not amused. "I don't want to go through another fight. That water was *cold*."

"I don't think we have a choice," Abazi said. She'd been re-braiding her hair while the others had been talking. "Oswald needs to explain himself. I think he owes us that."

"He's not going to see it that way," Gabe protested. "He's a bully. He'll just try another way to humiliate me."

"And me," Kris put in. "He threw that acorn at me, remember."

"You deserved that," Gabe said hotly. "Screwing around like that. We were on a mission, Kris, and you let yourself get distracted. Now look at us—stuck in a cave, our clothes soaking wet, and still clueless about what we're supposed to do."

Kris's eyes widened, his mouth opened to protest, then snapped shut again. Gabe felt quite satisfied with his brother's response, and maybe a little bit bad at how good that made him feel.

"I've got yer sack," they heard Hollie yell from down the tunnel. Gabe's bag, clutched in her thin hand, appeared, followed by her head. "And I've read the riddles."

"And..." Abazi prompted, taking Gabe's bag and opening it.

"I like his style."

"Or hers," Kimber pointed out.

Hollie laughed. "Right. Maybe *I* wrote them. I've been known to pen some wicked verse in me time."

The others looked at each other. "Well, the thought did occur to us..." Jer began.

The Dryad snorted. "I might like a bit of fun, but I wouldn't do this to ye. It's dangerous for us all, ye bein' here." The thought was sobering and everyone was quiet as they pondered it. "So ye tried the spiral in the woods, I take it, per the first riddle?"

"You had the same idea." Kris looked impressed. "But we didn't find a key or an answer or anything except—" He broke off, for once in his life showing some tact. "Well, we're sorry to say…"

Hollie frowned. "It were a horrid thing, what happened to Isis. It was Straif, of course, or his stupid sons. We don't even burn dead wood, not to mention live, or use it in any other way than defense." She patted the bata strapped to her waist. "And for that we have a ritual that asks for permission first, after which we give thanks."

"My people do that," Abazi said, looking at Hollie with an ambivalent expression on her face. She'd been busy unpacking Gabe's wet backpack and rolling out his supplies and sleeping bag to dry.

Hollie nodded. "We respect all things, as yer folk do. Anyway, I'm pretty sure I saw stupid old Dorn runnin' off after it happened."

"Pretty sure, or positive?" Jer asked.

Hollie shrugged. "I can't say nothing for sure. But I'm about as close to bein' sure as I can be." The others had to accept that for now. Hollie didn't seem in the mood to be challenged, and Jer, wisely, backed off. "As for the second riddle, well, I can see why ye came up here." She stopped talking and looked round at all of them.

"That's all you've got?" Gabe asked.

"The oaks are wise. I'm only clever."

"Well, I'm not talking to Oswald, Hollie," Gabe said more loudly than he meant to. "He came to my house, you know. He pretended to be my friend, in front of my mother. Then he threatened me. Which wasn't exactly wise, if you ask me. He was trying to stir up trouble."

There was nothing Hollie could say about what Oswald had done. In her way, she'd done the same thing when pretending to be a baby. "Well, Dame Hazel's wise, too," she mumbled.

"Is she up here with you?" Jer asked.

"She has her own place farther up on the ridge."

"Well, I don't know about the rest of you schmucks, but I need to eat," Abazi announced, pulling off her pack.

Hollie's green eyes lit up with interest as she watched Kris unzip his backpack. "So what did ye bring me, Kristofer?"

He pulled out a baggie. "Try these fruit chews. Blueberry-flavored, of course."

She fiddled with the bag for several frowning moments before he took it back and opened it for her. "Ah, yes, I knew there was a trick!"

The group gathered close to the fire and Gabe ate more than he should have. He hadn't figured on being in a battle, turning into a tree, or nearly dying. But it was only after eating everything he could find that this thought occurred to him, coming, as usual, too late. All his rations were gone. Rubbing a tired hand over his face, he felt as though he always made the wrong decisions, only thinking things through afterward. One of these times he figured he'd make the wrong decision and end up dead. The thought made him want to run home, climb under his covers, and hide out forever. He felt a new sympathy for those agoraphobic cat ladies who never left their house.

"Got any of those blue chews?" Hollie asked Gabe. He shook his head. He'd eaten those, too.

"Do you have anything left?" Abazi asked dryly. "You eat like a wild animal, you know."

Gabe blushed. His mom always teased him about what a messy eater he was. She took some of the blame on herself, telling him she'd made the mistake of not letting him make a mess when he was first learning to eat. And now she was paying the price, having to watch him make up for lost time.

"I was hungry," he muttered.

"One time he had pizza sauce on his ear," Jer commented.

"And once he had chocolate smeared on his back," Kris added, toasting his brother with a juice box.

"There's nothing wrong with bein' a healthy eater." Hollie patted him on the arm, then leaned low, "Though ye might want to slow down a bit, chappy. Ye're goin' to choke yerself." He scowled as she smiled broadly.

"I thought we were in a hurry." He pushed himself to his feet, then sank back to his knees as all the blood rushed to his head. *Crap, crap, crap*, he groaned, all the while hoping he was keeping those words inside his head.

Hollie plucked a chip out of Kris's hand. "Sit down, Gabe. There's no hurry. Dame Hazel won't be back until morn."

"Morn?" Abazi echoed.

"We were going to spend the night in the mountains anyway," Kris said. "Why not in here where it's warm?"

"Because we're trapped in here!" Abazi stood up, pacing back and forth and throwing suspicious looks at Hollie every few seconds. "Don't you see? This could be another trap and we're sitting ducks."

"You're right," Kris said, shoving his leftovers back into his bag. "I say we blow this joint. Scout the perimeter. Search out Oswald and demand to know what this is all about."

"Ye two are gettin' it all wrong," Hollie said with spirit. "Stay here and rest. Tomorrow ye'll be ready to do what ye need to do."

Abazi rounded on the Dryad. "Why are you so intent on keeping us here?"

Hollie met her glare with equal fervor. "Have ye ever thought I might be tryin' to help ye? Wanderin' around like ye never met Straif and his Ko-goks before. Ye're either mad or stupid. We need ye alive, not deader than Straif's heart."

"And what do you need us for?"

"Not *ye*!" Hollie spat. "We need Gabriel. Oswald is strugglin', but in the end, he'll do what needs to be done, and he'll do it *with* Gabriel."

"You have more faith in your friend than I do," Abazi retorted. "I think he's jealous, and I know what people do when they're jealous. They hurt you." She bit her lip and turned away from the group staring at her.

Gabe wondered how she'd learned that lesson, and from whom. Was it Jake Morrigan? Boy, he'd like to kick that creep straight to hell. That would teach him not to hurt anyone ever again. The moment Gabe thought this, a strange sensation washed over him. His skin prickled like a heat rash and he looked down to see black thorns pushing up through his flesh. He stared at the awful sight. So this is what was happening to him—this strange sensation. He looked like a Ko-gok!

Heart thudding and face hot with shame, he quickly pulled the blanket over himself to hide the thorns. Looking around he saw that only Hollie had noticed what had happened, and she looked quite pleased with what she saw. For some reason, that annoyed him.

He wrapped the blanket more tightly around his shoulders and said, "We'll stay here the night, but I won't be talking to Dame Hazel in the morning, or Oswald. I think we already know the answer to the riddles, so why stay? The notes were Oswald's idea of a joke—a way to show the 'Usurper' who's in charge. Well, I for one am not going to stick around and be made a fool of again."

"Why don't we just leave now?" Abazi demanded, turning on him. "We still have to scare off those surveyors, anyway."

He'd forgotten about the surveyors, but the prickling still bothered him, so he said in a shaky voice, "I don't think I can. I need more time to recover."

Abazi glared at him. "You're up to something, Hawthorne. I can tell."

"What? You think I like being like this?"

"I think that if you really wanted to leave this cave today, you'd find a way to do it."

She was right, but there was no way he was going to tell her the real reason he couldn't leave right now. At the moment, it was all he could do to keep himself from turning into a tree. And if he gave in, he'd end up destroying the cave, taking everyone with it.

Chapter Twelve

Stuck to the Thorn

Hours remained in the day and each one passed more slowly for Gabe than the last, especially since the thorns were taking their dear sweet time retreating. Hollie took turns leading people out of the cave to go to the bathroom. "I'll never pee on a tree again," Jer announced when they'd returned. "It just occurred to me I might be peeing on someone and that someone might not like it and do damage to my willy."

Everyone but Gabe laughed. He was too busy holding his pee in—he couldn't be seen like this. He figured he'd slip out later when everyone was asleep.

Kris, Abazi, and Hollie left again to scout the area and learn the layout of the land, as Kris put it, though more likely he just wanted something to do. Jer and Kimber were busy chatting to one another and didn't bother Gabe, meaning they didn't rile him up. The thorns still showed, but had almost completely sunk back beneath the surface by the time the three returned.

Gabe lay down and pulled the blanket over his head so no one would bother him. They spoke in low voices, no doubt discussing his strange behavior. *Well let them*, he thought. There was no way he was going to have them see him like this—thorns poking out all over the place. He looked like a Goth porcupine.

He hated that Hollie knew about his weakness. Would she tell Oswald and Dame Hazel? No doubt. But by then, he hoped to be gone from this place. Just thinking about being here, being trapped, started the prickling back up again and he forced himself to think of nicer things—running with Dad before he got sick, Sadie back in San Jose, eating sweet, sun-ripened blueberries, Abazi running her hands through her hair—

Whoa! Where had that come from?

He immediately switched to running the times table through his head. Math was good. Numbers were safe…as long as he didn't start thinking about measurements—

Agh!

There she was again.

This time he worked on staring at the glowing coals and letting nothing enter his mind but boring, non-provocative thoughts. In time, his eyelids grew heavy and he slid into sleep.

"I've found ye, ye dotey rapscallion!"

Gabe searched the shadowy woods, his heart beating in his throat, urging him to run. "Who's there?" he called, and his voice sounded echoey and hollow. He felt strange; his feet were heavy as cement and his mind light and dreamy.

"Follow the trail…Go on, I dare ye!" The voice was high-pitched and quavery, like an old flute. Gabe spun around, head tilted back to stare up at the looming trees. The voice seemed to be coming from up high.

"I'm trying to follow the trail!"

"Go round and round… Look high in the sky…"

"I *am* looking high in the sky," he called out. "I'm doing it right now!"

"The answer is up. Ye'll find the key."

What was high in the sky? The treetops? Was he supposed to climb a tree? If so, which one? There were thousands upon thousands in the Forest Immortal. Maybe he was supposed to have climbed Isis for the answer—but she was dead now, and there was nothing left to climb.

"Ninny, ninny, ninny!"

Gabe spun again and again, growing desperate. Suddenly he knew who his tormentor was. "Wildrr?" He shaded his eyes to scan the treetops. "Is that you? I'm really sorry about your tree! I only wanted to help her."

"Sorry won't save ye, ye wee feartie. Sorry only makes ye sorry."

"That doesn't make any sense!"

"Go round and round…"

Gabe spun about, unable to stop spinning, spinning, spinning like a child's top. Thorns burst through his skin, growing longer with each revolution until they reached the sky. "No! Please don't!"

One thorn stopped short, as though hitting a wall, and then slowly began to retreat. Gabe gazed up in horror. Something was stuck to the thorn. Something heavy.

Twenty feet away, Gabe realized what it was. A body. Wildrr. The thorn pierced his tiny torso like a pin through a voodoo doll and his bulgy eyes stared unseeingly at Gabe. His lips parted like a dummy's mouth, "Yer eyes are blind and so are mine... Ye'll see. Ye'll see..."

"NO!" Gabe sat up, panting, a layer of sweat coating his skin. Breathing hard, he looked around the cave. The light from the coal fire had died down to a cherry glow. Everyone appeared to be sleeping. Taking the blanket, he mechanically wiped off the sweat with a shaking hand. His frightened eyes took in his smooth skin and he realized his thorns had gone. Anger, not fear, appeared to be what caused them to erupt. Either way, it was awful not to have control over them. Anyone who knew Gabe knew controlling his anger wasn't exactly his forte. He got mad at the dumbest things and with the smallest of provocations. Though at the time, they never seemed dumb or little to him. More like the most important thing in the world.

Dry now, he crawled over to where his clothes were hanging. He found them a little damp, but dry enough to put on. His shoes and socks, next to the fire, felt warm and cozy on his feet. Dressed once more, Gabe felt a little better. Safer. He didn't know how nudists did it. To Gabe, clothing was like armor, and its absence was something to be feared. At least when around other people. Many's the time he dreamed of showing up at school in just his underwear. Sometimes, without even those. He hated those dreams.

Shoes tied, he realized he *really* had to go to the bathroom now. Checking to be sure everyone was still asleep, especially Hollie, whose tiny mound was still, he made his way toward the tunnel exit. He didn't much remember coming in and was rather glad for it. The going out was tough and a bit claustrophobic, if he let himself think about where he was, which he tried not to do as he pulled himself along.

Although it felt like forever, it wasn't long before cool air bathed his face. Twenty seconds later he was on his feet and leaving the cave. Free. He was free. For several moments, he just stood and pulled in lungfuls of fresh air as he looked around him. The moon was full as a ripe peach. A Hunter's Moon, he thought it was called. He shivered. Would its bright light benefit him as the hunter, or work against him as the hunted?

Either way, he made sure to be very careful as he slipped along the walk to find a relatively sheltered spot to empty his near-bursting bladder. He managed to find a place and urged his body to work faster as he peed into a crack in the stone, glancing over his shoulder, left to right. The snapping of a twig made him jerk and he almost watered his own shoe. Luckily he was pretty well done and he carefully zipped up and turned around, slow and steady. If he hadn't been seen yet, he didn't want to give himself away.

"If ye're done with yer duty, come join me. Up here."

Gabe was immensely grateful he had already emptied his bladder, for that eerie voice coming from out of nowhere was enough to make any normal person pee his pants. "Who's there?"

"Why, it's me, Hollie, of course! And Dame Hazel, too." So Hollie had been awake. He should have known. He turned around to face her.

"I thought you said she wouldn't be back until the morning," he hissed.

"Dame Hazel does stuff like this all the time…sayin' one thing, then doin' another. To keep us on our toes, ye see." He did see. Dame Hazel didn't sound quite all there. "Come on, then. Let's go talk to her. Tell her what happened to ye."

He took her extended hand and her long fingers gripped his firmly as she pulled him along a narrow trail that led up to where Dame Hazel waited for them. The noisy waterfall muted all other sounds and Gabe felt like he was standing inside a bubble. He didn't like this odd effect, not knowing what was coming, or from where.

"We meet again, Gabriel," Dame Hazel said when they reached the top. She had lit a lantern, which hung from a hook on her staff. The light showed her wizened features, the brown coils and fuzzy yellow bits of hair glowing against her purple cloak, the bristles growing from her cracked skin. She looked as strange as ever.

He nodded his head as a sort of bow. Being in her presence must be what it's like being presented to the Queen of England. Intimidating, formal, and hard to think straight.

"Are ye well?" she asked.

"I'm fine," he croaked, then cleared his throat.

"I saw what happened to ye."

His head swung up and he met her eyes. "You were there?" She nodded, a slight tilt of her head. "Why didn't you stop him?"

"I wanted to see what ye could do, Gabriel."

He couldn't help himself. "And what did you see?"

"That ye're a force to be reckoned with. Oswald has underestimated ye."

"Did you send the riddles? Did you set this up?" The prickling began and he tried to take a deep breath to coax it to go away, but the breath caught in his throat, making it hard to breathe.

"Riddles? What's this?" She looked at Hollie expectantly, almost angrily, judging by the jut of her chin.

"I haven't had time to tell ye, Dame Hazel," Hollie pushed out quickly. "Gabriel has received two mysterious riddles. He thinks Oswald sent them."

"He came to my house, too," Gabe added. "He—well, he—" He couldn't finish the sentence. He didn't like Oswald, but he wasn't about to go ratting on him for what he'd said. That was between him and Oswald. Not for Dame Hazel. And not for Hollie, who seemed to worship the screwed-up Dryad.

"I sent him to ye," Dame Hazel said.

"What?" Hollie and Gabe both cried. "Why?"

"I need him to get over his anger with ye, Gabriel. I need ye to work together to fight Straif."

"They were workin' together real nice today," Hollie snorted. "They were fightin' like they had brain rot, Dame Hazel! Ye saw it. They could've killed each other!"

"But they didn't," the little old woman replied, as if that meant something. "Tell me more about those riddles, Gabriel."

By now Gabe had memorized the odd poems and rattled them off to her. At the ending of each one, her nut-brown face would screw up and she'd rub her nose thoughtfully. "Interesting," she said when he was done.

"Do ye know who sent them?" Hollie asked.

Dame Hazel gripped her staff tightly. "I have me suspicions."

"And…" Gabe prompted.

"I never share suspicions, only certainties, Gabriel. Keeps others from gettin' hurt if I'm wrong."

"Can't you just give us a hint? So we know who to look out for?"

"Tell me about yer battle, Gabriel," she asked, sidestepping his question like a ninja.

"What about it?" he said sulkily. Her eyes narrowed and he amended, "I mean, you saw it. What else is there to say?"

"How did ye feel when ye were fightin'?"

His fingers curled as the familiar prickling started beneath his skin. "I almost killed him. How do you think I felt?"

"But ye didn't."

"I had no control over what I was doing. As a Dryad, I'm a killer."

"Ye can be a killer no matter what form ye take. Question is, can ye control yerself?"

"I don't know. I don't think so."

"I know about yer thorns—that they keep comin' out even though ye don't want them to."

"How'd you—?" He glanced over at Hollie, who didn't meet his eyes. "Of course you know," he heard himself sneer. "You have your eyes and ears right here."

Hollie turned on him. "I didn't tell her, ye skeevy! I looked away from ye now cause I didn't want to embarrass ye, not because I felt guilty."

He swallowed, not knowing what to believe. "I hate this, you know. I hate being this *thing*. I won't turn again. I *won't*."

"Ye can control it, Gabriel," Dame Hazel said softly.

"What if I get to a point where I don't want to?" he whispered, his real fear rising to the surface like bile.

"Ye must not give in. Ye must think of good things."

"I've tried that," he muttered. "I don't think it works."

He met her eyes and was surprised to see her looking worried. Then, just as suddenly, her knitted brow unknitted. "There's a way, Gabriel. Ye just have to find it." She banged her staff on the rock, like a judge about to make a ruling. "Ye *will* find it."

"I think I have found it," Gabe said. "We're leaving in the morning, and we're not coming back. That way I won't be tempted to change. I won't hurt anyone."

"Those people...are they comin'?"

He blinked, not expecting this response. He wasn't sure how she knew about them, but she obviously did. "You mean the surveyors? Yeah, they're coming tomorrow. We're going to scare them off."

Dame Hazel turned to Hollie. "Tell Oswald he's to escort them to the place."

"I don't want Oswald anywhere near me," Gabe growled. "He wants to humiliate me. He calls me the Usurper, which is a stupid name, by the way, and not true anyway. I didn't ask for this. I just want to be left alone." He paused, took a deep breath. "Please," he pleaded to the old woman, his hands stretching out. "Can't you leave me and my family alone?"

"Ye're not the Usurper, Gabriel." His hands retreated. "Some say Oswald is." Her eyes never left his face, assessing his reaction, as always.

"But...how? He's got more right to this place than I do even though, well, you know..." He wasn't going to say it out loud. That would make the fact that he and Oswald had been switched at birth too real.

"That may be so, but it doesn't matter when there's suspicion. After all he's done for this place, being doubted pains Oswald deeply. He disguises it as anger, and he takes it out on you."

Gabe crossed his arms over his chest, refusing to be sidetracked or pulled into feeling sympathy for Oswald. "He wrote the riddles, didn't he?" He asked the question quickly, hoping to catch her off guard.

It didn't work. "I'll not say one way or t'other, not til I'm sure."

Gabe straightened up, pulling himself to his full height. He towered over them and felt, briefly, rather powerful because of it. "Tomorrow we're going to scare off the surveyors, then we're going home."

"As ye wish, Gabriel. Good luck to ye." She turned to go, then swung back to face him. Somehow she'd managed to come to within a foot of him without looking like she'd moved. "Are ye worried about Wildrr?" she asked in a sly whisper.

"H-how did you know about him?" He mentally cursed his blunder. "I mean, who's Wildrr?" Dang stupid mouth of his. Might as well cross spy off his list of, "What I want to be when I grow up."

"Wildrr can be a bit of a troublemaker, see. He's spread a few stories about ye…"

Gabe leaned close, his stomach tight. "I didn't mean to hurt her."

She smiled up into his face. It was a satisfied smile. Not for the first time, Gabe wondered if he could trust her, or any of the Dryads. "Fairies are loyal and devoted. Very admirable, yes? But pigheaded to the point of idiocy."

Gabe swallowed, feeling a bit like he was being given a warning. "I'm sure I can handle him. I didn't do anything wrong, and besides, he's small."

Dame Hazel cackled. "Oh, Gabriel. Ye better learn now that not everyone'll like ye, and the ones who do like ye, won't like ye all the time. Bein' a leader means bein' both adored and hated, cause ye have to do things that aren't always seen as right."

"Well, good thing for me, I'm not a king." He pulled away from Dame Hazel and turned to Hollie, who was standing very still watching them. "Will you take me back to the cave?"

She glanced at Dame Hazel, then nodded. "As ye wish."

"Rest well, Gabriel," Dame Hazel called. "Ye're goin' to need it."

Gabe didn't look back as they walked away from the strange little woman. Where before she had seemed wise and comforting, she now came across as threatening. It occurred to him that she'd probably been the one who'd thrown that acorn at Kris. She'd wanted to test

Gabe and she had, forcing the fight with Oswald. She was lucky no one had been killed.

He sighed. He didn't know what to make of their conversation, and he didn't know how to get the Dryads to leave him alone. He did know he'd be happy to leave this wretched place far behind him. "What do you think about all this, Hollie?" he asked her when they reached the stream. "Do you really think I could be a king?"

"I don't know what to think anymore. Dame Hazel is wise, but tonight she was like smoke, a warning of danger to come." She peered up at the stars overhead, her thin face worried. The open sky between the stand of trees on both sides of the stream was like a river itself. A river of stars and darkness. "I'm comin' with ye tomorrow," she spoke to the night. "But ye'll not see me."

"You don't need to come, Hollie. I know you're loyal to Oswald and Dame Hazel, as you should be. I don't want you to have to pick sides. My brothers are always trying to get me to do that and I hate it."

She looked at him again and laughed. Her hand reached out and clasped his arm. He could feel its heat, even through his thick coat sleeve. "There are no sides in this, Gabriel. We—Oswald, Dame Hazel, me, and ye—we all are fightin' the same fight."

"I can't do it, Hollie," he said pleadingly. "I'll end up doing something awful."

"Ye'll get over that, Gabriel."

"Not me. I know that much about myself. I know I won't."

She squeezed his arm. "Ye're better than ye think, Gabriel. Stronger, too. Ye're afraid of what ye don't know. But what ye don't get is that ye know more than ye think."

"Was that supposed to make sense?"

She laughed again and let go of his arm. "It will. Now come on. We must rest. Tomorrow's a big day."

"I don't think it's going to be that bad. We're just going to scare off those surveyors."

"Oh, Gabriel. Do ye think ye're the only ones who'll be goin' after those surveyors?"

The breath left his lungs like swooping hawks. "Who else?"

"Why, Straif, of course. And all his dark ones, too."

Chapter Thirteen

What's She Up To?

The only way Gabe knew it was morning was from hearing Hollie's shouting to wake up. The cave was dark, the coals the only spots of light. "Eat if ye've got it. It's goin' to be a long day for all of us."

Kris groaned and stretched. "Six hours. Just give me six more hours."

Hollie ducked low and poked his head. "Get up, lazybones. Ye're worse than the Elms."

"Go away, Dryad wench."

She smacked him on the head. "If ye don't move yer behind, Kristofer Hawthorne, I'll be eatin' all yer food. And ye won't be wantin' my kind of fare in exchange, I can tell ye that."

That got him moving. Gabe grinned, watching his brother leap to his feet and grab his pack from Hollie. She laughed. Gabe struggled to sit up, running his hands through his hair, then down over his face in an effort to wake up. His grin faded as he reached for his own pack. He'd forgotten that he'd eaten all his food the day before.

A baggie full of beef jerky landed on the floor by his hand, startling him. Another followed, containing two donuts, which he caught mid-air. He searched the cave to see who had given him this godsend, but everyone was busy eating or talking. No one was looking at him. He tore open the bags and devoured the donuts first, then the beef jerky at a more leisurely pace, but only because it was harder to chew.

When he was done, he crawled over to where Abazi was eating a sandwich. "Thanks."

"For what?" she mumbled around the food. "For being my charming, lovely self?"

"Exactly."

"Hunh," she snorted, swallowing the last bite. "You're loony, Hawthorne."

"And you can be nice when you want to be."

She actually looked at him this time, her dark eyes narrowed. "Now I know you're crazy." Before she looked away, though, he thought he saw a little smile visit her enchanting lips. She shoved her baggie into her bag.

"I think you and Kimber and Jer should head back home," he said quietly, bracing for the reaction he knew was coming.

It was a big one, her whole body rearing like a spooked horse. "What? No way! Who do you think you are? Some sort of superhero? No, we're all going, or no one is." She shook her head in disgust as she fixed a braid.

"I think Straif is going to be there."

She frowned, still struggling with the braid. He felt a strange urge to take it from her and undo each strand until her hair was free. He shook his head to clear that image. "What makes you think that?"

"Why wouldn't he be? He can't possibly want the surveyors here, either."

"Then we can just let him do our job for us." She finished her braid and threw it over her shoulder.

"We can't. He'll kill them. People have disappeared in these woods. People will think the surveyors got lost and maybe go looking for them."

She grimaced and started on her other braid. "All right, fine. But I'm still not letting you go alone."

"Hollie will be there," he said, then winced, realizing his mistake.

She glared at him. "Well, isn't that sweet? You and your Dryad girlfriend saving the day. I don't think so, Hawthorne."

"She's not my girlfriend. And will you stop calling me by my last name?"

Her lips twitched. "Does that bother you?"

His skin started to prickle. "Not at all," he lied, struggling to keep his voice light and airy. "But as there are two other Hawthornes here, it might get a little confusing."

She smirked as she finished up her braid. "Fine." She peered into his eyes. "I'll call you Immortal."

"That's much better."

She bit back a laugh. "So who else is coming to the party?"

"Who knows? I imagine these woods are full of creatures we don't know about."

"Like that fairy you saw?"

"Exactly. So we better keep our eyes open and our ears to the ground."

She saluted him. "Got it. Eyes open, ears to the ground. I'll even get my nose involved, if you'd like."

"Very funny. You know what I mean."

She pushed his shoulder. "What'd you think I was going to do? I *am* an Indian. A Native American! I have no choice."

"Yeah, right. Tell that to your dad. He'll be happy to hear it."

"He just doesn't get that I'm an American first. And maybe the Native part just isn't my thing."

"Then you know how I feel. I don't want to be a Dryad. And even if I am one inside, that doesn't mean I have to have anything to do with it."

Her eyes narrowed as she considered what he said. "It's different for you," she finally decided.

"*How?*"

"If you ignore *your* roots, you're likely to end up as firewood or as a table for my kitchen." He waited for her to laugh at her bad pun, but she didn't.

"I don't think it's different at all. There's more than one kind of death, you know. If you ignore the Indian in you, not only will a part of you die out, your culture might die out, too. A whole people. A whole *history*."

Her lower lip jutted out. "One person won't make a difference. Indians won't go away just because *I* choose not to be all Indian."

Gabe pushed himself to his feet. "I'm going to go see when we're leaving. I'll tell the others what's going on." He felt Abazi's eyes on his back as he moved away. His mind was doing its best to erase their conversation, but certain parts of it nagged at him.

There's more than one kind of death.
One person won't make a difference.
Even if I am one inside, that doesn't mean I have to have anything to do with it.

The problem was, his arguments against Abazi worked against himself, too. They both wanted the same thing—to not be tied down by something they were born with. Though he supposed Kimber, with her cerebral palsy, didn't want that, either. But unlike him and Abazi, she couldn't simply repress it or forget about it. Though maybe they couldn't, either. Not without losing something.

His hand clutched his aching stomach. Maybe if he were meant to be Super Guy or something equally heroic, it wouldn't be so bad, but to be Tree Guy? That was just plain weird. Hollie, sitting by Kris, waved

to him at that moment, and his cheeks reddened. Crud. He forgot she
was one of those weird things he didn't want to be. It's just that she
seemed so normal. Wait…scratch that. Not normal exactly, but not
creepy, either.

"We'll be leavin' soon," she called to him.

He nodded nervously, hoping she couldn't read his mind. "Are you
up for a trek?" he asked Jer and Kimber.

Kimber smiled at him. "Ready when you are. Just stick me up in a
tree and I can make scary noises. I'm very good at making scary noises,
especially when my mouth doesn't want to work right." Her eyes widened mischievously.

"Are we going *now?*" Jer asked, his hands grabbing his backpack.

Gabe nodded. "But you should know that I think Straif might be
there." He didn't want to let on that he'd talked to Dame Hazel. Because then they'd want to know what she said—*I know about yer
thorns*—and he didn't want to share that.

"We can handle Straif." Jer puffed out his chest.

"Last time you met, Straif almost killed you."

"Yeah, and I owe him for that."

Gabe sighed. "Fine. What do you want written on your tombstone?"

"Jer will be careful, won't you, Jer?" Kimber's eyes caught his.

He jerked on his backpack's zipper. "I'm always careful. More careful
than those two jokers." He nodded at Kris and Gabe.

"There might be others—" Gabe went on.

"Then we'll be ready for them." Jer rolled up his sleeping bag in
quick, defiant movements. "You're not leaving me behind, Gabe."

"I didn't intend to." He turned and headed for his backpack. "Just
don't say I didn't warn you."

"You're always warning me. I'm sick of it, you know. I can handle
myself now. I'll be thirteen in four months!"

"I'm just saying…" Gabe knelt down to roll up his now dry sleeping
bag and gather his weapons. He'd done his job. If something happened
to Jer, it was his own fault. Though somehow the thought didn't make
Gabe feel any better.

"I'll be goin' with ye," Hollie announced when she saw that everyone
was ready, "but I must stay out of sight. I can't let the other humans
see me." Or Straif, she didn't bother adding.

"Where do you think the surveyors are right now?" Jer asked.

"This isn't the first time their kind have tried to do this job. They always start in the lower quadrant. We'll head there first off."

"And where's Oswald going to be?" Gabe demanded.

Hollie shrugged, doing her best to look innocent. "I don't know what Oswald's up to."

"Yeah, right," he muttered. "All right, then. We'll head to the lower quadrant, wherever that is. Everyone have a weapon handy and keep...well, stay alert."

"Eyes open, ears to the ground," Abazi said quietly behind him, laughter in her voice. "Though that will make it a bit hard to walk."

"I'm sure you'll manage. Ready everyone?"

"Ready to kick some butt!" Kris brandished his staff. "Let's do this thing!"

The group made their way out of the cave and into the bright sunlight, blinking and stretching. The air was crisp and so cold it felt like he was breathing ice crystals. Gabe was grateful that they didn't have to sleep outdoors last night. Being that his sleeping bag had gotten wet when he fell into the water, it would've been a long, cold night.

For the next hour, they followed after Hollie, each step down the mountainside bringing them closer to either the answer to their problems, or their death. "We're close," Hollie announced. "Can ye tell where we are?"

Gabe glanced around. This wasn't the same way they'd come in, but it looked familiar. "Near the main road, aren't we?"

She nodded. "The surveyors'll start their work where the small abode lies."

"Small abode?"

"Yer elder's home." Gabe nodded, though he was unable to shake off the feeling that something was wrong with that. "I'll be close," she went on. "Now get movin'. Ye've a lot to do before darkness falls."

"Dark's still a long ways off," Gabe pointed out, "and what are we supposed to be doing that's going to take all that time?"

"First off, smartypants, ye'll be meetin' *three* enemies in those woods, maybe more. There might be fights. There'll certainly be distractions."

"*Three* enemies?" The surveyors and the dark ones—that counted as only two. Unless Hollie meant Oswald, or she knew about Wildrr. But what about her saying, 'maybe more'? Who were *they*? Gabe suppressed a shudder. He really hated these woods.

"Later!" Hollie flipped a saucy wave at Kris, then disappeared into the woods. Literally. One moment she was there, the next she was gone.

"You've got to learn how to do that," Kris said. "It's like she went into stealth mode."

"She's probably just hiding behind a tree until we leave."

"Or until she *leaves*..." Abazi laughed. "Get it?"

"If you have to be a Dryad," Kris continued, ignoring her, "you should be the best Dryad you can be."

"Thanks for the commercial."

"Find your future," Kris sang in his opera man voice, "in the Forest Immortal Arrr-my!"

"Shh!" Gabe hissed. "We don't know who's close by."

"I'm just sayin'—"

"You're always *just sayin'*. Let's just find out where the surveyors are and then make a plan for what to do next."

Kris made a face. "Someone didn't get his caffeine fix this morning." He fingered his bata. "Aren't you the least bit revved up about this? I am *so* ready for a little paranormal action."

"I'm sure you'll get it. Now come on." Gabe motioned to the group and they followed him down to the main road. Making sure the way was clear, they hurried across, the bright sun outlining them clearly for anyone wanting to take them out. Thankfully they passed into the line of trees without a single loss of life or limb.

On this side of the road, the forest felt different from the woods up on the mountain. Here, the plant life was absent. No seedlings grew, no little animals scampered, no birds sang. Everything seemed darker, spookier—not as bad as farther into the forest, but bad enough. Gabe wondered how Grandma May could live in the middle of this place of death.

He made his way toward her house, stopping occasionally to scout around. His brothers and Abazi and Kimber were all staying on alert, which meant they felt as he did—that there was danger here. Even Kris was being unusually cautious, and that heightened Gabe's anxiety to new levels. As they crept along on the soft, thick moss, he wished his hands would stop shaking. He wished he could go home.

At the end of a long, dirt drive, Grandma May's cottage stood out like an oasis in a desert, like a star against a black sky, like a...well, it was very odd how lush and alive her yard seemed, surrounded as it was by dark trunks and death. With each step, the woods lightened; there were even plants growing here and there, mushrooms, too, and was that a squirrel? Life flourished in the woods surrounding Grandma May's home. A thirty-yard perimeter, actually. How did she do it?

He held up his fist and the others crouched down behind him, quiet and waiting. He looked down the driveway, a pale snake passing between hundreds and hundreds of birch trees. There were a lot of them, he realized. An unusually high number. He bit his lip. This was too odd of a phenomenon to go unnoticed. She *had* to know something.

"Kind of reminds me of Hansel and Gretel and the witch's cottage," Kris whispered behind Gabe.

He slowly nodded, feeling the same thing. "Maybe that's why she's been acting so weird lately, like she's nervous, or afraid. She must have noticed the woods creeping up on her."

"So we need to find out what she knows," Kris surmised. "I vote Gabe go talk to her."

"What? I can't talk to her!"

"You're scared of your grandma?" Abazi laughed. "She's, what, a foot shorter than you?"

"She's got crazy eyes," Gabe mumbled. "She knows magic. She's a witch."

"Come on, Gabe." Jer kneeled next to him, Kimber joining him. "She might be a bit weird, but she's family. She won't eat you."

"I know that," he grumbled. "It's just that she has a way of—" He broke off. He wasn't about to admit she had a way of making him feel like he was a little kid again. He wasn't about to open up that can of insults. "She isn't easy to talk to."

"But you're the one she gave the key to," Jer reminded him. "There has to be some reason for that." His disgusted tone made it clear *he* had no idea what made Gabe so special to get the coveted turret room.

"I know… But what if she won't talk?"

"Tell her we'll start having sleepovers every night since we're worried about her," Kris suggested. "That should get the old gal talking."

"I suppose…"

Abazi shoved him. "Just do it. We don't have all day. We've got to get prepared, scout out the area."

"All right, all right. I'll do it. You guys look around, see what you can find. I'll go talk to Grandma May." He stood up and made his wooden legs move out into the open. Feeling like a great big target with the words EASY PREY painted across his forehead, he forced himself to walk faster, until he was nearly running by the time he reached the little house. Standing outside its red door, he paused and listened, his eyes settling on the remains of Grandma's garden. He heard his own panting, but nothing else. It was surprisingly quiet here. Too quiet.

"Grandma?" he called, his voice no more than a whisper. "Are you in there?" Maybe she wasn't home.

He pushed on the door, which he discovered wasn't latched, and it fell silently open. He stepped inside the dark, earthy interior, which reminded him of being inside a hollowed out mushroom. A murmur of voices caught his ear. Was someone else here, or was Grandma talking to herself? She'd been known to do that.

Following the voices, he headed down a wood-paneled hallway that led to the living room. Just as he was about to step into the room, he called, "Hello?" in warning. No need to give the woman a heart attack.

Something screeched, and Gabe hurried into the room. A flurry of movement, like a whirlwind, charged toward him. Before he could duck out of the way, something hard smacked him on the forehead and he staggered backward, slamming against the wall. Head throbbing, he tried to steady himself with one hand while the other clutched at his wound. "Grandma!" he shouted, the word coming out slightly slurred. "Grandma, are you okay?" The smell of forest and something more pungent hung heavy in the air.

"Don't get your knickers in a bunch, Gabriel," her firm voice rang out. The effect was immediate. His mind cleared and the room settled down into normalcy. He blinked several times. There was no one else in the room. Grandma sat on her royal blue velvet couch, her matching blue eyes stern. "I don't remember you knocking."

"The door was open. I thought you were in trouble. I-I-"

"Don't stutter, Gabriel. It isn't attractive."

His mouth fell open. Grandma May wasn't always the sweetest woman in the world, but he couldn't remember her ever being mean like this. He pulled back, feeling hot and cold at the same time. "I was only trying to help." He turned around. "I'll go—"

"Oh no, you won't. Sit down."

Gabe froze. "I thought—"

"Sit down, boy."

Gabe slowly turned around and went to sit in the seat opposite the velvet couch—an oversized, overstuffed orange armchair. Sinking low, he had the distinct impression that the cushion was warm, as though someone had been sitting on it only moments earlier. The forest smell was stronger here.

"You scared King George. He must have run off into the kitchen." King George was Grandma May's very fat, very spoiled bulldog.

"I thought I saw...I thought a person was here," Gabe worked to push out the words before his nerves could stop them. When he got nervous, he had a habit of mixing everything up and repeating himself and saying 'um' half a dozen times. It was very annoying. Mom said practice would help him get over it. Unfortunately, in practicing he'd have to be willing to look like an idiot. Maybe back in San Jose, amongst friends, he'd be willing to take a chance, but not here in Ranger. No way.

"A person?" she echoed, as though he'd said 'alien.'

"Yes. He threw something at me."

"He did?" She laughed. "King George might be ornery, but he hasn't yet found a way to throw things. Lord help us if he ever does."

Gabe was about to back down and let the incident go when he noticed something odd…Grandma May was sweating. Several strands of black hair stuck in coils to her slick forehead. "Are you feeling okay?"

She laughed again and this time he heard the falseness in it. "I'm not the one imagining things."

Gabe rubbed the bump on his forehead. "I'm not imagining this."

She waved dismissively. "You always were a clumsy bird, just like your mother. She used to claim—"

"That the walls jumped out at her," he finished. "Yeah, I know. But that's not what happened this time."

She stood abruptly. "Shouldn't you be planning your attack on the surveyors?"

He flushed. "I am. We are."

"I have things to do, Gabe." She stood and headed toward the kitchen.

"Grandma, wait! How can you live here?" She froze. "There's something wrong with this place. Something odd."

"This is my home," she said coldly, without turning around. "And if you think it's so *odd*, then perhaps you should leave."

Tingles of humiliation zapped Gabe's body. "Fine," his voice trembled. "I'll leave. For good," he added under his breath. There was no way he was coming back to this cottage. When Grandma visited the house he'd hide out in the turret. He wouldn't ever be her target again. And if she lost her cottage to the forces of the forest, he'd laugh, that's what he'd do. Cause she'd deserve it for being so mean to him.

He practically ran down the hallway to the door. His hand was on the doorknob when her voice came roaring down the corridor to his ears.

"Hurry up and solve those riddles, you ninny. Or we're all in trouble."

Chapter Fourteen

The Surveyors Come

Gabe hurried out of Grandma's house, slamming the door shut behind him. As he ran toward the shelter of the woods—first time he ever thought of it that way—two disturbing thoughts hit him. Ducking behind the first birch tree he could find, he searched for the others, but could see no one. He wanted to tell them what had happened.

But maybe it was better to think first—about what Grandma May had said as he ran away. "Hurry up and solve those riddles…" How did she know about them? Even worse, she'd called him a ninny, just like the writer had done in the second riddle. His stomach churned. It couldn't be…could it? Was Grandma May the one writing the riddles? But why? Why did she want them to solve riddles she'd written herself? She must need Gabe and the others to do something that she couldn't, but *why* couldn't she? What was going on?

The snapping of a dead branch broke the silence of the woods, jerking Gabe's attention from this all-important question. His heart threatened to leap out of his chest as he crouched low, scanning the trees and bushes.

"Hiii-ya!" Kris leaped around a shrub. "Gotcha!"

"You idiot!" Gabe shouted, his fear quickly changing to anger. A foreboding prickling warned him he had to gain control, but he couldn't. All he wanted to do was beat the crap out of his brother for scaring him, for not being the one who had to deal with all of this.

"Sorry! I pulled back at the last second. Are you okay? You look kind of sick." He said it with real concern.

The thorns, deprived of a target, retreated, though Gabe's heart still pounded like death drums. "Where'd you guys go?"

"Just looking around. The others are coming." He jerked his thumb over his shoulder. "So what gives?"

Gabe forced himself to take a deep breath. *Inhale pink, exhale blue*, his mother jokingly told him whenever he got worked up. Pink is good, she explained, and blue is bad, and he needed to get rid of the bad. If only the breathing exercise would get rid of his tree spirit as easily. Or should he say, *exorcise*? Despite himself, he smiled. Abazi would've been proud.

"Did you find Grandma May?" Kris persisted.

"Unfortunately. I'll tell you about it when everyone gets here. In the meantime, do you have any food?"

"You ate all yours?"

"It's from turning into a tree. It took a lot out of me."

"Oh, sure. Take it all."

"Really?" Gabe looked up at his brother. For being so good at getting out of work, Kris was surprisingly generous. He knew his brother did good things, but sometimes he forgot the good things. "Thanks."

"Least I could do. You saved my life." He looked off into the distance.

It was all Gabe could do to stop himself from rubbing it in. He really wanted to. It wasn't often he bested Kris. But he decided to keep his mouth shut. No need to be a jerk about it, right? Besides, it couldn't have been easy to say those words. "That's what brothers do...be there for each other." He took the baggie of sandwiches Kris offered and settled down to eating its entire contents as quickly as he could before his brother changed his mind.

Abazi showed up seconds later, just as he was finishing off the first peanut butter and blueberry jelly sandwich. Gabe prided himself on being able to finish off a hot dog in three bites.

"Well?"

"Well, what?" he said around a wad of sticky bread.

She looked at him in disgust. "Did you talk to Grannykins? And could you fit any more food in your mouth?"

"I did." He took another bite. "And yes. Hi, Kimber," he said pointedly as she limped toward him. Her little face beamed. "Did you find anything out there?" He wasn't asking her simply to get at Abazi, well, mostly not, he was asking because Kimber had a rare talent of tracking and finding trails. It was like she had a map inside her head, or her own private GPS.

"The surveyors haven't arrived yet," she answered and sat down next to him. Abazi and Jer sat down next to her and began digging through their packs.

"That's weird. They should be here by now."

"Something must have held them up. Car trouble, maybe," Jer offered.

"That's possible." Abazi took a drink from her water bottle. "And we know how awful cell phone coverage is out here. They would've had to walk to get help."

Gabe nodded, chewing thoughtfully. "Well, that's to our advantage, but we're going to have to be on the lookout, not just for them, but for the dark ones and Oswald and his crew, too."

"This is a safe place, isn't it?" Kimber said. "Near your grandmother's home?"

Gabe looked at her in surprise. "Yeah. It's all those birch trees, like the ones lining the path through the woods to your house. They're protective."

"How do you guys know this stuff?" Abazi demanded.

"I read it in the book your dad gave you," Kimber replied with a sweet smile, but there was a hint of mischief in her blue eyes.

Gabe didn't bother to add that he just knew it, because then he'd have to explain how, and he didn't know how, exactly. When Mom had told them that the alder trees near the stream were protective, he'd already known it was a safe place. The tree book in his room, when he consulted it, had confirmed his intuition about the birches being protective, too. His knowledge probably came from a connection tree spirits had with each other. The idea of being a part of something so big and strange both disturbed and intrigued him.

He shook himself. No sense thinking that kind of incendiary nonsense. Encourage anything and it will grow.

"You read that snooze fest?"

Kimber nodded, her wide eyes amused. "It was actually quite interesting. I learned that birch contains aspirin-like qualities, which Native Americans used for their analgesic properties."

"So if I chew on a birch tree," Kris pointed at one, "it will help relieve my aches and pains? Wow!"

"I'm more impressed that you know what analgesic means," Gabe sniped.

Kris gave him a dirty look. "I guess I'm smarter than you think."

Gabe was surprised to see that his brother actually looked hurt. "I was just joshing you."

"Yeah, well, your joshing all seems to have to do with my lack of brains."

"I know you have brains. You just don't always use them to their full capacity."

"And you do?"

"Boys…" Kimber said in a warning tone. She sounded more like a teacher at that moment than a thirteen-year-old.

"Aw, who needs brains when you look like I do?" Kris grinned, back to his old self.

"Right," Gabe grumbled. "But if—"

"If you two could stop fighting like an old married couple," Jer interrupted, thrilled to finally get a chance to use the tried and true insult himself, "we could move on to talking about important things, like what we're going to do next."

"I want to know what happened with Grandma May," Kris said, shooting Jer a disgusted look. "And I'm not fighting like an old married couple. Baby Gabey started it."

"Oh, real original, snot."

"Are you gonna cry now?"

"I'm gonna knock your head off, that's what I'm gonna do."

Kris put up his fists. "I'd like to see you try."

Abazi walked over and plopped down between them. "Both of you need to shut up and grow up. Jer's right. We need a plan. But first," she turned to Gabe. "What happened with G-ma?"

He took a deep breath, willing himself to calm down. *Pink, blue,* he breathed. *Pink, blue.* "I think she had a visitor."

"Granny has a boyfriend?" Kris laughed in astonishment. "What's this world coming to?"

"I don't know if it was a boyfriend. I don't even know for sure if someone was there. I just saw movement, then something hit me on the head. When I looked again, whatever it was had disappeared."

"Are you okay?" Kimber asked, her eyes searching his head.

Gabe drew himself up. "I'm fine, just a little bruise. Thanks for asking, Kimber." She smiled sweetly and Jer glowered at Gabe. "Anyway, she told me it was King George—that's her bulldog. But this thing, whatever it was, was too tall to be a dog. Then she asked me to leave."

"She told you to get out?" Jer gasped.

"Well, I asked her how she could live in this place, that it seemed odd. And she told me it was her home and if I didn't like it I could leave."

"Maybe she's just touchy about her house. Who wants to hear that the place they live in is weird?"

"That could be it," Gabe acknowledged. "Though why didn't she just say that?"

Abazi shrugged. "Maybe she didn't feel the need to explain herself to a kid."

He bit down on a retort. "Fine. But that isn't all. When I was leaving, she said, and I quote, 'Hurry up and solve those riddles, you ninny. Or we're all in trouble.'" He took note of Abazi's surprised look and felt inordinately satisfied. He'd like to see her figure this one out.

"Your grandma called you a ninny?" Kimber said. "I can't see Mrs. May doing something like that."

"I can," Jer said. "But she wouldn't be mean about it. It's like our mom calling us a pack of monkeys when we get too loud."

"Don't you see?" Gabe cried. "The riddles... She knows about the riddles! And the second riddle called us ninnies. It's too much of a co-incidence. Grandma May must have written them!"

"Seriously?" Abazi popped a piece of dried peach into her mouth. "Why?"

"Why don't we go ask her?" Kimber suggested.

Gabe shook his head. "I've already tried that and—" He stopped. "What's that noise?"

"Vehicles!" Kris jumped to his feet. "And they're coming this way."

The rest of the group quickly hid themselves behind trees as a pink SUV roared down the driveway. A dusty black Jeep and a big bear of a car that closely resembled its driver, Mrs. Deacon, followed. Beams of sunlight bounced off her shiny brown Coupe De Ville, causing a weird, strobe-like effect as she passed.

The cars parked in front of the cottage and Candi Morrigan slid out on two pink hiking boots. Slamming her door shut with the strength of a weight lifter, Mrs. Deacon hustled after the slim blonde. Side by side, they looked like the odd couple, though the determined set to their shoulders—one rounded, the other squared—united them.

"Yoo-hoo!" Mrs. Morrigan called. "Mrs. May!"

She smiled back at the surveyors, a short man with curly brown hair and round glasses and a tall, slender, redheaded woman, who'd left their mud-spattered Jeep. Their khaki pants, brown leather boots, and thick canvas jackets from L.L. Bean made them look a bit like twins. The man left the woman to join Mrs. Morrigan and Mrs. Deacon on the steps.

"We're running late already—" he began.

"This will only take a moment, Jack," Mrs. Morrigan interrupted, a hard edge to her voice. "I just want to let Eleanor May know we're go-ing to be in the woods."

"But she lives here? In this cottage?" He indicated the place with his hand. "I thought you told me the land wasn't occupied."

"Most of it isn't. Anyway, it's only one little old lady," Mrs. Morrigan purred through pink lips. "Easily handled."

"Don't want to risk getting shot, do we?" Mrs. Deacon said briskly.

Jack went pale. "Shot?"

Mrs. Morrigan gave Mrs. Deacon a hard look. "She's ornery, Cornelia, not crazy."

Gabe thought he could argue that point, but decided now was not the time.

"I'm going to check our equipment," Jack said quickly, backing down the steps and scurrying over to the Jeep. Once there he began speaking to his co-worker and gesturing at the cottage. Gabe couldn't hear what was being said, but he thought he had an idea.

Kris crept up to his side. "She's not answering. What do you think she's up to?"

"Probably loading her shotgun."

"That I'd like to see."

"This is really getting weird. Grandma's up to something. Straif could show up at any time. Oswald's a wild card—who knows what he might do. And Mrs. Deacon and Mrs. Morrigan are very determined to go through with this survey. I have a bad feeling someone is going to get hurt."

Kris nodded, though the grin on his face conveyed his lack of concern. "Well, let's hope she bugged out and—"

"Get off my land, you bloodsucking harlots!"

Candi Morrigan looked up at the window Grandma was leaning out of, shotgun in hand. Gabe had to give the lady credit for not immediately running into the woods screaming. "Mrs. May, you're making this harder than it needs to be," she said in a sing-song voice that was meant to be charming, but only came off as condescending. "We came to let you know the surveyors are here and are going to be surveying this land."

"It's *my* land!" Grandma waved the gun. "Now get off it before I blow a hole in that butt-ugly car of yours!"

"Ugly?" Mrs. Morrigan gasped. "How dare you?"

For answer, Grandma lifted her gun and aimed.

"All right, all right! We're going. But like it or not," she shook her finger at Grandma May like she was a recalcitrant child, and which Gabe felt sure was not well-received, "we're still doing the survey."

Grandma released the safety and Mrs. Morrigan took off for her SUV, moving astoundingly fast in her tight red jeans. The surveyors piled into their Jeep, though Mrs. Deacon made it clear no one was going to make her hurry, gun or not. Climbing into her car, she called out, "You're standing in the way of progress, Eleanor! If we don't clear these woods, Ranger will become a ghost town. Mark my words…"

"Mark this!" Grandma cried, then shot into the air. Mrs. Deacon grimaced as she slammed the door behind her. The Jeep shot in front of her, racing down the drive in a cloud of dust.

Abazi kneeled by Gabe's side. "They'll park on the road."

"I can't believe Grandma May shot at people!" Jer cried as he joined them. "She's like a renegade."

"She's going to end up in a loony bin if she doesn't watch out," Gabe said dryly. "You can't just shoot at people and get away with it."

"She didn't shoot *at* them," Kris corrected. "She shot into the air."

"Same difference."

"Should we go let the air out of their tires?" he suggested.

"They can't survey while driving so that would be useless," Gabe replied. "We have to stop them from starting in the first place. And no, Kris, we can't kidnap them."

Kris rolled the tips of his pretend villain's mustache and everyone started snickering. Even Gabe joined in. It was pretty funny, after all, imagining Mrs. Deacon's expression when a bunch of kids came running at her with ropes in hand and determined expressions on their faces.

"Okay, okay," he wheezed. "We've really got to focus. Luckily the sun's out so Straif and his gang will probably lay low. Oswald likely isn't too anxious to be seen so I imagine they'll stick to guerilla warfare—acorns from the trees, tree branches knocking people over—that sort of thing. We can't use our masks to scare them, not in broad daylight. So we need to think of another plan."

"Steal their stuff?" Kris tried.

"If we take their equipment, they'll just get more." Jer's shoulders slumped.

"Maybe we don't need to stop them," Kimber said. "Just delay them…"

"Mom and Dad do think we're going to have an early winter," Jer said slowly. "How much surveying are they going to get done in heavy snow and frigid cold? So if we do take their stuff—maybe hide it somewhere—we can hold them off until we think of something better."

Abazi nodded. "Sounds good to me."

"But how are we going to take their things?" Kimber asked, looking worried. "I can't go to jail—it would kill my mom."

"Mom would kill *us*," Kris said forlornly. He straightened up, snapping his fingers. "But Gabe could do it! As a tree."

Gabe felt his heart expand three sizes. "No way. What if they see me?"

"They won't. We'll create some kind of diversion. Then, when they're not looking, *BAM!* your branch goes in, snatches their equipment, and gives it to one of us to dispose of." He used his fingers to make quotes around the word, dispose.

"I don't want to turn into a tree."

"Why not?"

"Besides the obvious reasons? Well, for starters, it takes a lot of energy and I'm out of food. And I don't like what I do when I'm a tree," he added quietly.

"The difference here is that you're not mad at them," Abazi pointed out, and Gabe mentally cursed her intuition. "So you shouldn't kill anybody."

He sighed. "Operative word here being *shouldn't*. No guarantees. I don't want to go to prison, you know."

"Not with those eyelashes," Jer joked and everyone snickered.

"I'm not kidding," Gabe grumbled.

"You don't have to turn into a tree, Gabe," Kimber said softly. "I noticed that Oswald was able to turn only parts of himself. Do you think you could do that?"

She said it so nicely and sweetly that Gabe found he didn't even mind that she'd mentioned Oswald. "I suppose I could try."

She smiled and patted his hand. "If I could, I would do it for you."

"Let's go, then!" Kris cried. "Time's a wastin' and I'm a growin' old."

"You're practically on your deathbed." Abazi laughed as she stood and brushed herself off. "So we're headed for the road?"

Everyone nodded their agreement and after a few scans, they headed for the driveway. When they reached the road, they spent precious minutes arguing about which way to head. Finally they agreed to split up. Kris, Jer, and Kimber headed in the direction of town, leaving Gabe and Abazi to go south. Gabe watched the others go with mixed emotions. He had the feeling they shouldn't be splitting up, but said nothing. It was too late now. Besides, he'd only be accused of being a scaredy-cat, or something equally stupid and unfair.

It didn't take long for him and Abazi to find the surveyors, already unloading their Jeep. They had parked less than a quarter mile up the road, unseen around a bend. Gabe felt queasy as he pondered how he was going to snatch their equipment without being seen. He beckoned to Abazi and they both slipped behind a large oak tree.

"They're going to see me," he whispered to Abazi.

"Not if you're quick," she hissed back.

He bit his lip. "All right, I'll try. But if I'm caught, I'm taking you down with me."

"Don't you know we Indians aren't subject to your white man's laws?"

"Why is it that you become an Indian whenever it's convenient for you?"

She grinned impishly. "It works for me."

He suppressed a sigh. "Just run back and fetch the others, okay? I'd like to at least have some back-up."

"Don't do anything stupid."

"I don't plan to."

She punched him on the shoulder. "I know you, Immortal. You pretend to be all 'I can't do this. I won't do this!' But when it comes down to it, you like being the hero."

Before he could respond to everything that was wrong with her assessment of him, she was gone—back down the road to find the others. *I don't like being the hero!* he argued to himself. *I just want to lay low and live my life. Like everyone else. Abazi is so irritating, and a hypocrite, too!* He would have gone on with his inner grumbling, but he noticed something bad happening—the surveyors were heading into the woods.

He glanced around. He had to do something now, before he either lost them or someone 'found' them. Steeling himself, he imagined his arm turning into a branch, hardening and expanding, with supple twigs to do the grabbing. The transformation was beginning to take place when he heard a snapping noise and a warrior shout.

And that's when he saw he had company. Lots of company.

Chapter Fifteen

Light the Bonfire

Oswald and his band of Dryads must be everywhere, hidden high in the trees, unseen and unheard. They were throwing acorns at the surveyors, and the missiles were coming fast and furious. Knowing how hard those nuts felt, Gabe felt sorry for Jack and the blond woman. They weren't evil; they were only doing a job. And while he didn't like Mrs. Morrigan or Mrs. Deacon, he also didn't feel they deserved to be attacked.

And maybe, on a more petty level, he didn't like seeing Oswald winning.

There was only one thing to do, and before Gabe knew it, he had turned himself into a tree. Unlike his first transformations, when he'd had trouble thinking clearly, this time, he felt more able to anticipate than just react. He felt more human. But a tree's natural instinct is to reach for the sky. So while he felt more in control, he still had to fight the lethargy that threatened his limbs as he made his way into the woods.

When he was between the fleeing surveyors and the oaks, he forced thousands of small twigs and thorns to burst from his trunk and limbs, creating a web to block the barrage of acorns. After getting pelted without mercy for longer than was necessary, the battery abruptly stopped.

"Get yerself out of the way, Hawthorne!" Oswald shouted. Gabe's hearing was better now, but still the words sounded thick, as though traveling through water. He looked around and spotted numerous figures perched high up in the trees. They gave off heat glows, but this time he could make out more detail, like Oswald shaking his fist. "Ye're blockin' us!"

Well, duh. Even a blockhead would get that. His trunk convulsed with treeish laughter. Blockhead. That wasn't bad. He'd have to be sure to tell…*hmmm*…well, someone that. What was her name? Or was it a him? Her, him. What did that mean?

"Gabriel!" a different voice called to him. "What are ye doin'?"

He wanted to explain himself, but he also didn't want to be heard by the surveyors. He'd have to send his thoughts another way. *THEY DON'T DESERVE PAIN!*

The glowing figures reared back, clapping their hands to their heads. "Ye don't have to shout!"

Sorry.

"How did *that* get there?" a human voice cried out, and a feeling of dread shuddered through Gabe's limbs. The other humans—the ones he was protecting—they had found him, and until they left, he was trapped as a tree. *Trapped.* The very idea of it made him want to scream in horror. What if he could never change back?

"Did it stop?" another wanted to know.

"What was all that?" a deeper, rather bossy voice demanded.

"That, my friends, was Eleanor May asking for trouble." This voice sounded like angry crows. "If she wants war, she's going to get it."

"We can't get to the cars. That thing has blocked our way."

"Then we head into the woods," crow voice replied. "And we get this done."

"Whatever that thing is," bossypants persisted, "it isn't right."

Thing?

"We just got turned about, Agnes. I imagine it was always there."

"Then how did we get around it, Candace?"

"How should I know? I'm not some tree hugger. In fact, I'll be the first to light the bonfire when we raze this woods." She made a shivering noise. "Creepy place."

Gabe agreed with crow voice until he realized that her scathing assessment of the forest included him. He was the 'thing' that wasn't right. He was part of what made this place creepy. It was not a nice feeling.

With lots of orders coming from the crow, the crew made their way into the woods, looking over their shoulder every few steps. When they were gone, Gabe released a pent-up breath and returned to his human form lightning quick. He was getting better at being a Dryad, and felt pleased at his success. Then he remembered what he was feeling pleased about and quickly emptied his mind. Exhausted, his knees crumpled and he fell to the ground. Within seconds he was surrounded.

"You idiot!" Abazi, of course.

"He was hurting them," Gabe pushed through his slack mouth.

"He was trying to scare them off and it was working until you got jealous!"

"Jealous! I know what those acorns feel like. He wasn't just trying to get rid of them; he was trying to humiliate and hurt them."

"Come on." Kris pulled on his arm. "Sit up."

"I can do it myself," Gabe mumbled, but he let his brother pull him upright.

"Are ye mad, Hawthorne?" Gabe spun his head to see Oswald marching toward him, seething from being outmaneuvered.

He felt a brief spasm of satisfaction as he shakily pushed himself to his feet. "Do you get a kick out of attacking defenseless people? They didn't stand a chance."

"We weren't hittin' them, ye knobby! So there's nothing to defend against!"

"Then how come I heard someone crying out in pain?"

"One of them tripped," Oswald snorted contemptuously, "and knocked his head on his measurin' contraption. I do me best, but I can't fix stupid."

"I think you were trying to hit them. Just like you had your lackeys hit me when we were by the birch spiral."

Oswald shrugged. "I can't account for all me band's actions. Sometimes they get ideas in their heads. I'm their leader, not their dictator."

Gabe worked to control his rising anger. He didn't want thorns popping out in front of this yahoo. "But they knew you'd be pleased, didn't they?"

"All right, all right." Abazi stepped forward, her palms facing each one as though holding them back from going at each other. "Enough of the pissing contest, boys. I vote we work together to scare off the surveyors. Without violence," she added, looking first to Oswald, then to Gabe.

Gabe met her eyes defiantly. "I just want to get this done and go home."

"That's just the thing, isn't it, Gabriel?" Oswald said. "Ye don't see the Forest Immortal as yer home. So how can it be that ye're the one meant to protect it? It's plain to everyone here that it means nothing to ye."

"You think I want this? My whole idea of who I am is a joke. Am I human? Am I Dryad? I don't even know. All I know is that those surveyors have to be stopped, but I won't hurt them to do it."

"That's where ye and I differ. I'm willin' to do whatever it takes to protect me home."

"Yes, Oswald," Gabe said quietly. "That's where we differ. I won't become like our enemy."

"Are you two done?" Abazi demanded. "Because those surveyors you both are so fired up about are getting away."

"Abazi's right," Kris said. "Time to move it or lose it."

Oswald gave Gabe a long stare. "If ye're so capable, then I leave ye to it." He turned away to face his band. "To the trees," he ordered, and the Rogues slipped away like shadows at dusk. He turned back to Gabe. "Next time we meet, ye be sure to stay out of me way, cause I won't stop me band from takin' ye out."

Kris placed his hand on his bata. "You mess with my brother, you mess with me."

"Me, too!" cried Jer.

Oswald gave them a cold smile. "Just understand that I be yer *real* brother, not this pitiful imposter…this *Usurper*." And then he was gone.

"Come on," Gabe said shakily. He had to move; he needed action to clear those awful words out of his head.

"Don't listen to him," Jer said. "You might be a pain in the butt, but you're still my brother. Besides, I've invested too much time training you to do what I want you to do."

"Jer's right, Gabe," Kris said, joining them. "I'm on your side. No question."

"He's just trying to get your goat," Abazi added. "Don't listen to him."

"He can have my goat," Gabe managed to joke, though it was an effort. "But he can't have my family, or my friends. Right?"

"Right!" everyone echoed fervently.

Feeling better, he gripped his bata and headed deeper into the woods. "If we move quickly, we should catch up to them soon. They have to start their surveying around here somewhere."

His prediction turned out to be correct. After a few minutes trek, they spotted the two surveyors as they attempted to set up their equipment amongst the thick moss and tightly packed trees. Mrs. Morrigan and Mrs. Deacon stood together about ten feet farther on, arguing. He held up his fist and everyone squatted low. Man, he loved doing that.

"Let's spread out," Abazi whispered. "Make sure you're well-hidden, then start making weird noises. Use the bullhorn if you can. Kimber and Jer, go together. I'll stay here with Gabe to take the equipment.

Kris, can you manage on your own?" He gave her a grin and a quick salute. "Good. Ready, everyone?"

Gabe took a deep breath and nodded. When the others had left, their footsteps silent in the thick moss, he whispered to Abazi, "I'll do better up in a tree."

"Just don't let it be an oak," she whispered back.

He smiled. "Definitely not."

He spotted an elm tree not far from where they crouched and silently made his way toward it. A low hanging branch made his climb easy and soon he was about fifteen feet in the air. He glanced down and saw Abazi waiting beneath. She gave him a thumbs-up and he returned it. Then she made a circular motion with her finger—the 'let's speed this up' sign. He nodded and attempted what Kimber had suggested—transform only one part of his body into a tree. He inhaled deeply, then focused on turning only his arm into a branch. The mental effort made him sweat, but within a few seconds, the change was complete. He was surprised to see his first attempt at a partial transformation work, and rather proud of himself.

Not knowing how long he could hold this form, he sent his branch-arm speeding toward a piece of equipment the female surveyor had momentarily left unattended to consult with Jack. Gabe easily roped his 'calf' and lifted it into the air. The hard part was watching everyone to be sure no one saw what was happening, but he was doing pretty well despite the difficulty.

And then the strange noises began. The surveyors stopped what they were doing to scan the woods nervously. Soon the yellow tripod Gabe had grabbed was in Abazi's hands and she dashed off to hide it. But Gabe couldn't wait for her to return. Someone was bound to discover the missing equipment sooner rather than later.

With a bit of maneuvering, he managed to snag three orange equipment bags. While pulling them up into the tree, one of the bags hooked on a branch. He yanked on it, but it didn't let go. He pulled again, but nothing happened. Heart pounding, he tried another one. It was stuck, too, so was the third one. *All* the bags were caught in the tree.

Relax, he warned himself, feeling dizzy. *You're going to fall if you're not careful.* He took a moment to scan the branches, wondering what to do, when it hit him—the tree was taking the bags from him! He could leave them here. He unwound his tendrils and, bit by bit, pulled in his branch-arm. The tree lifted the bags upward, going above Gabe's head, until soon all three bags were a hundred feet in the air.

He almost laughed aloud. *Let's see you find those, Mrs. Morrigan!*

"The tripod!" the female surveyor shouted. "Where is it?" She sounded frightened and he regretted scaring her. But it was best that she and the others leave this place now before they met with Straif and found out what scared really meant.

"Look in the moss, Kate," Jack told her. "It probably just tipped over. This stuff is so thick, it'd hide anything." He sounded a bit repulsed by the idea, and Gabe couldn't blame him.

"But isn't it weird that the tripod disappeared after we heard those noises? First we get acorns thrown at us, then this?"

"Candi warned us some locals were against taking down the forest. It's probably only an environmental group trying to scare us off. Just ignore them so we can get this job done and get out of here." Jack sounded gruff and in charge, but even from this distance Gabe could see from the way he kept looking around that he was nervous.

"I do feel like I'm being watched." Kate hugged herself and shivered. "This place is creepy. I haven't heard or seen one animal since we entered the woods. And this moss is like quicksand. And didn't a surveyor go missing last year? I thought I read something about that."

"That was Andy Sorbo. He was an arrogant idiot who didn't think he needed GPS. But in a place like this, well, that would be stupid. I'm sure he got lost and died from exposure."

Kate didn't look too convinced. "I'm not so sure that's all it was, Jack. There's something about these woods that's different from anything I've ever encountered." She turned around. "Hey! Our bags are gone!"

Jack spun about. "What? My dad's going to be furious! There's thousands of dollars of equipment missing now. *Mrs. Morrigan!*"

Gabe gulped and hoped Abazi hadn't done anything stupid to the tripod.

Candi stomped over, followed by Mrs. Deacon. Both women looked fierce. "What is it?"

"Our equipment's gone."

"What? How? Weren't you watching it?"

Jack twitched nervously. "We were looking for a place to set up the tripod." Mrs. Morrigan's nostrils flared. "And, y-you did say there might be trouble from the locals."

"Yeah, locals," Mrs. Morrigan replied vaguely. "Right. Search for the bags. We need to get this done."

"They can't have gotten far," Kate pointed out. "Not in this maze."

They headed in the direction the noises had come from and Gabe felt his stomach drop. That's likely where his brothers and Kimber were hiding out.

"Look!" Kate pointed away from Gabe toward a section of the woods that looked dark and daunting. "Over there! Someone's running through the trees!" Gabe knew right away that it was Kris. This was just the sort of thing he lived for—the chase. Undoubtedly he was leading them away from Jer and Kimber.

"Let's see if this will make a difference." Mrs. Morrigan expertly hoisted the hunting rifle she'd pulled off her back, flipped off the safety, and fired a shot into the air. The bullet sliced through several branches and Gabe heard a groan. She was hurting the tree.

He glanced down to see Abazi gaping up at him. "Bring it back!" he mouthed to her.

She shook her head. "Can't," she mouthed back.

"What do you mean?"

"It's stuck," she hissed through cupped hands.

Gabe was wondering what else could go wrong when he heard angry shouting. "Let me go! I didn't take anything!" He looked down to see Jack dragging Jer toward Mrs. Morrigan. Kimber wasn't with him.

"Well, well, well..." Mrs. Morrigan tapped the barrel of her gun with a long, pink fingernail. "If it isn't one of the Hawthorne boys." She approached Jer and ran her fingers over his blond hair, as though he were a pet dog she no longer wanted to own. "Taking a walk?"

"I didn't take your stuff. I don't even know what they're talking about!"

She tutted. "Young man, do you really think I believe that?" She shook her head. "I imagine you and your brothers—" Here she paused and watched with amusement as red blotches bloomed on Jer's cheeks. "Just as I thought." More fingernail tapping. "So...you and your brothers thought you'd entertain yourselves interrupting official town business? You know what kind of trouble you're in?" Jer scowled at her, but kept his mouth clamped shut. He wasn't talking. "I'll tell you what..." she purred. "Return the equipment and all this will be forgotten. The acorns...the theft..."

"That wasn't us!"

"Why don't you get your brothers to bring everything back, hm? Gabe's old enough to be tried as an adult for this sort of criminal behavior." She gazed upward, as though thinking deep, serious thoughts. "Being convicted of theft and assault, serving time. Now that wouldn't look too good on his resume, would it?"

Jer's shoulders slumped, though his expression remained defiant.
Gabe had to do something. He mentally urged Jer to hold on for a few
more minutes and began to climb back down the tree.

"We need to return that tripod!" he hissed to Abazi when he met her
on the ground.

"Tell me something I don't know!"

"Just show me where it is."

She frowned, then ducked into the woods. He followed after her,
grateful to see she hadn't gone too far when she stopped and pointed
at a large stone, split in two. "It's in there."

Gabe stared at the crack. How had she managed to fit the tripod in
that tiny space? And why had she thought it would be a good idea to
put it in there in the first place?

"Before you ask," she whispered, "I didn't put it in there. I set it
down, turned around to be sure no one was following me, and when I
turned back, it was gone. I found it in the crack...wedged in tight."

"You didn't see anyone?" he asked, already knowing the answer.

"If I had, he'd be dangling from his feet by now." She indicated the
trees. "They're definitely on our side in this. Could it have been one of
those little guys you met? You know, a...well...a fairy?"

He shrugged, feigning ignorance. "I've no idea." He peered down
into the crack. "But whoever did this was either very strong or very
determined." He looked up at the trees. Had one of them done it? It
was likely they understood what was going on with the surveyors, so
why not? Unfortunately, they'd done more harm than good. But he
wasn't about to point that out. His reputation in the Forest Immortal
already stunk as it was.

He grabbed one of the tripod legs and gave it a yank. It didn't even
shift. He gripped two of the legs and pulled hard. Nothing happened.
He tried using his staff to wiggle it out, but again, nothing. He needed
to think of alternatives. But the only alternative that came to mind involved, once again, becoming a tree. He sighed. This was just not his
day, week, or year.

The problem was, what could he do as a tree? Tickle the rock with
his twigs? Whip it into submission? Or... He found he was staring
right at the answer. On top of the boulder grew a young tree, its roots
reaching down into the crevice. He could do that himself, reach into
the crack with his tree-arm, but that would mean he might kill the sapling. He couldn't do that. In the Forest Immortal, young trees were
practically non-existent. In fact, this was the only one he'd seen so far.

He studied the scrubby little thing. It wasn't the prettiest of plants and was likely not going to survive, especially if Straif found it. Still, despite its low chance of survival, Gabe couldn't destroy it. *But what if I do the opposite?*

Before he could overanalyze the idea, he wrapped his hand around the tiny trunk, no thicker than his big toe. *Grow*, he implored the tree. *Reach for the sun and for the earth. Arise and burrow, my friend.*

The tiny pine tree trembled beneath his fingers and Gabe watched in amazement as it began to expand. Its rough, crooked trunk thickened, its limbs reached upward and its roots downward, like a river spilling over its banks. The roots filled the crack and pushed against the hard stone. Behind him, Abazi gasped as the tree grew and grew, until finally a cracking sound told Gabe what he wanted to hear—the stone giving way. With his free hand, he grabbed hold of the tripod and pulled. The metal inched upward.

"I know you're out there!" Mrs. Morrigan's voice rang out from close by—*too* close. "You'd better show yourself before I call the police."

Come on, Gabe urged the tiny tree, but its progress was slowing, and then, just as abruptly as it began, the growing stopped. The sapling could do no more. Not today. Gabe patted the determined little soul. "Thank you," he whispered, then grasped another tripod leg. With all his strength, he yanked, and the tripod shifted, but it didn't give.

"I can hear you, you little imps!" The words were playful, the tone was not. Mrs. Morrigan sounded really close now, and she sounded mad.

Abazi wrapped her slim arms around Gabe's waist and he stifled a tremor. He wasn't sure his heart could take it, but somehow it managed to keep beating. "We'll do it together," she whispered in his ear. "Now pull!"

They yanked as hard as they could and the tripod shifted, then pulled free. With its abrupt release, they flew backward and Gabe nearly squashed Abazi before twisting away from her at the last second and landing on the ground close by.

"Thanks," he breathed. "Now let's get out of here."

They scrambled to their feet. Heading away from Mrs. Morrigan's voice, which was growing more and more threatening, they circled about and returned to the tree where the bags awaited them. Once there, Gabe handed the tripod to Abazi, then encircled her waist with a tree-arm and lifted her into the tree. Then he pulled himself up to sit next to her.

Once they reached the bags, Gabe gathered them up, the tree relinquishing its hold, and took the tripod from Abazi. The surveyors had gathered into a half-circle to watch Jer and keep an eye on the woods. Mrs. Deacon and Mrs. Morrigan were missing. Gabe didn't want to think about where Mrs. Deacon had gone and could only hope she wasn't watching the area.

Forcing a branch to grow out of his main tree-arm, he sent it toward a tree about twenty feet away. Grabbing hold, Gabe gave it a good hard shake. Jack and Kate jerked toward the sound, their eyes wide as they stared upward. Behind them, Gabe replaced the bags and tripod and snatched Jer around the waist. He started to fight to get away, but stopped when he saw who had him. Getting him through the branches took some careful maneuvering, but Gabe managed it with only a few minor collisions.

When Jer was sitting on a branch, rubbing his head—one particular collision was maybe not so minor—Gabe retracted his branch. Feeling as though he'd just run a mile at the pace of a 100-meter sprint, he sagged against the tree trunk, not sure he had the strength to climb down.

"Where's Kimber?" Abazi asked Jer.

"Far away, I hope," he replied. "Mrs. Deacon was heading our way and I had to distract her. I left Kimber close to a big rock. Not long after I started running, that survey guy grabbed me."

"Where's Mrs. Deacon now?"

"I don't know. Going after Kris? He'll easily outrun her, but you know what happens when he thinks things are a little too easy..."

"He ups the ante." Gabe cursed his brother under his breath. "We need him to stay clear of them, and we need to fetch Kimber. This idea isn't working. I hadn't counted on Mrs. Morrigan and her shotgun."

"I'll bet you hadn't counted on something else, either," Abazi said in a wobbly voice.

"Something else?"

She turned her head and pointed. "The Ko-goks are here."

Chapter Sixteen

Shoot-Out

Gabe wondered how long it would take for his puke to hit the ground if he threw up. It was his typical gut reaction whenever he thought about Straif. Ha. He couldn't even bring himself to look—not right away. When he did, he saw dark cloak after dark cloak, all hidden from the sun as they perched in the shadowy canopy. Enough leaves remained to protect their skin from burning, and besides that, clouds were gathering, turning the sky a hazy gray.

One of the cloaked figures, one tree over, was staring at him and it took all of Gabe's fortitude to return the gaze. Crap. It was Feltry. Why couldn't it have been his bumbling brother, Dorn? Feltry was as ruthless as his father, Straif the Hideous, though not as wily or skilled. But what he lacked in talent, he made up for in meanness.

"I've been waitin' a long time for this, Freak." Feltry's voice was thick as spoiled stew.

"You're calling *me* a freak?" Gabe retorted. "Have you looked in the mirror lately?" Feltry looked worse than ever. With his fish belly skin, dark holes for eyes, and tiny black thorns sprouting from his flesh, he looked like a skinned porcupine.

"I'll be teachin' ye some respect soon enough," Feltry sneered. "But first me and me boys have a job to do."

"Where's Dorn?"

"Don't say his name to me. He's a clod and a disgrace."

"You don't know where he is, then?"

"I do!" Feltry spat. "He's takin' care of the little imp…the one with the white hair. He's quite taken with her. Thought she looked right tasty."

Gabe fastened a restraining hand around Jer's arm. There was nothing he could do up here. To be frank, there wasn't much he could do to Feltry on the ground, either. Feltry didn't have a conscience—none of the Ko-goks did. They wanted to rule the Forest Immortal and were willing to commit unspeakable acts to achieve their goal—genocide and cannibalism, to name just two.

"We have the same goal, Feltry," Gabe said as loudly as he could without drawing the attention of the others below. "We want to get rid of the surveyors. But if you kill them, you can bet people won't put up with it this time. They'll torch the woods and you and your dark dorks will go up in flames."

Feltry's hellish eyes narrowed a fraction. He was actually listening. "But yer *friends* would die, too."

"Oh, I would warn *them* in time to get out."

"If I let ye live that long."

"That didn't work out so well for you last time, Feltry. You'd better watch yourself because I'm ready for a fight. Aching for it, in fact."

Feltry gave what might be mistaken for a chuckle. "Ye threatenin' me?"

"I'm giving you a friendly warning." Gabe was glad for the shade of the leaves himself—Feltry wouldn't be able to see that Gabe was bluffing like crazy. He couldn't start anything now. Kimber was nowhere to be seen and Kris was off on some wild goose chase with Mrs. Deacon. Before Gabe could make any kind of move, he had to be sure they were safe.

If only I hadn't pissed Oswald off.

The admission didn't sit lightly in Gabe's head, but it was true. He'd sent away their only hope for winning this battle. Kris, Jer, and Abazi were good fighters, and stubborn, too (though the second trait could be a limitation, especially in Jer's case), but they couldn't fight off all the Ko-goks, even if Gabe turned into a tree. Last time they'd had the Rogues fighting with them and they'd gotten lucky. Luck like that didn't last.

Crack!

Gabe's body jerked and he nearly fell out of the tree at the sound of a gunshot.

"I see you kids! You'd better come down right now or my aim is going to improve real quick. I'm champion in the women's division at the gun club. I'd be champion in the men's, too, if I pushed the point."

Mrs. Morrigan.

Gabe glanced over at Feltry, wondering what he was going to do now, only to find the Ko-gok staring down at Mrs. Morrigan hungrily. Now was Gabe's chance. He grew his tree-arms, wrapping one around Jer and Abazi's waists and another around a birch thirty yards away, threading the narrow space between the trees as precisely as a surgeon.

When Jer and Abazi realized what he was going to do, their mouths dropped open, but not before their arms grabbed hold tight. Taking a deep breath, Gabe yanked hard and they flew through the air with astonishing speed, directly at a thick, very solid looking, white pine.

Move, move, move! The tree hesitated, then leaned to its left. The trees behind it followed suit, until only one remained between him and the birch. An oak.

I'll land on you if I have to, Gabe relayed. *And I won't leave, absolutely no pun intended.* The oak shook fiercely before shifting a few inches to the right. Gabe swung the branch holding Jer and Abazi around the tree, just missing smacking them against its trunk, and set them down. As they scrambled to grab hold, Gabe's shoulder smashed against the stubborn oak and he plummeted to the ground. With a flick of his wrist, he sent up a thin branch and grabbed hold of one of the oak's branches. His body jerked to a stop, then zipped back up again. With his feet, he pushed off from the oak, which was thrashing about as though in a seizure, and grabbed hold of the birch.

Shaking, he clung to the smooth white tree. *One more time*, he promised himself. *And then…never again.*

He grabbed Abazi and Jer and lowered them to the ground, joining them moments later. "Run," he whispered as soon as his feet hit the soft moss. "Fast," he added, unnecessarily.

Crack!

"Holy crap, she's shooting at us. Run!"

"Mrs. Morrigan!" Jack shouted. "For Pete's sake, you can't *shoot* them!"

"You know how much money is riding on this, O'Reilly!" she howled. "Now get out of the way!"

Gabe didn't stick around to hear any more. He just ran. Hopefully the surveyors would be safe from the Ko-goks. Mrs. Morrigan had her gun and obviously wasn't afraid to use it. When Straif showed up, things would change. But until then…

"This way," Jer hissed over his shoulder and Abazi and Gabe chased after him. Moments later, Jer slid to a stop near a massive boulder, then darted around it. When he came around the other side, his expression was sick. "She's gone! I know this is the place. I pulled up some moss while we were making noises so I'd know which rock was ours."

"She's got to be around here somewhere," Abazi said in a low voice.

"You don't think the Ko-goks took her, do you?"

She shook her head. "I think they would've said something. Come on," she motioned. "We have to get out of here."

An angry screech pierced the air and they spun around. "Mrs. Morrigan!" Gabe gasped. "That was her." A shotgun blast boomed out.

"Grab the equipment, Kate!" Jack yelled, not far from them. Gabe could see glimpses of him through the trees. He pushed the others back behind the boulder to hide. "We're getting out of here."

"But it's—" Kate began. "Oh, no! It's back!"

"It's just me!" Mrs. Deacon shouted. "Candace is on her way back right now."

"Well, we're not waiting for her," Jack retorted. "Kate and I are getting out of here. When you can guarantee our safety on this job, only then will we come back."

"We're paying you a lot of money!" Mrs. Morrigan screeched. Gabe peeked around the rock to see her striding toward the surveyors like an Amazon warrior. "You either stay and do the job, or we'll find someone else." Gabe had the feeling it was an empty threat. No one else would do this job.

"There's something wrong with this place," Jack said, "and I won't have you shooting at those kids, either. You're going to kill someone."

"It was a bear," she replied, her voice trembling slightly, and Gabe wondered if she'd seen Feltry. "I scared him off. He's gone. Hey! Where's the boy?"

"He got away," Kate blurted. "I hope he'll be all right with that bear out there. I saw it, too. Just a few seconds ago. Mrs. Deacon said it was her, but she was coming from a different direction. It didn't really look like a bear, actually. More like a human."

"It was definitely a bear," Mrs. Morrigan emphasized in a low voice. No one said a word, and several seconds passed like this, casting an eerie silence over the woods. "All right, you win, Jack! I'll get you some protection. We'll return tomorrow."

"It'll have to be after next weekend. The tripod needs adjustment."

"Is it broken?"

"No. But, um, I'll need some time to recalibrate the instrument." Gabe wondered if he was making that part up, giving himself some time to make up a better excuse.

"Well, what about next weekend?"

"I have another job I need to do next weekend."

There was a calculating pause followed by a whispered argument that Gabe couldn't decipher. Neither could Abazi, judging by her frown. "All right, a week from this coming Monday then!" Mrs. Morrigan said loudly. "And I'll add another grand to the final price…for your trouble today."

Jack cleared his throat. "It's a deal."

Gabe couldn't believe their luck. Another whole week to plan. Another week to find a way to stall Mrs. Morrigan and Mrs. Deacon. For the first time in a while, he felt hopeful.

Jer's next words effectively doused his growing optimism. "Kris and Kimber are still missing and the Ko-goks haven't left."

"I'm sure Kris is all right," Gabe said uncertainly. "And Kimber's smart. She probably just found herself a better hiding place."

Jer's worried expression looked about as soothed by this as Gabe felt. Feltry had said Dorn was going after Kimber. Since neither of them was at the boulder, the only alternative was that Dorn had found her and carried her off. Enough time had passed that he might even have done to her what the Ko-goks did to any animal they could catch.

"Come on," he said shakily. "We'll go look for them. They're probably not far."

The weary group turned and headed further into the woods. The soft moss showed no evidence that anyone had passed this way. Gabe turned to go another direction. Then another. Finally they stopped and stared around them. The trees, it seemed, were moving about, and now they were hopelessly lost. Just like that. So easily. Like small children. Gabe didn't think he could carry on much longer. Not without food. He felt so hungry and weak. Food and sleep. That's all he wanted, all he craved.

Gabrielll.

A groan slipped between his lips. Not *now*!

Gaaabriel, come to me. Come to yer mother.

"Mother?"

"Not again," Abazi muttered behind him. "Snap out of this, Hawthorne. You're just tired. No one's calling you. No one's there. Your mom's at home."

"Not my other mother. My real mother."

Her hand grabbed his arm, holding him back. "It's an illusion. You're delirious. All this changing back and forth. You need to rest."

"And eat…I need to eat." He sighed. So tired.

She looked at him worriedly. "I don't have anything left."

Shouting came from somewhere up ahead of them. "Abazi!" the voice sharpened. "Jerome!"

"That must be Kimber! Thank goodness!" Abazi let go of Gabe's arm. Without looking back, she headed toward the voice, Jer joining her as though hypnotized.

"Come to me, Jerome! Come to me, Abazi!" Gabe's guts turned to ice. That wasn't Kimber…that was the woman. His real mother. She was luring them away.

On the verge of collapse, his arms were seized from behind and the world turned black.

Chapter Seventeen

Kris Pulls a Runner

Kris had always liked being chased. The challenge of eluding his pursuers, of using his speed and wits to get away, was better than any drug. Back in San Jose, whenever he made the attempt to hang out with Gabe and his friends, they'd want to play *Catch Kris*. He learned to get very good at the game, very quickly. They could never catch him. Over time, he grew to enjoy the chase, especially the part about being able to irritate the crap out of boys two or three years older than him. That part was awesome.

So, at first, running from Mrs. Deacon had been fun. Unfortunately, it didn't take long to lose her. She couldn't help being slow; she was pretty ancient, after all, at least forty-five or fifty. Still, the old gal could've tried a little harder. He decided to circle back and see if he could pick up a new pursuer. Halfway along, he realized he had a new shadow…one who wanted to do more than just scare him off.

Let the games begin! He began to run. Out of the corner of his eye, he glimpsed a black shadow and his heart beat a little faster. He remembered his last encounter with the Ko-goks. The fighting had been exhilarating, and he liked that, but he'd also learned a little something. The Ko-goks were good at inflicting pain. And pain hurt. Kris wasn't a chicken—he'd fight them, but he preferred no-contact warfare. Either weapon on weapon, with only *his* weapon connecting to *their* flesh, or him chasing, or getting chased. Either way was a thrill. Getting hurt, not so much.

He ran faster, skirting around trees as though he were in an obstacle course. The moss slowed him down, but he had long legs, and fortunately for him, the Ko-goks had short ones. Plus, those cloaks couldn't help speed their progress. Besides, trees weren't exactly known for their speed. Kris grinned. He had them beat, no problem.

He hadn't counted on one thing, though. Dryads may not be fast runners, but they had another way of getting from place to place quite rapidly. When he saw a mass of dark cloaks swing past him, as though flying, he just about choked. How the heck were they doing that?

Eyes darting about, Kris finally figured it out. The Ko-goks had transformed their arms into branches and were using them to grab hold of tree limbs high in the air. In this way, they were able to swing through the woods like Tarzan. And they were getting ready to surround him.

He could only be thankful that he'd taken a wooden staff with him. Stopping abruptly, he turned about with a roar and started swinging at anything that moved. The Dark Dorks hadn't counted on this maneuver and those who were following him shrieked and leaped out of the way. Two didn't make it in time, and the staff slammed into their midsections, flinging them backwards.

"Take that, you mutants!" he howled and swung at three charging him from his left.

"We got ye surrounded, so ye'd better give up." One of the cloaked ones took a step closer.

Kris laughed. "You're kidding, right?"

"Father don't like it when Dorn joke. So Dorn don't."

Dorn...Feltry's brother. Gabe had told them about him. Apparently he was a bit of a screw-up. The front part of Dorn's hood had slipped back, revealing his face, pale as a grub and pitted by dark holes. Kris studied Dorn with fascination. He'd seen the Dark Dorks' faces while fighting them in the field, but not this close up. It was almost as though Dorn wanted him to see his hideous face, to be scared. Which meant he wasn't as sure of himself as he wanted Kris to think. Resorting to intimidation usually meant you didn't have the goods to deliver.

"Come a little closer, why don't you?" he taunted. "I've got someone I'd like you to meet." He swung the staff in a wide arc.

Dorn shook his head. "Dorn isn't stupid. Dorn has ye outnumbered, twenty to one."

Kris lifted an eyebrow. "Only twenty?"

Dorn frowned. "What do ye mean?"

"I mean, twenty is about what I do for a warm-up."

"He's a right scary one, Dorn," another spoke up. "Remember the Battle at Fallow Field? He were like a berserker, he were!"

Kris couldn't help himself. His chest puffed out, his smile widened, his guard dropped, as did his staff. And that's when the Dorks rushed him. Kris lifted his staff to swing it, but Dorn caught the blow with a large metal shield—the top of a garbage can.

Crap.

Kris swung again, but the Dorks ducked and spun about him as though they'd choreographed the fight. Every few seconds, one would duck in and punch or kick him—in the gut, in the small of his back, on the kneecap. Sweating now and in pain, Kris cursed himself for letting his pride get him in this position. He was losing! He never lost.

It was time. With a bellow like a Wookie, Kris swung the staff back and forth in front of him as he plunged through the crowd of black hoods surrounding him. Pale, long-fingered hands lunged at him, but none could grab hold. Then Dorn got lucky and knocked the staff out of Kris's hand. Kris had only his fists now and he used them with abandon, yelling and growling.

Howls of pain and anger followed him as he broke free at last, bruised and bloody and mad as hornets. He wanted to fight, but his brain told him to run. Staggering, nearly falling, he plunged through the woods, almost unable to see through the haze of rage and sweat dimming his eyesight. He had to do something different—they had their branch-arms to chase him. Soon they'd do that again.

Stupid tree spirits! It wasn't fair!

His foot caught at a tree root and he only had enough time to re-member his mother's warnings about bad Karma coming back to haunt a person before hitting the ground. As soon as he landed, they were on him. A hand wrapped around his arm and began dragging him along the ground like a sack of garbage.

What fresh hell is this?

He had little time to answer as he and his captor picked up speed and were soon skimming over the moss like a Hovercraft. Where were they taking him? And how? He felt like he was flying, the only reminder that he wasn't was the pain in his arm socket. He tried to look around but could see little beyond tree trunks zipping past.

Just when he thought his shoulder socket was going to pop free, he stopped abruptly, sinking down in the moss. "Come on!"

Seeing his captor, he almost started laughing, but his arm hurt too much. "What took you so long?"

Hollie, standing over him, beamed. "I come when I'm needed. And ye looked to be in a right pickle."

"I had things under control." He grabbed her proffered hand and she pulled him to his feet. The thought registered that she was awfully strong for a girl. Then he remembered thinking bad thoughts about tree spirits only moments earlier and it hit home that Hollie was a tree spirit, too.

Well, she might be a tree spirit, he told himself, but he didn't see her that way. In fact, in his mind, it was like she really wasn't a Dryad. He wasn't quite sure that was a good way to think about her, but if it helped any, he didn't think of Gabe as a Dryad, either. To Kris, he was just Gabe, and Hollie was just Hollie, a gorgeous, mysterious girl he liked a lot.

"Under control, eh? Well, then perhaps I should be leavin' ye to fight on yer own?"

He shook his head. "Nah. I've already embarrassed them enough for one day."

"All right." She laughed. "I'll let ye off the hook. Now come on. Yer brothers and yer friends are lookin' for ye."

"Did they scare off the surveyors?"

She looked up at the sky. "For now." Her eyes came to rest on his. "But Feltry's out there. We have to get ye home. All of ye. The Ko-goks are hungry, especially with the Dark Night comin'."

"Dark night? You mean when the sun sets?"

"This is longer. The time when we must slumber."

"Ah. Winter." He stared at her. "Do you really go to sleep during that time?" He didn't like the idea of that.

"We have little choice."

He didn't like that, either. "So you sleep all winter?"

"When the last leaf has fallen and the snows blow, then we can move no more. Not til the spring comes again."

"That really bites."

She smiled impishly. "I imagine so."

He leaned forward. "You said little choice. Does that mean there are ways to avoid going comatose for months?"

She glanced around. "That means, *I* have ways."

He laughed softly. "Why am I not surprised?"

"They are not easy, mind… And there's a price if ye do it wrong."

"But there's a chance…"

"If ye know the secret."

He took a step closer, grabbing hold of her thin arm, which should be unbearably cold in the wispy shirt she wore, but it wasn't. It was as warm as his own. "And that would be…"

She smiled. "*My* secret."

He was disappointed…and intrigued. He loved secrets. What he loved more, though, was trying to find out what they were. He ducked down low and whispered, "Then I'll just have to find a way to get you to spill it."

Her green eyes tilted up at him. "In yer dreams."

"Yes, you'll be in my dreams." Her eyes flickered with an emotion he couldn't quite read, though he had the feeling he'd said the right thing.

She pulled away from his grasp, laughing. "Oh, Kristofer, ye're a charming one." He grinned, feeling suddenly buoyant. "Now come. We must hurry. Time is short."

"What's the hurry?" he asked, sprinting after her.

"Straif grows hungry, and it's dinner time, that's what's the hurry."

Kris frowned, but could ask no more. Hollie was fast and he needed all his breath just to keep up. As he ran after her, focusing on not tripping or getting stuck in the thick moss, her smile stayed in his mind, warming him all the way to his toes.

Chapter Eighteen

Mother

Gabe awoke with someone's arms wrapped around him. Human arms. Black patches peppered the skin, which was dusty from a fine layer of dirt.

"Eat this…"

Before he could refuse, long fingers shoved a sticky wad between his lips. He tried to spit it out, but a rough palm covered his mouth, forcing him to chew before he choked. Trying not to think about what was in there, he made his jaw work to chew up the crunchy, gummy mass. He was surprised to taste sweetness, and with each chew realized that he actually liked whatever it was in his mouth. When he was done, he croaked, "More," and opened his mouth like a baby bird.

Whoever was holding him chuckled softly and popped in another chunk. After several more mouthfuls—he lost track after the tenth one—he began to feel better, almost pumped up. He held up his hand to stop the latest delivery.

"Ye're better?"

"Much. Thank you." He lay there for a moment longer. "Um, can I sit up now?"

"Ye won't run away?" The voice was desperate and tinged with a sadness that caught at his throat.

"No, I won't," he promised. "But I will have to leave in a bit. My brothers and my friends will be worried about me."

She didn't respond, but she did let him go. He sat up, then slowly turned to face his captor. "Gabriel," she whispered, and her hand reached out to caress his cheek. "Ye came back to me."

The woman before him wore a simple brown shift, sleeveless and falling to just above the knees, and leather moccasins to protect her feet. She had a thin face and a narrow nose and bits of leaves and brambles poked out from the twenty or thirty braids covering her head like a bird's nest. Her lips, like his own, were full. Her skin was an indeterminate color, covered as it was with dirt and dark patches. She looked worn and tired, as though she'd spent the day working in the fields. Her brown eyes were wary, almost paranoid, as they darted about, searching his face for two or three seconds, then looking over his shoulder at the woods behind him. Despite all this, she was beautiful.

"Are you…are you my mother?"

She nodded and a smile split her lips, but only for a moment. The smile quivered and died and her hand dropped. "I-I…tried to get ye back, me child. I tried to find ye. But ye went away and me mind has been troublesome, givin' me an awful battle for so long." She shook her head, as though trying to dislodge a drove of bees inside her brain. "I can't seem to remember things." She stared at him hungrily. "But I remember ye. Yes…" She frowned.

Gabe started to feel worried. *More* worried, anyway. Despite a frailty about her, she looked strong. Her long bare arms were sinewy and muscular, her legs sturdy. She had to be pretty powerful to drag him far enough away from Jer and Abazi, through this thick moss, which was hard to walk through without carrying a load. And she didn't look too stable—not with those darting eyes, not with those strange patches on her skin. All these things added up to danger, and Gabe knew he was in trouble.

But he was also curious.

"So you missed me?" he asked hesitantly.

She leaned forward and grasped his arm. She seemed driven to touch him, connect to him. Her other hand beat her chest. "I've been dead inside without ye. Ye were me only one. Me only child." Her dark eyes welled up. "When ye were taken from me, I lost me soul."

This emotional declaration both stunned and saddened Gabe. To be the cause of this pain, even if unintended, was a heavy burden. Still, it was nice to be missed, though that felt a bit selfish considering what she'd gone through. "I'm sorry that this happened to you."

"Do ye feel it?" she demanded. "Do ye feel our connection?"

He tried to, but he felt nothing, and felt bad for that. He wanted to feel connected to the woman, because she wanted it, but it just wasn't coming. She was a stranger to him. A rather strange stranger, too. "I, um, well, I always heard you calling to me."

"Ye were scared of me," she accused, though her eyes were sad.

"I was scared of the woods, actually."

"I'd never hurt ye, Gabriel. And now that we're together, I can watch over ye, just as a real mother would do."

Gabe's lower jaw dropped a fraction of an inch. "Together? You know I have to get back? My friends…they'll be looking for me."

Her chin swung up and her eyes glowed like a demon's. "Then I'll take ye somewhere they can't find ye!"

He shook his head, slowly getting his body into position to flee. "I can't just leave them. There's Straif and his dark ones, and we have to scare off the surveyors, and there are other things in this wood. I can't leave them alone to fend for themselves." He didn't bother explaining about Wildrr. If she was like any mother, she'd be furious and ashamed of him for what he'd done to the Lady.

Her features crumpled into distaste. "Straif's a blight on all trees. He killed yer father, ye know!"

Gabe jerked back, stunned. "What? My father's dead? I'll never meet him?"

She gazed off into the woods, her lips parted. "He were a hero, too. A leader, like yerself. He gave his life to save ye, ye know." She looked back at him, her brown eyes melting in sorrow.

"Me? How?"

"He—" Her body tensed and she sniffed the air. "Come on!" She grabbed his arm and yanked him to his feet. His unwilling feet stumbled after her as she dragged him along with surprising strength.

"What is it?" She didn't answer, just continued her relentless escape through the moss. After a minute of this, Gabe finally came to his senses, and he dug his heels into the moss. "Please, stop! I need to know what we're running from."

She abruptly let go of his hand and he fell backward into the moss. He scrambled to his feet as she turned around. "From the other one," she said softly. "He's comin' after ye. He does not like ye."

"A Ko-gok?" he questioned.

She shook her head. "The other one," she repeated, her dark eyes bewildered. "The oak."

"*Oswald?*"

She nodded solemnly. "He's full of anger, poor wee thing. I feel his pain, and I know it well. But I can't let him hurt ye."

"How do you know Oswald?"

Before she could answer, thumping noises and patches of dark green surrounded Gabe as ten or twelve figures dropped down from the trees. The Rogues. "Greetings, *Mother*," Oswald spoke, his tone bitter.

"Mother?" Gabe stared at the wild woman. "But you said…" She ducked her head low, as though ashamed. Or afraid.

"Who do ye think raised *me*, Gabriel?" Oswald snarled.

Gabe flinched at the hatred in the Dryad's voice, but he asked, "Did you know your, well, our father?"

Oswald nodded, two short jerks. "Did Faeth," he flung his thumb at his mother, "tell ye how he died?"

"She said he was a hero. That he died while..."

Oswald's mouth was so twisted he looked as though he wanted to spit the evil right out of it. "While savin' yer life. Yes. Ye took me father away. Now me mother wants ye. And me real parents have no idea I exist." He stopped, a slow smile spreading across his brown face. "Well, yer mother knows me now. She likes me, too, doesn't she?"

Gabe felt sick. "Do you think I want this, Oswald? I didn't ask for any of it, that's for sure. How many times do I have to tell you that? Trust me, if I could change things, I would. But what would you have me do?"

"I'd have ye leave this place and never return."

"I'd love to do that! But things keep happening that drag me back here. First I was kidnapped by the Ko-goks. Then I got those notes..." He stopped suddenly, a terrible realization spreading through him. "You wouldn't have sent me those notes...not when you don't want me here."

"Now ye're catchin' on, Sloe."

"He's not sloe!" the wild woman cried.

"I'm a straight-A student," Gabe added, feeling a bit stupid for defending himself. But still, he was sick of Oswald always implying he wasn't too bright.

Oswald snorted. "Sloe's the fruit of the blackthorn."

Blackthorn—that was the type of tree the Ko-goks were. So now Oswald was grouping him with the dark ones. "You say I shouldn't be King of the Forest Immortal because I don't see this place as home," Gabe shot back at him. "But you're the one who's got it backwards. You're fighting the wrong battle, Oswald. You're wasting all your energy fighting me when you should be focusing on your real enemy— Straif. If you really cared about the Forest, you'd drop this fight with me. Yet you continue a battle that only *you* want to fight. It makes me wonder where your loyalty really lies." He lifted an eyebrow in challenge.

Oswald's band all took a step forward, in unison. It was quite intimidating, being surrounded by a group of angry Dryads, but Gabe didn't regret what he'd said.

The muscles in Oswald's cheeks flickered as he clenched and unclenched his rigid jaw. "I don't need to defend meself to ye, Usurper.

But I will tell ye this." He took two steps toward Gabe, seemingly growing taller within that short distance, so that he towered over Gabe. "I hope Straif takes ye out, because then I won't have to."

"Oswald!" Faeth shouted. "I raised ye better than that!"

"Ye didn't raise me hardly at all, did ye?" he said coolly, meeting her fierce gaze with derision. Gabe looked into Oswald's eyes and he saw something in them he didn't quite understand. He saw fear.

Faeth blinked and took a step back. "I-I did me best, Oswald. I hardly knew meself those days. But now—" She broke off as though she didn't know the ending to the sentence she'd started. Perhaps she didn't.

"Ye spent yer days lookin' for him," Oswald nodded at Gabe. "Leavin' me to fend for meself."

"I didn't mean to," she said, her outstretched hands pleading. "I wasn't meself!"

"So ye keep sayin'." His words were dry as desert bones. "But even now ye search for him. And ye found him. Yer life is finally perfect!"

She shook her head, looking more confused and wild by the second. "No, no, no, Oswald, me bairn! Ye don't understand!"

"I'll never understand, Faeth. But know this, from this day forward, ye're not me mother, and I'm not yer son."

She gasped, her face collapsing in pain. "No, Oswald. I want ye both! Ye're both me bairns. I need ye both!"

"Now that ye have him, ye need nothing from me." He turned his back on them. "She's dead to us from here on." The other band members nodded, but Gabe found comfort in the fact that more than a few looked doubtful, glancing warily at each other when Oswald wasn't looking.

"But she's sick, Oswald. Surely even you can see that? You can't abandon her."

Oswald didn't bother to turn around. "She's yer problem now, Usurper."

"But I have to go home! I can't watch her. I can't keep her safe."

Oswald spun around, triumphant. "I'll tell ye what... I'll keep her safe, if ye stay out of the forest."

"I'll do my best," Gabe promised. "But I have to figure out those riddles, both of which have led me to these woods, and I still have to scare off the surveyors. They're coming back next week to finish the job."

"Me and me band'll handle the surveyors...with no harm comin' to them," he added, seeing Gabe's doubtful expression. "As to those riddles, they're nothing but someone's idea of a bad joke. Not mine, but somebody who wishes ye harm." He grinned suddenly. "And that could be a lot of somebodys in this wood." With that, and a devilish laugh, he and his band leaped into the air and disappeared.

Gabe stared into the dark trees before turning around and facing the woman who was his true mother. She looked scared. "I have to go. I promised Oswald, but he said he'll look after you and I believe him."

She stepped forward and her shaking hand cupped his cheek. "I can't let ye go, Gabriel."

"You have to. I have things I must do." He stopped, searching for the right words. "Did you...did you send those riddles, Faeth?"

She smiled, her eyes crinkling with humor. For a brief moment he saw the young girl she had once been, full of life and mischief, and his heart clutched painfully. "I know nothing of these riddles of which ye speak. I can't write, anyway. Oswald learned from Filidh, ye see. Not from me."

Gabe blinked. "Did you say Filidh? The strange little man who lives in the gorge?"

She nodded. "His price was high, but it was worth it for me son." Her expression was filled with pride. "Oswald's a good boy. He'll come round. He's mine, even if I didn't bear him. I'll have him back."

Gabe swallowed. It seemed as though Oswald had charmed both his mother and Faeth quite thoroughly. "What was the price?"

"I don't remember, but it were high. That I recall."

"Do you know who sent the riddles?"

She sighed softly. "I wish I did. Are they good riddles?"

"In the sense that they're hard to figure out, yes."

Her smile grew dreamy. "Yer Father loved riddles."

"He did?"

"He loved Filidh's best of all."

Filidh. A riddle maker. It made perfect sense. Kind of...because why would Filidh want to lead him here? Into the forest?

Gabe grabbed hold of Faeth's arm. "I have to go. I promised Oswald not to enter the Forest Immortal again. But you can come to me—to where Shambolic Stream meets the willow trees. I don't count that as Forest Immortal territory and you should be safe there. All right?"

Her eyes brightened. "Yes, Son. I'll come to ye there."

"Just call my name."

"I will."

"Goodbye, Faeth."

"Goodbye. And remember, ye know more than ye realize, and ye're clever, too." She gazed off into the distance. "I know I'm addled right now, but I once were sharp as quartz and brighter than sun through dewdrops. I *know* that." She clasped a brown fist to her heart.

Gabe nodded. "I know *Mooo...ther* Faeth." The 'M' word came out stilted and he kind of sounded like a baby cow, but he said it all the same. If anyone needed a consoling word, this woman did. Gabe was as hopeless as most teens at seeing the plight of others, but even he could see her distress. And this was all he had to offer her. He hoped it was enough.

The smile she gave him told him he'd done the right thing, even if he felt slightly guilty about the mother who'd raised him—the one he thought of as his true mother. What she didn't know wouldn't hurt her, though. And as far as he was concerned, she would never know he'd called another woman Mother.

He stepped away. "I'll see you again."

"Yes, ye will."

But as Gabe turned his back, he wondered if he would. There was something about Faeth that exuded tragedy. She'd lived a hard life, filled with suffering. Could things really be turning around for her, or was she setting herself up for another loss?

And who would she lose?

Him, or Oswald?

Chapter Nineteen

In the Midst of Lions

"If that wasn't Kimber calling us, then who was it?" Jer demanded for the twelfth time. "And where did Gabe go?"

Abazi stopped walking and faced him. "They're both fine, Jer. You'll see. I have a feeling about it." She looked almost pained as she said this.

Jer knew she was just trying to make him feel better, but boy did he want to believe her. The reality, though, was that they'd been searching for an hour now with no luck. Weapons drawn and voices low, they'd made a sweeping arc through the darkening woods, each step dreaded, knowing it could be their last. The Ko-goks were out there, but they'd yet to make a move.

"You can feel them, can't you?" he whispered, keeping his eyes fastened on Abazi's back. "They're all around us, aren't they?"

She nodded, though he could barely tell in the dark woods. "But they must not have Gabe or the others," her voice was soft. "Otherwise they'd have taken us by now, don't you think?"

"I think you're right. So it's time to stop being quiet. They already know we're here. We need to make them believe we think they've moved on. And then we whistle."

She grinned, her straight white teeth glowing in the dim light. "Brilliant, Jer."

"I only wish I'd thought of it before."

"Let's go."

They began walking at a more normal pace, whistling an eerie lament that carried through the thick air. Abazi had taught them the song, passed down to her from her ancestors. When she sang it, her low voice was hypnotic, and Jer loved to listen. His mom used to sing to him at bedtime and he remembered those times with a warm glow in his chest.

There was a story to the song, Abazi had told them, before teaching it to them. It had to do with a young man who'd lost his love in the forest and spent the rest of his life wandering the woods searching for her. Some believed white men stole her away; others claimed it was a starved wolf. But the young man believed it was the Ko-goks who'd taken her and he vowed to search for her forever, even after he died. He was determined to save, if not her mortal life, then her immortal soul.

Abazi declared it a sappy love story, but Jer couldn't help noticing that she told it well, as though she'd thought about it a lot. He also noticed how she kept looking at Gabe as she spoke. Gabe, as usual, was clueless. He listened, but often he didn't hear the nuances. She was trying to tell him something. How Jer could see it, but Gabe couldn't, he didn't understand.

Not a good whistler, he worked hard to hold the complicated tune. Luckily Abazi was a natural and the sound coming from her lips was pure and strong. He only hoped someone would hear it as they headed east, toward home. But so far, only the shadows followed.

Where is she? he wondered again when the whistling produced nothing. His brothers could handle themselves, at least that's what they were always telling Mom and Dad. But Kimber was a delicate flower. A kitten in the midst of lions. She was too precious and kind—she could never survive in these woods. No doubt Straif had her and was doing horrible things to her.

Jer's fingers curled into fists. He would kill that jerk if he so much as laid a finger on her! And he'd like doing it. His whistling faltered then died altogether. It was no use. She was gone. Perhaps dead. And it was his fault. He should've insisted she stayed home. Why didn't he? His scowl deepened, if only to keep the sobs at bay. If she *was* still alive, he'd make sure she never came with them again. He'd keep her safe.

Feeling slightly better, he began to whistle again, more loudly this time. When several thumps hit the ground around him, he nearly choked on his own spit. In the small clearing, four hooded figures closed around them. "Not so fast," one of them growled.

Jer swung both his bata and his staff hard and the dark ones back-pedaled. "One step closer and you'll get a taste of my fury!" It was a hokey thing to say, but it just might work. The Dorks glanced at each other. It was hard to see their faces, lost in the folds of their hoods, but an occasional glimpse of white flesh and sunken shadow was more than enough to remind Jer of who he was dealing with—nasty, foul

Ko-goks. A part of him wanted to rip off their hoods. Another part fought that urge like a shrieking beast.

Abazi gripped the handles of her bata and tomahawk tightly. "Who wants to be the first?"

"Where's Gabriel?" one of the Ko-goks demanded.

She shrugged. "He's gone."

A cackle came from the opening of the hood, conjuring up the bloodcurdling image of a demon. "So ye're all alone?"

"You already know that, idiot," Abazi growled. "So what do you want? If you try to capture us, you'll leave here hurting…and without either one of us, to boot."

"Why must ye fight Dorn? It'd be easier on everybody if ye'd just come along nice-like."

"Nice isn't in my vocabulary," Abazi spat. "I'll fight to the death."

"And get yer friends killed, too? I especially like the golden one."

"Where is she?" Jer howled as he rushed Dorn. Screeching filled the air around him as he swung his bata and staff. "Tell me!"

Abazi swung her tomahawk like a warrior, but the dark ones were fast. They ducked out of the way, narrowly avoiding its sharp blade. The batas had more success in landing, but really only made a difference when hitting bare skin. Jer went after exposed wrists and the Ko-goks bare feet the one time he got knocked to the ground.

It was no contest—there had to be fifteen of them now—but Jer and Abazi fought on, even though both were tiring against the constant onslaught. Dorn had something to prove in his competition against his brother, and seemed determined to prove it today.

Suddenly, there were fewer cloaks throwing themselves at Jer. Afraid to take his eyes off the action too long, he glanced around. It was Gabe! He was swinging his staff like a madman and knocking back dark ones left and right. Jer grinned gratefully. He might fight with his brother and think he was an annoying turd more often than not, but he was sure glad to have him on his side.

With renewed vigor, he swung his club hard, connecting with a Ko-gok's arm. The fetid thing clutched his shoulder and ran off, screeching. The timing was not right for doing a victory dance, but Jer wanted to—things were turning around.

"Don't make me change, Dorn!" Gabe shouted. "Cause I can't control myself when I'm a Thorn."

"Kowabunga!" came a shout from behind Jer. He spun around and saw Kris leaping into the fray, his staff swinging like a horizontal pendulum. Several of the Ko-goks froze for a moment, then turned and

hightailed it into the woods. Only four remained—Dorn and his closest lackeys.

"Um, Dorn," one of them spoke up. "I think we should be givin' up.
I'm awful sore right now and ye know I can't heal so good."

"Shut yer yapper, dingleberry!"

"But the others are all gone!"

Dorn swung around to look and Jer tackled him. "Where is she?" he
yelled into Dorn's hideous face. It would star in his nightmares for
months, he knew, but right now he didn't care. "What did you do to
her? So help me, I'll kill you if you so much as touched a single strand
of her hair."

Dorn's lip—if you could call the red that lined the black gaping hole
of his mouth a lip—curled into a sneer. "Ye think she'd fancy a Drisk
like ye? She be needin' a real Dryad like Dorn. Not some jejune like ye.
Dull as dirt and about as smart, ye are."

"Nice coming from someone who refers to himself in third person!"
Jer shouted. "Now tell me!" He stuck the bata in Dorn's face; its tip
hovered over a sunken cheek, white as chalk and thin as rice paper.

Dorn followed the bata with the holes that were supposed to be his
eyes. "Dorn doesn't know, ye log lover!" With a violent twist, he threw
Jer off and bolted to his feet. "Ye haven't seen the last of Dorn!" he
hollered, as he and his remaining minions raced away.

A hand appeared in front of Jer. He looked up. Hollie. He grabbed
hold and she pulled him up. "Ye proved yerself today, little warrior!"
She clapped him on the back.

He grinned proudly, then looked around her. "You didn't find Kimber?"

Her little face scrunched up in concern and she shook her head.
"Sorry. Didn't know she was missin'."

He glanced around at the little group. Kris and Gabe seemed all right,
though Gabe looked tired and distant. They both shook their heads.
"Feltry found me," Kris explained. "Hollie came along just in time to
see me kick their butts."

Her thin eyebrows shot up. "I believe *I* saved yer keister today,
Kristofer Hawthorne."

"Yeah, maybe." He laughed. "Let's just say she came along at the
right time."

"How about you, Gabe? What happened to you?"

It took a moment for Gabe to focus on Jer. "Hm? Oh. I'll tell you
about it later. It's growing dark and we should be looking for Kimber
now."

Abazi gave him a funny look, almost like concern, before it trans-formed into her typical bossy glare. "We'll form a line and head toward your grandma's house."

"What if we don't find her?" Jer asked, feeling chilled, and not just from the growing cold. "She can't stay out here overnight."

"We'll find her," Kris assured him.

But what if we don't? I'll never forgive myself, he determined. *Never. And I'll search for her forever…just like Abazi's song.* He shivered as he took his place in line. To his left, spread out ten feet apart, were Gabe and Abazi. To his right, Kris and Hollie took their places.

Never.

The closer they came to Grandma May's cottage, the louder they yelled. Each of Jer's shouts sounded increasingly frantic to his ears. At the edge of the woods, close to the drive, he found it—a pink mitten. Kimber's. Blood pounded through his brain. Breaking ranks, he pelted down the gravel drive as fast as he could.

"Kimber!" he cried. "Where are you?"

Ten feet from the cottage, the door opened wide, spilling warm light into the night. "Thank you, Mrs. May!" a voice called sweetly. "I'll come visit again soon."

"See that you do. Are they all present and accounted for?"

"I see everyone."

"It's about time." The door shut, cutting off the light.

Jer stopped in his tracks, his mouth hanging open as he panted loudly. "Kimber?"

"Jer!" She hobbled toward him, her arms wide. He ran into them. She felt warm and soft. "I'm so glad to see you!"

"What happened?" he demanded, a part of his mind dancing in de-light that she was worried about him. "Why are you here?"

She laughed breathily, pulling back to look at him. "Your Grandma May found me. Or should I say, I found her. She told me she was checking up on the surveyors. Mrs. Deacon almost caught me, you see. But just as she was about to come around the boulder, a tree grabbed me, lifted me up, and handed me off like a football! I was set down right behind your Grandma May. She nearly shot me, I startled her so much!"

"You were rescued by trees?" Gabe had joined them, along with the others.

"I believe you have a lot of friends in the Forest Immortal," she said, smiling up at him. "Some that would surprise you." Gabe stared at her uncertainly, wondering what she meant.

"I'm just so glad you're okay!" He was about to add that from now on she was staying home, but Kris interrupted.

"I'm gonna go say goodbye to Hollie, then we'd better get home."

"Will she be safe?"

Kris looked pained. "I don't know."

"I'll be fine," a voice called from the woods. "I've got me own escort."

Kris hurried toward the voice and Jer and the others followed after him. "What do you mean?"

Oswald jumped down from the trees. "She means me." He was alone, but Jer knew his band was out there, watching and waiting. He faced Gabe. "So we're clear on our deal?"

Gabe nodded. Jer was dying to ask what Oswald meant, but judging by the serious look on Gabe's face and the triumphant one on Oswald's, he figured he'd better wait until later.

Kris wasn't as sensitive to nuances. "What's he talking about?"

"I'll tell you when we get home." Gabe turned to face Oswald squarely. "You stop the surveyors from doing their job and watch after Faeth and I'll do what we agreed. I swear on the Forest Immortal."

Oswald nodded. Jer didn't like how satisfied he looked. "As do I." He cocked his head toward the forest. "Come, Hollie. We've better things to be doin'."

"I'll be comin' when I'm ready, Bossy. Go on. I'll catch up to ye." He didn't move and she sighed with annoyance. "Fine. Stay, for all I care." She nodded at the group. "Goodbye, one and all. I don't know what ye promised, Gabriel, but I hope it isn't what I think it is. And if it is, I won't hold ye to it. Neither will the rest of the forest."

Oswald glared at her as though she'd just turned into a dark one. Then they were gone, as though they'd never been, leaving everyone in the dark.

"What was that about?" Abazi asked.

"I'll tell you as soon as we get into our yard. We aren't out of the woods yet, you know." His smile was tired, but it was still a smile.

Abazi reluctantly laughed. "All right. I'll wait."

No one said a word as they trudged down Grandma May's drive. They followed the road until they reached the Hawthorne's driveway, weapons ready, eyes darting like little birds hunting for seeds. When they saw the big red barn, Jer breathed a sigh of relief. They had made it home. Even though it was only about five o'clock according to his watch, the barn light was on, guiding them.

By unspoken agreement, they hurried toward the circle of light. Once there, Gabe told them what had happened to him. "My mom took me," he began, then related the strange story of how he had met his real mother and how fragile she had seemed to him. "And that's why," he finished, "I promised Oswald that if he took care of the surveyors and watched over Faeth, I would stay out of the forest."

"Why'd you do that?" Kris demanded. "What if I want to see Hollie?"

"*We* didn't make the promise," Jer pointed out what should have been perfectly obvious.

"Hey, you're right!" Kris brightened. "And he'll take care of the surveyors?"

Gabe nodded. "And he said he would do it nicely."

"Too bad we didn't get to use our costumes," Kris sighed. "But at least now I know what I'm going to be for Halloween." He struck a ninja pose. "A Dark Dork Slayer."

"I didn't get to use my megaphone, either," Jer bemoaned. "I was too busy running. So what are we going to tell Mom?"

"I guess we just say we scared them off for a while," Gabe replied. "Which we did, in a manner of speaking."

"Well, too bad they aren't doing it next weekend," Abazi said. "That's when the tribe's meeting at our house for a powwow. I really wanted to get out of it, especially as they're holding a ceremony for me." Her mouth twisted in annoyance. "I told my dad I didn't need some hoodoo ritual telling me I'm an adult. I already know that. But he insisted. He's normally pretty easygoing, but on some things, he puts his foot down. Usually it's the wrong things."

"Where are you going to put everyone?" Jer wanted to know.

"Oh, they have their teepees and lean-tos. They love that crap. Pretending it's the old days. Having their campfire. Eating their venison. Bo-ring!"

"That sounds awesome!" Kris exclaimed. "Can we come?"

She stared at him. "You're serious?"

"Yeah! I love Indian stuff. So does Jer. Do they do any warrior ceremonies? Smoke the peace pipe? Ride horses?"

"Yeah, and there are classes on how to make bear hide rugs and feather headdresses and how to survive in the wilderness on one pouch of dried jerky."

"*Really?*"

She gave him an exasperated look, then sighed. "You guys are seriously interested in all that crap?"

"Who wouldn't be?" Jer asked, starting to feel just as excited as Kris.

"How about you, Immortal?" she confronted Gabe.

He bit down on his lip. "Sure. Why not?"

"So you think I should embrace my roots?" She smiled mischievously, and Jer wondered what that was about.

"I think you should at least know where they lead."

She tilted her head to the left, then swung around to face the rest of the group. "Then it's decided. Party at the Wanibagw's house. Next weekend."

Chapter Twenty

The Ranger Rag

The last day of their holiday weekend was busy, which was good since Gabe didn't want to think about what had happened in the Forest Immortal. He didn't want to think about meeting his real mother, about when she might come to see him, about promising Oswald he'd never return.

And then there were those stupid riddles. Oswald had been dismissive of them, but Gabe couldn't get the rhymes out of his head. He'd pretty much decided that his grandma hadn't written them—the handwriting wasn't hers, and besides, she was more likely to just come out with it than to write dumb poems and wait around for him to figure them out. But if she hadn't done it, she had to know who had. Her secret visitor, perhaps?

On Monday—Columbus Day—he worked at the store from seven to noon. It was busy and the credit card machine was acting up. The few tourists that happened to find Ranger were out in force, buying up anything that had the word Maine printed on it. Abazi didn't make an appearance, even though for once he wished she would. Her smart remarks always kept his mind off his problems, if only because it took all his wits about him to keep up with her. Her dad, Mozi, noticing Gabe glancing at the door every few minutes, told him with a grin that she was working on some mysterious project, leaving Gabe to wonder what she was up to now.

While he was at work, Kris and Jer picked the last of the apples and Mom made applesauce and dried cinnamon apple slices, with Dad working right alongside her. At supper the night before, Mom and Dad had accepted Gabe's version of how they'd scared off the surveyors— loud, spooky noises, moving their equipment about, throwing a few acorns. Mom, of course, didn't like that they'd touched anything and told them not to do it again. They all solemnly promised not to. He didn't mention talking to Grandma May, and since neither of his parents said anything about hearing gunshots, he left out Mrs. Morrigan firing at them, too. He ended by saying that the surveyors would be back a week from Monday. Dad was happy about that, but Mom looked both annoyed and worried that their plan had only delayed the issue, not taken care of it.

That afternoon Grandpa Hawthorne took them and their dad fishing because Mom and Grandma May wanted fish for smoking and for making pickled herring. The boys fished with rods, catching a mackerel for supper, along with six haddock, and Dad helped Grandpa H. with the small seine net as best he could. Grandpa was in his element, spouting tales of all the fishing adventures he'd had before retiring, and Dad's cheeks were full of color and his smile stayed put nearly the whole time.

At the end of the day, everyone begged Grandpa to take them out again soon, with Gabe the loudest. Being with his dad and Grandpa Hawthorne made all his troubles disappear. They were so normal and down to earth, so solid and good-humored. More than that, he just plain liked being with them.

~~~~~~

School started up again on Tuesday, and with it, Gabe's trouble. He was trying to open his locker when someone behind him started talking to his back. Gabe nonchalantly turned around.

"I heard you were being a pain in the ass for my mom, Hawthorne." It was Jake Morrigan, naturally wearing the most expensive name brand clothes, from his Nike sneakers to his Abercrombie and Fitch shirt. His sister, Jen, hovered nearby, her blue eyes lingering on Gabe. She was very pretty and certainly nicer than her brother, but he wasn't interested. Especially not when she came with Jake attached. She fluttered her fingers and her heavily mascaraed eyelashes at him and he gave her a nod before facing Jake.

"Is that her story?" He was tempted to add, "Oh, and next time your mom starts shooting at me and my brothers, we're calling the cops." Unfortunately, the Chief of Police was Mrs. Morrigan's younger brother, Carl. Still, it would've felt good to have that bit of news spread around town, especially if it never met his parents' ears. He decided to keep it in his back pocket for now. Who knew when he might need that kind of information?

"Are you calling my mother a liar?"

Gabe raised an eyebrow. A large crowd had gathered in the hallway around them, eager for action, camera phones at the ready. "I'm saying, 'Is…that…her…story?" The kids laughed, but they quickly shut up when Jake threw his glare around.

"She told us you were trying to stop her from doing her job."

Gabe pretended to think. "Oh, *that*. You mean when she hired surveyors to survey land that isn't hers?"

Jake's face turned an ugly shade of puce, making it look like a squished grape. "She's a real estate agent. That's what she does!"

"Trespass? Wow. I wish I had a job like that. What does your lawyer dad think of her doing something illegal?"

Jake raised a tight fist. "Take that back, Hawthorne, or I'll grind your face into the floor."

Not long ago, Gabe would have felt sick at the thought of such a confrontation. But after facing Straif and his goons, he thought he could pretty much take on anybody. "You and whose army, Morrigan?" He took a step toward Jake and the senior flinched, just a little bit, but enough for Gabe to notice. "Because I could really use a fight right now. Great stress reliever, beating the crap out of people." He grinned inwardly. *If only Abazi could see me now!*

The thought was barely complete when he spotted her serious brown face in the crowd. She did not look impressed. More like annoyed. The five-minute bell rang, but nobody moved. They were waiting to see how Jake would respond.

Just when Gabe thought he might have won, Jake grinned. "You better be stressed out. Because when you find out what I know, you're going to crap your pants." With that, he hitched his backpack up onto his shoulder and strutted away. His groupies followed after him and the crowd, disappointed at the way things had turned out—*boring*—began to break up. Gabe watched Jake go, his top teeth chewing on his lower lip.

Abazi joined him. "You had to antagonize him, didn't you?"

"He started it," Gabe argued as he headed toward his chemistry class. Abazi followed after him. She had English, which was right across from the science room.

"And you fell for it."

"Fell for what?"

"He set you up. Made you look like an idiot."

"He did not!"

"No, I guess you did that all on your own. I wonder what he knows."

"I didn't look like an idiot," Gabe persisted, knowing all the while that he was fighting a losing battle when it came to dueling with Abazi.

"Maybe she actually got permission to do the survey," she mused.

"Then why wouldn't he say that?"

They stopped outside their respective classroom doors. "Well, whatever it is, I'm sure we'll find out in the worst way possible."

"Probably. Say—" Gabe was about to ask Abazi what her project was when the bell rang. Without a backward glance, she strolled into class while Gabe dashed to his. The last thing he needed was another tardy. He'd gotten two already today when his lock wouldn't work. Three and he'd have detention, which was bad enough, filled as it was with a bunch of goons, but worse than that, his mother would kill him.

As he tried to concentrate on an experiment that involved way too much sulfur, he thought about what Mrs. Morrigan might have done. Called a meeting with the town council? Threatened Abazi and Kimber's dad and mom? What?

He managed to avoid Jake for the rest of the day, though Jen and her friends sat near him during lunch...and giggled. He ate alone and fast and after he was finished, went searching for Abazi. He didn't find her. He spent that evening working on a paper and worrying—about his mother, about Oswald, about the fate of the forest, about impending fairy attacks—all the things he'd been so successful avoiding thinking about over the last couple days.

The next day pretty much went the same as yesterday—sucky. Gabe wasn't sure how much longer he could stand this not knowing. He hated being in limbo, and he hated not seeing Abazi all day long. To his relief, he found her waiting for him on Thursday in the lunchroom. Relief, that is, until he saw her expression. She was livid. In her hand she clutched the town's newspaper, *The Ranger Rag*.

"Ronald Pruspin is dead to me!" she cried, making her beaded earrings fly back and forth.

Gabe hurried to her side. "What happened?"

"He printed this drivel!" She shoved the paper at him. "How can he call himself a newspaper reporter? This is so one-sided, it's insane!"

Gabe read the headline. "Morrigan and Deacon Save Ranger." This didn't look good. His eyes skimmed the article.

Ranger, Maine - Candi Morrigan, owner of Ranger Real Estate, and Cornelia Deacon, upstanding citizen and member of too many committees to list here, have devised an ingenious plan to save the languishing town of Ranger. The delightful Candi Morrigan told *The Ranger Rag* all about it.

"Ranger needs to expand," Candi, wife of Dick Morrigan of Morrigan & Halston, LLC, told *The Ranger Rag*. "To do that, we must clear the forest—and we all know which one I'm talking about. It's a hazard and an eyesore. Frankly, I find the whole place creepy. Is that the image Ranger wants to portray to tourists?"

I should think not. The Ranger Forest, a veritable jungle, boasts a mess of trees that *literally* block the sky—not a pretty picture, folks. Unable to penetrate this thick maze, Route One had to be re-directed around Mount Vidar, causing endless delays for residents and keeping tourists from stopping in and supporting our struggling business sector.

Not only that, but Ranger Forest has a history of claiming hundreds of lives, dating back to Colonial times! In the 1950s, two young citizens of Ranger, 18-year-old Jessica Payer, and 17-year-old Matt Townsend, went into the woods and were never heard from again. Over the decades, several out-of-towners have gone missing. The last disappearance of a local occurred twenty years ago. Bruce Holt, aged 49, went for a walk in the woods and never returned.

The message Ranger Forest sends is this: If you're smart, you'll stay far away from Ranger.

The much-esteemed Cornelia Deacon added her two cents, "This town needs a good shake-up. We have to breathe new life into our businesses or run the risk of becoming a ghost town like Grimston, our neighbors to the west."

None of us Rangerites want that, do we? Which is why Mrs. Morrigan and Mrs. Deacon have been such dedicated advocates for a survey of the woods to determine what the town of Ranger is dealing with.

"We have no clear idea who owns this property," Candi Morrigan explained. "A trust fund was set up to pay the taxes, and at the time I'm sure the landowner was hoping to preserve our natural landmarks. But clearly the moment has come for Ranger to move on. This is the twenty-first century! Those woods are more profitable to Ranger cleared and developed. Just imagine...a movie theater, museums, condos overlooking the ocean, perhaps a golf course, and a hotel to accommodate the rise in tourists we'll be sure to see once those woods are cleared. What profits we'll make and what fun we'll have doing it!"

When asked what's to be done about the trust, Mrs. Morrigan was quite candid. "We break it. I'm sure we can convince the town board that developing those woods is in the greater interest of this town. Property value will double! New jobs will be had!"

Mrs. Deacon, no less impassioned, said, "The timber in that wood will pay for the survey, for the zoning and planning, and for countless other projects, like improving our schools. We only have our citizens' best interests in mind."

As you can see, Rangerites, we are in good hands! In fact, a survey team has already been hired and the survey was completed just before *The Rag* went to press. Keep up the good work ladies, and as always, keep us informed!

Gabe lowered the newspaper. The survey was *completed?* He looked at Abazi, her face an unnatural shade of red. "How?"

She glared at him. "You said Oswald would take care of it."

"That's what he said! But he didn't know...I didn't realize...Crap." The newspaper made a scrunching sound as his fist tightened. "Mrs. Morrigan outsmarted us, didn't she?" The vague thought passed through his mind that a Morrigan outsmarting him stung worse than the reality of the survey. "She must have said next Monday to throw us off. At the time I wondered why she was talking so loud. I'm not sure why the Ko-goks didn't eat them, but maybe Feltry held them off. I think he wants her all for himself."

"I'm not surprised. It's like she's a pile of crap and he's the fly." Abazi's palm slapped the table. "We are *so* screwed!"

"It's just a survey, Abazi. They still have to claim ownership of the property. I can't see how they can do that."

"That snake will think of something," she growled. "We have to stop them. I have to—" She stopped talking, her nostrils flaring.

He peered at her closely. "Your dad said you were working on some kind of project. Does it have anything to do with all this?"

Her dark eyes slid to the right. "Maybe."

"Come on, Abazi. What's going on?"

"I can't tell you yet, Hawthorne, because I don't know anything yet. When I do, you'll be the first to know."

He finished crumpling up the newspaper. "Well, that makes me feel so much better."

"My life is complete then," she spit back.

"I guess I'll have to return to the Forest Immortal," he said, after opening up his lunch bag and taking a few bites of his pb & j sandwich.

"What about your promise to Oswald?"

"He didn't hold up his end of the bargain so I don't need to uphold mine."

"When are you going?"

"During the powwow. There'll be a lot of people there, right? A lot of coming and going? I should be able to slip away and return without anyone noticing I'm gone."

"And what do you plan on saying to Mr. High and Mighty?"

Gabe shrugged, not bothering to correct her mistake. He had no plan of talking to Oswald. "I'll come up with something."

"Is that the best you can do? We need a plan, Gabe. Oswald is smart and Straif is a defective lunatic."

"I said I'll come up with something," he growled.

She snapped off a bite of carrot and studied him as she chewed. The crunching wore on his nerves, as she probably knew, but he didn't give in. "Don't get caught," she said at last.

"I won't."

That was the hope anyway. It was a dim hope, though. If the Kogoks didn't catch him, Oswald and his gang would. And if they didn't, well, Wildrr was still out there, bearing his grudge as proudly as a boy scout and his Eagle badge. Although the revenge-focused fairy hadn't actually done anything, Gabe figured he was merely biding his time, drawing out the agony like any good little imp would do.

The simple truth was that there were too many creatures in the forest interested in tracking Gabe down and taking him out. And even though Kimber had been rescued by a tree and had come to believe many of them were on his side now, he knew the woods were not where he should be going. But he was going into them, anyway. He had an idea, his only idea at the moment, and probably not a very safe one. But he had to do something, because if he couldn't stop all this trouble soon, he was going to change over. And once he did, he would hurt someone very badly.

Maybe even someone he loved.

Chapter Twenty-One

Like a Ghost

At supper that night, the Abenaki powwow came up. "I got a call from Mozi this afternoon," Mom said as she sawed at a piece of pork chop with the intensity of a woodcutter. "He says his tribe is holding a powwow—well, he called it a Heritage Gathering—this weekend and wondered if you three boys would like to attend as their guests."

Gabe, Kris, and Jer all looked at each other. "Hell, yeah!" Kris threw his fist into the air.

"Watch your language," Mom replied automatically, frowning as she worked around a gristly bit.

He grinned. "Sorry."

She speared a piece of meat and pointed it at him. "It doesn't count when you say it with that unrepentant expression on your face."

His lips curved downward. "I am so very sorry, Mother. My heart hurts to have offended you."

Gabe kicked him under the table. "Don't screw this up," the kick conveyed.

But Mom seemed to be in a good mood for once. The typical worry lines that always accompanied her expression these days had smoothed out and her eyes were bright. "Very funny, smart aleck."

"So we can go?" Jer ventured.

"I don't see why not. You'll have to pack warm. I can't believe it's October and it only got up to 40 degrees today. It should be in the 50s." She shivered and rubbed her arms through her wool sweater, which was the color of pine needles and brought out the green in her eyes. "Your father's still going to put the woodstove in here this week-end, right?" she asked their dad.

He chewed thoughtfully on his pork chop. "Last I heard. It's cherry red, if you can imagine that. Very stylish." While Gabe and his brothers were being hunted by Ko-goks, Dad and Grandpa Hawthorne had been in Portland picking up a used stove they'd tracked down on the Internet. The house where it was located was being remodeled by city folk, who apparently had no need for a woodstove. Grandpa had turned on the charm and got it for even cheaper than the asking price, so it was no wonder Mom was happy.

"At this stage, I don't care what color it is as long as it keeps me warm." She indicated the hallway leading to Gabe's tower. "It might even throw some heat all the way down there. Definitely upstairs to our bedrooms."

"We'll dress warm," Gabe promised, glad his parents were going to be otherwise occupied this weekend.

"And you'll spend next weekend chopping up that pile of wood out back?"

"We promise." He crossed his heart, giving her a solemn look.

"We'll chop enough wood to heat the house for the whole winter," Jer piped up.

"We have a deal then." She shivered again and wrapped her arms around her torso. "I personally think you're all nuts, but as the saying goes, to each his own."

"To each his own what?" Kris asked. He'd tuned out after getting permission to attend the powwow, shoveling down mashed potatoes covered in melted butter as fast as his arm would go. He loved his mashed potatoes.

"To each his own nuts," Jer snickered.

"His own preference," Dad clarified. "And your mother and I prefer not to freeze our patooties off. We'll have to find some way to keep each other warm." He flashed a mischievous grin at her.

She rolled her eyes back at him, but she was smiling. Seeing how much his parents loved each other made Gabe feel that the world was safe and good, and his resolve to end things with the residents of the Forest Immortal strengthened. Ayla and Keith Hawthorne might not be his biological parents, but in every sense, they were his *real* parents. He wouldn't give them up without a fight.

His plate wiped clean, he pushed back his chair and stood up, then took a moment to breathe in the smell of home—fresh bread, melted butter, warmth, laughter, and togetherness. He refused to let anyone take this away from him.

After he and his brothers cleared the table and washed the dishes, they went their separate ways to pack for the powwow. By now, they each knew what was needed on such adventures. Neither Kris nor Jer were aware of what Gabe planned to do while they were at the

Abenaki gathering and he had no plans to tell them. If he did, they'd want to come along, and no way was he going to risk having them there if he changed. He scared himself when he was a tree, so he could only imagine how his brothers must feel.

A strange noise coming from the secret passage interrupted his packing. He shoved the bata he was about to pack in his back pocket and raced to the bookshelf. Someone was trying to get in and he was going to catch them at it, whether it was Hollie, Oswald, or Wildrr. He was tired of these games.

The metal pole burned his hands as he raced down it, his socks doing little to slow his progress. When his feet hit the ground, his breath caught in his chest and pins and needles pierced his ankles.

The moment he wasted trying to recover from hitting the floor so hard was enough to let his visitor escape. Gabe could tell. Ever since he'd transformed into a tree, his senses had changed, not always for the better. Some things came to him more clearly; others felt like he was looking at them through Jell-O.

One thing that had definitely improved—he was able to sense anything that emitted warmth, which meant everything living, be it plant or animal. Sometimes the feeling overwhelmed him, like at school, and other times, it was like being surrounded by the sun. He imagined the feeling depended on the objects around him, and maybe, more importantly, their intent toward him. Good intent equals sun feeling. Bad intent equals hellfire. Maybe that's why he didn't particularly enjoy going to school anymore. The only plus was seeing Abazi. Her warmth was like a thousand suns, but if he ever told her that, the feeling would very likely rapidly change to fire and brimstone from all her gloating.

Even though he knew his visitor had left, he still crawled outside to look around, hoping he was wrong and the intruder was nearby. But whoever had come was gone, disappearing into the night like a ghost. Feeling the cold nipping at his nose and his toes, Gabe headed back.

He was on his hands and knees when he saw the paper nailed to the little entry door, its ends curled up like old parchment. He yanked down the note, knowing at once what it was. Another riddle. He rolled it up and pulled the door close behind him, tugging once more to be sure it was shut fast.

In his room, he sat down on his bed and uncurled the paper with shaking hands. A dull ache forming in his gut, he began to read...

Clue Number Three
(for you incredibly dull-witted saps)

Check under the surface
Within the wood walls
Listen to the tinkling
You'll hear its calls...

But hurry, you dingbats!

Gabe groaned. Why didn't the idiot just come out and say what he or she wanted to say? Why the secrecy? The riddle form? *Because he doesn't want anyone else to know what he's talking about*, Gabe answered himself. He sighed in frustration. That was probably true, still, couldn't he have been a little less cryptic? Under the surface? Within the walls? Tinkling? Sounds like he was writing about a toilet. Gabe shook his head. The last thing he wanted to do was search a stinky old toilet.

Well, he knew one thing for sure. If this turned out to be Oswald pulling his leg, Gabe was going to introduce him to the toilet by way of the swirly...and he wouldn't flush first.

Which brought him back to the 'why' behind the riddles. Why would Oswald write these notes, other than to piss Gabe off? Was that reason enough to take the risk of delivering them? Besides, his reaction at the gorge had seemed pretty sincere when he'd denied knowing anything about the riddles.

Then again, weren't con men great at deceiving others? Sure, they were. But the thing was, as much as Gabe didn't like Oswald, he couldn't bring himself to see him as a con. Arrogant, yes. Deluded, yes. But two-faced? That just didn't fit the Dryad. Maybe Gabe wouldn't have admitted that when he was so angry before, but he could now. Just because he wanted Oswald to be the one who'd written the riddles, that didn't make him so.

Gabe pushed himself to his feet to go tell his brothers about this latest riddle. Then he sat back down, deciding it could wait until tomorrow. He was tired, and he had a math test he really should be studying for. If he wanted to go to college, and he did, he'd need all the scholarships he could get. No way would Mom and Dad be able to help.

After staring at the riddle for several more minutes, he stood up and fetched his math book. By 10:30, he could no longer keep his eyes open. He shuffled off to the bathroom, brushed his teeth and washed his face, then shuffled back, more asleep than awake. As soon as his head hit the pillow, he was asleep and dreaming. At first he dreamed about trigonometric equations that went on for pages. Then Mr. Boos, his pre-calc teacher and a pretty decent guy, appeared and scolded him for not studying enough. "You're a dull-witted sap!" he taunted Gabe, handing the test back with a giant red "F" on it. Devastated, Gabe took the test and ran.

He ran, as one does sometimes in dreams, without feeling the ground beneath his feet or noticing how quickly he moved from one place to the next. Now he was at the old mill without remembering how he got there. He was just there, listening to the waterwheel spin around and around as its paddles slapped the black surface. Water dripped from the paddles, making a sort of tinkling sound as it hit the river.

Check under the surface
Within the wood walls
Listen to the tinkling
You'll hear its calls…

Someone was singing the words to the riddle, over and over, and the disembodied voice echoed in the hollow old building. Gabe shivered. He hated it here. He hated…

He sat upright, wide awake. The mill…the riddles were talking about the mill! Round and round meant the waterwheel, and probably where they could find the key. *The answer is up* meant above the waterwheel. *Look high* from *the sky* meant they'd have to be *above* the secret spot to find the key. The key undoubtedly unlocked the door to an underground secret room in the mill, being 'under the surface' and 'within the wood walls.' The tinkling had to do with water. He'd solved the riddles!

His mood soared, then, just as quickly, it took a dive. The old mill. That horrid place gave him the willies, and was almost worse than facing Straif. But that's where he had to go. The question was, did he go before or after he went into the woods to carry out his plan? *Before.* And then maybe he wouldn't have to do the other thing at all. That would be ideal. Gabe had no desire to make a promise he wasn't sure he could keep.

The mill it is, he decided, then closed his eyes and fell asleep to the clamor of the wind billowing about the house, a sound not unlike the howl of hungry wolves descending on their helpless victim.

Chapter Twenty-Two

Under the Surface

The next day at school, Gabe tried to catch Abazi to tell her about the riddle, but he could only track her down long enough between classes to get her to agree to meet after school at the barn. She appeared distracted and only responded after he'd repeated twice that he had something to tell her.

"I have something to tell you, too," she'd replied with a frown. "I'll bring Kimber," she added quickly, before hurrying off to her next class, books clutched tightly in her arms. Gabe was glad he'd already taken his math test because his ability to concentrate was now shot. What had she meant? What did she have to tell him? Judging by the perturbed look on her face, it wasn't good.

On top of that, he'd meant to tell his brothers about the riddle before school, but as usual, Kris had turned off the alarm and gone back to sleep. So he had overslept and Jer only discovered him when he found Little Joe meowing to be let out of Kris's bedroom. In their race to get to school, Gabe completely forgot about the riddle. He'd meant to read it to them on the drive, but while his driving had improved greatly, he still had to concentrate on what he was doing or risk ending up in the ditch when the truck acted up, as it liked to do.

On the way home, he told Kris and Jer, who were bickering about the seating arrangement, as *they* liked to do, that they were meeting Abazi and Kimber at the barn. "So as soon as we get home, grab a snack and get out there. I found another riddle and Abazi has something to tell us."

Jer stopped mid-rant. "Another riddle? What did it say?"

"Something about wood walls and under the surface and tinkling."

"Our clue has peeing in it?" Kris slapped the dashboard. "A pissy poem!"

"I hope that isn't what it meant," Gabe sighed. "It's weird, but probably not that weird. I think I have it figured out, though, thank goodness. Whoever is writing the riddles is getting annoyed with us. He, or she, has now called us both dull-witted saps *and* dingbats."

"Well, we can rule Abazi out for sure," Jer replied. "Her insults would be meaner than that."

Gabe glanced over at him. "You're right. Those words are pretty archaic."

"Ark-whatic?" Kris echoed.

"Old-fashioned," Jer explained. "Nobody these days would use them."

"Oh. I know that word, but I thought it was pronounced like the word arch. But anyway, maybe whoever used them wasn't exactly human."

"Right," Gabe said thoughtfully as he parked the truck next to the barn. He had just remembered another creature who'd used the word dingbat. Wildrr, the mad fairy. "Let's get something to eat and head to the barn."

After saying hi to their dad, who was washing dishes, they dropped their bags in their rooms, then returned to the kitchen for handfuls of animal crackers and a Macintosh apple each.

"Bye, Mom!" they called to her as they headed single file out the door.

She was emerging from the basement with a basket of laundry. "You have laundry to put away!" she shouted after them. "And homework!"

"We'll do it after supper," Jer yelled back. "Promise!"

They escaped to the sounds of her muttering something about, "Yeah, right, when pigs fly."

"Where's the fire?" Grandma May barked as they dashed past her. She was parking her colorful three-wheeled bike near the porch.

"We're meeting friends," Kris told her, taking a bite of apple.

She scowled at Gabe. "You failed me, you know."

Gabe, recalling their last meeting, felt his stomach clench up. "Mrs. Morrigan tricked me."

"Not hard to do."

"Why are you being so mean to me?" he cried, suddenly losing it. "What did I ever do to you?"

Her piercing blue eyes flashed and Gabe wanted desperately to turn and run to the barn and hide. But he stood his ground. He'd done nothing wrong. No way was he going to take the fall again.

And then, just as he thought she was going to go off on him, she was the one taking a step backward, up the steps. "Have you figured out the riddles?" Her voice was low, almost soft, as she stared at his hands.

Gabe looked down at them in horror, fearing his thorns had popped out without him even realizing it. To his relief, his skin was smooth and free from the black protrusions. "I might have. How do you know about them?"

Her eyes flicked toward the woods. "I have my ways."

"If you know something, you have to tell me, Grandma. Something's going on with you. I just want to help make this go away."

She grabbed his arm and pulled him away from the house. Jer and Kris quietly followed, not saying a word. "If you want to help me…help *all* of us," she hissed, "you'll figure out those riddles."

He tried to pull his arm from her tight grasp, but she had strong hands. "Why can't *you* do it? You know who's writing them, don't you? Just ask him, her, *it*. Whoever!"

Her eyes blinked rapidly. "Believe me, I've tried to get it out—" She stopped suddenly. "If I had the answer, Gabe, don't you think I'd tell you?"

"I don't know what to think. It'd be just like you to act all ornery and keep the answer to yourself."

To his surprise, she laughed. "That *would* be like me." She quickly sobered. "But not this time. I can't tell you any more. Not yet. Not until I'm certain. I'm fri— I'm worried," she amended, though Gabe was certain she'd been about to say frightened. He suddenly felt frightened himself. If Grandma May was scared, that meant the end of the world was likely heading their way. She released his arm. "As soon as you solve the riddles, come to me." She spun about, pushed past Jer and Kris, and marched resolutely up the stairs into the house.

Gabe, Jer, and Kris stared after her. "What was that about?" Kris broke the silence.

"I don't exactly know," Gabe answered after a few seconds. "She's acting so weird. You heard what she said, right?"

"She sounds scared," Jer said.

"I know. That's what worries me."

A shout came from behind them and they turned to see Kimber and Abazi heading toward the barn. They ran to meet them, and together they climbed the stairs to the loft. When everyone had found a hay bale to sit on, Gabe pulled two apples, the nicest ones he could find from their stash, out of his jacket pocket. He handed one to Kimber, and then, not quite able to help himself, presented the other to Abazi as though it were a diamond.

She took it and grinned at him, her white teeth flashing as she bit into the juicy apple. "I love Macs best of all. Thanks, Immortal."

He nodded at her, hoping he was projecting the suave, sophisticated image he'd been working on in the mirror. "No problem."

"I would've brought you an apple, Kimber," Jer spoke up, giving his brother the stink eye, "but Gabe beat me to it."

"I know, Jer. You're so sweet." She smiled at him and he ducked his head, blushing.

Kris's eyes sparkled. "Sweet as poison-laced honey."

Jer glared at him. "You're such a jerk, Kris."

Gabe held up his hands. "We don't have the time or energy to waste on bickering, you guys. Lives are at stake." The two brothers nodded, looking suitably sheepish.

"So what did you want to tell us?" Abazi asked.

He pulled out the riddle and handed it to her. She looked at it a moment, gave a martyred sigh, then took it from him. She read it aloud, her expression sour and her words mincing like a high society lady.

Clue Number Three
(for you incredibly dull-witted saps)

Check under the surface
Within the wood walls
Listen to the tinkling
You'll hear its calls…

But hurry, you dingbats!

"What an idiot!" she finished. "Why doesn't he just out and tell us what he wants us to know?"

"Because he, or *she*, doesn't want anyone else to figure it out," Gabe answered, glad to be able to know something for once.

"Including us," she snorted. "This makes no sense."

"I thought maybe it meant the old mill down by Shishiqua River."

She looked up at him, her eyes narrowing thoughtfully. "Wolka Mill? I suppose it could. Surface for the water. Wood walls for the building. Tinkling for the water." She looked around at all three boys. "But I'm sure at least one of you mentioned peeing, didn't you?"

They laughed. "You hit that one on the nose, sister." Kris grinned.

"I thought we could go check it out," Gabe said. "You know, before we do anything else." He gave Abazi a meaningful glance, letting her know that he preferred to try out the mill before going through with his plan to return to the forest.

"Of course we're going to go check it out," she replied, picking up on his message instantly. She handed him the riddle and he folded it and stuffed it into his coat pocket. "We'll go tomorrow morning, before the festivities really get started." She shivered and wrapped her arms around herself. "It's going to be cold in those teepees."

"We're sleeping in teepees?" Jer cried excitedly. "Yes!"

"You're an odd bird," she told him, her tone affectionate. "Though, technically, they're wigwams. I called them teepees so you palefaces would know what I was talking about."

"I like teepees," Gabe heard himself saying and immediately wishing he hadn't.

She gave him an exasperated look. "Well, I don't. They're confining, smoky, and sometimes downright stinky. Can you imagine living like my ancestors did? Where was the privacy? If you wanted to be left alone, you were supposed to turn your back, but that wouldn't do it for me. You couldn't even pick your nose without someone catching you."

Gabe didn't exactly know what to say to that. He really did like teepees, but he also had this stupid desire to please Abazi even though she didn't seem to possess the same desire to please him. "Maybe nose picking was more accepted back then," he suggested.

She leaned toward him. "What if you had a girlfriend? What would you do then?"

He felt his cheeks go hot. "I'd go kill a bear and make my own teepee, that's what."

She pulled back, her eyes dancing. "I like your style, Hawthorne. Maybe I'll come join your tribe."

A rush of warmth filled his chest. He wasn't sure why he liked Abazi so much, but he did. She was prickly and seemed to enjoy poking him whenever she could. But then, when he thought she'd gone too far, she'd say something like that. She was a temptress, that's what she was, and he liked it. Which was probably going to be the death of him.

Jer was looking back and forth between them, his eyes suspicious. Gabe figured it was time to change the subject, fast. "Abazi, what was it you wanted to tell us?"

The sparkle in her eyes fizzled out. "It's totally crappy news, I'm afraid." She fingered the hem of her coat. Gabe stared at her, disconcerted. He didn't think he'd ever seen Abazi looking uncomfortable. "I've been doing some research and I found something out," she continued. "It's about your grandma."

"If it's about the riddles," Jer interjected, "she just told us she didn't write them and she doesn't know what they mean."

"But she might know who's writing them," Gabe added. "I think she's scared and that scares me. Grandma May never gets scared."

"She might get scared if she were about to lose her house," Abazi said in a soft voice. She held out her hands and gave an apologetic shrug. "She doesn't own it, you see."

Chapter Twenty-Three

Lovers Dance

For a brief moment the loft felt like a church, still and profound, then Abazi spoke into the stunned silence, which had descended over them. "The house was built in the part of the woods outside your property. That's why Crazy Candi and the Deaconator were surveying so close to it."

Gabe couldn't quite get his head around it. "So you're saying she stole a house?"

Kris grinned. "It's the heist of the century."

"Well, I guess I would be scared if I was living in a house that wasn't mine," Jer remarked.

"So that's it," Abazi concluded. "That's why she's been acting so strangely. She's fighting for her freedom. She's a rebel with a cause."

"But she stole a house," Gabe couldn't help repeating. "How'd she think she'd get away with that?"

"Grandma May's a ballsy woman," Jer said with a big smile. "Gotta love that."

"It explains why she was so anxious for us to get rid of the surveyors."

"So now what do we do?" Gabe wondered.

"We have to find out who owns that land," Abazi answered him. "I looked at the town hall, but I couldn't find anything out. It's like someone took the documents—" She snapped her fingers. "I'll bet someone did!"

"Did what?" Gabe asked.

"I bet someone took the documents!"

"But who?"

"My best guess is that twerp, Ronald Pruspin, hack journalist and Candi's toadie, to boot. He's just the kind of loser who'd do something like that. We need to get those papers back."

"We can't break into his house," Gabe protested. If Mom was mad at them just for touching someone else's stuff, imagine how she'd react if they actually snuck into someone's house.

"That would be a waste of time, not to mention being a felony, Gabe. I'm surprised you'd even think of it." She gave him a saucy look.

"So we're screwed," Kris moaned.

"I think we should stick to our original plan," Gabe said, ignoring Abazi's needling. He needed a clear mind to work this out. "We head to the mill and see what's there. I think someone is trying to tell us something, and maybe it has something to do with those missing papers."

"Good thinking, Immortal." Abazi smiled mischievously at him.

"Glad you agree."

"When?" Kris asked.

"Same plan," Abazi decided. "Tomorrow morning while everyone is sleeping off the night's festivities." She paused. "Which means you guys should come tonight. Then we could get an early start."

"Let's do it!" Kris cried.

"Sure, why not?" Gabe agreed. He thought it actually sounded fun.

"Even better," Abazi smiled. "You'll get to see me dance."

"I'll bring the video camera," Gabe said with a grin, then raced down the steps before she could change her mind. "Gotta pack!" He could hear her grumbling all the way through the barn.

After supper, their mom helped them by directing what to pack. "You'll be careful," she said to Gabe when she came up to check on him. "Watch your brothers."

"It's just a powwow," he replied casually, being careful not to give anything away. "But I'll watch out for them."

She crossed her arms and shivered. "Make sure you bundle up. You're a human furnace, I know, but even furnaces break down."

"Nice analogy, Mom."

"Thanks. I worked hard on that." She smiled at him. "You're getting so grown up. I like that, and I don't."

"You don't?"

"No, because it means you'll be leaving soon, heading off to college. I like my boys around me."

"I'll be sure to move back home after college."

"Your father and I will be touring Europe by then."

"Jer will still be in high school!"

"I'm sure he'll graduate early."

Gabe smiled as he shoved a sweatshirt into his backpack. "Then I'll run the farm for you while you're gone."

"That sounds good." She moved towards the stairs, then spun back around and enveloped Gabe in a hug. "I love you, Gabe. No matter what." With that, she broke away and hurried down the stairs with him gaping at her like a stuffed fish hanging on a wall. What had that been about? Normal parental worry, or something else? Maybe Grandma May had been talking to her. He shook his head. Likely not. Grandma May had her own secrets to protect, which meant protecting Gabe if she wanted his help.

Maybe Mom sensed something was up. Or maybe she'd somehow figured out that he wasn't her real son. A cold chill washed over him. She couldn't possibly have figured that out, could she? She could. He'd heard that parents possessed an intuition about their children that went beyond the ordinary. Maybe she'd guessed the truth when she'd seen Oswald. Maybe she'd always sensed something, but meeting Oswald had confirmed her intuition.

Gabe shuddered miserably. He had to make things right with the Forest, and with Oswald, before things went too far and he lost his family forever. If he couldn't do it by solving the riddles, then he'd go through with his plan to confront Filidh about the riddles. And if Filidh hadn't written them, then maybe Gabe would give him what he wanted—whatever that was—to find out who had.

A warning bell sounded in his mind. Maybe Filidh had been the visitor in Grandma May's cottage. Gabe remembered smelling the scent of woods and something foreign in the air, both suggestive of the strange forest man's presence. Add to that the fact that he liked creating riddles and Gabe had his answer.

On the other hand, and even worse, it might have been Wildrr come to seek him out. That could be why Grandma May had been so scared. But then, why not say so? Wildrr had gone by then. She could have warned Gabe, scolded him, anything, but she'd said nothing. It seemed as though she wanted to protect her visitor, keep his identity a secret, which was rather disturbing if he thought about it.

It was all too confusing. He couldn't wait to get to the mill and solve the riddle. He was getting sick of this wild goose chase. Well, sick might not be the best term. It was actually kind of fun trying to figure out the clues. But it would be more fun if he weren't so worried about how much he had to lose if he failed.

At the very least, going to the mill might help him stop feeling so anxious all the time. At most, he might get his old life back. That would be really awesome. And the best part of going to the mill? It wasn't in the woods, where simply entering could get him maimed or killed.

~~~~~~

The three brothers arrived at the Wanibagw's to a scene of wonderful chaos—campfires and teepees (aka wigwams) dotted the spacious lawn, and laughter and music filled the air. The walk through the woods had been a bit unnerving, being dark out, but Gabe hadn't felt nearly as worried here as he did in other parts of the woods.

Abazi and Kimber must have been watching for them because as soon as Gabe and his brothers left the trees, they came running. "It's about time!" Abazi exclaimed. Along with matching leggings, she wore a heavily beaded, tight-fitting buckskin dress that Gabe felt sure wasn't made from a traditional pattern. A multi-colored shawl, decorated with beadwork, fringe, and ribbons, was draped loosely over her shoulders. She looked amazing. "The dancing is about to begin." She led them toward two small teepees, where a small campfire burned. Abazi's father waved to them from a lawn chair.

"Welcome!" he cried, his smile emphasizing the moon-shaped scar on his cheek. According to Abazi, he'd gotten it as a kid. Mozi told people it was from fighting a bear over a blueberry pie, but the real story was that he and his older brother had been playing cowboys and Indians and Uncle Atso forced Mozi to be the cowboy. His punishment for existing was to get pushed off a cliff, which was only a rock, but he'd landed on a tree stump, gouging his face. "The hawk is looking good." Mozi pointed at Kris's Mohawk with a two-pronged metal roasting stick.

Kris ran a hand over it. "Thanks. Just trimmed it."

"I'd have one, too, but my hair's too fine. It'd just keep flopping over. Marshmallow?" He indicated an open bag on the lawn chair next to him.

"Yes!"

Mozi laughed at Gabe's puzzled expression. "We Indians like to mix the old and the new. If marshmallows existed back in our ancestors' time, I'm quite sure they would've eaten them whenever they got the chance." He popped a perfectly browned one into his mouth.

"Yeah, right, Dad," Abazi said. "Right along with potato chips and diet soda." She turned to the others. "Throw your bags into that teepee," she nodded at the one on the right, "then eat up. I don't want you distracted when I'm dancing." She looked pointedly at her father.

"Since I *have* to do this dance, then I need to be sure everyone witnesses it so I won't ever have to do it again."

The three brothers slipped inside the dark teepee, dropped their bags, weapons, and staffs on the ground, then hurried back out. Everyone picked up a stick and joined in the roasting. There was much jockeying for the best positions and whoops of dismay when a marshmallow burst into flame. The first time one went up in smoke, Kris exclaimed, "Look, it's a dark dork!" and they all had a good laugh. It didn't take long to go through the entire bag, especially since sometimes they'd purposely burn a marshmallow just for the thrill of pretending it was a Ko-gok. It was grisly, and great fun.

"So what dance are you doing?" Gabe asked Abazi, spinning the marshmallow stick in his hand. At the school library, he'd found a book on the Abenaki—Abazi's tribe—and had read about their various ceremonial dances. The Two Step, or Lovers Dance, had caught his attention, as it was the only dance, it seemed, where a man and a woman could touch. The woman gets to choose her partner and he wondered if Abazi would pick him. Probably not, if only to annoy him.

"The Shawl Dance," she replied, fingering the fringes on her shawl. "I move pretty fast so watch closely."

She didn't have to tell him twice.

Jer asked Mozi about the different costumes and teepees spread around the small field and he told them about the various symbols and colors and what they represented. Smoke from the fire drifted upward, blending into the dark sky. A log popped and scattered sparks of red and orange into the air; the sparks flew and danced about before flickering out. Gabe spent his time shifting pieces of wood around and glancing over at Abazi when she wasn't looking. One time she caught him peeking and gave him a mischievous smile. "Watch closely," she mouthed.

They were on their second bag of marshmallows when the drums began to beat. "It's time," Mozi said. He rose, wrapped up the bag, and indicated for the others to follow him. Gabe stuck his stick into the ground and joined the exodus toward the largest bonfire in the middle of the meadow. When they reached it, he could see what appeared to be the tribal elders. They either wore wool blankets wrapped around their shoulders or beaded shawls. A number of musicians seated off to one side were playing pipes and flutes and the tom-toms. An old Indian, with skin like a walnut, chanted a mournful song and his voice, low and keening, filled the fire-warmed air.

Gabe was surprised at how excited he felt. The mood around the fire was exuberant, yet serious, and deeply spiritual. He was not an Indian, yet he felt connected to all the people around him, like he was one of them. They smiled and welcomed him to join their circle. The Indian children, dressed in native costume, and Jer, Kris, and Kimber, looking a bit out of place in their modern jackets and hats, sat closer to the fire. Gabe stood a little farther back, reluctant to miss seeing Abazi dance. She had left them to join a group of young women on the other side of the fire. At school, she typically held herself back from the other girls, interacting only when it seemed convenient for her. But with these girls, she was different, more joyous, her teeth flashing in the firelight. She actually seemed friendly. It was a side of her Gabe had never seen, and it gave him hope.

No words were spoken, but as though hearing a signal, all other sounds ceased, until only the drummer remained drumming. Then the elders stood and entered the empty ring around the fire. They began to dance, slow and rhythmic. Gabe watched, fascinated, as they circled the leaping flames, around and around, then around again. At last, the tempo changed and the elders left, making room for the next round of dance.

Several groups performed, each one unique. Finally it was Abazi's turn. She and the other young women stepped confidently into the cir- cle. The children scooted back, making more room, and the dancing began. Gabe's eyes fastened on Abazi and didn't leave her form once, even though the intensity of the dance was fantastic. The drumming was fast and furious, in rhythm with Gabe's heartbeat, as Abazi leaped and whirled around the fire like a wild creature. By the end of the dance, he was breathing almost as hard as the dancers. Abazi at last came to a rest, dipped her head slightly, then raised it to look directly into Gabe's eyes. She seemed to stare at him forever before breaking away from the circle with the other girls, her lips curved into a satisfied smile.

As the next dance began, Gabe looked around, grinning broadly, wanting to see everyone else's reaction to Abazi's amazing perform- ance. But everyone was already absorbed into the next act, so no one saw what Gabe saw—Oswald, standing at the edge of the woods, watching Abazi with covetous eyes. All Gabe's pleasure drained away as he hurried over to her side. Seeing him coming, she separated from her friends to meet him halfway. Together they pushed their way through the crowd toward the edge of the woods.

"Well?" she demanded, her breath coming in quick pants. Sweat beads shimmered on her forehead and her shawl had slipped down to her elbows. "Wasn't that the stupidest thing ever?"

For a brief moment, Gabe forgot everything else. He reached out and grabbed Abazi's arms; her heated skin warmed his hands, even through knit gloves. "That was amazing, Abazi. I don't know why you don't want to embrace your heritage, but you looked really good out there. Your ancestors would be proud. Your mother, too, I bet."

Her brow wrinkled and her dark eyes narrowed in warning. "You don't know anything about it, Tree Man." She pulled out of his grasp. "I danced that stupid dance because it will get my dad off my back. All right? And I certainly didn't do it for my mother."

"But you really looked like you were enjoying yourself!" Gabe persisted.

"Well, I wasn't. And everyone here," she indicated the crowd, "only came to watch me blow it."

"Blow it? But you were awesome!"

Something in her eyes flickered, like flashbulbs going off. "What would you know, paleface?"

Hurt, Gabe took a step back. "Why do you do that?"

"Do what?"

"Put distance between yourself and other people?"

"Because I'm not good for other people." She pointed at his chest. "And you'd better get that through your thick skull before you become just another one of my victims."

What sounded like a pleased chuckle echoed around Gabe and he suddenly remembered Oswald. He searched the edge of the woods until he spotted the Dryad leaning against a birch tree, his arms crossed and his expression smug.

"Looks like I'm not your only admirer," Gabe said bitterly, pointing at Oswald's dark figure. Just seeing him sparked Gabe's anger...at the Dryad, at Abazi. Luckily his spikes stayed put.

Abazi's head swung toward the woods. "What are you talking about?"

"You have an audience. I'll leave you two alone, all right?" But he didn't move. No way was he going to leave Abazi alone with that creep. He might be thoroughly pissed at her right now, but leaving her with Oswald would be like leaving her alone in the jungle, covered in gravy.

"I don't see anyone," she said, her eyes roaming the woods.

He pointed again. "He's right there. It's Oswald."

She glared at Gabe. "Now you're trying to trick me?"

His mouth dropped open. "Are you kidding?" He looked again to be sure he wasn't imagining things. He wasn't. It was definitely Oswald and now he was smirking. "He's standing right by that birch tree and he's looking entirely too pleased with himself."

Abazi took a step backward. "He…he's watching me?"

Gabe looked at her closely. For the first time since he'd met her, she sounded uncertain and his anger deflated. "Like you were dinner."

She gave Gabe a strained smile. "I guess some people have nothing better to do with their time. I'm going to bed."

Before she could flee, Gabe grabbed her arm and swung her back around. "I don't know why you think you're bad for people, but with my screwed-up life, I don't think I'm any better than you. I nearly drowned Oswald, you know." He left out that he was also a tree kil-ler—he wasn't ready to go that far with his confession. "And if it wasn't for me, you guys wouldn't be in this mess with the Ko-goks. So you're not going to get rid of me that easily." He took a deep breath—this next part wasn't going to be easy. "Cause I like you, Abazi. I just wish you'd stop trying to drive me away. I wish you'd tell me why you'd want to. If you don't like me, fine. I'll have to live with that. But if you think it's because something's wrong with you, I won't accept that. Ever."

Abazi's eyes welled up. "You're a good guy, Gabe." She pulled away, but more gently this time. "But you just don't get it." She started walk-ing away, her shoulders bowed as though she'd aged in seconds.

"Then explain it to me!" Gabe shouted, forgetting to be quiet. "Tell it to me like I'm five!"

She didn't stop walking, her steps matching the beat of the drum. Gabe stared after her. What had just happened? Had he really told Abazi he liked her? Despite the fact that she'd walked away from him, Gabe felt his spirits lift a little.

Then he felt a presence behind him and he plummeted back to earth. He slowly turned around. "Have you come to gloat?"

"I don't need to. When I want to be with Abazi, I will. It's that sim-ple."

"She doesn't want to be with anyone, idiot. She just said so."

"I've never let people tell me what to do. Why should I start now?"

Gabe sighed. "You let the surveyors finish their job."

Oswald's confident swagger deflated a little. "That was an unfortu-nate outcome."

"Really? You think so?"

Oswald scowled. "I sometimes forget that yer kind can, on occasion, be somewhat intelligent." It was funny how easily Oswald could forget that he was that 'kind' himself. "Their ruse threw me off track…and I was distracted by other things."

"What other things?"

Oswald stared off into the woods. "Not yer concern."

"Then why'd you mention it? Making excuses for your incompetence?"

Oswald came at Gabe so swiftly that his head swam wildly. "Ye messed Faeth up. She was well enough before she talked to ye. What did ye say to her?" His breath, which smelled of apples and acorns, came in fitful starts. "She was fine until ye showed up."

Gabe thought it had been a long time since Faeth had been fine, but he didn't say that out loud. "What's happened to her?"

"She's run off. Me and the Rogues can't find her anywhere. I'm afraid that Straif has got her, that he'll be wantin' to use her as bait."

"You were supposed to watch her!" Gabe shoved Oswald backward, feeling furious and afraid at the same time. He was angry with Oswald for messing up, afraid for Faeth, and afraid of the spikes that would be coming soon. He tried to calm down, but his heart was racing.

"Things are happenin', Gabriel. I cannot be everywhere all the time."

"You could if you were who you think you are."

"Even kings are fallible."

Gabe kicked the dirt, breathing hard. "Do you really think Straif has her?"

"In these times I cannot be certain of anything. I do think she's still alive. I've not felt the wrench."

"The wrench?"

"When two souls are parted…it's the tearin'. If ye're connected, ye'd feel it."

"Would *I* feel it?" Gabe breathed. "With Faeth?"

Oswald's lips twisted. "It's likely."

"I didn't feel anything. Nothing weird. Not like that."

Oswald searched his face and what he saw must have both irritated and reassured him. It was strange to see both expressions cross his features, kind of like watching oil and water try to mix. "I have to go now. Say goodbye to Abazi for me, would ye?" His swagger was back.

"I thought you liked Hollie," Gabe said, refusing to be drawn.

"Ways are different in the forest, Gabriel. We're not like ye and yer kind."

Gabe smiled and Oswald's eyebrow rose. "That amuses ye?"

Gabe laughed outright. "No, it pleases me. Two different things." Oswald wouldn't understand that Abazi was the type of girl who needed to be the one and only in someone's life. If she couldn't be that, you might as well give up now. "Goodbye, Oswald. I hope we don't meet any time soon."

"Not so fast. I came to tell ye something else."

Gabe's smile dropped. "What?"

"Beware the Freeze."

"What's that supposed to mean?"

"Prove me wrong about yer kind and figure it out yerself."

Gabe was getting awfully sick of riddles. "Why can't you just tell me?"

"Because that wouldn't be very fun, now would it?" He flicked a mock salute at Gabe and dashed off into the woods before Gabe could say anything more.

When Oswald was gone, Gabe turned back and joined the crowd to watch the final dances. He felt tired and confused, and he was worried about Faeth. He hadn't felt anything strange or worrying, nor had Oswald, but that didn't mean she was safe. What if Straif really did have her? Or Wildrr? Or she could be injured or lost, wandering the forest looking for him. The thought of her hurting and in distress disturbed him more than he thought possible.

Before the dancing ended, he headed to their teepee. He really didn't want to talk to anyone right now and the best way to do that was to avoid people. Once inside, he unrolled his sleeping bag and climbed in, fully dressed. It was cold outside, freezing, in fact. Besides that, the sense that he needed to be ready for something to happen was growing inside him, and he didn't want to be caught in his boxer shorts when the time came.

Chapter Twenty-Four

It's Mill Time

The next morning Gabe awoke early feeling groggy and out of sorts. Jer was sleeping in his usual position, on his back like a mummy, and Kris was sprawled half-in and half-out of his sleeping bag, and upside down compared to everyone else. Something had awakened Gabe, a flash of light, actually. He looked toward the teepee flap and just as he did a bright light caught him square in the eyes. His hand flew up to block the glare.

"Put that thing down, Abazi," he hissed. "You're going to blind me."

The beam dropped to rest at her feet. "It's time to go. I want to move out before the others wake up. I left a note for my dad, so he won't worry, too much anyway, and Kimber's already waiting outside."

Despite his addled brain he noticed that she didn't sound as bossy as she usually did. He lowered his hand to study her. "Are you all right?" Her hair hung loosely around her face as she stared down at the beam. He liked it that way; it made her seem softer, less prickly.

"I'm fine," she muttered. "Let's get moving, all right?"

"All right." Now was not the time to challenge her. He scooched out of his sleeping bag and crawled over to Kris and Jer. "Wake up, guys." He took turns shaking their shoulders and was met with groans. Taking advantage of their freedom, they'd stayed up later than usual, eating marshmallows, drinking root beer or lemonade, and dancing with the other kids. They had woken Gabe up when they'd climbed inside the teepee, snickering and pushing each other.

"We have to go now, before the others wake up."

Kris pulled the sleeping bag over his head, and Jer sat up and looked around. "Where's Kimber?"

"She's outside." Abazi pointed. "Grab your weapons…just in case. The mill isn't in the woods, but you never know."

Hearing Abazi's voice, Kris emerged from his cocoon. "What time is it?" he groaned.

"Early, dope," she said, sounding a little more like herself. "I have food."

Kris pushed off his bag. Like Jer and Gabe he had opted to sleep in his clothes and was ready to go. "Why didn't you say so?"

In five minutes, they were assembled outside the teepee, eating blueberry muffins and talking in whispers. Abazi spent the time braiding her hair. Gabe wished he could tell her to leave it down, but after last night he wasn't going to push things.

"We'll take the shortcut," Abazi indicated a one-lane dirt drive on the other side of her house, "which should make it only about a half-hour walk to the mill."

"Through the woods?" Gabe questioned. "Are you sure that's a good idea?"

"It's faster, and we don't have a lot of time. My dad put this whole powwow thing together for me, so I can't exactly not be here."

Gabe pulled in a deep breath. "All right, we'll do it."

"I know you don't like being carried, Kimber," Kris said around a mouthful of muffin, "but I could do it."

She smiled at him. "I'll take one for the team." She glanced at Jer. His face was tense, but he nodded. "As long as I can yell giddy up a few times."

Jer laughed and relaxed. "I might have a willow whip you could use."

Kris poked Jer in the arm. "Dude, if you were about four inches taller, I'd be happy to let you carry Kimber." He took another bite of muffin, followed by several swallows of hot chocolate from one of the thermoses Abazi had brought along. Gabe realized she must have gotten up extra early to prepare everything.

"Thanks for the food, Abazi."

She looked at him, her eyes dark circles in the glow of the flashlight. "Yeah, well, I didn't want to hear any whining."

Kris patted his stomach. "The only whining you'll be hearing from me is how full I am. I think I ate six of those muffins."

"Then it's just as well you're carrying Kimber, you pig," Jer said. "Work off some of those calories."

"Let's get going, guys," Gabe urged. He just wanted to get this over with.

"I'll take the lead," Abazi said. "Jer, stash the food in your teepee." He took the bag and thermoses and disappeared inside the flap. When he emerged, Kris bent low for Kimber to climb onto his back. As he straightened up, Jer silently handed Kimber Kris's staff.

Gabe glanced around the sleeping, temporary hamlet of teepees and lean-tos; the remains of several fires still smoked, lending the air a fragrant, homey smell. It was a safe smell, one that spoke of warmth and comfort and safety. But he knew it was a false sense of security he was feeling. They were heading into the woods soon and he couldn't help worrying that the Ko-goks lay in wait for just this moment.

"You bring up the rear, Gabe," Abazi whispered. "If you see anything strange, other than your reflection, let us know."

"Very funny," he scowled, but inside, he felt a little better. After telling Abazi he liked her, it was good to see she was still talking to him. "After you." He waved his arm before him.

She gave him one last look, then ducking low, headed for the woods. They weaved in and out amongst the quiet teepees until at last they broke free of the settlement. Abazi started to run and they chased after her, eyes focused on the bobbing glow from her flashlight. The woods loomed before them, but before Gabe could even entertain seconds thoughts, Abazi plunged into the forest and they followed, *like sheep to slaughter*, Gabe couldn't help thinking.

He was glad to see birch and alder trees lining both sides of the drive. They were safe trees. Even so, they'd only gone about a quarter mile when he heard something—whispering. All around him. He couldn't make out any words, but he didn't have to know what the whispers were saying to get that they were bad. Just the sound of those sibilant hisses, like evil snakes, made his skin crawl and his hackles rise.

"They're here!" he shouted. "Run!"

Abazi glanced back, her eyes wide. "Here? But this is protected space!"

"I don't think they care," he yelled. "Now move!"

"It's not much farther to the road," she gasped.

And let's hope they don't follow us onto it, Gabe finished in his head. The whispers had stopped, replaced by thudding footsteps. Lots of them. He tried to run faster, but the hot chocolate sloshed about like a tempest in his stomach and the muffins weighed him down heavily as lead. If he was hurting, then Kris was likely ready to puke. He'd eaten more than any of them, and he was carrying Kimber. As though reading his mind, Kris stumbled and fell. Kimber rolled off him, landing in a heap beside him and both lay still on the ground.

Jer spun back around and ran to Kimber. He pulled her to her feet while Gabe helped Kris up. The sound of footsteps grew to a roar and Gabe grabbed Kimber around the waist and threw her over his shoulder. "Move, move, move! Don't stop for anything!" He took off down the trail after them, his breath coming in short, quick gasps as his shoes slapped against the ground. Kimber might be small, but she wasn't exactly light, and her hipbone was digging into his shoulder like a knife.

"We're...almost...there," Abazi's voice drifted back to him.

Up ahead, the way grew brighter, a literal light at the end of the tunnel. Gabe focused on that light and nothing else. A hand touched his back and he nearly screamed. He willed his arm to transform into a whipping branch, but nothing happened. His arm remained an arm, refusing to change. He gritted his teeth and wished for the spikes to appear...just for a moment, so that he could at least frighten his pursuer. But again, not so much as a pimple popped up. What the heck was going on now?

"Keep moving!" Kris panted in his ear and Gabe relaxed in relief. It wasn't a Ko-gok, just Kris. He had somehow ended up behind Gabe and was pushing him forward. "Just a little ways to go."

The footsteps sounded so close it felt like they were in his head, pounding on his brain. The whispers picked up again, dizzying him as they swirled around and around him. He was going to pass out. Kris pushed him harder. "Almost there, almost there," he chanted.

And then they were out of the woods and on the main road. The footsteps and whispers stopped, but Gabe did not. He kept running, panting and nearly gagging, but still moving forward.

After another five minutes, Abazi slowed, then stopped. She turned around, catching them in the beam of her flashlight. "I think they're gone," she wheezed, then bent in half as she tried to catch her breath.

Gabe slowly lowered Kimber to the ground.

"Are...you...all...right?" he pushed out.

She nodded, her face pale. "Are you?"

"I'm fine. They were so close."

Abazi straightened up. "So what did you see exactly?" Her tone sounded suspicious.

"I didn't see anything. I just heard them."

"What did you hear, then?"

"Whispers at first, then footsteps."

"Really? Cause I didn't hear a thing."

He stared at her in disbelief. "But they were so loud. How could you *not* hear them?"

"I didn't hear anything, either," Kris said.

Jer shook his head. "Me, either."

Kimber looked at him, her eyes sympathetic. "I only heard us, Gabe. Are you sure it wasn't your imagination? I mean, it would make sense," she hurried to reassure him. "Things haven't exactly been friendly toward you in the woods. You're on high alert. One unusual sound and your mind would automatically turn it into something more. It's a survival technique."

"That was *not* my imagination."

"You know, you said you saw Oswald at the gathering when I didn't see a thing," Abazi went on. "Your eyes were probably playing tricks on you."

"But he was there! He talked to me!"

"Oswald showed up and you didn't tell us?" Kris was obviously not happy about that.

"You were watching the dance," Gabe replied. "I was going to tell you at the mill, when we had some time."

"What did he want?" Jer asked.

"I don't know. I think he just wanted to show me he's still in charge. But I pointed out to him that I'm allowed in the forest now because he didn't hold up his end of the bargain." He paused for a second. "That's it! What I heard was him and his band chasing us. They did this to keep me out!"

Abazi looked skeptical. "I still don't see why you're the only one seeing and hearing these things."

He could only shrug helplessly. "I don't know why, either. Maybe Dryads can do something so only other Dryads can see them."

She regarded him warily. "I don't understand what's going on, but we still need to get to the mill." She turned and walked away and the others followed her. She was acting like the topic was closed, dealt with. But he knew it wasn't.

Exhausted from running, they walked the rest of the way, passing the only stoplight in town. But instead of taking a right and heading downtown, they kept walking. The rare time a car approached, its headlights bright in the darkness that still surrounded them, they slipped into the ditch and let it pass.

Finally they turned down the long gravel road that led to the mill. On one side, a rotting sign loomed before them.

Wolka Paper Mill
The Way to a Better Future
Est. 1843

Abazi flashed her light on the orange sign next to it.

Trespassers Will Be
~~Prosecuted~~
Shot

Well, Gabe thought, *that's a good sign.* He snickered, half-hysterically.

"Ignore it," Abazi told them. "Everyone else does. Besides, Jake Morrigan was the one who crossed out 'Prosecuted' and wrote 'Shot.' So it's not like we're going to actually get shot."

"Great," Gabe muttered. "I'll tell that to the doctor when he's picking buckshot out of my butt."

"Don't be such a sissy," she snipped. "Now come on. The sun's up in about forty minutes. I want to be out of here before it rises." She marched down the gravel drive.

Gabe didn't answer, just tightened his grip on his staff and followed after the rest of the group. For being abandoned, the road to the mill was fairly well-kept. There weren't many trees here and most of them had the bad fortune of being covered by bittersweet vines. Their relative absence was a welcome relief. No trees meant no place for Kogoks or vengeful fairies to hide. The closer they grew to the mill, the fewer trees popped up, until at last there were none, just a vast expanse of salt marshes and mud flats.

As they neared the river's bank, the not unpleasant smell of rotting vegetation and brine hit Gabe. Abazi's flashlight caught glimpses of the black water flowing fast and furious past them and Gabe found himself nearly hypnotized watching it. "Why isn't the road on the other side?" he asked when Abazi stopped at the foot of the rust-pitted bridge. Strangely, the mill had been built on the far side of the river, meaning they would have to cross a bridge to get to it. It didn't seem very convenient.

"To cut down on the attacks," she answered shortly.

"Attacks?" Kris echoed. "Who was doing that? And why?"

"Nobody ever found out. For a while people blamed the Indians. Of course. One night, the mill owners had their goons round up the entire local tribe and place them under guard. But then it happened again, worse than ever. So the owners built a new road and let the old one return to its natural state." She pointed at the mud flats, which Gabe knew from Grandpa Hawthorne could be treacherous. Like quicksand, anyone attempting to walk on a mud flat risked getting swallowed up forever. "This bridge is the only way to get to the mill."

"But how's the bridge going to stop them?" Gabe asked. "They could just cross it."

She pointed. "It's a drawbridge. At night, it was raised so nobody could get through."

"Don't you see?" Jer cried, snapping his fingers. "It had to be the Dryads. If they destroyed the mill, the woodcutters would eventually stop killing their kind."

"My people call the mill Passagassawakeag," Abazi said, "which means the place of ghosts."

"This place does remind me of a graveyard." Kimber shivered a little.

Gabe shivered too in the cool breeze that whipped off the river. "I remember Dorn talking about getting banished to the 'Other Side.' Could this be it?"

"Hmm… No trees, place of death, and cut off from everything," Kris counted off on his fingers. "I'd say it would work as an effective place of banishment."

Gabe relaxed suddenly. "If the Ko-goks avoid this place, then we have nothing to be afraid of. Come on," he motioned. "Let's do this."

The group's mood lightened as they raced across the bridge, their footsteps echoing hollowly. The river rushed beneath them, but Gabe ignored its whispers, calling him closer, urging him to join it on its journey to the ocean. He was here to do a job and nothing was going to distract him from doing it. At last they were going to solve the riddles. And then he'd be done. He had to be done. The riddles had to be the answer to all his problems. He was counting on them.

On the other side of the river, they left the bridge and raced toward the mill. The massive building rose up before them and Gabe's steps slowed. He might not have to worry about Ko-goks here, but this place still gave him the creeps. He remembered when he'd first seen it from the safe distance of downtown, probably a mile or two away. Even from that distance, he'd felt there was something wrong with this place.

"Do you know how to get in?" he asked Abazi. Despite being so late in the year, thick ivy still covered the red bricks and windows. Soon enough the green would turn to brown and the plant would sink into sleep, but right now, the leaves acted as a barrier, covering everything as effectively as a sheet.

"Around this way." She pointed to her left. They followed after her as she slipped around a corner of the building. "Watch out for stuff on the ground," she called out, too late for Gabe, who stubbed his toe on a brick hidden in a tuft of grass.

Another twenty feet and she stopped outside what looked like a side door, a back entrance into the building. Her waving flashlight caught the rusty handle of a blue metal door covered in dents, scratches, and graffiti. "The lock's broken and no one has ever come out and fixed it."

Kris accidentally kicked an empty beer can and they all jumped as it clattered across the cracked cement. "Party central, huh?" He laughed.

"Only when they're idiots, and totally wasted, too," Abazi told him. "Nobody smart and/or sober enough comes here if they can help it."

"Well, now we can tell people that we did it and we weren't drunk," Kris bragged.

"No, we're just idiots," Gabe joked.

"Right." Abazi reached for the handle. "Well, here goes." The door squealed as it opened, letting loose the smell of damp and misery. "You should probably get your flashlights out."

As she held the door, they fished them out and flicked them on. Gripping the cool metal cylinder in one hand and his staff in the other, Gabe entered what felt like a monster's gaping mouth. The floor was strewn with torn, yellowed papers, cracked acorns, and slivers of glass—everything broken to bits as though caught in mid-chew. All the machinery was gone and only vast open spaces remained. There was an eerie feel to the place, as though it were haunted. It was likely that more than a few mill workers had died while working here. Factories held a bad reputation for dangerous work, especially ones back in the old days before OSHA came along to enforce safe working standards.

"Where do we start?" Jer whispered. He, too, sensed the need to stay quiet, to not disturb anything for fear of what it might provoke.

It was a good question. Gabe thought about the riddle. It said to check under the surface, within the wood walls. But where? Which walls? There were too many of them; there had to be something more, something a little more leading. He concentrated for a moment and the rest of the words came back to him. *Listen to the tinkling...* Well, the only thing that would tinkle around here was water falling off the waterwheel. Nothing else in this dreary place could make such a light-hearted sound. And the wheel was high up, the top of it anyway.

"It has to be the waterwheel," he said aloud. "It's all I can think of."

Kris twirled his staff. "Sounds good to me. Let's do it."

"I'll lead the way," Kimber volunteered.

Abazi motioned her forward. "Go ahead. I don't remember much from our last visit, nor do I especially want to. A group of us came out here on a dare a few years back," she explained. "I swore to myself that I wouldn't ever come back, and yet, here I am." She didn't sound happy about it.

Kimber started off and Jer followed after her. The only sounds were the crunching of debris underfoot and the river outside, its roar drifting in through broken windows high up near the ceiling. Once in a while Gabe thought he heard voices, but this time he was sure it was his imagination. Anyone who might be sneaking up on them wouldn't talk so openly. The only other option was ghosts and he wasn't quite sure he believed in ghosts. Though, at one time, he hadn't believed in fairies or tree spirits, so he kept his ears and eyes open.

As they picked their way across the cavernous room, he wondered if the Dryads really had attacked the mill at one time. It was disturbing to think about…that this place had served as a morgue for all those dead trees. "You drop 'em, we chop 'em." But did the Dryad die with the tree? Couldn't it separate itself, maybe turn into a spirit and run away before was too late? He thought it should be possible, especially back when there wasn't this plague that seemed to be weakening the tree spirits. Then he remembered what Dame Hazel had said, when he'd first learned they were Dryads. She'd told him that tree spirits couldn't survive without their shells, their homes. So the answer was no. Without the tree, Dryads would die. Gabe wasn't sure he liked that.

"Over here," Kimber interrupted his thoughts. She motioned to them, then disappeared through a doorway. He followed after her, stepping into a room where a mass of gears and levers connected to a huge iron spoke, upon which the wheel rotated. In one corner, a pile of old tools and a sledgehammer sat rusting and forgotten. The smell of damp and rust and algae was almost overwhelming, though Gabe rather liked it. It reminded him of Grandpa Hawthorne's boat. Kris and Jer were already inside, eagerly exploring.

"That door must lead outside to the waterwheel." Abazi pointed her flashlight at a small, rust-stained black door. "That's how they did repairs and cleaned the rungs. The wheel is locked right now, which is why it doesn't turn."

Gabe had been wondering about that. He supposed it had to be done for liability purposes, but the pressure from the water all those years must likely be doing some major damage to the wheel itself. Still, from this position, things looked pretty sturdy. "Let's go check it out. I'll go first, make sure it's safe. No sense all of us falling in."

Abazi turned the handle easily. Apparently they locked the wheel, but not the door that led to it. Seemed kind of dumb to him. "Have fun," she said.

He stepped outside into the cold, fresh air. In the short time they'd been inside, the sky had grown lighter and he could see enough to make his way onto a mesh platform. It groaned when he stepped on it and he looked down, suddenly dizzy. The mesh's see-through effect highlighted the water rushing under his feet. He looked up and inhaled deeply. He needed to relax and concentrate or he'd end up in the river.

He flashed his light upward. The waterwheel, attached to the spoke that drilled through the wall like a giant bolt, stood about ten feet out from the wall and seemed as big as a Ferris wheel. It made Gabe feel small…and nervous. What would happen if it suddenly started to turn? He shook off that thought and looked around for a place to search 'within the wood walls.'

Unfortunately, the wall of the mill didn't look promising. While having been exposed to water for over a century, it appeared to be surprisingly solid, plus the building rose up from a rock and cement base, which was obviously impenetrable. From this perspective, nothing stood out that said, "This is the place!"

He poked his head back inside. "It seems pretty sturdy, but we should only have a couple people at a time out here. Maybe someone else can see something I can't."

"I'll come out," Jer and Kris both volunteered at the same time and were already halfway out before Gabe could change his mind. He managed to step back and let them through before they knocked him over the railing.

"Don't trust anything," he told them. "We don't know how sturdy anything is out here. The place is falling apart."

"Yep, sure," Kris mumbled, staring up at the giant wheel, and Jer responded, "Uh, huh," in a vague tone.

Gabe sighed. "I'm serious, guys."

Kris poked the wheel. "I wonder if we could climb it."

"We're not going to climb it! I promised Mom I'd keep an eye on you. If anyone dies she's going to kill me." Then he remembered the part of the poem that said something about looking high from the sky, so perhaps someone *was* going to have to climb the wheel, even though a number of its lower planks were missing. Maybe he could just use his tree powers to pull himself up…if they were working again.

Jer joined Kris. "It'd be more fun if it were running."

Gabe had to admit the idea was intriguing, but only to himself. "We're looking for the clue, remember?"

"Yeah, yeah," Kris replied. "I'm on it."

"Find anything?" Abazi called from the doorway.

"Nothing. There's too much wall and…" Gabe stopped. "There's no tinkling."

"What?"

"This can't be the place. The waterwheel hasn't been running for decades, which means no tinkling sound and no going round and round. And even if we could climb the waterwheel to search the wall, we wouldn't be able to actually reach the wall—it's too far away."

"So you're saying we've been on a wild goose chase?" Abazi demanded.

"It would seem that way. I mean, it made sense before, but now that I'm here, I just don't see how it will work." Gabe paused, feeling strange. "I don't like this. Maybe someone wrote those poems to set us up. But why send us way out here to the mill? It's like they wanted to get us out of the way—" His blood froze. The three riddles all had one thing in common—they'd all lured them away from the farmhouse, away from unsuspecting victims…Mom, Dad, Grandma May.

But who was doing it? And who were they going after? "We've got to get back," he breathed, feeling sick. But where should they head—to their house or to Grandma May's? Who was in danger this time?

An image of Grandma May filled his mind. The perspiration on her forehead, despite her claims of being all right. Her unusually rude behavior. Something wasn't right with her. She'd always been brusque and honest to the point of painful, but never mean. He should have caught that right away! Feeling sorry for himself, he'd missed all the signs that she was in trouble and now she could be in grave danger because of his stupidity.

"Grandma May's in trouble," he said aloud, his voice trembling. "We have to go right now. Before it's too late."

Chapter Twenty-Five

Finding the Key

Strangely, no one asked Gabe any questions about why he thought Grandma May was in trouble. They simply followed him as he led the way out of the empty, echoing factory and across the river. Kris, with Kimber on his back, was lagging behind. It didn't help that he'd stopped briefly to fiddle with something on the bridge.

"Hurry up, Kris!" Gabe yelled, fervently hoping that they'd be in time to save Grandma May. Faeth had been right about him knowing more than he realized. The knowledge had been there in his head, but he hadn't been able to put it together fast enough. The other part—that he was clever—was a joke. It had taken him far too long to figure out that the riddles were tricks. Like a lot of mothers, Faeth expected far more from him than he had to give.

The sun was rising up over the ocean as they raced down the highway, but its muted light, blocked by a thickening cloud cover, gave Gabe no comfort. His worry at the moment was not the Ko-goks, but reaching his grandmother in time.

He stopped running, and a few seconds later, Kris and Kimber caught up with them. "We have to stay on the road," Gabe said through gasps, each breath creating a white puff in the chill air. "It might be faster to go through the woods, but I don't trust them. I don't really trust the road, either, but it will give us more room to maneuver. Even though it's daytime and the Ko-goks will be less likely to brave the sun, I think they're getting desperate. Straif might force his minions to attack, even though they could be seen or get caught in the sun."

"It's getting cloudier, too." Jer pointed at the sky. "So that will make them braver."

"What's going on, Gabe?" Abazi demanded, no longer able to just follow along without asking questions. He was surprised she'd made it this far. "I can sense things, too, remember, and I didn't hear anything in the woods, and I didn't see Oswald last night. So why are you getting so freaked out?"

He shook his head, feeling increasingly frustrated. "I don't know, Abazi. What happened in the woods earlier was different than what I've experienced before. And when I thought about trying to transform, just my arm to help fight off the attackers, nothing happened. I haven't even gotten any spikes lately, either." As soon as he said the word spikes, he realized he hadn't told the others about them coming and going as they pleased. Hopefully they wouldn't pick up on his slip.

"Something's definitely up," Jer said. "Maybe something's blocking your powers in one way and increasing them in others? But why?"

Kris shifted Kimber to his left. "We don't have time to figure that out right now. I want to know why you think Grandma May's in danger. If we're going into battle, I want to be prepared."

"I think the riddles were meant to get us out of the way," Gabe explained, "so whoever is writing them can do something. Remember how I said she looked scared? That she was being so mean to me? Well I have this bad feeling she was trying to tell me something, but couldn't, because whoever is doing this was close by."

"But why would she tell you to solve those riddles?" Abazi pushed.

"Because he made her."

"Who's *he*?" Kimber wondered. "Or *she*?"

"That's the million dollar question," Kris answered. "Come on, we need to keep moving."

Gabe nodded, though he didn't like the suspicious looks Abazi kept giving him, like she didn't trust him. But there wasn't time to reassure her, or argue with her, or whatever it was she wanted him to do.

Despite the looks, she didn't say a word, simply joined the group as they jogged down the road. But Gabe noticed she stayed as far away from him as she could. There wasn't much he could do about the way she felt, and that made him want to yell and stomp his foot like a thwarted child.

Just beyond the stoplight, a brown car passed them going the same direction, and the four people inside, even the driver, turned to look at them as they drove by. The car swerved a bit before the driver straightened out the wheel and the car accelerated, roaring off.

"That's Mrs. Deacon's car!" Abazi shouted. "They're heading toward your grandma's house."

"They've found out, haven't they?" Gabe increased his speed. "They know the house isn't hers, and they're going to kick her out."

"What if she starts shooting?" Jer's voice was small. "She's got that shotgun."

Gabe screeched to a halt, then bent over to catch his breath. "Jer's got a point. We're going to have to split up. Jer, Abazi, and Kimber, stay on the road and head toward Grandma's. Kris and I are going through the woods. It's our only chance to catch them before they try to evict her, or before she turns them into Swiss cheese." Kris grinned at the idea, but no one joined him. He shrugged and lowered Kimber to the ground, solemnly taking the staff she held out to him.

"Just don't get yourselves shot," Abazi warned, looking at Kris. Gabe felt his heart sink. She was really mad at him, wasn't she? She probably thought he was lying, or something insane like that. "Now move it, you two. We'll meet you there."

Gabe didn't like separating the group, but Jer and Abazi were good fighters. And Kimber, if she wasn't pushed to run, could hold her own. He'd dueled her a couple times over the summer and found her upper body strength surprising. He just hoped she could surprise the Ko-goks.

He and Kris entered the woods at full speed, likely thinking the same thing—that if they ran fast enough, the Ko-goks wouldn't be able to catch them. The forest was silent all around them, which made Gabe nervous. He picked up his pace, and Kris did, too.

A strange birdcall sounded to his left. Then another, to his right. "Did you hear that?"

Kris shrugged. "I only hear us."

"It sounded like birds, but not the kind that would live around here."

"Maybe you're imagining things again."

Gabe's lips pressed tightly together. What was going on? He didn't think he'd *ever* be asking this, but where were his thorns? How come he couldn't turn into a tree anymore? And why was he seeing and hearing things no one else could? Had Wildrr placed some kind of spell on him?

The more he thought about the spell theory, the more it made sense. Gabe decided that if he saw the little turd, he would give him a knuckle sandwich, hand-delivered with a smile. He was so small the punch would likely knock him to the moon.

Gabe felt a huge wave of relief when they burst out of the woods and onto Grandma May's driveway. They dashed down it, immediately spotting the brown caddy parked outside her door. His relief withered away. He'd been right. Those two interfering biddies were up to something.

Kris passed his staff from hand to hand as he ran. "It's time to kick some butt."

Without bothering to knock, they pushed open the unlatched door and headed straight for the living room. The tableau that greeted them was strangely innocent compared to what they'd been expecting—something along the lines of spattered blood on the floor and broken chairs and bullet holes in the walls. Instead, Grandma May held a tray with coffee mugs and a pot of coffee and was about to set it down on the coffee table. Ronald Pruspin, the newspaper reporter, sat primly in a high-backed chair, his hands folded over the knee of his crossed legs. He was a small man, with slicked back, sandy-colored hair, and a thin mustache. He wore a preppy pink shirt, collar turned up 80's style, under a black blazer. Light brown eyes blinked suspiciously at them from behind black-framed designer glasses, which he no likely wore to appear smarter than he actually was.

Opposite him sat the surveyor with the curly brown hair—Jack. He eyed them warily, and a bit sleepily—it was very early for a social call—but otherwise seemed unthreatening. Candi Morrigan and Cornelia Deacon shared the small couch. They all turned to stare at the brothers, their expressions obviously displeased at the interruption, but there was no murderous intent in their eyes.

Gabe's cheeks heated up. Only Grandma May looked welcoming...kind of.

"Did you figure out the riddles?" she asked hopefully.

"Yes!" Gabe answered, feeling he'd finally gotten something right. "That's why we're here."

She looked hugely relieved. "Finally! Well, hand it over." She set the tray on the coffee table and held out her hand.

"Hand what over?"

Her eyes narrowed. "The papers."

Mrs. Morrigan laughed. "Didn't you know, Eleanor? The papers are gone. Someone stole them."

"We know that," Kris snorted, his gaze fixing on Ronald Pruspin. Ronald looked away, his close-set eyes fluttering guiltily.

"I need those papers, Gabe," Grandma May said through clenched teeth. "I need them now."

"But I don't where they are. They're probably ashes by now."

"The riddles," she hissed. "You said you figured them out."

"I did... They're distracters, Grandma. Someone was trying to keep us away from you so these vultures could make their move. But we figured it out just in time, and here we are."

"The riddles are not a distracter," she groaned. "You need to figure them out so I can—" she broke off. "Oh, just please figure them out!"

"Look here," Mrs. Deacon spoke up. "What are these riddles you're talking about? Sounds like some sort of game. I don't like games."

"It's not a game," Grandma May ground out, her eyes focusing on Gabe. "Mrs. Morrigan is about to call the Chief of Police and tell him to come arrest me for trespassing. That's if she can wake him up."

"Very funny," Mrs. Morrigan drawled. "But what's more funny is what you can get done when your husband is a lawyer and your brother runs the police force."

"You're saying more than you need to, Candace," Mrs. Deacon warned.

"Oh, Aggie. They're just kids. What are they going to do to us?"

"Just make the call," Ronald urged, looking more and more uncomfortable. "I have other things to do than to sit around this dump talking to children. I've got deadlines." He stretched and yawned. More likely he just wanted to go back to bed.

Kris banged his staff on the floor. "Who you calling a child, rat?"

Ronald pulled back, offended. "Did you just call me a rat?"

"Yes, I did. Because I'm pretty sure you're the one who stole the papers."

Ronald didn't answer, but his reddening cheeks were answer enough.

"That's it!" Mrs. Morrigan shouted, standing up. "I'm making the call. Progress is being held up as we speak. I plan to put Ranger on the map, and the sooner, the better. If we move fast, we can get those woods cleared by spring and the condos started soon after. Early to bed, early to rise," she trilled, "makes me healthy, *wealthy*, and wise!"

Gabe felt sick. Condos? Here? Just the idea of it was horrid. Even worse was the thought of all those trees, that weren't just trees, being destroyed. Even though Dame Hazel scared him a little and he wasn't sure he could trust her, he didn't want her to die. Heck, he'd even hate to see Oswald reduced to a pile of planks. Of course, he might not feel upset about Oswald right away, but the melancholy would surely begin sometime soon after, like when Oswald was a dresser or a bookshelf.

"You can't let them do that, Gabe," Grandma May hissed. "Figure out those riddles, or we'll all be ruined!"

But Candi already had her cell phone out. It was, of course, pink. She frowned, banged it against the palm of her hand, then put it back to her ear. "No reception! I hate these woods. I swear they fight me at every turn. I'm going to try it out on the road." She turned to Jack. "Come out with me, Turner."

He nodded, obviously relieved to be leaving the tense scene, and followed her out the door like a puppy dog. Gabe looked at Grandma May. "I'm really sorry I failed you, Grandma. I thought I'd figured it out, that it was all a trick."

"It isn't too late!" she cried. "Now go. Use that brain of yours!"

"Come on." Kris grabbed his arm and pulled him outside. "We'll work on it together."

As they stumbled down the steps they heard, "Pssst!" from around the side of the house. Jer, Kimber, and Abazi poked their heads out and Gabe and Kris ran to meet them.

"I was wrong," Gabe told them, feeling stupid. "The riddles aren't a distracter, they're the real deal. And Mrs. Morrigan is calling the cops as we speak to come arrest Grandma for trespassing."

"What aren't we getting?" Kris wondered aloud.

"Give me the riddles," Jer demanded, holding out his hand.

Gabe reached in his pocket and handed them over. Jer and Kimber bent over them, taking turns reading them out loud.

Follow the trail
You'll find the key
Go round and round
And then you'll see…
it.

~~~~

The answer is up
But your eyes are blind
Look high from the sky
And then you will find…
it.

~~~~

Check under the surface
Within the wood walls
Listen to the tinkling
You'll hear its calls…

"We have to look at the words," Jer said after a minute's silence. Obsessed with becoming a spy, he'd spent a stretch as a kid working on breaking codes. "What other meanings they might have. Like the word key."

"There's a key for a door," Kimber said. "That one's easy."

"And a key for a map," Abazi added.

"Pianos have keys," Kris said absently while swinging his staff left and right as though fighting an invisible enemy.

Jer's blue eyes grew excited. "And pianos tinkle!"

"We have a piano," Gabe said slowly, his heart thumping. "And there's a picture above it. I remember looking at it. It shows the forest and the spiral going—"

"Round and round!" Abazi yelped excitedly. "That has to be it."

"Check under the surface and within the wood walls…" Gabe put in nervously. "Are you saying we have to take down a wall?"

"I'll do it!" Kris volunteered.

"Mom will kill us," Gabe moaned.

"Grandma May will kill us if we don't figure this out," Jer reminded him.

Gabe heaved a sigh. "I suppose you're right. Damned if we do, damned if we don't."

"Well, what are we waiting for?" Abazi cried. "Mr. Gabeachev, let's take down that wall!"

"Hold on. I think I heard someone following us when we were cutting through the woods. We should stick to the road and the driveway. We can't take any chances."

Abazi turned to Kris. "Did you hear anything?"

Kris glanced at Gabe. "Oh, sure. All sorts of things."

Her eyes narrowed suspiciously. "I think—"

"I think Gabe is right," Kimber interrupted, stepping forward. "We can't take any chances. Not now. Not with Chief Mara coming to arrest Mrs. May. You know how he is, Abazi. He's been waiting to get back at her ever since she told him to his face that a monkey could do his job, and better."

Abazi rolled her eyes, then gave a grudging sigh. "I suppose you're right, Kimber. But something weird is going on, I'll tell you that."

Gabe totally agreed with her, but he wasn't going to say a word. "Come on," he urged Kimber as he knelt down. "I'll be your chariot this time." She climbed onto his back, and once she was secure, he started running. He wanted to get moving before Abazi could change her mind and start asking questions.

For once, he heard nothing as they ran down the driveway to their house. No strange noises or bird calls. No rustling in the bushes. No ghostly footsteps. Their absence, rather than comforting Gabe, made him feel more nervous than ever, as though their enemy had hunkered down to wait for just the right moment to attack.

In the yard, Gabe noticed that the truck was gone and he hurried into the house, feeling both worried and grateful. A note on the table explained that Mom and Dad had driven to Payton, a tiny town about half an hour away, to pick up a cheap computer that they'd found on Craig's List—Dad missed having his own—they'd sold his fancy one to help pay for the trip out to Maine. Afterwards, they were meeting some old friends for lunch and wouldn't be back until mid-afternoon. It seemed somehow too convenient that they would decide to leave now, but Gabe was determined to look at it as a blessing in disguise. It would be much easier breaking down that wall without Mom trying to stop them with her body.

After Gabe read the note aloud, Jer motioned to them, "It's this way," and they followed him to the parlor. Gathering around the piano, they stared at the aerial photograph hanging on the wall. It looked just as he remembered it—an overhead shot of the woods, then the spiral. When his eyes settled on the clearing, he remembered poor Isis and her horrible demise. His resolve to figure things out deepened. He would not let Straif win, nor Mrs. Morrigan or Mrs. Deacon. And especially not that weasel, Ronald Pruspin.

Kris, never one to hesitate, put his shoulder to the upright piano and began to push. When he'd moved it most of the way out from under the photo, he stopped to rest. "Someone fetch the pick-ax. It's out in the barn." He threw back his hand to indicate the way and as he did, his long fingers caught the edge of the photo. There was a snap, and Gabe watched in horror as the picture smashed on the floor, spreading glass everywhere.

"Kris, you idiot!"

"Don't yell at me! You're always breaking things."

It was true, so Gabe decided he'd better move on, and quick. He squatted down and gently picked up the photo, still in its frame, careful not to cut himself on the jagged pieces of glass. "The photo's still okay. No scratches on it." He turned it over. "I think if we just replace the glass and the rope used to hang it, it will be good as new."

"Hopefully Mom won't notice it's gone," Jer said worriedly.

"Mom notices everything," Kris replied glumly. "She should be a spy."

"We'll just say we were goofing around and it fell. If we offer to fix it and pay for everything, she won't get mad."

"She won't get *as* mad," Jer clarified. He held out his hand. "Let me look at it." He examined it carefully. "I can take the glass out, tie the string together, and rehang it. She might not notice the glass is missing before we can replace it." He carefully removed the glass from the frame and picked up the pieces on the floor. "There. I'll just dump this in the recycling."

When he was gone, Gabe picked up the photo and stared at it forlornly. Why couldn't just one thing go right for them? Oh, what did it matter? Mom wasn't going to notice the damaged photo because behind it would be a gaping hole. Though maybe the piano would cover it up until they could get Grandpa to help them fix it. He might aid them in covering up their crime if it was for a good cause.

He stood up and cracked his elbow against the piano, jarring the photo loose. The frame hit the floor, bounced, and separated from its backing. Then the whole thing seemed to fall apart as a packet of papers skidded across the floor.

Holy crap. Kris was right. He *did* always break things. He even broke broken things! He bent down to pick up the papers, his cheeks red. "I made it worse!"

Kimber squatted down to help. She picked up the aerial picture and examined it carefully. "No, you didn't, Gabe. The photo looks fine. We just have to tuck it back in the frame."

He grabbed a handful of papers. "What are these?"

Abazi plucked them from his hand, and as she scanned the pages, a slow smile lit up her face. "You did it, Kris!" She grinned at him and he returned it, though his grin looked slightly baffled.

"Did what?"

"You solved the riddles! These are the papers your grandma wants. It's a deed to the land her house is sitting on, one acre, and..." She shuffled through a few more papers, her eyes bright. "*And* a deed to the house!"

"A deed to the house and an acre of land?" Gabe repeated dumbly. "But whose name is it in?"

She kneeled down and gathered up the papers on the floor. She handed a wad to Gabe. "Look through them," she ordered. After a few seconds, with only the sound of whiffing paper, she spoke into the expectant silence. "I've found it. His name is...holy crap."

"Whose name is Holy Crap?" Jer demanded, returning to the room. "Cause that is awesome."

"No, no." She laughed. "The guy who owns the woods and your grandma's house is none other than Bruce Holt."

"Bruce Holt? Who's that?" Kris asked. "Sounds like some kind of movie star."

"He went missing about twenty years ago. He was a bit of a recluse and very rich."

Jer snapped his fingers. "Mom and Dad talked about him. Didn't he have a heart condition?"

She nodded. "I'm sure he's long dead. If the cold didn't get him, Straif would have."

"So what are his deeds doing in our house?" Gabe looked at the sheaf of yellowed papers in his hands. "These look pretty old. He must have stashed them here before he disappeared. But why?"

Abazi shook her head. "You got me. A better question is, what good will they do your grandma?"

Kris picked up one remaining piece of paper. "Maybe because her name is on the deed?"

Gabe snatched the paper. "I hereby will this house and accompanying one acre of property to Eleanor May of Ranger, Maine." It was signed, witnessed, and sealed.

"My grandma owns the house," he breathed.

"Let me see that!" Abazi plucked the paper from his limp fingers. "I don't know any of these people, not the lawyer or the witnesses," she said after reading through it. "I'll bet this took place in Portland." She turned to look at the others. "Which leaves only one person who could possibly know about this."

Jer's eyes widened. "Bruce Holt. He's still alive!"

Chapter Twenty-Six

Smells Like Snow

Abazi looked around at everyone. "If Bruce Holt didn't die from his heart condition or from the elements *or* Straif, then where's he been all this time?"

"He could've been living in Grandma May's cottage," Gabe suggested. "Though that's kind of a weird thing to do, don't you think?"

"Exactly. If he's still alive, why hide from everyone? That's taking the recluse thing a bit too far. Not to mention the fact that the old dog and your grandma would've been living together when she moved into the cottage this spring." Abazi grinned. "Your granny doesn't waste any time."

"But if he lived with Grandma May," Jer said, "then why didn't he just tell her where the deeds were hidden? Why the subterfuge?"

It was a good point, and Gabe felt more confused than before they found the deeds. "I have no idea. It probably wasn't him, then."

"I agree," Abazi said. "There's no way he could have survived. I think my dad said he'd suffered a couple of heart attacks before he disappeared." She frowned. "Which means we still don't know who did it."

"We'll figure that out later," Gabe determined. "We have to get these deeds to Grandma May before Chief Mara comes to arrest her." He started sorting the papers. "Jer, would you fetch a plastic baggie? The gallon size." When Jer returned with one, Gabe slid the stack of papers inside, sealed the bag shut, and slipped it into his jacket's inside pocket. "All right, that's done. Does everyone have their weapons ready?" Heads nodded all around him. "Good. Cause we're going to have to go through the woods. There's no time to waste."

The gang jumped to their feet and headed outside, marching like an army on a mission. Despite the rising sun the sky had grown darker.

Kris sniffed the air. "It smells different."

They all looked up at the sky. "Smells like snow," Abazi confirmed.

"Snow!" the three boys echoed. "Yes!"

She shook her head. "It might sound exciting, but it's really bad timing. If we get a winter storm, we won't be able to fight the dark ones. Snow can get awful deep around here, and they can turn into trees and we can't. Well, Gabe can." She glanced over at him and he looked away. He wasn't so sure he could do that anymore. Something had happened to him, something had changed. He wasn't sure if he should be happy about it, or scared.

"Then we'd better get moving," Kris urged and took off down the driveway.

"Follow the path that cuts through the woods," Gabe shouted to him, and after a few yards Kris veered off into the trees. They followed him along a narrow path, overgrown with bittersweet and littered with broken tree branches. They had spotted it one day during the summer, but after exploring for a short time, had avoided it ever since. It wasn't like the Forest Immortal, and it wasn't like the safe woods by their house. It was a sort of no-man's land, neither here nor there. From its overgrown state they determined that no one ever took this way—not the Dryads, not the dark ones, not even Grandma May. She only rode her bike on the roads.

Halfway along the path, Kimber stumbled and fell. As Gabe stopped to help her up, he heard a riotous rush of noise, like what he imagined evil spirits would sound like. He straightened up and pulled Kimber to her feet, then noticed the others had stopped, their weapons drawn. He pulled out his bata and tightened his grip on his staff.

"Looks like we've got company," Kris whispered.

From behind the trees, splotches of black materialized, quickly forming into bodies and limbs. The dark ones had arrived.

"I've been bidin' me time," a voice came from behind Gabe and he spun around to see Straif standing a mere five feet away from him. He wore his typical dark cloak, but its hood was thrown back, revealing his awful, spiky head and the terrible black holes that represented his eyes and mouth. Red oozing patches dotted his skin. "Oh, yes. I've been waitin' for the right moment to get me revenge on ye, Gabriel. Don't like that it's here in Bittersweet territory, but here we are."

Bittersweet territory? Uh, oh. Gabe knew from his mom that bittersweet was a vine that, given free reign, slowly took over trees and eventually killed them. Great. Not only did he have to deal with homicidal vines that even the Ko-goks avoided, he had to face a furious and desperate looking Straif. The only good thing about this situation was that there was no sign of Faeth anywhere. The Ko-gok leader obviously didn't have her, or he'd be using her as bait.

"I never did anything to you, Straif. You caused your own problems."

"Oh, really? I'm still tryin' to recover from what ye did to me. I was burned awful bad, as ye can see." He pointed to the angry red splotches.

"You were burned because you were trying to kill me and my friends. That's your own fault!" Gabe's voice echoed around him, as though he were in a cave. The bittersweet growing overhead was so thick that the vines formed a ceiling. "And then you killed Isis the same way, by burning her."

"What are ye goin' on about, cretin?" Straif growled.

Suddenly Gabe knew what had happened. "You were torturing her, weren't you?"

"If I were, I'd have gone about it differently." He chuckled evilly. "Burnin's too quick."

"You're a jerk, Straif."

"That may as be, but it weren't me. Not this time."

"Then who?" Gabe glanced at Dorn and Feltry. Both were staring at him, but neither looked like they were gloating. So if none of the dark ones had done it, then who had? Wildrr? Filidh? Both were a good possibility. Perhaps in a moment of madness, even Faeth might have done it.

"Ye know the best way for a Dryad to heal?" Straif asked, moving easily on from the topic of Isis.

"Aloe vera?" Gabe suggested, hoping to stall. They had to be close to Grandma May's house by now. If he yelled while the police were arresting her, they might come to help.

"Yer blood."

Gabe gulped. "I'm afraid I don't have any to spare. I seem to need it to stay *alive*." He practically shouted the last word and it sounded like a shotgun blast in the waiting woods. A strange stirring came from the trees—a slithering sort of sound. Gabe glanced around, but could see nothing.

"Ye think ye're funny, don't ye? Ye think ye can just use fancy words and confuse me. What ye don't get is that I've seen it all, heard it all, been through it all. I know too much, and I won't be stopped by some git who thinks he's got me all figured out."

Gabe held up his hands, forgetting he was still holding his weapons. The dark ones closest to him stepped back. "You're right. It's a bad habit of *mine*." The word blared out of him, again sounding strangely like a gunshot. More slithering hissed through the woods.

Instead of responding to Gabe, Straif looked up, and his expression, never good, grew ominous. "Keep yer voice down," he warned. "Ye're wakin' them."

Abazi stepped up to Gabe's side. "What are you doing?" she whispered.

"Stalling." His eyes followed Straif's gaze and this time he spotted movement in the trees. The bittersweet vines were waking.

"You're just making him mad."

"He was mad *long* before I showed *up*."

"Ye need to stop yer shoutin'!" Straif roared. He stepped toward Gabe, and without thinking, Gabe swung his staff. The dark leader ducked, the staff just barely missing connecting with his hideous skull.

"*No!*" Gabe yelled. "I *won't* stop shouting!" This time the shotgun blast effect of his voice waited a few seconds before sounding off.

"Someone's shooting a gun!" Kris yelped excitedly, and Gabe realized that it hadn't been his voice making such a grand noise, but a real shotgun. Sometimes he wondered a little about his intelligence. "I think Grandma May is shooting at the police!"

Oh, crap. His own grandmother was ruining Gabe's plan. Two more blasts sounded and Straif looked around, his black hole eyes narrowed. "What are ye up to now, *Gabriel?*"

"We brought in reinforcements," he pushed out, trying not to look like he was bluffing, and likely failing miserably. "Don't you hear them coming? We thought there might be trouble from you. You were following us earlier, weren't you?"

"What are ye talkin' about? We've been searchin' for ye these many days and been led astray too many times to count. We've finally found ye and we're not lettin' ye go." He took a menacing step forward. "So stop tryin' to put me off with yer stupid delays. And the only thing I hear is the Bittersweet, lookin' for a meal."

Bittersweet *looking* for a meal?

Another shotgun blast rang out and Gabe knew it was now or never. "Immortal!" he hollered loudly, and at the same time, swung his staff in a wide arc. Immortal was their code word to run and the others took off toward Grandma's cottage. Gabe pulled Kimber up onto his back and dashed down the path swinging his staff from side to side. Kris, Jer, and Abazi, following the drill they'd planned out over the summer, cleared the way, shouting and swinging their weapons like Amazon warriors.

Fearing the touch of dead wood, all the dark ones backed off. Except Feltry. Next to Straif, Gabe feared him most of all. Feltry carried a wood chip on his shoulder the size of a car. He didn't like Gabe and he was also in competition with his older brother, Dorn, to bring Gabe in, to get Straif's weird approval, and to become the next King.

He stood directly in their path, neither flinching nor backing down—playing his own perilous game of chicken. Gabe knew exactly what was going to happen next and Feltry didn't fail him. In two blinks he had transformed into a tree. Where before he stood shorter than Gabe, he now loomed over him, his long black limbs covered with deadly thorns and cracking through the air like whips. Gabe slowly lowered Kimber to the ground. He felt, rather than saw, the dark ones move in to surround them.

"We're not giving up without a fight," he called out. All around him he could feel the vines of the bittersweet spreading their net. He tried not to think about them, hoped they were on his side, but the web was tightening. He wondered if any of the others had noticed them, as he and Straif had.

Feltry's face, strange and distorted within the trunk of the tree, seemed to grin. "I was hopin' ye'd say that."

"Change," Kris said. "Do your tree thing."

Gabe knew his changing over was their only hope, so he closed his eyes and concentrated. But nothing happened to him. When he opened his eyes, his hands were still hands; his feet had not turned into roots. He should be happy about that, but he was only frightened. He didn't want to kill anyone, but he also didn't want to be killed.

Maybe if he got mad that would help him change. Anger did seem to bring out his spikes. But he wasn't feeling angry, more like terrified.

"Do *something*, Abazi!" he shouted, hoping to provoke her.

"What do you want me to do, dipwad? Tackle him?"

"You're always going on about how talented you are. So show us what you've got!"

"And take the spotlight off you?" she spat back. "I know you love it too much."

"Screw you," Gabe ground out.

"What did you just say, half-wit?"

"I said, screw you and that high horse you rode in on."

But instead of getting angry and letting him have it, her eyes teared up. Gabe stared at her in horror. "I-I didn't mean that…"

he stuttered. "I need to get mad. I can't explain why, but I—" She didn't answer, only turned her back on him, effectively cutting him off.

If only Oswald were here, then Gabe could get really angry. For once, though, the annoying twit was nowhere to be found.

"What are you doing?" Kris hissed at him. "She's your friend."

Gabe was about to explain himself when a whooshing sound passed over his head. He looked up to see one of Feltry's branches flying by. "Now that I got yer attention, I'm ready to kill ye. I want to see the expression on yer ugly mug right before I take off yer head."

"Why can't I be the one to take him?" Dorn whined. Even though Dorn was the older of the two, his tree form was smaller and less intimidating than his brother's.

"Ye can't even kill a seedling," Feltry snarled. "So just stay of me way."

Gabe wasn't sure how Dorn managed it, but his tree mouth turned sulky. The two brothers couldn't seem to get along, and their behavior distracted each other and the whole group. Which was to Gabe's advantage. They might have a chance to get away, if only they kept up their bickering for another few seconds...

"Shut yer trap, ye two rotters, or I'll shut it for ye," Straif growled. "I'll not have ye ruinin' things for me *again*." Gabe's hopes plummeted. He hadn't heard a gunshot for a couple minutes now, which meant Grandma May had likely been arrested for trespassing *and* attempted murder, and the bittersweet had yet to make its move, hovering above them like a lion waiting for its prey to make a mistake.

Straif took two steps toward Gabe, looked up at Feltry, and nodded, like a king giving the signal...*off with his head!* On cue, Feltry began swinging his arms like an angry squid. Before Gabe could lift his staff to defend himself, one of Feltry's branches smacked him upside the head, sending him flying through the air, right into Kris.

"Two in one!" Feltry bellowed. Gabe's arms and legs were tangled with Kris's long limbs, and he could only watch helplessly as Dorn grabbed Kimber and Jer around the waist, lifting them high into the air.

Dorn's expression was triumphant. "She's mine now, and I'm keepin' her!" Kimber screamed as Dorn stuck his face in hers.

Come on, change! Gabe ordered himself, finally gaining his feet. *Turn into a tree!* But the change didn't come, not even a flicker of one. *What's going on with me? Have I been tricked? Was I never really a Dryad in the first place? Was it all an illusion, or some kind of magic from that drink Dame Hazel gave us?* There were no answers to his questions, and no time to pursue them.

Abazi charged Dorn. "Let her go!" She swung her staff at him, but Dorn whipped out a branch and caught hold of it, wrenching it from her grasp. Kimber screeched again, her face pale and her eyes wide.

"Leave her alone!" Jer screamed, struggling to free himself.

"Use your tomahawk," Gabe shouted. "Pound him with it!"

Struggling to breathe, Jer jerked his tomahawk from the strap on his back and began to pummel the limb holding him. Dorn shrieked and immediately dropped Jer, then started swinging his limbs even faster. "Stay back! I'm keepin' her!"

"Get out of me way!" Feltry roared. "We need Gabriel, not those two puny seedlings."

"I'm not puny!" Jer cried and threw his tomahawk at Feltry. The metal blade struck the wood with a satisfying whack and Feltry bellowed. Kris took the opportunity to attack, and within seconds, had climbed up Feltry's trunk and wrapped his arms around his face.

Jer ran in, grabbed his tomahawk, and retreated, then turned on Dorn. Pulling back his arm, he hurled the tomahawk with all his might. The blade drove into the branch holding Kimber and Dorn convulsed in pain, dropping her like a hot potato. Gabe ran forward to catch her and she landed in his arms, toppling him backwards.

Abazi pulled Kimber off Gabe, then helped him to his feet. "Get behind us," she told Kimber. "And stay low! We have to get out of here," she panted as she swung her willow whip in broad arcs. "Now, Gabe!" The dark ones were closing in on them. Feltry yanked Kris off his face and threw him to the ground. At the same time, Dorn swatted Jer into the air, where he landed at Gabe's feet.

"I know that!" Gabe replied as he pulled his winded brother to his feet. "But we're surrounded, and not just by dark ones." He pointed upward. Abazi's eyes followed his finger and seeing the bittersweet, thick and writhing, her face turned pale.

"Turn into a tree!"

"I can't, Abazi."

"Oh, get over yourself, Gabe! You're a Dryad. Just accept that it's who you are!"

"Says the Indian girl who doesn't want to be Indian," he growled. "I'm telling you, I can't. Not because I don't want to, but because I *can't change into a tree!*"

Suddenly there was silence and everyone stopped moving. The sound of laughter, low and cruel, filled the air. "Well don't that beat all. The King of the tree spirits can't turn himself into a tree."

Gabe slowly turned around. "I don't know what you're talking about."

Straif's thorns quivered and his red spots oozed puss. Gabe felt sick. Straif had heard him. He'd given himself away through sheer stupidity. "Ye know exactly what I'm talkin' about. Ye can't change."

"I-I was just making that up! I didn't really mean it."

"Is that so?" Straif cocked his head. "Then show us what ye can do. I've been waitin' to see ye unleash yerself again. So let's see it."

Gabe bit his lip. This was not going well. "I don't feel like it."

Straif chuckled. "No worry. Ye just showed me what I needed to see. That ye're a mere mortal and nothing more."

"Then why do you need to kill me? I'm not a threat to you anymore, and my blood won't do you any good, either." Gabe was grasping at straws here. Very flimsy straws.

Straif gave a horrible grin and smacked his lips. "Because I'm hungry and ye're meat." He waved his lackeys forward. "Grab him. Grab them all."

The dark ones advanced on them like starving hyenas and Gabe's insides turned ice cold. Beside him Kimber trembled and Jer put his arm around her. Gabe knew he had to do something to save them, but there was nothing left to do. He'd gotten his wish—he'd stopped the thorns—but now he couldn't turn into a tree anymore. And even though he didn't want to be a Dryad, being a tree ninja would come in handy right about now. The dark ones were advancing and the bittersweet was about to spring.

"Help!" he cried desperately. "Somebody help us!"

Straif's hand shot out and slapped him across the face. The dark leader's skin was cold and dry, and small thorns scratched Gabe's cheek. Straif stepped forward and his eyes fastened on the blood trickling down Gabe's jaw. "Ye do that again, and I'll eat ye right now, tear ye limb from limb while yer friends watch. First I'll suck out yer eyes, then eat yer tongue. And all the while, ye'll still be alive."

Gabe stared at his foe in horror. "Somebody help us!" Straif lifted his hand to strike again, but Gabe was ready for it. When Straif swung,

Gabe blocked his arm with the bata and the sound of something breaking hit his ears. "Immortal!" he shouted. *"Immortal!"*

Kris lowered his head and ran forward, knocking aside dark ones like a battering ram. Gabe gathered up Kimber and they slipped past the slowed down Feltry, still in his tree form. Behind them came a fearful roaring sound and the pounding of footsteps. And then came the slithering. The bittersweet was on the move. Gabe ran faster. Their best hope was to reach Grandma May's cottage and hole up inside. But the dark ones had other ideas. The pounding footsteps were gaining on them.

Just as Gabe felt sure either the dark ones or the bittersweet was about to pounce and tear them to pieces, something strange happened.

"Ow!" someone cried out behind him. "Ow, ow!" Hundreds of small objects showered down from the trees. They were being attacked from above! He tried to run faster, but Kimber was awkward in his arms. He hadn't had time to swing her onto his back and was carrying her like a baby. Her eyes were closed and at that moment, he could truly feel what it was like to be her, how humiliating to have to rely on someone else, to be helpless as a baby. In that moment, Gabe hated Straif, hated that he even existed.

"Faster," he gasped, just as Kris screeched to a halt. Gabe barely stopped in time, nearly taking out Abazi and Jer in front of him. "Go, go, go!" he shouted at them, but they remained frozen. He peered over Kris's shoulder and what he saw on the path made him wish desperately for a hole in the ground to open and swallow him up.

Chapter Twenty-Seven

Mouth-Watering Ducks

Wildrr stood blocking the trail, his tiny hands planted on his hips, his face scrunched into a ferocious snarl. "Get movin', ye imps!"

Gabe could only stare at him, unable to move, unable to speak.

"Who's this?" Kris asked, breaking Gabe's spell.

"He's that fairy I was telling you about. And he's mad at me. *Really* mad."

Wildrr's scowl deepened. "As for that, boy, we've lots of things to be straightenin' out betwixt the two of us." He held up a slingshot with an acorn lodged in its strap and let it fly. In less than a second, another had replaced it. "But I'm right busy, if ye caint see the truth of it for yerself. Now get!" He shot another acorn. "I caint hold off both the bittersweet and the dark ones with all yer blabbering goin' on."

Gabe had no idea why Wildrr was being nice to him, but he wasn't waiting around to find out. He pushed the others forward and together they raced toward Grandma May's cottage. The sound of a flute fluttered after him, but this time, he felt no inclination to follow it.

Within half a minute they broke free of the trees and into Grandma's yard. Mrs. Deacon's car was gone, and near where it had sat were several empty shotgun casings. There were no dead bodies, however, or any blood, so Gabe felt a little hopeful that no murders had taken place. Not yet, anyway. Maybe Grandma would attempt to kill Chief Mara on her way to the town jail.

The door to the cottage was unlocked and they hustled inside. Gabe lowered Kimber onto the couch, then returned to the windows facing the woods. He peered out, but saw nothing moving. Where were the dark ones? And what was going on with Wildrr? Why hadn't he taken out Gabe when he'd had the chance?

Everyone was gasping for air after their mad dash, but no one sat down. Kimber was already standing again and patting her pockets. "Let's do a weapons count," she suggested as she pulled out her bata.

She looked better now, Gabe was glad to see. "And make sure all the doors and windows are secure."

"Good idea," Abazi said. "Wouldn't want those little buggers overrunning the place."

"Do you really think they'll try to get in?" Kris looked excited at the prospect. "And what's this bittersweet that fairy was talking about?"

"It's a vine that takes out trees," Gabe quickly explained.

"So it won't hurt us? Just you if you turn into a tree?"

"I'm not sure. I wouldn't take any chances. It looked pretty lethal out there in the woods."

"Would've been nice to know about them at the time," Kris remarked drily. "And you still haven't answered my question. Will the dark ones try to get in here?"

"Straif seemed pretty desperate to me," Kimber answered him. "I think he needs Gabe's blood to heal himself and won't stop until he gets it."

"But I'm not a Dryad," Gabe protested. "My blood is worthless."

"Oh, Gabe," she sighed, and the look she gave him made him feel like he was two years old again—not childish, just not very bright. "How can you not see what's in you?"

"Because there's nothing there?" Before she could elaborate, a clattering noise came from the kitchen. He put his finger to his lips. Maybe Wildrr had found a way into the cottage and was hunting Gabe down at this very moment. Bata firmly gripped in his hand he took a step forward. The kitchen door swung open and a figure burst through, pointing a shotgun at his chest. "Grandma!" He automatically threw his hands in the air. "What are you doing here?"

"It's my house," she countered, lowering the gun.

"Don't you mean it's Bruce Holt's house?"

She narrowed her eyes, then for the first time in a long while, she smiled at him. "You found them." She held out her hand and Gabe felt like pretending he had no idea what she was talking about just to make her sweat a little after how she'd treated him.

Kris ruined that. "Show her what I found!" he crowed, claiming all the glory for himself, of course.

"You didn't find anything," Gabe couldn't resist saying. "You just broke a picture."

"Yeah, you big goon," Jer put in. "Gabe was the one who cracked the riddles. You just cracked some glass."

Kris laughed. "Details, details."

Gabe reluctantly pulled the plastic baggie out of his jacket and handed it to his grandmother. "Here." She took it from him, but before she could make yet another snarky comment about what a loser he was, he turned to the others. "We need to cover all the windows and watch from all sides. Oh, and what do we have for weapons?" Everyone called out what they had, which was fairly paltry, much being lost in their scuffle with the dark ones. Only Abazi still had her staff, Kris and Gabe had their tomahawks, and everyone, except Jer, had a bata, but luckily he still had his bow and a quiver of arrows.

"What's going on, Gabe?" Grandma May demanded.

He turned around to face her, but didn't meet her eyes. "Oh, just keeping an eye out for Mrs. Morrigan and her goons, in case they return to try and take you away. What happened to them, by the way? And who was doing all that shooting?"

She cackled. "The hussy couldn't make her phone work, so when she came back to get the others to drive into town, I made sure she understood, in no uncertain terms, what she'd be up against if she came back."

"So she could still come back?" Gabe didn't like the sound of that. The dark ones were coming, Wildrr was coming. Mrs. Morrigan and Mrs. Deacon and the others would be sitting ducks for Straif. Juicy, mouth-watering ducks.

"She could…if she wants to have to buy herself a whole new wardrobe." She chuckled smugly.

Gabe made up his mind. "I want you to stay here, Grandma, just in case. If you're not in the house and Chief Mara comes, you might have a hard time getting back inside in time. Possession is nine-tenths of the law, you know, and I wouldn't put it past Mrs. Morrigan to have you bodily removed, deed or not, and stake her claim."

"And where are you going, young man?"

"To watch the woods…make sure they don't start anything."

She stared at him for what felt like a long time before nodding. "All right, but don't stay out too long. It's going to snow."

"Sure. Right. Snow." He motioned the others to follow him.

"We should stay inside!" Abazi hissed.

"We can't let her see them. Straif or his miserable sons might tell her what I am and I can't deal with that right now." If he was even a Dryad. He couldn't be sure of anything anymore, but he wasn't taking any chances.

Abazi opened her mouth, then closed it again. Maybe she was about to tell him he shouldn't be ashamed of what he was, but then realized she couldn't say a word because she was doing the exact same thing. Maybe. But probably not.

They stepped outside and the air felt even colder, as though at any moment it could turn to ice. "Do you hear anything?" Gabe whispered.

Kris shook his head. "Should we be worried about that little guy?"

Gabe had been hoping he could just forget about what he'd done to the Lady, and that maybe Wildrr would forget, too, but now was the time to fess up. "Yes, we should. His name is Wildrr, and I killed his tree."

Abazi spun on him. "What? When were you going to fill us in on that little detail?"

"I was hoping for never, but that didn't work out quite like I'd planned."

"What did you do?"

"He wanted my help and I tried to give it and she freaked out at my touch and *died*." To his horror, he felt his eyes welling up. "I didn't mean to kill her! It seems like all I do is hurt people. I'm glad I can't do the Dryad thing anymore. I was a walking death sentence for everyone around me."

Abazi pretended to wipe at her eyes with her fists. "Wah, wah, wah." She shook her head in annoyance. "So you're saying, because of you, in addition to a horde of dark ones and their murderous sidekick, Bittersweet, plus Can-Head, the Deacon, and the police, we have a pissed-off fairy to worry about?"

"Pretty much." He sniffed, but no longer felt like crying. The 'wah, wah, wah' had pretty much dried up that impulse.

"Then I can only say you'd better get over this 'I can't change into a tree anymore' right now. Without you we're board for the dark ones. Get it? Like room and *board*? Food...we're tree food." Everyone groaned.

"There really ought to be a law against your puns," Gabe said. "Cause that was so bad it hurt."

A tree limb snapped behind Kris and he spun around, his tomahawk swinging. "Come out and show yourself!"

A tiny figure broke from the line of trees and stumbled toward them. It was Wildrr, and he had a streak of blood running down the side of his grizzled face.

"He really is real!" Jer shouted excitedly. "I *knew* it!" He sniffed the air. "But I don't smell strawberries or lemonade." His nose wrinkled. "More like sweat and old guy smell."

"They're comin'!" Wildrr panted, stumbling. "Turn, Gabriel! Turn!"

"Is this some sort of trick?" Gabe demanded, getting ready to run.

"No trick! Now turn!"

"But I can't change anymore! Maybe I never really could in the first place."

"Have ye eaten anything strange lately?" Wildrr cried, still running.

"Other than Mom's surprise meat casserole?" Kris joked.

"Not that I can think of…" Gabe stopped, suddenly remembering Faeth, in the woods. "Someone gave me something. It was sticky and sweet and after I ate it the thorns stopped coming." What had she given him? What had she done?

"Aha!" Wildrr crowed triumphantly. Five feet from Gabe he catapulted himself into the air and, like an idiot, Gabe caught him. The fairy pulled something out of his pocket and stuck it in Gabe's face. It was a glass vial filled with a blood red liquid. He pulled out its stopper "Drink this!"

Gabe pursed his lips and shook his head. "Un, unh!"

"Drink it, feartie, or we all die!"

"You promised to seek revenge on me for killing your tree," Gabe dared to open his mouth to say. "You're trying to kill me!"

Wildrr groaned. "Ye're thicker than an oak and yer brain's more knotty than a pine tree. Now open up before I make ye."

"No!"

"If'n I wanted ye truly dead, ye'd be six feet under by now. Or Straif meat. Or flower food. Or wood chips—"

"He gets the picture, Wildrr," Kris interrupted. "Gabe, you owe him for killing his tree, and honestly, as much as I like fighting, I've discovered I like living more. We need you as a tree."

"Listen to him," Abazi urged. "He's one of the little people. Like he said, if he'd wanted you dead—"

"What about the acorns?" Gabe demanded, suddenly putting two and two together. "You threw them at our house, didn't you?"

Wildrr shrugged. "I got a wee bit angry, is all. Wanted to teach ye a lesson, or three."

Lovely. "And was that you following us this morning?"

The little man heaved a sigh. "I was needin' to speak to ye. I told ye that. Now I caint be leadin' the dark ones on a merry chase much longer, so hurry, lad. The spell willna hold forever."

"Spell?" Jer echoed. "You can do magic?"

Wildrr's expression turned sour. "Do idiocy run in yer family?"

"According to Oswald," Jer explained, a little hurt, "we're not really brothers. And I'm not being stupid, just impressed that you can do magic."

Wildrr's expression mellowed instantly. "Oh, well. That be all right then. I like impressed. Though stunned and bedazzled are much tastier morsels to swallow." He looked up into Gabe's face, his large eyes sincere. "I swear on me Lady's honor that I'll do ye no harm."

Gabe's heart beat rapidly. What did he have to lose? He could die by poison, or by Straif's hand. At this point, poison sounded the better way to go. "Okay, fine." He opened his mouth. "Do your worst."

Wildrr grinned and poured the contents of the vial into Gabe's mouth. The taste was both sour and sweet, thick as honey and light as water. It was the strangest, most wonderful thing he'd ever tasted. He swallowed it down, hoping for more.

"That be enough, ye pig! Ye think this stuff grows on trees?" Wildrr laughed, stoppered the vial, and leaped out of Gabe's arms. "Now we be even." Before Gabe could process what the little imp meant, Wildrr took off toward the woods, then stopped at its edge and looked back. "Get yerself ready, because here they come." He whipped out his panpipes and began to play, softly at first, then with increased passion. Beneath the whimsical notes stirred other sounds. Footsteps, breaking branches.

They were coming.

Chapter Twenty-Eight

The Whole Forest is Moving

"You snake!" Gabe shouted at the retreating little man, his skin prickly and hot. He'd been poisoned and now Wildrr had summoned the dark ones to finish him off. It was the ultimate revenge and Gabe was helpless to stop it. He didn't want to die. He didn't want his dad to die. He didn't want the trees to die. But what could he do? Death was inevitable for every living thing in this world.

Still, even if he was dying, he couldn't let the others down. He'd fight to the end, if only to prove to the world, or maybe just to himself, that he wasn't the coward he felt he was.

He felt strange and shaky now, but he pulled back his shoulders anyway and prepared to attack. Releasing a warrior's cry that would rival a Viking's, he raced into the woods, brandishing his bata like a magic wand.

He was only ten feet in when everything went dark and his steps slowed to a crawl. He felt as though he was working his way through waist-high mud. The poison was already doing its worst.

He stopped running and waited for the pain, waited to fall to the ground in agony. But he did not fall, nor did he feel agony. All around him came a cacophony of noises he did not understand, until one sound broke through the growing haze in his mind.

"I've come to save ye, Gabriel!"

Oswald? Well, that explained all the acorns flying at Straif and his goons. Gabe had wondered how the fairy had managed to launch so many at once. Feeling a growing fury, he spun around, whipped out his arm, and grabbed Oswald around the waist.

Wait a second…how did I manage to do that? The words were strange in his mind, so he dismissed them, and continued lifting Oswald high into the air, only now seeing what he'd missed before. Black spikes and dark gray bark had replaced his skin and his arm had grown to twelve feet long.

He was a tree.

"How'd ye do that?" Oswald sputtered from high up in the air. "And ye can put me down, Hawthorne!"

"Doooo whaaat?" Gabe forced out through stiff lips. His mouth, this time around, tasted woody and bitter. But the deep, authoritative tree voice was the same, if a bit slow in coming out. It hadn't exactly stuck when he returned to being a human, but he thought he sounded a little cooler these days. More manly, anyway.

"Ye shouldn't be able to change into a tree anymore!"

"Whooo told you thaaat?"

Oswald shook his head stubbornly. "No one."

"Where's myyyy mother?"

"I don't know! She's gone, and she won't come when I call. Now put me down. Straif is comin'."

Gabe lowered his arm, then released his grip, letting Oswald fall. The Dryad landed nimbly on his feet, disappointing Gabe, who was hoping he'd land on his butt. "Youuu chaaange," he demanded. He liked that this time he could actually think some rational human thoughts. Last time he'd been too distracted by the sun to think of anything else. Now, there was no sun, no warmth to reach for. In fact the air felt like it was growing colder by the minute. Gabe wanted nothing more than to find somewhere to curl up and go to sleep.

Oswald looked up at him. "And risk the—" He stopped himself and grinned at Gabe. "Not just yet."

Something caught at Gabe's slow working mind, but he couldn't pin it down. "Youuu are afraaaid."

Oswald scowled and drew up his shoulders. "There's not enough room here. An oak is mighty. I'd crush ye beneath me feet."

"Afraaaid," Gabe said one last time. "Because youuu know I'll beeeat youuu."

Oswald turned his back on Gabe. "They're comin'," he announced to his band. "Take yer positions!"

"Holy crap," Kris breathed. "The whole forest is moving!"

Entire bunches of trees marched toward them like an army, swinging their branches crazily. Straif must have spelled them! Riding on the branch of a blackthorn sat Straif himself, dark and ominous. "Take them. Take them all!" he howled. Gabe peered around, his tree eyes observing the shadows advancing on him like a dust storm. The Kogoks had transformed into trees, too, becoming giant, spiky weapons of destruction. "Get Gabriel!"

Gabe's heartbeat doubled and his anger soared. "Geeettt baaack!" he cried, then started to whip one of his branches over his head like a lasso. It whooshed louder and louder with each swing until he let go and it cracked through the air, wiping out a line of Ko-gok trees. Screams filled the woods and several of the dark ones transformed back to their 'human' forms, writhing on the forest floor in pain.

Total chaos broke out and Gabe's human mind shut down as he let his anger take over. He slashed and whipped his enemies while the Rogues jumped from the trees, taking out any untransformed Ko-goks. He thought Kris and Jer and Abazi and Kimber were fighting in a tight little pack to his left, but he couldn't be sure. It was hard to make out much of anything through his haze of rage.

At one point, his mind cleared and he made out Straif on his tree, pointing and directing like a diseased general. He didn't look the least bit worried, urging on the mass of trees, coming wave after wave. Straif, it seemed, was sending the majority of his forces to take out Gabe. And since the Rogues weren't changing into trees—*why aren't they changing?*—Gabe was on his own.

He swung and he roared and he whipped his branches every which way, but at last he realized he couldn't fight them all. There were just too many, even with the Rogues on their side. They'd have to retreat. But how? They were surrounded and he was growing more tired with each new line of trees that advanced on them.

For the first time since the fight started, Gabe felt pain. It radiated upward through his trunk and into his head, threatening to split it in two. He looked down to see a massive spike piercing his trunk. He shook his head, trying to concentrate, trying to figure out what to do. When he looked back up again, he was facing Feltry. The blackthorn pulled his branch back and swung again. Weak from the pain, Gabe moved too slowly and a fresh wave of torture overwhelmed him as a giant thorn ripped into him.

He pulled back a branch and smacked Feltry across the face. Feltry barely reacted, advancing steadily, his thorny limbs swinging violently as a tree in a hurricane. Gabe kept whipping branches at Feltry, deadly as bullets, but nothing seemed to stop him. He moved as though under a spell.

And then one of his branches wrapped around Gabe's trunk and jerked tight. The pull grew stronger and stronger, and Gabe realized he was having trouble breathing. How could that be? He was a tree! But he was also a spirit living within the tree—a human one. Feltry must be cutting off the air supply for the human part of him. Gabe didn't like that he wasn't one or the other, that he was both at the same time. It seemed a stupid frailty to have to deal with.

Feeling perilously close to passing out, he grabbed Feltry's branch and yanked on it, trying to weaken his insanely tight grasp. But instead of loosening, Feltry's grip tightened as he advanced on Gabe. His other branches flew in and grabbed Gabe's weakening ones, effectively tying him up. Gabe thrashed and fought, but he couldn't shake Feltry off.

Maniacal laughter, coming from Straif, filled the air. Close by, on the ground, stood Dorn, looking mutinous. Unlike his brother, he had reverted back to his human form and didn't look like he had any intention of changing over to a tree again any time soon. Gabe wondered why. He would certainly be a better fighter as a tree…bigger, anyway.

"A little longer, Feltry!" Straif shouted. "Hold him tight. Our time is so close." He glanced up at the sky and Gabe followed his gaze. It was raining, he saw, and the wet felt cold on his limbs. Icy cold. He started to shiver.

"Let him go!" a fierce voice cried. Jer! He pulled back his arm and seconds later an arrow flew through the air, hitting Feltry between the eyes. He roared in pain, one of his branches swiping at the arrow.

"Get him!" Straif screeched. "Crush him!"

"Protect the little one!" Oswald called out to his Rogues, then turned to Gabe. "Ye have to turn back into a human. Leave it to me to take care of this mess!"

Feltry's hold had loosened on Gabe's torso, allowing him to breathe, to think more clearly. Another arrow flew through the air, followed by another. Feltry's branches retreated, and as they did, Feltry changed back to human form, the arrows dropping harmlessly to the ground. Blood oozed from the wounds between his eyes, and he did not look happy. But he did look alive.

"Change over, Dorn!" Straif tried again. "It's yer turn! Make yer father proud!"

Dorn looked uncertain. "The freeze is too close, Father! Dorn'll be stuck here! And besides, ye said Gabriel weren't a Dryad."

"Do as I say!" Straif ordered, his voice deadly. "Or I'll strip ye bare!"

Dorn's face scrunched up and he began to turn. Just as his arms transformed into branches, an arrow struck one and he instantly changed back. "I've been hit!"

An arrow struck the tree Straif was sitting on. With a screech, it changed over, and Straif dropped to the ground looking murderous. "Can any of ye do anything right?" His arm whipped out, turning into a branch as he cracked it at Jer.

Before the branch could strike, Kris leaped forward and hacked it off with his tomahawk. Straif pulled back his stunted arm and advanced on Kris, but Abazi ran forward and hit him on the head with her staff. His expression, twisted and horrid with fury, Straif turned on Abazi and threw out a branch. She ducked, but not before the tip caught her cheek. Hand clasped to her face, she went down.

Furious, Gabe shot out a branch and wrapped it around Straif's waist like a boa constrictor. Seeing Abazi lying on the ground, alone and helpless, Gabe squeezed as hard as he could, hoping with all his might to snuff out everything that was alive in Straif. He wanted to kill him. He wanted him dead as the stones beneath his feet.

I truly am a killer, he realized, and did not feel ashamed. He knew what he was about to do and he kept doing it anyway. Was that good or bad? He didn't yet know, and didn't really care.

Straif struggled and kicked, but Gabe held on. Then the Ko-gok leader shot out another branch and whipped Gabe hard in the face, startling him. His hold loosened and Straif dropped to the ground. "Curse ye!" he screamed at Gabe. "Fall back, fiends!" he ordered his dark ones. "It's gettin' too close to the Freeze. Retreat!"

All at once the surrounding trees transformed into dark ones, and like a swarm of bees, they tore off into the woods. Gabe watched them go, stunned. "Whaaat is the Freeeeze?" he called out. He felt so cold, so stiff. Something was wrong with him. He tried to transform, but nothing happened. He thought of everything human he could think of—his home, his friends, his parents, eating hotdogs—and still he remained a tree. "Whaaat is the Freeeeze?" he tried again, barely getting the words out.

"If ye were King of the Forest Immortal, ye'd know about it, wouldn't ye?" Oswald taunted.

"What are you talking about?" Kris demanded, sounding winded. "What's he supposed to know?"

"It's time we trees took a little nap." Oswald held his hand up to the sky and smiled. "The Freeze has come."

"What?" Abazi cried, looking around. "So that's why none of you turned! You'd better turn back, Gabe," she said. Her voice was shaky, which wasn't like her at all, and got Gabe feeling very worried. "Now! Before you're trapped as a tree."

"I caaan't!" he moaned. "I've triiied."

Abazi faced Oswald, her whole body quivering with anger. "What did you do to him?"

Oswald held up his hands. "I didn't do anything. It's nature. It's what happens to us Dryads when the Freeze comes. When it's time, we find our place and we change over. We stay that way for the winter and come out of it in the spring. But once we change, we can't change back until our sap is warmed and runs fast as Shambolic Stream. If we try, it can do harm. Great harm."

"Why didn't you warn him this could happen?"

"I did before, but then Straif attacked and…" His words trailed away. Even Gabe's tree mind could tell he was making excuses.

"You didn't change yourself, nor did your band," Jer reminded him, his arm around a shivering Kimber. "So you knew what was going on and could've stopped him before this." The freezing rain was coming down harder, coating Gabe's limbs, freezing them. His mind was growing fuzzier by the second. He wanted to go to sleep. He sensed it was the only way to stop feeling so cold. "You *tricked* him."

"I didn't trick him!" Oswald cried. "I figured he knew. He should've known…" he ended less vehemently.

Kris lifted his bata in a threatening gesture. "So what are you going to do to fix this?"

Oswald held up his hands. "I don't know if I can—"

"Help him change, Oswald," Abazi said, her tone of voice soft, coaxing. Even Gabe's foggy mind picked up on the strangeness of it. "Please, Oswald! If anyone can do it, you can." Was she fluttering her eyelashes at him?

Oswald's whole demeanor changed, becoming almost cocky. "Well, now that ye mention it, I do have an idea. It might work. Might not." He glanced up at Gabe. "I'm going to climb ye. Don't move." He smiled charmingly. Gabe didn't smile back. He didn't want to, and besides, he couldn't because his face felt tighter than a drum, like he'd just gotten a Botox injection.

In only a few seconds, Oswald was level with Gabe's tree head. "Remember that I'm savin' yer hide, Gabriel," he whispered. "Remember that I could've left ye like this." Then he shoved something strange looking into the hole that seemed to be Gabe's mouth. "Chew it."

Gabe tried, but he couldn't make his jaws work. He was so cold, nearly frozen, and his will to fight drained away. He stopped trying, and the sticky sludge slid down his throat, catching in his windpipe. He started to gag, but the wretched stuff wouldn't budge, cutting off his air. He was going to choke to death, and Oswald would be King.

Just like he always wanted.

Chapter Twenty-Nine

Not King of Anything

Seeing Gabe's struggle to breathe, Oswald stuck his arm in Gabe's mouth and shoved the wad of gunk farther down his gullet. Gabe tried to fight him off, but Oswald wasn't having it. "Stay still, idiot! I'm tryin' to help ye." It didn't feel like it; felt more like he was trying to finish off the job of killing Gabe. But Gabe was so weak, he could do little but go along.

Having Oswald's arm down his throat felt really weird, and a desire to throw up almost overwhelmed Gabe. He knew that would only make matters worse, so he tried to concentrate and force the stuff to stay where it was. He remembered it now, sweet and sticky, like what Faeth had given him, and then he knew what it would do to him.

His guess was confirmed when Oswald pulled out his arm and soon after Gabe started to tingle all over. Oswald jumped down, and in a few, long moments—the change seemed to take forever this time—Gabe was back to his human form.

"You did it!" he gasped gratefully, bent over. "You saved me!" He clapped Oswald on the back. His mind was still a little fuzzy, like he'd been drugged, but his euphoria was real. "And I didn't kill anyone."

"Just ye remember what I did," Oswald hissed, then motioned to his band. "We must hurry before it's too late." As one, the band turned and disappeared into the woods.

"That was close," Kris breathed. "I thought you were going to be a tree for the winter, Gabe."

"Me, too!" He laughed, feeling light with relief.

"Of course, if you were a pine tree, we could've brought you inside for Christmas and decorated you."

Gabe felt so good, he was actually amused. "Luckily Oswald had that stuff—whatever it was."

"Yes, lucky," Kimber said, her voice shaking from the cold.

He knew what she was thinking. He remembered what Jer had said about Oswald tricking him. He remembered how Oswald and his band and Straif hadn't changed over. How Dorn didn't want to. He remembered. He just wished he didn't.

"Booooys!" a distant voice called. "Abaaaazi! Kiiimmmber!"

"Grandma May!" Jer said. "She's looking for us!"

Gabe wrapped his arms around himself. "Then we'd better let her come to us, or find ourselves getting shot at."

~~~~~~

Once everyone had changed into some old clothes Grandma May kept around "just in case," Gabe placed the call to his parents to leave a message, then handed the phone to Abazi. After she left a message telling her father she was safe at Mrs. May's house, Kimber took the phone and called her mother. She reassured her she'd be just fine, and if she could tell Mr. Wanibagw where they were in case he didn't get Abazi's message, that would be great. Finally, after talking to Grandma May, Kimber's mother agreed not to call out the National Guard to come rescue her baby.

After the phone calls were made, everyone gathered around the fire and tried to get warm. Grandma May made hot chocolate and they drank it gratefully. Not once did she question their story—that while looking for Mrs. Morrigan and Mrs. Deacon, they got turned around in the woods and were caught in the ice storm. Kimber, they explained, had led them back to the cottage to safety.

Grandma didn't question anything, which was odd in itself, so Gabe decided to push his luck a little. He needed to figure out just how much she knew about the forest and its secrets. "So you knew about the riddles all along?" he asked casually, after downing the last of his hot chocolate.

She was tending the fire, stirring up the coals before adding three more logs. The flames snapped at the dried bark like voracious dogs. "I overheard you kids talking about the riddles. That's how I knew about them. No mystery there."

Really? he wondered. *When?* "But who sent them?" he asked aloud, hoping she'd say Bruce Holt so they could get somewhere.

She shrugged. "Beats me. I thought it was someone in town who knew something, but was afraid to talk because of those two troll women, Deacon and Morrigan, always being about."

Gabe didn't believe her, but her expression in response to his raised eyebrows told him she didn't really care whether he believed her or not. She wasn't going to tell him anything. Still, he had to try. "But why would you think the riddles had anything to do with this place, and were the answer to saving you from getting kicked out?"

"I just had a feeling. With Morrigan hounding me about the house, I took a guess that the riddles had something to do with this place." It was a terrible reason, but again, she didn't look particularly concerned that she wasn't persuading him.

"What I don't understand," interjected Jer, "is why Bruce Holt gave *you* the house." There was a collective murmur of "yeahs."

Her face grew soft. "We were best friends, all through school. Still are."

"Still *are?*" Gabe pounced. "Isn't he dead?"

Her expression pinched closed. "Just because someone dies doesn't mean you stop caring about them. So, yeah. Still *are.*" She pushed herself to her feet with a groan. "Now I'm going to start lunch. You all can come help do some chopping and table setting."

Gabe took in the stubborn set of her chin and her blue eyes were steely, daring him to try and ask more questions. He sighed. He wasn't going to win this battle, though he knew there was definitely something fishy going on with her.

The others stood and followed her into the kitchen. Gabe was the last to go, so he was the only one to hear the knock on the front door. A very soft knock. He waited for the swinging door to shut on Kimber before he headed down the short, dark passage to the door. Taking a deep breath, he opened it a crack. Cold air whooshed in and he shivered convulsively. Despite being dry now and full of hot chocolate, he still didn't feel warm, didn't think he'd ever feel warm again. And winter was only starting. What had happened to his internal furnace? He hardly ever felt cold.

He peered out the door, but saw nothing. Just as he was about to turn around, something at the bottom of the steps straightened up. Gabe quickly flipped on the front light to see better and discovered, to his shock, that it was Filidh. The strange man was covered in a coating of shiny ice, with the beginnings of snow peppering his shoulders and head. He must have knocked, then retreated in case the wrong person came to the door.

"Filidh's here to do a little trade," he announced, beckoning Gabe to come outside. "I'll tell ye what ye want to ken and ye give Filidh something only ye, as King, can give."

"I'm not King of anything," Gabe protested, tiptoeing down the steps. He didn't want anyone, especially Grandma May, overhearing their conversation. But if that were true—that he wasn't a king—he could promise Filidh anything and not have to follow through. Though somehow that didn't seem quite right. What if he did have some say? "What is that you want from me?" he asked warily. The snow was already growing more intense and he wrapped his arms around his shivering torso.

"I ken who yer riddle writer is."

Gabe's interest was caught. "You do? Who?"

"Hold yer spirits there, human. There's a price."

Gabe nodded at him, urging him to go on. "Well, what is it?"

"It's a small thing to ask for. Ye see," Filidh wheedled, "I has got to get rid of those hooligans once and for all. They make too much noise, which makes me head ache, and they're full of pomposity and always goin' on and on about nothing." He rubbed his temples as though they were aching from just talking about the hooligans and their noise. "So I guess what I'm sayin' is that I want the gorge back to meself."

"Is that all?" Gabe asked casually. It was a lot to ask, and Gabe knew it. Giving Filidh control over the gorge would start a war with Oswald, bigger than the one they were already engaged in. Did he want that? *Of course I do*, he thought hotly. *He's been nothing but trouble to me since I met him.*

But he did save your life, he counter-argued, *by helping you transform back into a human.* That was true, but there was something about the whole thing with Oswald saving him that was troubling Gabe. He couldn't put his finger on what it was, but something about it didn't seem right, something more than just him not telling Gabe about the Freeze.

Even so, this decision didn't just affect Oswald; it affected Hollie and the rest of the Rogues. None of them seemed to dislike Gabe. Yes, they typically avoided looking him in the eye, and followed Oswald's orders, but usually never with any animosity on their part.

"That be all, King," Filidh said with a modest bob of his head. Then he fixed Gabe with his ancient eyes. "Ye see, Filidh never once thought ye were a Usurper. But that's neither here nor there. What I have to tell ye'll make everything so clear. *Everything*." His bushy eyebrows wriggled knowingly, provocatively. "Yer secret riddler. Yer history. Yer entire life. Yer real parents. Filidh kens it all."

It was *so* tempting. "Well…"

A figure burst through the line of trees. "Don't do it, Gabriel!" Hollie shouted, her eyes wild. "Don't do it!" She raced up and grabbed his arm, pulling him away from Filidh. "Ye can't trust this rascal, and ye can't give him our home."

"I wasn't planning to," he said, and realized he meant it. "As much as I want to know the answers to my questions, I couldn't screw you and your friends over. On the other hand, if it were just Oswald…"

She squeezed his arm, then gave Filidh the stink-eye. "Ye're an old busybody, Filidh of the Forest, and a mischief-maker, to boot. Ye threw the acorn, didn't ye?"

Filidh's eyes shifted away. "Might've accidentally tossed it. Didna mean to make the spike-haired one fall, as such."

"Ye did it to throw blame on Oswald, so ye can have the gorge!" Filidh didn't deny it, which was pretty much the same as admitting to it. Hollie sighed. "We've just as much right to the gorge as ye do, ye old codger. There's plenty of room for us all."

Filidh shook his head regretfully. "Ah, well. Twas worth a try." He winked at Hollie. "Just to be clear, I'd let *ye* stay. Ye're a sight for sore eyes and feisty as a trapped coon." Hollie clamped her lips down on a pleased smile. Filidh turned to go, then said over his shoulder, "But I'll find ye again, King Gabriel, of that ye can be sure. I've things to tell ye, things no one alive kens. Only Filidh." He stabbed at his chest, then started coughing. "Only Filidh."

Gabe nodded solemnly. He was actually sorry to see the old man go. He wanted desperately to know the answers, though what he'd do with them, he'd yet to figure out. "I'll keep that in mind, Filidh. See you next spring?"

"Spring? Oh, I suppose. It's all the same to me. Spring, summer, winter, fall. It's all the same to me," he mumbled again as he shuffled off into the dark woods. When the trees had swallowed him up, Gabe turned to Hollie.

"Should you be out in this?" He pointed at the sky.

"I'll be all right. If I can turn meself into a baby, I can handle a little cold." He stifled his grimace, remembering the ugly baby form she'd taken to spy on them. "And ye can keep all yer comments to yerself about that." She scowled at him and he wiped his face clean of the big grin that was forming.

"I'll try."

"I know who wrote the riddles."

He stared at her. "Really?"

"No, I just wanted to be standin' here in the freezing cold lookin' at yer ugly mug."

"Oh, well. Then look away," he joked.

She glared at him in disgust. "Are ye ready to hear it?"

"As ready as I'm going to be," he answered, wondering what name she would speak.

"The human. The man. His name's Bruce Holt."

Gabe shook his head, disappointed. "We thought about that, but it can't be him. He's dead. You know he had a heart condition? Everyone's pretty sure he wouldn't have lasted the winter, much less twenty of them."

She sighed and patted him on the arm as though he were a simple child. First Kimber, now Hollie. Had he shrunk or something? "Use yer brain, Gabriel."

"I thought I *was* using my brain."

She looked at him skeptically, then relented. "He found a way to become one of us."

"One of us? You mean— No way!" Gabe couldn't believe what he was hearing.

She nodded importantly. "He turned himself into a Dryad. Up until lately, Dame Hazel has always been able to keep him in check. He's a bit odd and he takes a lot of chances, which is why she watches him. But this time, he managed to elude her. That's where I was all this time…helpin' her to find him."

That explained the smell in Grandma's house, of woods and wildness. But did Grandma know Bruce Holt was a Dryad? And could he ask her that question? Well, he could, but it was unlikely she'd answer him. "Maybe Dame Hazel let him go on purpose," he replied, the curious thought coming from out of nowhere.

Hollie looked thoughtful. "It's possible. I never do know what Dame Hazel's thinkin' half the time. But why send me after him?"

"To get you out of the way?"

Her green eyes darkened. "Get me out of the way for what?"

"I don't know." He had his guesses, of course, but if they were right, that meant Dame Hazel was conspiring with Oswald, and he didn't like that one bit. Was this why she'd sent Oswald to Gabe's house? She said she'd done it so he could get over his anger with Gabe, but that hadn't worked. In fact, it had created the opposite effect. Or maybe it was the old "keep your friends close and your enemies closer," with Gabe as the enemy. "So why didn't you tell me about Bruce Holt when we were at your cave?"

"I'd only just learned about the riddles, Mr. Suspicious. Ye confronted Oswald with them, remember? And at that point I didn't know Master Holt had written them. I figured it out after askin' Dame Hazel a lot of questions. And even then, it took me a while. Since then I've been tryin' to let ye know, but Oswald's been keepin' a close eye on me. Partly because he's jealous and worried I'll join yer side, and partly because once I got caught by Straif's sons." Her eyes shifted away for a moment. "I managed to slip away from Oswald for a bit, but I was too late."

"Too late?" Gabe echoed. "For what?"

"Faeth found ye, and after that, I lost track of ye."

Gabe remembered them running from someone. At the time he'd thought it was Oswald, and Faeth had confirmed that, but it must have been Hollie. "But she saved me, and she was really nice. So I was okay, Hollie." He didn't like how distressed and guilty she looked.

"No, ye weren't, Gabriel." She paused and the expression on her face made Gabe's stomach churn. "Oswald set ye up. I'm pretty sure he made her give ye sloe berries. I heard ye in the woods, about not bein' able to change, and I worked it out. I saw him pickin' them, ye see, from some blackthorns that can't change over. They stopped yer thorns, didn't they?"

He didn't answer for a moment, thinking it through. True, he had stopped sprouting thorns every time he got angry, and it was after his meeting with Faeth that he'd been unable to transform into a tree. Also, the stuff Oswald had given him to help him change back into a human had been the same as what Faeth had given him, so what Hollie was saying made sense. "But why would he do that?"

"He wanted revenge on ye. He took away yer powers and figured that at some point ye'd need rescuin', and he'd be the one to do it. Then he'd get his title back. I heard about what happened when I was gone lookin' for Master Holt, about Straif and the dark ones and yer battlin' them. I think Oswald planned all that, then led Straif to ye."

"I told him he could have the title!" Gabe cried, frantic with anger. "He's being such a jerk! Why, Hollie? What have I ever done to him?"

"Nothing, Gabriel," she said in a soft voice. "Faeth raised him alone, remember. And she isn't exactly all there, if ye know what I mean." A long finger tapped the side of her head. "But the sloe berries do wear off, and he did warn ye about the Freeze, did he not?" she added hopefully.

"He warned me, but he didn't tell me what it meant until it was almost too late. How was I to know trees hibernate in the winter? That if you let yourself get too cold in your tree form, you lose your mobility, your ability to change back? I would've been stuck as a tree all winter. My parents would have thought I was dead." This notion, just occurring to Gabe, bothered him more than all the rest. News like that would have hit his father hard, and he wasn't strong enough to withstand a blow like that.

"I see," Hollie said, looking troubled. "Ye have a good point there. But I did try to let ye know what he'd done. I think he suspected I knew something and wouldn't let me out of his sight. And then, when

I finally did ditch him and catch up to ye in the woods, that Wildrr ran me off. I think the addlepated goof thought I was tryin' to do Oswald's work and get ye gone from the forest."

So, Gabe thought, those voices in the woods on the way to the mill had been Wildrr going after Hollie. But why would he think Hollie was a threat to Gabe? It didn't add up.

"Are you sure it was Wildrr? I think you've got the wrong guy. He'd happily feed my carcass to Straif, so I can't imagine him doing anything to protect me. Do you know what happened…did Dame Hazel tell you?"

"Tell me what?"

He lowered his voice. "That I killed the Lady."

She pulled back from him. "She never said. And why did ye do that?"

"I didn't mean to. Wildrr asked me to help her—she was dying—and I tried and she started going mad. That's when he went after me."

"Then why did he keep me away from ye?"

"I suppose cause he wanted me for himself."

"Are ye sure about that?"

Gabe nodded. "He set me up today—gave me a drink that undid what Oswald did with those slow berries you mentioned. Then he called up the dark ones. He probably knows about the Freeze and figured if the dark ones didn't get me, the Freeze would."

"But Wildrr was the one who saved me from Straif," she said. "He even took a wound."

"He did?" Gabe was surprised, though he remembered now how Wildrr hobbled as he walked. "Well, he was probably just hoping to cash in the favor later on."

"I didn't get that feeling, Gabriel." She looked thoughtful. "Maybe ye should go talk to him."

"And lose my head? No thanks." None of this made sense. First, Wildrr saves Hollie, then he runs her off. What was going on with him, with both of them?

She laid a hand on his arm. "Just talk to him."

"He did say we had some things to work out, though he probably just meant he had to do it with his fists."

"Give him a chance. He's got a temper, and he's terribly mischievous, but good-hearted in the end, I'd say." She turned to go, then turned back. "Say hello to Kristofer for me, will ye? Tell him I'll look for him when the waters run fast."

"I take it that's springtime?" he ventured.

"Tis. Now I must go. It's time to settle. The others already have and I must join them."

"How come I don't have to hibernate?" he asked.

"Because ye're different, Gabriel."

"Because I've spent so much time as a human?"

"Perhaps, and something else, too. We all see it. That's why Oswald is so afraid of ye."

Gabe laughed. "Afraid? He's not afraid of me."

"He's afraid of what ye can take from him."

Gabe didn't have a reply for that. There was nothing Oswald had that Gabe wanted, so what would he take? Then he remembered when Oswald was talking to Faeth, how he'd looked afraid. Could it be possible? Perhaps. Because if others bestowed what Oswald wanted—to be King—upon Gabe, Oswald would have no choice in the matter. It was likely that he did feel very frightened indeed. The fact that he might not be a real Dryad didn't help, either.

"Goodbye, Gabriel," Hollie whispered. "Enjoy yer rest. Springtime'll come soon enough, and with it, great trouble."

"Great trouble? That doesn't sound good."

"Many of us are afraid we'll not wake come buddin' time. Ye'll be on yer own against the Ko-goks."

"*Not*...wake up?" He couldn't be hearing this right.

"It's the sickness. This year it's the worst it's ever been. We've all been feelin' its effects. And if this time of snow and ice is as bad as the old ones predict, we'll not revive. We'll not have the strength to get our sap flowin' again."

Gabe grabbed Hollie's hands and held them tight. "Then stay awake! Come live with us. We'll tell our parents you're a distant cousin or something. I don't know—"

Hollie gently pulled her hands away and lifted her long, thin limbs into a stretch. Her mouth widened into a yawn. "It's too late for me. Just be ready..."

"But you told me to tell Kris you'll look for him at—"

"What I say and what'll happen are two different things." And before he could stop her, she was gone.

He stared into the woods for several long seconds, feeling scared and alone. She couldn't really mean it, could she? She was just trying to scare him into staying alert for when Straif came after him again. Of course the Dryads would wake up again.

"Gabe!" Kris called from the doorway. "I don't think Grandma's going to buy the 'he's in the bathroom' excuse for much longer."

Gabe spun around. "Huh? Oh, yeah. I'm coming."

"Who were you talking to?"

"What?"

Kris pointed to the footprints. Hollie's footprints. "Oh. Um, well…"
He didn't want to tell Kris he'd missed Hollie.

"Don't bother trying to spare my feelings. It was Hollie, wasn't it?
She hates me, I suppose, probably for fooling around up on the waterfall and nearly getting us all killed. It's probably why she didn't come
along with Oswald this time."

"She was helping Dame Hazel, and she doesn't hate you, Kris. In
fact, she told me she'll look for you when spring comes again."

Kris brightened. "She did?"

Gabe swallowed hard and nodded. He didn't like not telling his
brother what Hollie had said about the trees not waking again, but he'd
already left out telling him about Filidh. Besides, maybe Hollie was one
of the Dryads who'd be spared. "Now let's go in before Grandma gets
out the laxatives."

Kris laughed and pushed Gabe inside.

~~~~~~

After the table was cleared and the food put away—what was left of
it—Grandma May made them haul wood inside. When they were
done, they changed back into their now dry clothes and assembled in
the living room. Grandma gave them blankets to wrap up in and left
them with two big bowls of popcorn and a couple liters of soda, along
with a warning to behave while she made some phone calls.

With Kris promising to act like an angel, she went off with a disbe-
lieving snort, but looking like a new woman. The riddles had been
solved and her home was safe. For now, anyway. She'd confided at
lunch that she was quite aware Candi Morrigan would be back, with
the 'Chief Idiot' in tow. Bruce Holt's Will and deed to the house would
hold Candi off for a bit while her lawyer husband figured out some
way to get around it. Or she'd discover a way to threaten Grandma
May. But for now…life was good and she planned on savoring it.

When she was gone, the five of them burrowed under their blankets
to warm up, popcorn bowls within reach for easy dipping. After a
minute or two of munching and the sounds of crackling from the roaring fire, Kris asked the question Gabe knew he'd get to eventually.

"So are you going to tell me what Hollie wanted?"

"Hollie was here?" Abazi cried, looking more peeved than the an-
nouncement warranted. "Why didn't you tell us?"

"In front of Grandma May?"

"Okay, fine," she reluctantly acceded. "But she's not here now."

"I was working up to it. There's a lot to tell. Not just about her, but about a couple of things."

It wasn't easy owning up to the fact that he'd kept stuff from them. He told the whole story about Wildrr and his plot for revenge. They listened carefully, then argued about whether or not the fairy was still seeking vengeance when he made Gabe drink the potion that allowed him to change into a tree again. Opinions were divided evenly down the middle.

They weren't so willing to rationally discuss Filidh and how Gabe hadn't said a word about him. They also didn't accept his excuse that he was only trying to protect them, maybe because it wasn't the truth. He hadn't wanted them to know about Filidh, and especially not meet Filidh, because he had this sense the old man had heard about the Lady and would have used that knowledge as leverage against Gabe.

To distract them from their understandable anger, he quickly moved on to what Hollie had told him about Bruce Holt and how the recluse *was* alive and had somehow become a Dryad. The change of subject did the trick, inviting discussion about how Mr. Holt had managed to turn into a tree spirit and if anyone else could do that. No one had any good answers, though Jer wondered aloud if Wildrr might have a magic potion for making it happen. The consensus was that he just might.

They did figure out one thing, or at least made a good guess. Gabe had asked, "But why would anyone voluntarily want to become a tree spirit?"

"He was dying," Kimber answered simply. "And being a tree made him strong," she added wistfully.

"Ah," was all Gabe could think of to say to that.

At last the talk wound down and he was able to voice an apology. "I'm sorry, guys. I wanted to tell you everything, but I thought... " He paused and took a deep breath. "Well, I was afraid I was going to hurt one of you. You see, every time I got angry, thorns would come out of me. I couldn't control them and it didn't seem to take much to trigger them. It was pretty freaky—I looked like a dark one. And then, when I became a tree, I almost killed Oswald."

"But you didn't," Kimber pointed out.

"True, but I wanted to. Let's face it—I'm a homicidal Dryad."

"So what?" Abazi said, twirling a strand of hair around her finger. "You can't help who you are so stop whining about it."

He stared at her incredulously. "And you accept who you are?"

"It's different for me. People can see I'm Indian. They can't see that you're a tree. You can pass."

"Not when I start sprouting spikes out of my forehead!"

"Point taken." She paused. "Get it? Point…as in spikes have *points*?" She roared with laughter.

"That was really pointless," Gabe said.

"I thought I got right to the point."

"No, that was me."

Abazi groaned and threw a pillow at him.

Kris's eyes were distant, still thinking about Gabe's spikes. "That would be so cool if you could just summon them up at will."

"Yeah, imagine if you could use your tree-ness when you play basketball?" Jer mimed shooting a basket. "If you could control your powers, you'd be unstoppable. You'd have a longer reach than Kevin McHale."

Kris nodded. "Yeah, that dude is like Stretch Armstrong."

"I doubt I can just make my arms go longer then bring them back again without anyone noticing that they're branches. Same with the spikes."

"Why not?" Kimber wondered. "Although it might be considered cheating."

Kris caught a piece of popcorn in his mouth. "All's fair in love and basketball, kiddo."

She tossed a piece of popcorn at him. "Who you calling kiddo?"

"You, shrimp!" A handful flew back at her.

Jer jumped up. "You jerk!"

A wad of popcorn hit him in the face and he sank back down. Abazi grinned at him, then threw another handful. By the time Grandma May poked her head out, it was too late. Popcorn was everywhere. Five flushed, contrite faces took in her startled expression.

"We'll clean it up!" Gabe promised.

"Don't bother." And with a whistle she summoned King George, who waddled out and cleaned up the mess with surprising speed and efficiency.

As Gabe watched King George make the popcorn disappear, he wished taking care of his problems would be as easy as that. There was something big he still had to face, but he didn't want to. In fact, he'd rather stick one of his thorns in his eye.

But he had to do it, or spend the rest of his life looking over his shoulder.

Chapter Thirty

I Won't Forget You

The freezing rain soon turned over to snow, but luckily they were able to get home before the worst of the storm struck. Mr. Wanibagw had a plow and he arrived late that afternoon to give everyone a ride home and return their bags to them, left behind in the teepee. He took Kimber and Abazi first, then returned for Gabe and his brothers. On the ride back, they apologized for making Abazi miss the powwow. *They'd gone for a walk*, was their story, *and had gotten a little lost.*

After admitting he wasn't too worried, or surprised, after finding Abazi's note, Mr. Wanibagw joked, "Though maybe I should make all of you sleep in the wigwam tonight as penance."

"Are you and the others still staying in them?" Kris asked.

"Are you kidding?" Mr. Wanibagw laughed. "We're Indians, not crazy. You'd think we'd stop listening to the forecasters, though. This storm is a day and a half early. Strange, huh? So everyone packed up and bugged out this morning before it got too bad. Abazi didn't miss anything, other than the pleasure of our company."

Relieved that Abazi wasn't going to get into trouble, Gabe hardly listened to the rest of the conversation—Mr. Wanibagw was answering Kris's questions on how to make a wigwam. When Abazi had left, things were still strange between them. He'd hope to talk it out with her, but she'd avoided being alone with him. It was almost a relief. What would he say? *Please like me? Or, at the very least, don't hate me? Or, please don't like Oswald.* He remembered the look on her face when he'd told her Oswald had been watching her, and the soft, sweet voice and fluttering eyelashes she'd used to convince him to help Gabe. She seemed to like Oswald, and the very thought made Gabe want to kick in a wall.

Abazi's father dropped them off with promises to invite them to the next powwow and they thanked him for the night before. Gabe was able to truthfully say that it had been one of the neatest things he'd ever done. Mr. Wanibagw drove off with a honk and a pleased smile on his face.

Mom and Dad were inside, trying out the new woodstove Grandpa had installed yesterday (which threw a lot of heat). They'd made it back from their lunch, just barely, with the slippery roads.

After telling their parents about their experience sleeping in a wigwam (surprisingly warm) and seeing the powwow (very cool) and roasting marshmallows (delicious) and owning up to the broken photo in the parlor (they'd been horsing around, they decided to tell her— Grandma May said she would explain about Bruce Holt and the deed and Mrs. Morrigan's attempts to boot her out when the time was right, which might be never, Gabe figured), his brothers headed to their rooms to unpack and Mom went upstairs to sew up one of their winter jackets. Dad followed behind her, anxious to tinker with his 'new' computer in his office. Mom, despite her strange behavior before— telling him that she loved him no matter what—seemed back to her old self. Maybe she'd just been worrying like any parent would. Maybe she hadn't really sensed anything unusual about him. He could only hope so.

He was about to head up to his room when the phone rang. "Hello?" he answered, feeling tingly.

"Hey." It was Abazi. He'd sensed it was her, hence the tingles. "Everything okay with the rents?"

"Yeah. They don't suspect anything."

"Good." There was a long pause. "So was Oswald really watching me…at the powwow?"

Gabe's stomach plunged. "I wasn't lying," he replied, feeling a desperate urge to crush the phone with his bare hands. Oswald! He was always there, always standing between Gabe and happiness, between Gabe and Abazi. Even though Oswald could change into a tree, he wasn't a real Dryad, and Gabe was. And since Abazi likely preferred humans to Dryads, she would pick Oswald over Gabe.

"Oh, I believe you. Just wanted to be sure. Watching me like that, it's kind of creepy, like a stalker, don't you think?"

"Definitely," Gabe breathed, almost unable to believe what he was hearing.

"By the way," she said hurriedly. "You're right, you know."

"I am? I mean, of course I am."

She ignored that. "I tell you to accept who you are, but I won't do it myself."

His breath caught in his chest. Was this the reason she'd been so cranky after the powwow? He had to tread very carefully here. "So do you know why you don't want to be Indian?"

"It's not that I don't want to be Indian," she hedged. "I just don't want to be labeled and judged as some kind of stereotype."

"Your dad isn't a stereotype. He owns a store and a car, not a horse, and he wears blue jeans instead of buckskin. Heck, he even eats marshmallows. But I also know that he's an Indian who prides himself on being an Indian." Abazi didn't respond, so Gabe tried another tactic. "Besides, you wear your hair in braids and you wear beaded headbands."

"I wear those because they look cool on me."

"Well, I think being an Indian is cool. I loved the powwow, watching you dance—" here he blushed "—and how everyone knew all the steps. Everything felt so connected. I wish I had that in my life."

"But you do—" She stopped herself. "Okay, I know your parents aren't really your parents and your brothers aren't really your brothers. But they are!"

"Make sense, please."

"If you were adopted, would they *not* be your family just because you don't share the exact same genes?"

"No, I guess not."

"Then how is this different?"

"Because my real mother lives in the woods and I don't know what to do about her. Oswald got her to give me something and I'm beginning to suspect she knew exactly what it would do to me and still she did it. So if I end up losing my real family, all I'll have is her. And she betrayed me!"

At that moment, it all came together for Gabe. His fears, his worries, his confusion, all hit him at once. He felt like he was standing on the edge of a precipice and only the slightest of breezes would blow him into it…and there'd be no one to catch him.

"Okay, I get that being betrayed by your mother is pretty awful. But from what you've told me, this Faeth chick isn't all there. She might have thought she was doing you a favor."

"Some favor."

"This from someone who doesn't want to be a tree in the first place! She granted your wish, Gabe. Have you thought of that?"

He hadn't. "But how would she know I wished that?"

"Because she knows the life you lead. She understands. She took you once, remember? She might have seen something, then. That you weren't entirely hers. That you didn't fit into her world." Gabe nodded absently. What Abazi was saying made a twisted sort of sense. "I also wanted to say something else," she went on. "And it isn't easy, so keep your mouth shut until I'm done."

"Okay."

"That's not keeping your mouth shut." He refrained from apologizing. "I wanted to say that I'm sorry I didn't believe you about seeing and hearing things. As you might have figured out about me, I'm not a very trusting person. And…well…if you want to go out some time— somewhere that doesn't involve woods and flesh eating creeps—then that'd be cool with me."

All the air sucked out of Gabe's lungs. Was she messing with him? Did she really want to go on a date? With him?

"You can say something now, idiot."

The air returned and with it a gush of warmth. "That would be awesome," he managed to say, despite his heavily beating heart, which was clamoring to climb up his windpipe.

"Good. Now did you say you played basketball? Forward, I'm guessing? I play point guard."

Gabe didn't remember much of the details of what they discussed after that—the 80s Celtics and how they could never be replaced, ways to screw with Jake Morrigan, where Abazi wanted to go on their first date—but he would never forget the feeling in his chest as they talked…like he had gained new roots. They hadn't yet dug deep, but they were heading in the right direction.

~~~~~~

The snow finally stopped on Sunday afternoon and he and his brothers spent hours cleaning it up, mainly because half the time was occupied by snowball fights and building snowmen. When they were done, Gabe told them he was heading into the woods. He had something to do. His brothers seemed to know that it was best if he went alone.

"We'll be waiting for you to come back," Kris told him as Gabe strapped on snowshoes. "In case, you know, you want to talk about it."

Then, with a clap on the back that was more like a shove, he sent Gabe off towards the woods. He glanced back one last time and saw both his brothers staring after him morosely. Seeing their expressions, something tugged at his heart. Sure they fought a lot and Kris was great at getting out of work and Jer had a knack for saying exactly what Gabe didn't want to hear since it was usually to Gabe's detriment, and often true, to boot, but when push came to shove, he had to admit he couldn't do any better for brothers. And he wouldn't want to.

The trek out to the Lady was quite a struggle. Halfway along he finally got the hang of the snowshoes and it went a bit easier after that. He wasn't sure how he'd find her, but he just placed one foot after the other, trusting that his tree senses would steer him.

After an hour of trekking through the deep snow, he stopped. An unusual scent filled the air around him. After the metallic smell of snow, the sweet odor caught his senses right away. He looked up and saw her—the Lady. She was covered in white flowers and pale petals drifted through the air like giant snowflakes. She was alive. Not just alive, but thriving.

"What in the world…" he breathed, unable to finish the sentence because he didn't even know what to say. While staring at her, she transformed into a human. Her hair, white as her dress, reached up toward the sky like an angel in flight. Her eyes, a silvery gray, stared into his, drawing him to her like a lassoed calf. A long, delicate hand reached out to him.

Without thinking, he searched his pocket and retrieved the little bit of branch that had broken off in his hand when he'd tried to help her. He'd kept it all this time. He placed it in her hand, which was so white, it shimmered like the snow around them.

"Thank ye, Gabriel." She spoke in an ethereal, echoing voice that filled the woods with its haunting melody. "Ye've begun the healin'."

"The healing?" was all he could say in response. She was so beautiful that his head spun, as though in a dream. And just now, he realized that he recognized her—she was the carved figure on the door leading up to his tower room.

She only smiled, then retreated from him, floating backwards like a ghost. When she neared where she had stood as a tree, she leaned down and stuck the branch into the ground. Then, with a leap and a whirl, she was a tree once more. Petals drifted down and silence froze the air.

"*Ye* did that," a familiar voice came from behind him, breaking the spell.

Gabe spun around. "Me? But I was the one who killed her!"

Wildrr shook his little head. "Yes, well…about that. After ye left, I ran from her. I couldna bear what I'd done—that I'd asked ye to help her and it ended up bein' her death. So I ran, and I plotted me revenge. I wanted to hurt ye as ye hurt me. Scare ye silly."

"Like with the acorn attack in the woods and on our house. Was all that your idea?"

Wildrr's eyes shifted to the right. "Maybe," he hedged. "I didna participate in the first attack, but I did witness it. The second round, well, that were me and the Rogues." Wildrr spat on the ground. "That Oswald's a piece of work, volunteerin' his band right away when I put out what I be wantin'. Then he had poor wee Hollie doin' his dirty work, tryin' to run ye off all by herself. Took care of that, I did."

Now it was making sense. "Actually, she was trying to warn me about him, what he might be plotting."

Wildrr cocked his head to one side. "I thought it were something like that. She's a good lass, and I be fond of her."

"I think we all are. Oswald, especially."

"Oswald doesna want to share what he thinks is his. He be a bit greedy that way."

Gabe wouldn't argue that. "He really does hate me, doesn't he?"

"Hate's a strong word. More like, he's afeared. I ken about that sort of thing. The Lady is me life. I thought ye took her from me, leavin' me with nothing. Leavin' me to *be* nothing, and it drove me to act in ways other than what be right." His head drooped low and his pink hat slid over his eyes.

"It's all right, Wildrr. I understand. But just so you know, I don't want to be the king. I just want to be me. Oswald doesn't want to hear that, though."

Wildrr's head swung back up, and with it, the hat. "Sometimes we caint choose what we are, we just have to make the most of what we be."

"Do you think I'm a Usurper, Wildrr?"

Wildrr looked slightly abashed. "I might have...once. But not after what ye did for me Lady." Gabe shivered, then felt suddenly very tired. "Ye should go," Wildrr told him. "Ye've enough of the Dryad to thicken yer blood in this cold. Get yerself home and warm up."

Gabe nodded. "I will. And Wildrr... Since we don't know for sure that I was the one who did this for the Lady, maybe it's best we keep it under wraps."

Wildrr frowned. "But I ken ye did it. 'Oo else?"

"Oswald, maybe?"

Wildrr looked skeptical. "I'll tell ye what. I won't say nothing, and I won't say something. Yer secret is safe with me, for now." He waved Gabe off. "Now go. Ye look right peaky."

"Will I see you again?"

"Ye'll see me in yer dreams, at the edges of yer sight, out of the corner of yer eye. I'll be around. Ye've only to call me name and I'll come."

"Good to know." Gabe stifled a yawn. "Goodbye, Wildrr. I'm glad you're not trying to take me out anymore. You're a formidable opponent."

Wildrr grinned. "As are ye." The grin suddenly disappeared and Wildrr's eyes widened. "Oh, bugger!"

Gabe's heart skipped a beat. "What is it?"

"I forgot to call off the others!" Wildrr dashed away, looking fit to be tied. "Stay safe and rest up, King Gabriel," he shouted over his shoulder. "For with spring comes the awakening. And danger everywhere. And you'd better hope I reach everyone with the message that the attack is off before they sleep!"

"Are you kidding me?" he shouted at the running figure. Wildrr didn't stop, and soon disappeared into the woods. Gabe decided to be on high alert when he walked back, and hope that everyone got the message that Gabe was no longer on Wildrr's hit list.

As he turned to go, his eyes landed on the Lady in all her glory. *If I was truly the one who saved her, then maybe there's something I can do for the Dryads that doesn't involve killing anyone.* It was a pleasing thought. Come spring, he realized, he'd have to return to the Forest Immortal to be there for any Dryads struggling to come back.

For all of them. Even Oswald. Maybe if he could save the Lady, he could at least coax the others to wake up. He'd do it for the trees, for Hollie, for Dame Hazel—even though he wasn't sure he could trust her—for Isis, who'd lost her life, for his dad. For some reason, it seemed the least he could do.

Feeling lighter, he followed his tracks back home. Soon it would be dark and he hurried a little faster. He knew the Ko-goks were hibernating, but that didn't mean he shouldn't be careful.

"Don't forget me," a wavery voice floated toward him as his foot caught a snowdrift and he stumbled. He caught himself and spun around, only now realizing where he was. Shambolic Stream—where he'd promised to meet Faeth if she needed him. "Please don't let me go."

"Faeth?" he called, and his voice sounded loud and uncertain in the stillness of the woods. "Mother?" he called more softly.

"Don't forget me," she whispered again. And then he could see her, half-hidden behind a tree, as though afraid of him.

"I won't forget you," he called out. Had she really betrayed him, or had Oswald taken advantage of her addled wits? She wasn't herself, probably hadn't been for a long time, and Gabe realized he couldn't hold what she'd done against her. Besides, he needed her and she needed him. He was her real son. They had to look out for each other.

"Take care of him," she entreated.

"Take care of who?"

"He'll need ye now more than ever."

"*Who* will need me?"

But he already knew. She meant Oswald. Gabe was never going to be free of him. Never. His fingers curled into fists. "He can take care of himself!" he shouted to the trees, and with that, he turned and walked away from his mother, back toward home.

Back toward the only family he'd ever known…a family that wasn't his.

About the Author

When author, Kristina Schram, was growing up she wanted to be a star. When that didn't turn out quite like she expected, she turned her mind to achieving other goals: Earning her Ph.D. in Counseling Psychology, working as an Artist-in-Residence at local schools, being a free-lance editor and reader, coaching parks & rec basketball, protecting the earth through recycling and using green products, and publishing her first novel, a YA fantasy called The Chronicles of Anaedor: The Prophecies.

Knowing what it's like to struggle with self-doubt and lack of confidence, her biggest dream (in addition to owning a castle) is to stamp out low self-esteem for everyone, especially young people. She lives in beautiful, wooded New Hampshire with her husband, three boys, and various pets, and can also throw a tomahawk, if need be. One of her favorite things to do is walk with her dog in the woods, where she searches for the impossible around every corner. Sometimes she finds it.

For more information on Kristina Schram, feel free to make a trip to her website: www.kristinaschram.com. She's also on Facebook, Twitter, and Pinterest.

Other Books by Kristina Schram

<u>The Chronicles of Anaedor: The Prophecies (Book One)</u>

Strange things happen to fifteen-year-old Lavida Mors. Maybe that's why her father sends her to Portal Manor, a mysterious family estate she never knew existed. Lavida quickly discovers that not everything at Portal Manor is as it seems when she stumbles across a secret passage to a hidden world—Anaedor. Long ago, humans drove the Anaedorians, a civilization of magical and strange beings, into the dark world of huge caverns, frigid rivers, and bottomless pits deep within the earth. Malevolent forces, led by the evil Malvado, seek to control all of Anaedor, but an ancient prophecy tells of a hero who will save them from destruction. While trying to escape the dark realm, Lavida must battle overgrown leeches, survive a poisoned arrow, and outwit a giant, all while trying to convince the hopeful populace of Anaedor that she is not the savior they believe her to be.

<u>The Chronicles of Anaedor: The Return to Anaedor (Book Two)</u>

After escaping from Anaedor, fifteen-year-old Lavida Mors starts a training course with her guardian, Mrs. Keeper, in hopes of improving her magic skills before the dreaded Malvado returns. But while trying out a new spell, something awful happens, and she vows never to do magic again. When an unexpected discovery forces her to return to Anaedor, she is faced with her most terrifying challenges yet. Strife reigns in the hidden underground world as lootings and burnings break out, and numerous enemies conspire to capture Lavida, fight her, even kill her. Without magic, how can she possibly flee from dragons, escape the Goblins, outwit the ruthless Frio, and fight a duel with a young rebel intent on proving she's not the One? Time is running out. If Lavida doesn't learn to trust herself and her skills, a series of catastrophic events will ensure that she and her friends never make it out of Anaedor again.

The Chronicles of Anaedor: The Lost Ones (Book Three)

Sixteen-year-old Lavida Mors is in for a long, hot summer. With no way into Anaedor, the Lost Ones seeking refuge at Portal Manor are taking over the house, creating havoc and misery. Lavida is overwhelmed trying to keep up with her chores, learning magic, and fighting off the Pixies—tiny creatures who have made it their mission to harass Lavida at every turn. Meanwhile, unbeknownst to the residents of Portal Manor, the AAK is hard at work opening a Portal to the Upland. They are successful at last, and the twins, Loria and Darian, on the run from Malvado, and the AAK leader, Trey, manage to make it through the opening only to have it collapse behind them. With no way back into Anaedor, they are forced to take refuge at Portal Manor. As they try to settle into this strange new life, tensions between the humans and the Anaedorians grow, creating rifts between Lavida and her friends. To make matters worse, Frio, Amoral Hunter Leader, is hiding out in the Upland, and when he goes after Lavida, he starts in motion a series of events that could end up costing Lavida her life.

The Chronicles of Anaedor: The Uprising (Book Four)

In this final book of the Anaedor series, sixteen-year-old Lavida Mors is placed in grave danger when a group of young Anaedorians infiltrates the Upland. Their orders are to eliminate the evil one, whom they believe is Lavida, and then launch an Uprising to take over the Upland. Disguising themselves as humans, they befriend the unwitting Lavida and her friends, allowing them easy access to Portal Manor. Darian and Loria, Blendar twins and Lavida's friends, and Trey, ex-AAK rebel leader, have come to the Upland to warn Lavida about the intruders. But before they can, Darian learns something about Lavida's past that turns him against her. Surrounded by betrayal and danger, and faced with an astonishing revelation that makes her question everything about her existence, Lavida feels increasingly alone and afraid. If she cannot convince Darian and the others that she is not the evil being they think she is, she will lose everything to the Uprising.

Mayhem at Nepenthe Manor: A Pandora Belfry Adventure
(Book One)

Precocious and morbidly obsessed with death, Pandora Belfry has spent her entire life at Nepenthe Manor, a dark, Gothic mansion also known as the local loony bin. Recently turned fourteen and growing exasperated with her stifling life, Pandora wants two things more than anything else in the world—to make her escape from the asylum, and to get her mom to finally act like a real mom. Until these wishes are granted, she acts as self-imposed ringleader to a wayward posse of inmates. Known amongst themselves as the Secret Six, Pandora and her friends spend their time at Nepenthe Manor stirring up trouble—holding weekly Midnight Meetings to concoct schemes, sneaking into places like the Nepenthe family cemetery and the forbidden attic, and generally doing everything they can to avoid the curse of living a mundane life. But when a mysterious new inmate arrives at the manor, things change for Pandora, and not for the better. In retaliation for a trick she plays on him, the charming and handsome Xavier connives to take over the posse, threatens to divulge one of Pandora's biggest secrets, and refuses to tell her what he did to get himself locked up. This boy is obviously hiding something, and it's up to Pandora to use whatever nefarious means necessary to find out what it is, before he destroys the only world she's ever known.

The Labyrinth of Lunacy: A Pandora Belfry Adventure
(Book Two)

Pandora Belfry, along with the eccentric members of her posse, is back, and looking for trouble. The posse's first order of business is to break into the off-limits labyrinth, even though they can't find its door. Against her mother's wishes, Pandora also works to solve the mystery of her father's identity. Perhaps he's a staff member, or maybe he's the stranger haunting the beach late at night. Topping the list of possible dad candidates is the new therapist, Dr. Steele, who keeps popping up in Pandora's life like an annoying, but handsome, nanny. To add to her problems, Pandora's date with the slimy, but oddly fascinating, Dougie Daft, is fast approaching. She isn't sure how to get out of it, or even if she dares to. Her new acquaintance, Giganticus, certainly doesn't want her to go, but if she doesn't, she'll be obligated to Dougie Daft, and that's the last thing any sane person would want... Come join the posse on their latest, a-maze-ing adventure. Just one warning: Watch out for snakes!

I Shall Return: A Paranormal Gothic Romance

 Journalist, Lily MacKenzie, is off to the Highlands of Scotland on a newspaper assignment. But in reality, she has another mission in mind, one she desperately needs to keep secret. Her arrival starts off unexpectedly when she encounters Greg Huntington, a stranger who seems to know her even though they've never met. Things grow more peculiar as she gets to know the Derings of Dundeid Castle, the lodging where she's staying. Andrew Dering, the god-like laird, is welcoming enough, but appears to be hiding something. His cousin, Vivian, seems intent on sabotaging Lily's efforts, while another relation, Ophelia, sees Lily as her savior from a mysterious illness. As Lily works to unravel the mystery that set her on her journey, events grow increasingly complicated and dangerous, and she finds herself caught between two very different men. The reason behind her mission makes it difficult to trust either one, but when she finally ends up choosing, things go very wrong, and Lily ends up fighting for her sanity and her very life.

The Wrath: A Paranormal Gothic Romance

 When a cryptic letter arrives from Evalina Filmore's two aunts, she travels to England to find out what they want, figuring this will be the chance to experience the romantic adventure she has so often read about in her beloved gothic novels. When she arrives, she finds the eerie mansion, the strange atmosphere, and the adventure, as hoped. But there are troubles. On the train, she meets a man who, upon learning her name, walks away without a word of explanation. Not long after, she passes unharmed through a wood called the Wrath, even though, as she later learns, no one ever has. While in the Wrath, she meets a tantalizing and seductive stranger, one who just might be her gothic hero. But he has a secret. It seems everyone in the village does, including her aunts, and it's up to Evie to figure out what is going on before the Wrath lures her in and never lets her go.

The Battle to Become an Author:
When Great Expectations Go Awry

 Are you looking to find an agent and/or get published? Are you a published author frustrated with the whole process? Or have you simply heard the horror stories and are looking for a ray of light before plunging into the fray? In this short booklet, author Kristina Schram discusses how one's unrealistic expectations about becoming an author can contribute to feelings of negativity and isolation. Dr. Schram offers a real-world discussion of this growing issue, humorously incorporating her own experiences throughout. She also offers insights and ways to cope with the increasingly difficult battle to become a published author. Come prepared to challenge your own expectations, to laugh and to cry, and to battle against the forces conspiring to keep you from reaching your writing potential!

www.ingramcontent.com/pod-product-compliance
Lightning Source LLC
Chambersburg PA
CBHW020753250626
47155CB00003B/1050